She was no longer alone...

At first Catrian could see nothing, though her widened gaze searched frantically from shadow to shadow, bush to bush, seeking movement. Her blood iced in her veins, as a dark shape resolved itself from the gloom, moving in a shuffling gait that belied the powerful speed it was capable of.

A Stalker!

It must have caught her scent when she had created the storm. She had exploded with so much energy that she had drawn it to her like a fly to dung. Fear shivered her flesh, for she had drained so much of her Godsmagic that she could barely lift her legs to walk, let alone defend herself magically!

The Stalker's scaled snout was to the ground, snorting and snuffling at the trail she had left that morning. "Sorcerer, thou art a woman!" It mumbled. "A pretty succulent for my feast!" Its chuckle sounded like chains rasping against stone.

She reached deep within, seeking her residues of Godsmagic. By draining herself of power she would destroy her body's ability to keep her heart beating, and her lungs expanding with air but she was going to die anyway at the hands of Doaphin's creature!

For Catrian, it was no choice. If she was to perish, then she was going to take the Stalker with her!

Other Books by L.G.A. McIntyre

Lies of Lesser Gods Series

The Exile

The Rebel

The Sorcerer

The Prince – arriving in 2017

The King – arriving in 2018

The Sorcerer

Lies of Lesser Gods

Book Three

L.G.A. McIntyre

Per Ardua Productions Inc.

Vancouver, Canada

Published by Per Ardua Productions Inc

www.perarduaproductions.ca

First time in print
Trade Paperback edition December 2016

ISBN: 978-0-9919120-4-9
eBook ISBN: 978-0-9919120-5-6

To all the aspiring authors out there.

If it isn't scary to *try*,

it doesn't mean as much

when you *succeed*.

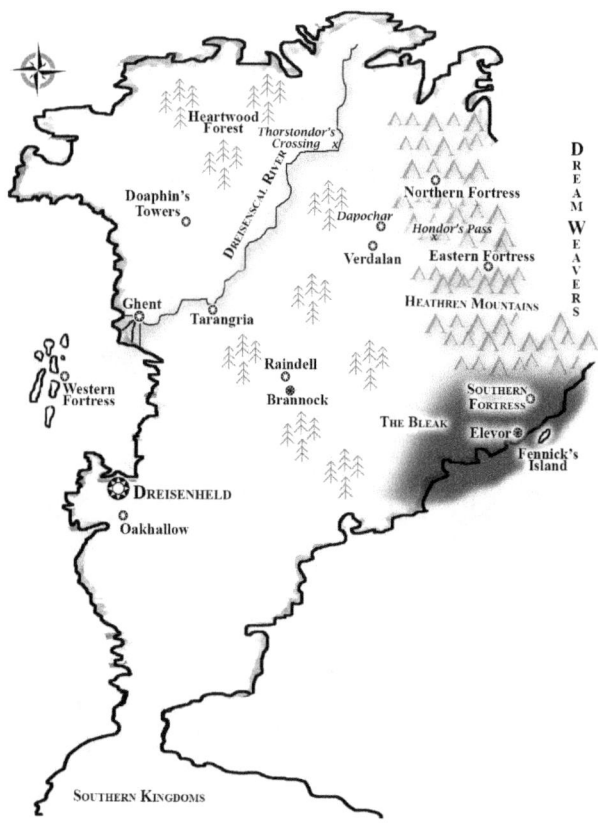

PROLOGUE

DREISENHELD – LATE WINTER

The throne room of Dreisenheld teems with creatures, great and small. Some are early creations, misshapen mistakes that slather and slime, kept for sentimental reasons more than anything else. Later years saw a growth in skill and execution, personified in the shining pantheon of Demon Lords, beings of great beauty and powerful darkness, who answer to no one but the throne. Of highest status, they stand nearest to the dais, their faces uplifted in adulation. The ones they were created to supplant, the Stalkers of nightmares and madness, skulk in the shadows, hidden from the light of the crystal sconces and massive candelabras flanking the dais, resentful still, even after centuries have passed, that they are no longer the favored ones.

Spaced throughout the chamber fifty white marble columns, veined in rich gold, support a ceiling two hundred lofty feet above where stained glass windows, curtained by nightfall, gleam dully in candlelight cast by twenty crystalline chandeliers the size of pleasure barges. Save for the Demon Lords, and the common troops of Demon Riders, who are too lowborn to be attending this audience, none present can survive in sunlight - a flaw that was also corrected in later years.

The gathering is packed shoulder to shoulder so that even the rivers of gold in the white marble floor beneath their feet, and claws, and tails cannot be seen. The multitudes even spill through the massive, thirty-foot tall, hammered gold doors opposite to the bejeweled throne, into the antechamber without. The throne room seethes with wealth, power and magic, but none present are as mighty as the Master.

"It is time. We make an end of it at last. Muster our troops. What sallow remnants of Mankind reside in the land shall at last serve the purpose to which we spared them. Glut yourselves upon death! Kill! Kill! Kill!"

The echoes of the edict are eclipsed by the roar of approval from the assemblage, from the throats of all save one.

As the noise settles, he sidles nearer, his arm crossing his torso that he might hide his withered hand within a slit in the middle of his rich, blue velvet tunic. He believes his position as Supreme Commander grants him certain rights and privileges, and he boldly stands upon the lowest step of the dais, holding himself above all others.

Carmine lips twist in displeasure and disdain. Is he still needed? Perhaps like the other first mistakes he is kept for sentimental reasons, though like it or not, he is the only one with the experience to lead on the field of battle.

He bows low, addressing his feet. "You are all seeing, all powerful. There are none who can challenge you! You are the deepest darkness of the moonless night, the Master of..."

"Enough! Your words pleasure us little."

He straightens, his face a mask of careful consideration for the words he will speak next. "My Master, have you forgotten the curse? You know that I dare not leave Dreisenheld while the sword remains out of our reach."

"Your cowardice is as consistent as your uselessness." A mighty concussion rocks the throne room. Creatures great and small scatter, creating a bottleneck at the heavy, gold doors in the wild rush, trampling upon each other to escape the Master's wrath.

The chamber is soon empty of all save the supplicant and the maimed and dying littering the doorway. To his credit, he did not flee with the others. Perhaps there is mettle remaining after all.

A negligent wave takes care of the dying - a burst of sorcery and they collapse back into the dust from whence they came.

"My Master, may I ask what has changed? After so long, why kill the last of mankind?"

Glee stretches the red mouth wide, and white teeth gleam cruelly. "He has returned." The reaction to the news is more entertaining than could have been hoped for.

He flinches as though struck, and his face becomes a portrait of terror and shock. To catch his balance, the withered hand appears, a disturbing claw of flaky, diseased skin stretched tautly over bones. It has never healed.

"My Master! I am doubly cursed! Please, I beg of you, do not ask this of me!"

"You live for but one purpose. You are the mask we wear."

"But if he has returned, he must be seeking the sword!"

"Yes."

"When Dragon is perched on vengeful fist..." his voice is obsessed and panicked, as he recites the stanza of the curse.

"Silence!" A tremor starts deep in the earth. "You will not speak that twaddle in our presence!" In the upper corner of the chamber a stained glass panel shatters, and shards rain down onto the marble floors in a rainbow clatter.

He falls off the bottom step into the filth and muck discharged by the creatures so recently assembled, and clings to the floor, anchoring himself as best he can until the trembling ceases. From hands and knees he raises his head to beg. His fine blue velvet tunic is now smeared and filthy, his thinning blond hair plastered to his face from the sweat of his fear. "Have you no mercy for me at all? The curse...!"

"You are a disgrace! A failure! In three hundred years, you have been unable to retrieve the blade for us. 'Tis clear to us now that Fennick has defeated you. Only one man may reach it."

"My Master! Please! Send a Stalker for him before he can reach Fennick's Island! He will be in hand, and you need never disturb the sword again! You will have what you have always wanted."

"Dare you order us? The Man is but part of our desires! We need that sword. We want its powers. It is ours. We will add its strength to our own."

"But only consider, my Master. Once he has the sword again..."

"He will trade it for the lives of his people, to keep us from exterminating the last of the vermin. That is how we will gain both of our prizes!"

"My Master, I beg of you…"

"Fool! There is nothing to fear here, save that he is unable to reach the Island before the Solstice! When we have both the sword and the Man in our thrall the curse cannot be fulfilled." The ground rumbles again. "Our patience wears thin."

The supplicant falls forward onto his belly. "My life is your life! Always has it been, my Master! Always and forever!"

"Find your spine, and ready our armies for war. Your next failure will be your last."

CHAPTER ONE

NORTHERN REBEL FORTRESS – LATE WINTER

The Gods of Fortune were rolling their dice while humanity scrabbled for any weapon with which to stave off genocide. The dice landed with thunderous cracks of inevitable destiny. No escape now, the wagers had been made. The unattainable quest for the magical talisman, the Dragon Sword of Lyre, had begun.

Catrian shivered, as from atop the battlements of the Northern Fortress, she watched the column of horses snake down the mountainside along the switchback trail towards the tree line, and sought the fortitude she would need in the coming year. Even at this distance, she could easily single Gralyre out from the pack of sixty riders. The proud set of his shoulders, and the graceful control of his steed set Gralyre apart from all others, even if the black, canine figure of Little Wolf, loping easily alongside Gralyre's horse, had not marked his position.

Long after Gralyre had vanished into the forested valley below Catrian continued to watch and to grieve what was to come. The wind plucked at her hair, gusting the scents of hopelessness and winter into her senses.

War was upon them. Even should Gralyre defy all the odds set against him by the Gods of Fortune, and succeed in his quest to return with the Dragon Sword, Catrian knew it would count for naught. The Rebels were not rank and file soldiers; they struck from the shadows and retreated from the enemy after making a small cut. Doaphin's forces outnumbered the Rebels' by at least five hundred to one, and in open warfare, on a field of battle, there was no question of if the Rebels would lose, it was only a matter of how many people they could save ahead of the grinding maw of Daophin's battalions before their strength was spent. Without Gralyre's magic by her side Catrian feared that this number was rapidly dwindling. But save them to where? There was no place beyond the reach of Doaphin's evil!

'What have I allowed to happen?'

Periodically, Rebels brushed by on the narrow walkway, murmuring a polite "Good morn, lady" as they strolled onward along their circuitous watch walks atop the palisade wall, but she paid them scant mind. The wind quickened, and she watched solemnly, as the promised storm finally rolled over the distant, encircling mountains, and heavy clouds slid down into the valley, filling the bowl until naught but the tips of the trees could be seen, isolating the Rebel's mountain, taller and broader than the rest, in a sea of undulating grey. Lightning cracked in the distance, and the boom of the thunder rolled out, echoing and re-echoing against the mountains. The wind increased to a squall, and stings of sleet began to pepper her face, as restless fog boiled and churned below; a winter cauldron of mal intent.

"He is gone, lass, and none too soon! Look at ye here, standing a vigil for him. Ye are making a spectacle o' yourself."

Catrian turned to face her uncle. Her rage had been spent

alongside her tears so that now she only felt regret as she looked up at the man who had raised her from a child.

She could not remember her mother beyond an impression, an idealized thought. 'Twas Boris' face, careworn and stern, that she had always seen if she thought of family, as solid a presence in her life as an ancient oak, and just as steadfast. It had been a distressing shock to discover he had not the same regard for her.

She folded her hands gravely in front of her waist, standing firm against the buffeting wind. "Ye have ne'er trusted me, have ye, uncle? At least no' beyond how ye could use me." The purple and blue bruise from his blow, the one delivered when he had discovered her interlude with Gralyre, marred the fine skin high on her left cheekbone, swelling painfully.

Boris' face flushed red from anger, perhaps from shame, or maybe only from the cold gusts. "Stop being dramatic. Ye know I love ye like a daughter," he muttered.

In her disenchantment, her uncle's declaration sounded naught of affection, or even a rough apology, but the snap of a chain attempting to clasp her ankle with obligation.

Whatever it was that he read in her face made Boris scrub roughly at his short, grey hair, as he turned away, and stepped forward to gaze out over the shrouded valley. His hands clenched upon the wooden crenels, and he blinked against the wind driven ice, measuring the intensity of the oncoming storm, both the one in front, and the one behind that brewed within his niece. The wind rolled the mists against the fortress walls like the crests of a ghostly tide, raising higher and higher as each wave broke. When it reached the top of the palisade, it would spill over and drown them all.

Catrian forbore to block the sleet that began to spatter down in thicker sheets, as the tempest gathered momentum. Her cynical gaze never left the profile of Boris' craggy face. "That is no' what I asked. Ye do no' trust me. 'Tis why ye sent him for the sword. Ye did no' trust my judgement."

Boris reeled to face her, his voice strengthening to compete with the boom of the wind that had started to hammer against the Rebel fortifications. "Your judgement? Matik caught ye and he…! How far had it gone, girl? Did ye…?"

Catrian's mouth twisted with a flash of pain, and her chin snapped up proudly, her grey-green eyes glowing with outrage. "Gods! I am four and twenty! Women o' my age have a husband, and a score o' children. How is it that I have t' explain my actions to ye, or t' anyone else! I am left t' wonder if ye would have disapproved o' any man gaining a foothold in my heart, or if 'twas Gralyre in particular t' whom ye objected. Well, ye got what ye desired, Commander," she acknowledged bitterly. "My undivided attention and commitment t' the cause. As though it were e'er allowed out o' my thoughts."

"Keep a civil tongue, girl! I *am* your commander, and ye are my weapon against Doaphin and his Demon Lords. Ye are too important t' waste upon a man!"

Catrian swiped her hair back, as the wind lashed the brown strands against her face, loosened from her long braid. "Against one, maybe two Demon Lords, if they are no' expecting my attack, I might protect us. Against the assembled might o' Doaphin's forces?" Catrian shook her head in disgust. "Gralyre is powerful beyond measuring. I do no' think that even he knows the limits t' his strength. He has no' the skills, but he is learning at a pace that may have turned the tide. Ye fool," Catrian's voice was frosted with condemnation enough to rival the icy storm, "your greatest weapon is riding away from ye as we speak."

The Commander's expression curdled further at her scorn.

Catrian smiled grimly. "Would ye care t' adorn the other side, uncle?" She turned her head slowly to present the unmarred right side of her face while her eyes bored into his, daring his fist to fly. "'Tis no' your fault. I was the fool who did no' fight for what I knew t' be right. I told ye many times that I would ne'er allow my powers t' be ruled by another. I always thought I referred t' a husband or lover, I ne'er thought it would be ye, Boris."

The Commander's breaths heaved in heavy white plumes, as he worked for words that were lost to him in disbelief at her uncharacteristic defiance. "Aye, I rule ye," he bellowed. "As it should be! Power run amuck has ruined this land, and brought its people t' the brink. Sorcery is evil, and I would rather have seen ye dead than become another such as Doaphin! I will no' apologize for it!"

"Is that the real reason that ye ne'er allowed me t' leave the fortress without a contingent o' men? Ye told me it was for my protection. What were their real orders, Boris?"

The Commander's gaze slid away from hers, and the rift in

Catrian's heart widened.

"Ye told me t' think about what I had done. I did. I thought about a great many things, uncle, and I realized how *witless* I have been! 'Tis only now that Gralyre is gone forever that I realize my mistake. I trusted your judgement o'er my own." Most of Catrian's temper was directed at herself.

"Ye were so clever t' warn me against him from the first, and I continued t' tell myself t' beware o' Gralyre. All the while ye were giving me a nudge o' fear here, and some mistrust there, fanning the flames o' my suspicions, and I never suspected it, no' until the fog cleared from my hindsight! With all his power, and mastery o' the blade, Gralyre could have escaped this fortress at any time, ne'er t' be heard from again, but he did no'. He stayed. And now he is serving himself up t' your ambitions because he is a man o' honour!"

"He was dangerous t' ye, girl!"

"No! Gralyre was dangerous t' ye! Ye plotted and schemed behind my back because ye feared ye were losing your hold o'er me. Gods! I even asked ye t' advise me, and ye left it t' me t' decide his fate. Ye knew that if ye told me t' kill him ye ran the risk o' making me defy ye, but leave the matter t' me, and against my every instinct, I would continue t' treat him as an enemy, though he never once, in thought or deed, betrayed our cause, no matter how harshly we treated him! I held tight t' my suspicions just t' please ye."

Boris bared his teeth in a snarl. "And was I no' right? Look at ye now that ye have lost him! Ye will stop this idiocy at once!

He had magic! He could have turned on us – on ye! - at any time. I had t' keep ye safe, so I did what had t' be done. Gralyre's fate is sealed!"

Catrian's lips curved into a slight, sad smile, as her ire drained away. "So is ours. We will no' survive the year. All o' it has come t' ruin, though we will struggle, and fight the inevitable. Without more magic beside us whatever we accomplish will be but a drop o' water in a river."

"Get a hold on yourself! Can ye no' longer hear your words? 'Tis as I feared! Your affection for that man has tainted your judgement! The resistance needs ye! We canno' afford t' lose ye!"

As he spoke, Catrian slowly turned her head back to the left, so that Boris was forced to confront the evidence of his miscalculation. "Ye had no' lost me, uncle. No' until this." She brushed her fingers across the painful welt on her cheekbone. "How is it that ye ne'er realized that ye held me with bonds o' kinship and love, no' obligation t' the cause. What ye have shattered will no' be so easily mended."

Boris shivered as her words struck home with flawless precision. He stood mute before her, unable to atone for what had come before, as Catrian abandoned him atop the battlements, taking the stairs that would lead her back down into the avenues of the Rebel's Northern Fortress.

Let the storm twist his thwarted schemes! She had her own strategies to implement.

ഓരു

After the initial eager speed with which they had departed the fortress, the Rebels settled into a ground eating gait that would keep the horses sound over the coming weeks of hard travel.

The grunting of the horses, and their pounding hooves echoed throughout the winter-held forest, shattering the serenity with the rush of their passage. The men spoke little, huddling in cloaks and heavy woolens to protect vulnerable skin from the wind chill that plummeted the ambient temperatures. Beards were frosted thick with icicles, formed beneath mouth and nose from the fog of their breath.

The sky was the color of sorrow, soon to be shedding bitter tears. It was a miserable day to be journeying, but there was no time to stop, make camp, and huddle around the warmth and cheer of a fire to await finer weather. There would be no haven from the oncoming storm. Most of the Rebels journeyed homeward to prepare for war, but the small group of eight that traveled with them raced the Spring Solstice to Fennick's Island, a contest that they could not afford to lose.

Gralyre stared, unflinching, into the future, his course set, his determination absolute. He replayed his parting vow to Commander Boris, his last defiance in the face of the Rebel's taunt.

"Your death is certain. Your influence over Catrian has ended."

"I will retrieve my sword, old man, and return to claim all

else that is mine!"

But nothing was certain, and this quest was meant to be a death sentence, a convoluted political maneuver on the part of the Commander to appease his Generals, and reclaim the full devotion of his Sorceress. Gralyre was not meant to return, and it was likely that he would never see Catrian again.

The memory of her grew vivid in his mind's eye, so that as he blindly followed the horses ahead, he replayed every conversation, every nuance of light upon her face, her smile, her laughter, and her kisses. It was a torturous pleasure, a grief filled tease of what would never come again.

He fought the instinct to turn his horse, and ride back to her, to stand at her side when the Rebels went to war, and Boris be damned by the Gods! Should Gralyre choose to leave, the combined might of the surrounding men would have no chance of staying him to this fool's quest.

But 'twas for Catrian that he stayed, for the slim chance that he would retrieve the Dragon Sword and return, and that she would consent to be his for what time remained before Doaphin razed the house of man.

It was no form of heroism, for true heroics come from places of selflessness. Gralyre's need for Catrian went beyond. For her, he would challenge the dark gates of the underworld. For Catrian, he would storm Dreisenheld, and fetch her Doaphin's head should she but ask it of him, with no coin of payment save for her smile. And without hesitation, he would ride into certain death for a magical sword.

At mid-morn, clouds rolled in to shroud their path, lightning cracked overhead, and the sky began to weep thick sweeps of sleet that first saturated their outer garments then froze in the wind of their passage. Their cloaks were soon iced hard as boards.

The rough forest path grew treacherous, slowing their progress, but the promise of warm fires and hot food should they reach the outer defenses by nightfall kept them pushing onwards.

The day waned, and the temperature dropped further. The storm became a blizzard, as the mountain and weather sought to turn the Rebels back from their folly. The grey day ebbed to blackness telling them of a sunset come and gone, and still they rode onwards until in the distance there appeared a ruddy light reflecting off the low-bellied clouds, beckoning and guiding them towards safety. They had traversed the forested valley, and had reached the sentry outpost of the southern pass.

As the riders approached, flickers of flame from large bonfires glimmered at them through the trees, the origin of the orange and red glow that fought back the stormy night.

At any one time, each of the Northern Rebel outposts that guarded the west, east and south passes into the valley, held a contingent of fifty Rebels who rotated in and out from the Northern Fortress every fortnight. Over the course of winter, the men spent their time, when not on sentry duty in the passes, shoveling tall banks of snow to surround their outposts with an extra degree of protection. By this late in the season, the snow walls of the southern outpost rose to the height of a man's shoulders, and spanned three hundred feet from corner to corner in a rough square.

The timber gates set into the icy wall swung wide in welcome at their arrival, and the sixty riders, and their spare steeds, swelled the small camp to bursting, as they rode through, and were hailed by the outer defensemen of the Northern Fortress.

Three bonfires snapped and sparked, shooting flames dozens of feet into the air, and sending waves of heat towards the weary, cold travellers. The glow of firelight on the storm of thick snowflakes made cascades of red and gold fall amongst the men, a shower of tribute upon the new arrivals. Spitted venison had been set to roast, and a keg of ale had been tapped. It would seem that the sentries were set to give them a warmer sendoff than that which they had received during their departure that morning from the fortress.

The master-at-arms formally welcomed General Ryes and General Kierdenan, giving up his tent to their comfort. All other travellers, those who were not billeted within the few tents of the off duty sentries, would make due with rolling themselves into bedrolls upon open ground beneath simple canvas tarps. The extra weight of tents had been sacrificed from their packs for more speed and stamina from their horses, so these rude shelters would be their only nightly protection from the weather over the coming weeks.

Gralyre, Rewn, Aneida and Mayvin fell into their comfortable routines, shaped by their numerous hunting forays throughout that winter. Together, they saw to their horses' stabling before claiming ground for their beds, taking advantage of the snowy earthworks and stringing their tarps in the lee of the wall for protection from the worst of the wind and weather.

Rewn and Aneida used the edges of shields to dig sleeping hollows in the new snow, a task made difficult by an icy crust formed only a few inches below the surface that had been laid down by the earlier onslaught of sleet. These they lined with soft evergreen bows to insulate against the cold, before rolling out the bedrolls into the depressions.

By the time their work was done, Gralyre and Mayvin had collected firewood from their hosts. Over the long cold winter, the dry stores of wood had been spent, so it was unfortunate that the provided firewood was both green from the cutting, and damp from the storm.

Gralyre crouched over the wet kindling, frustrated as his attempts with iron and flint fizzled to nothing. The wood was ill suited to accept a spark. Finally, he was obliged to use a subtle burst of magic to ignite an ember.

He bent his ear low to the ground, and blew softly over the wood to stoke the flames, cheating with his sorcery now and again to keep the fire growing in the saturated kindling. To anyone watching, he was just having more luck lighting a campfire than they.

Catrian had warned Gralyre to avoid using sorcery as he travelled, as it would alert any of Doaphin's creature's to his presence, but this near to the Rebel fortress he was willing to risk the smallest trickle needed to ignite a much needed fire.

The flames gained momentum, and the wood was soon crackling merrily, though the fire smoked and sparked with abandon. Gralyre set the spare logs near the heat to dry as much as possible before their use later in the evening.

Aneida grinned at Gralyre, as she warmed her hands. "I knew there was a reason we invited ye along." She coughed, as the wet wood sent a plume of grey smoke upwards to pool under the tarp. She had the appearance of a feral cat, wet and disheveled from the cold. Her red hair, damp and limp, clung to her head while the end of the one fat braid that fell down her chest, began to drip in the thawing heat.

Rewn pulled off his woolen cap, wet and useless now after the day of travel, and slopped it over one of the ropes holding the tarp taut. His mitts followed suite and began to steam, as the heat from the fire began to boil off the icy wet. His brown hair stood on end from the removal of the cap, as he stretched with a mighty yawn. "I am done in. If we do no' eat soon, I will be asleep where I stand." He scratched lethargically at his thick, winter beard for a moment.

Gralyre envied Rewn his beard, missing his own after the day of freezing travel. Catrian had taken it from his face with a burst of magic during their tryst; not that he regretted their heated kisses, only that his face felt naked and cold without the luxurious, black beard he had so recently sported. He rubbed a hand over his chin, feeling the bristles, and sighed regretfully. Everything reminded him of her.

The bonfires set in the middle of the outpost crackled, as the blizzard tried in vain to snuff the large flames with swirls of falling crystals. Mayvin nodded towards them, and her hands danced gracefully. *Aneida and I will get the bread and ale, if you men fetch some of that venison.* Her large dark eyes were overshadowed with exhaustion and that, along with her roughly cut, short, black hair, gave her a waifish look that was at odds with the heavy sword at her hip. Though her voice had been silenced forever, she had taught Gralyre and Rewn enough of her hand language that they were easily able to decipher the gestures.

Gralyre fed a stick of wood to their hungry fire, and stood. "Sounds like a plan." He dusted his hands and looked to Rewn. "Shall we go get some supper?"

While the sisters hied off towards the line forming in front of the keg of ale, the two men sauntered over to the central bonfire, where the majority of the men had congregated in jovial camaraderie for heat and meat. As they awaited their turn for the hot food, many weary Rebel came and went, lifting flaming brands from the bonfires with which to light the smaller campfires that would warm them as they slept, for they had not Gralyre's magic with which to aid them. Throughout the darkness, small dots of flickering light began to appear, marking the places that the others had claimed for their bivouacs.

When Gralyre and Rewn reached the front of the food line, Rewn held a wooden plate, while Gralyre used his dagger to slice meat from a haunch, piling it high enough to serve the women as well. The succulent meat steamed in the cold, and

Gralyre had to swallow the water in his mouth, as his stomach twisted with hunger.

"Stand aside, lowlander. Ye will no' eat afore good Rebels," Cian, General Kierdenan's contribution to their quest for the Dragon Sword, elbowed Rewn out of his way, deliberately knocking the overfull plate to the ground, and spilling the hot meat into the snow.

Cian shook his thick brown hair back behind his shoulders, and his teeth flashed mockingly through his beard. He deliberately stepped upon a goodly hunk of meat, and ground it into the snow with his boot. "Pick that up, lowlander. Ye are wasting food."

"Sod off!" Rewn snarled, as he bent down to retrieve the now empty plate.

Cian gave him a hard shove, sending Rewn staggering towards the bonfire.

Rewn jerked upright, regaining enough balance to avoid the last fatal step. His hands fisted for battle, his face hot with outrage, he lunged forward but halted when Cian's hand came to rest upon the pommel of the short sword sheathed at his side.

Rewn was unarmed. He had left his sword with his pack back at their campfire.

Cian's blue eyes narrowed, glowing with twin flames in firelight, and the grin fled his face. "For that ye will eat it off the ground, like the dog ye are!"

Conversation suspended, as the assembled men at the bonfires watched the outcome of the rude challenge.

As Rewn stared at him defiantly, not moving to obey, Cian began to draw his sword but Gralyre's sharp knife pricking his throat halted his rash action. Cian froze with his chin raised to the point of the knife, and he swallowed thickly, as his eyes cut sideways to view Gralyre's impassive face. Gralyre's blue-black gaze was sharp with intent, and though the angular features showed little emotion, Cian had no doubt he was staring into the face of an executioner.

Gralyre evaluated Cian's fear, as from out of the darkness and swirling snow, Little Wolf materialized on silent paws, an otherworldly sight with his massive shoulders rolling with sleek muscle at every tread.

"There are no dogs here, Cian. Just wolves. If you move, I will let him have you." The threat was made all the more powerful, as it was delivered quietly and without heat.

Cian's nod of compliance was more of a jerk of dread, as he released his sword, and held out his hands in open surrender.

Little Wolf attacked the spilled meat, and devoured it with quick snaps of his powerful jaws, the sound graphic and primal. When he was done, he focused on Gralyre, his tongue circling his pointed snout to capture the last of the savory juices.

"Guard him," Gralyre ordered, though it was all for effect. He had already told Little Wolf precisely what was required through their mind link.

As Little Wolf sat, his gaze shifted to the Rebel, and a low growl lifted his muzzle, showing off dagger teeth of gleaming white. The black fur on his back bristled with threat. He was a terrifying sight for he had almost reached his full growth, and even sitting, his head now rose to the impressive height of Gralyre's waist.

Cian grunted in fear, and his hands began to tremble.

Rewn retrieved the fallen plate, while Gralyre removed his knife from Cian's throat, and casually turned his back to slice more meat to replace their dinner.

Cian swallowed again, his throat bobbing beneath his beard, for Little Wolf's threatening gaze never faltered.

The atmosphere remained tense, and the surrounding men silent, until Gralyre stepped away from the fire, and Little Wolf sprang up to melt back into the darkness beyond the ring of firelight.

Cian's breath whooshed from his lips, as the wolfdog disappeared, and his hands dropped limply to his sides.

Rewn's face remained bland, as he joined Gralyre, but he could not resist elbowing Cian from his path as they left.

"*Ooof!*" Cian doubled over as Rewn's blow connected. The tension broke and men went back to their own business, laughing and talking, as though the incident had never occurred. Cian glared after Gralyre and Rewn, shoving off his friends, as they tried to help him stand upright.

They thumped his back with laughs, turning their attention to filling their plates with food, but Cian continued to glower.

Across the flames, Dotch watched Cian's dramatics, and rubbed idly at an old injury in his shoulder that was exacerbated by the weather. Though still in his prime, he had age and experience over the younger warriors that Catrian had united in the quest for the Dragon Sword. He frowned, as he considered the incident he had just witnessed.

'Twas obvious that Cian's agenda had little to do with their quest, and it set Dotch to wondering what General Kierdenan was scheming. Something was off there that would bear minding, but the lowlanders looked as though they could handle aught that Cian sought to afflict them with. Dotch could have warned Cian that Gralyre was not the sort that you trifled with, but he doubted that the younger Rebel would heed him.

"Come Dotch! Leave it. Tell Mikil about the time ye were in the lowlands, and came across those four Demon Riders. Ye know the time... in that village... What was it called?"

Dotch smiled, brought back to his present to spin tales of his past. He had found his good friend here on outpost duty, and was glad for the merriment to keep his mind from missing his wee lads, and his sweet wife.

"Trevon, ye idiot, ye know good 'n well 'twas Aleburn, and there were eight 'Riders, a maid, and a cart full o' swords." Dotch drained his stoup of ale, and passed his sleeve over his lips to sop a drip. "I killed the Riders, married the maid, and lost the swords in a river. And if I am going t' tell *that* story, I am going t' need a lot more o' this!" He waggled his empty tankard.

The off duty sentries laughed, and drew Dotch away with them back to their tent to continue the drinking and sharing of old war stories.

General Kierdenan eyed his counterpart with disgust from over the rim of his tankard, as General Ryes listed in his chair on the opposite side of the table. Ryes was drunk again, a state the man seemed to enjoy, though Kierdenan had to admit that the florid color the drink brought to the man's ashen cheeks was an improvement over the unusual paleness of his flesh.

Ryes was no specimen of leadership even when sober. With a pallid, moon-shaped face now flushed from the drink, and a slack, red mouth that seemed to sag further open with every sip, he looked the part of the village dolt instead of the Southern General of the Resistance.

Their borrowed tent billowed from the wind, the inhale and exhale of the storm. Outside the walls, the conversation of the men was a background jumble of voices and laughter. Periodically, monstrous shadows slid across the canvas, as men walked past between the tent and the flickering light of the bonfires.

"So 'tis impossible then?" Kierdenan felt obliged to prod to keep Ryes on topic, as the silence stretched. He preferred to get his information from the source rather than rely on what Commander Boris and his pet Sorceress, Catrian, had decided he needed to know. "Ye are sure?"

General Ryes nodded loosely. "Ab-solu-lely. Canno' be done. Tried t' tell 'em, but they would no' listen t' me." Ryes leaned forward on his elbows, and lifted an admonishing finger, not quite able to focus enough to point accurately in Kierdenan's direction. "Heed me, Keeyured-enen," Ryes hiccupped, his arm weaved, and his elbow slipped off the table. "Demon take it!" he snarled, then grinned mistily, before adjusting his expression to stern seriousness once more. "Heed me, Kierdenan. There is no coming back from Fennick's Island. Boris knew it. Ye heard him at the war council. Ye saw it. 'Twas a ploy t' kill this Gralyre fellow. If ye ask me, Boris is afraid o' 'im."

Ryes took a swig from his tankard, spilling more down his shirt than went into his mouth. He brushed his pudgy arm across his face to soak up the drips with his sleeve. "Ye know what is good for ye, ye will pull your man out o' this venture. 'Tis a waste o' a good Rebel if ye were t' ask me. And us going t' war soon." Ryes shook his head despairingly. "Going t' war. What is the point o' it?" His eyes slid back in his head, and he pitched sideways out of his chair, hitting the floor with a soft thump and a groan before a drunken snore burbled from his loose, drooling lips.

General Kierdenan took a contained sip of ale. "What indeed." He blew out the lamp, leaving Ryes where he had fallen, and took himself to bed.

ഇൽ

The sisters had not been idle while Gralyre and Rewn had been foraging for meat. As promised, they met back at their campfire, having gathered some crusty bread and tankards of frothy ale for them all.

The smoke from the wet wood rolled thickly up under the tarp before escaping out the sides, yet despite the choking fumes, the heat was most welcome in the cold, and there was no complaint from the exhausted travellers, as they supped upon the last hot meal that they would share for a long while. Snow continued to fall, flurries and eddies of large flakes that seemed disinclined to stop anytime soon.

Little Wolf, satiated upon the fallen meat, curled nose to tail by Gralyre's side, and was soon deeply asleep, as unaccustomed as they to the distance they had travelled. Gralyre ran his hand through the wolfdog's thick, black coat, his face lost in thought, as he stared deeply into the small flames of their smoking fire. With no distractions remaining, it was all he could do to keep from succumbing to his despondency at leaving Catrian behind.

Rewn nudged Gralyre, jerking his chin to address his attention to a small distance away, where Jord sat alone by his own small blaze, his back to a tree. Glittering knives reflected the golden firelight, as they tumbled and twirled in Jord's hands.

Gralyre knew nothing about the man, other than General Baldric, the spymaster, had conscripted him to join their quest. His ragged dark brown hair looked as though he had cut it himself with one of the knives he was juggling. His face was clean-shaven, angular and clever, and his dark gaze was piercing above a generous nose that he was currently glaring over at an interloper.

Trifyn, the bowman gifted to the quest by General Laurazon

of the lowland north, had approached Jord with a trencher of meat, and his bedroll, and made as if to join him. They were of an age, and Trifyn gravitated naturally towards a peer, though his blond hair and guileless face made him seem years younger than Jord could ever have once been.

A long dagger materialized in Jord's left hand, pointed at the bowman, while his right hand continued to juggle the two blades he had previously held. "No." Jord stated flatly, his knives whirling, tumbling.

Trifyn, already halfway crouched to the ground, bolted upright again. Stammering an apology he withdrew a few paces, hovering undecided for a moment before drawing a tremulous breath for courage, and approaching the tight knit group surrounding Gralyre's fire.

Gralyre said not a word, just shuffled nearer to Little Wolf to leave an inviting space.

With a sigh, the young bowman plopped down his bedroll and sat on it. "Thanks," he mumbled, as he began to bolt his food.

Trifyn's gaze darted amongst Gralyre, Rewn, Mayvin and Aneida, as he chewed and swallowed, made nervous by the easy silence surrounding the fire that seemed to exclude rather than include him. He racked his brain for something to say. "So, how about that ride today?" He smiled nervously.

Aneida snorted derisively, and rolled her eyes. "I am going t' sleep." She ensured that her aggravated snarl gave Trifyn the impression that he was somehow at fault. She twisted and flopped down into her bedroll, the rustling slowing as she found a comfortable position.

Mayvin stared stonily, then made a deliberately rude gesture that needed no interpretation.

Rewn chuckled quietly into his tankard.

Trifyn, his face flaming a bright red, sought to rise but Gralyre placed a heavy hand on his shoulder, and forced him back down with a tired smile. "Stay, Trifyn. Tell me how you came to be so good with your bow." Gralyre needed the distraction of conversation. Also, it would do well to remind the others of the lad's special talent.

Trifyn's smile was pure youthful enthusiasm. "Really?" he set aside his plate, and licked his fingers clean while he settled himself. "Well, there is no' much t' tell," he began.

Big surprise, Mayvin signed.

From out of the darkness, Aneida snorted. Though she was wrapped in her bedding, she was still paying heed.

This time, Trifyn manfully ignored the heckling. "My Da was a bowman, with General Zewan, who lead the Lowland Northern Rebels before the massacre at Thorstondor's Crossing. My Da died there too, and never knew me. A few months later, my Ma gave birth, and raised me herself."

Gralyre nodded encouragingly, though he had no clue who the people and places were that the bowman cited. Just another bit of his past lost to his amnesia, but his encouragement was real enough, though it seemed Trifyn needed little to share his life's story.

Trifyn reached over his shoulder, brought forth his unstrung bow, and caressed it reverently; six feet of gleaming re-curved yew, well-polished with wax, resin and tallow against the elements. Within ready reach, the small leather pouch attached to Trifyn's belt held the woven bowstring, precisely folded to prevent it from tangling.

"This bow was my Da's. He could fire three arrows into three different targets at the same time!" he boasted. "With this very bow, he killed a Demon Lord at over three hundred and fifty yards."

He passed it over to Gralyre. "My Ma gave me my first bow when I took my first step, and I have ne'er been without one since." He held out his left arm and patted his enlarged bicep. "I have bent the horns so many times that I have developed a curve in my arm," Trifyn held up two fingers of his right hand, "and my fingers have flattened t' hold the string." The two fingers were noticeably distorted in thickness and shape, compared with the others.

Gralyre passed the bow back. "What is the weight of the draw?"

"A hundred and fifty pounds. O' course I could no' draw this one back then. My Ma brought me bows according t' my age and strength, and as I increased with both, so my bows were made larger."

Rewn took a swig from his tankard. "'Twas an impressive shot ye made at the tournament, striking that little wooden discus in the air the way ye did."

Trifyn smiled enthusiastically. "Ye are good with a bow?"

Rewn shrugged. "I am alright, but no' at your level, I think."

"How many arrows can ye shoot in a minute?"

"Six. Eight if I do no' care t' save my strength."

"I can shoot twelve," Trifyn declared. "All because I save my arm by no' adding t' my work by pulling the string t' me, but by pressing the bow away."

"I do no' see the difference," Rewn frowned in confusion.

"My people call it *'Bending the Horns.'* Ye keep the bowstring at your cheek, and press your weight into the horns o' the bow. Your bodyweight draws the bow, no' your arm, ye see, so your arm ne'er grows tired."

Rewn still seemed doubtful, but gave the bowman his due. "'Twas a fine shoot ye made at the tournament. I would say that your Da would be proud o' ye."

Trifyn's smile faltered. "Aye, but I think my Ma is no'. She did no' want me t' ride with General Laurazan. She said that I was too young, and would only come t' harm." Watery tears threatened in his innocent, blue eyes. "I guess she was right," he whispered.

His fingers tapped nervously against the gleaming yew of the bow. "Are we really going t' die? Do ye think that we can do it? Get the sword?"

Rewn tossed the dregs of his tankard into the fire, raising a spitting hiss of steam. "Ye should have thought o' that afore ye agreed t' this madness," he growled peevishly, and settled himself deeper into his pallet, covering his body with a worn fur by way of withdrawing from the conversation.

Gralyre frowned at Rewn, then shrugged. "All things are possible, Trifyn. Get some sleep. Tomorrow is another long day."

Mayvin rolled into her furs, as Trifyn dug a hollow of his own and bedded down. Gralyre, about to settle into his snug hole, happened to glance over at where Jord was sitting, but the man had vanished, leaving no trace but for the weak, smoking fire, and an empty bedroll beneath a tarp that undulated in the brisk wind of the snowstorm.

Mystified, Gralyre arose, and walked over to investigate Jord's camp, reaching out with his senses to discover where the man had gone. There was an impression from where he had been sitting on his bedroll, but no footsteps in the fresh snow to show which direction he had hied off to. The man had the skills of a thief.

Gralyre stared out at the night, watching as the bonfires died down, and the men rolled into their beds, the outpost quieting of its revelries. Loneliness filled his heart, and he reached into his woolen overcoat, seeking his most precious possession. By the light of Jord's dying fire, he was able to see the plates he had painstakingly braided into the lock of golden brown hair stolen from Catrian after Matik had interrupted their kisses. He raised the token to his nose and breathed deeply.

It still held the scent of wild heather. *Catrian.*

After a moment, he returned it to its place of safety above his heart and turned back to seek his bed.

As though summoned by his heartache, Catrian's voice called to him from out of the darkness, a hollow, thin sound that did not match her usual rich tones.

"Gralyre."

Gralyre's heart thumped heavily in his chest, and he took an instinctive step forward, his eyes searching over the wall into the dark woods beyond the outskirts of the outpost. How was this possible? How was she here?

"Gralyre, come to me."

"Catrian," he breathed, her name as honey on his tongue, and bolted forward unheedingly, scaling the protective snow fortification with ease, and sliding down the far side. Within several leaps of deadfalls, and weaving between trees, he was completely engulfed by the shadowed forest, and swirling storm, and halted in bewilderment for there was no sign of her. He could not sense her, and even the minds of the beasts, the ones that flew in the night sky, or that prowled under trees for prey, spoke of no other. He was alone.

"Catrian!" he yelled. He pivoted in place, waiting, straining to hear a sound. Madness.

"I am here."

Gralyre whirled, his stomach flipping over in surprise when he beheld a wavering, ghostly figure, glowing gently against the darkness. "Catrian?" he whispered in awe, and reached out with his hand, his fingers splayed wide.

She smiled, and matched his actions. As their fingertips met, Gralyre felt a slight electrical zing, and his hand tingled as though it had gently fallen asleep, but Catrian's flesh held no substance.

He swallowed against a lump in his throat. "How? What magic is this?" She had promised that she would remain in contact with him to provide more training as he travelled south, but Gralyre had expected only a mind link from the Sorceress, as in the past. This was something new.

Catrian's voice was muffled, as though she spoke to him through the wall of a tent. *"My flesh is sleeping within my bed at the Fortress, and 'tis my soul that has left it behind, and flown here t' be with ye."*

Gralyre gently pushed his hand forward again, and shuddered, as her ghostly fingers passed through his. "Here, but not here," he murmured, his disappointment crushing the breath from his chest, as his eyes glittered with thwarted yearning.

Catrian dropped her hand, her fingers clenching into a fist. *"Yes."* She moved away like a leaf on the wind. Her feet did not shuffle beneath her cloak, nor did they leave a mark in the snows that she passed over.

"How long do we have? How long can you stay?"

Catrian shook her head and glanced back over her shoulder at him. *"No' long. We must hurry, for walking outside my body will sap my strength. I am sorry I did no' come t' see ye off, but..."* her chin dropped, and she brushed her hand over her left cheek, as she turned back to face him, *"I could no'. Please say ye understand!"*

Gralyre tried not to surrender to the overpowering ache in his heart for being unable to touch was almost worse than not seeing her at all. He nodded even as his hands clenched to fists.

She drifted back towards him to rest her insubstantial fingers against his cheek. *"Your training must continue."* There was urgency to her tone that forbore any arguments. *"I do no' know what it is that ye will face, but I will do everything in my power t' keep ye safe,"* Her eyes searched his. *"so that maybe..."* Her voice trailed to silence.

Unthinking, Gralyre tried to trap her fingers against his cheek, but was thwarted, as they passed through his cupping hand with numbing tingles. Drawing a deep breath, he stepped out of her reach. "What must I do?"

"Ye must work further on your control, but I will also teach ye how t' form weapons and defenses. The further ye travel from my side, the more difficult it will become for me t' reach ye, and the more dangerous it will be for ye t' practice your magic. So we have no' much time, yet much t' accomplish afore ye reach Fennick's Island."

"What of the Commander? Catrian, I will not have you placing yourself in..."

"I will deal with my uncle. What I will teach ye is only what ye should have been taught all along if no' for my fears."

"Will I learn enough to kill a Demon Lord?" Gralyre asked. Beyond any other, he wanted that power. Should he ever fall into the clutches of another like Lord Mallach, the Demon Lord who had been dragging him to Doaphin's Towers before Catrian had intervened and rescued him, he wanted to be able to kill the evil creature.

Catrian shrugged. *"Ye have the strength Gralyre, but it will depend on how quickly ye master your gifts, and how versatile your skills become."*

Gralyre could well understand her meaning. A large sword would cause a large wound, but wield it without skill, and small knives applied with expertise would cause far more damage than brute force.

Gralyre sat upon a deadfall, watching her through the swirling snow. "I am ready."

"Tonight, I will describe t' ye the mechanics o' forming a globe o' fire, that will no' burn your flesh, yet will incinerate all else, so be certain at what ye toss it at. 'Tis a versatile weapon, easily formed and controlled, that will stand ye in good stead for defense or attack. I have always found it t' be very useful."

Gralyre smiled in anticipation, and sat forward on his log.

Catrian smiled back, and hovered nearer, her body undulating slightly as though she were a piece of silken fabric blowing in a slight breeze. *"Ye are aware that fire can be drawn from any object, even stone. Some things have more o' the right energy than others, for example wood ignites with less effort than a stone will, yet still a stone will burn."*

Gralyre nodded attentively. Even a man could be caused to burst into flame. 'Twas a dangerous power to possess.

She held out her arm, her hand palm up and stared at it with frustration. *"Unfortunately, in this form, I canno' show ye, but I will talk ye through the steps, as ye do the work."*

Gralyre held out his own hand in mimicry.

Catrian nodded. *"Form a hollow sphere made o' air. Ye will be able t' feel its touch on your hand. 'Tis the same method as the cage ye used upon the thieves that attacked ye at the fortress, but small enough t' sit in your palm."*

Gralyre nodded, "Done." He could not see it with his eyes, yet he clearly felt it resting against his skin. "Now what?" As he watched, snowflakes accumulated against the surface of the orb, giving it a vague shape until a gust of wind sent the flakes fluttering and tumbling away.

Catrian's eyes narrowed on her palm, seeing in her mind's eye what was to happen next so as to describe the lesson as clearly as possible. *"Set the air within the orb, and only the air within, on fire. Ensure that the outer crust o' the globe remains intact so as t' protect your hand. Then ye throw it at something. The fuel of so little air will be quickly consumed but as ye grow in skill, ye will learn how to feed more air into the globe to maintain the fire without allowing the flames and heat to escape. Given enough time, the flames will condense and become almost liquid, sticking to and igniting anything that they strike."*

Gralyre grinned in delight. "That is all? 'Tis simple!"

"Careful Gralyre! Find your control! Do no' use too much power...!"

WHOMP!

The globe detonated, a burst of flames that lasted only a moment. Gralyre cursed and doused his hand in the snow.

Catrian giggled girlishly, her eyes dancing. *"Oh, Gralyre..."*

He glared up at her through the purple after-images that seared his vision. "What?" he asked testily.

She chortled again, bending double, and huffing for breath before she could speak. *"Your eyebrows are singed!"*

⁊ʀɢ

From where he sat, high upon the limb of a tree set far back from the small clearing, Jord watched Gralyre practice his sorcery. The knives flipped and twirled, the only movement within the stillness that Jord cloaked himself with.

Gralyre was conversing with the air. Who did he talk to?

General Baldric had warned him to beware of the man, that there were concerns over his allegiances. From what Jord could see those fears were well founded. Magic was not to be trusted.

CHAPTER TWO

Daylight heralded clear skies. The storm had worn out overnight, but had left behind its legacy of a foot of new fallen snow. The black, scorched circles that had been the bonfires still crackled occasionally from embers kept alive within deep piles of ash.

The outpost had not yet begun to stir from its evening revelry, when Lieutenant Vetroy awakened Cian with a hard nudge of his boot.

"General wants ye." The cold air fogged in front of Vetroy's face, but Cian could still see the sly blue eyes peering out from behind the lank blond hair contained under the knit cap of Kierdenan's lieutenant.

"Gods! 'Tis cold!" Cian griped, as he emerged from his heavy furs in a puff of loose snow, and rolled up to his feet.

"Keep quiet, and get moving!" Vetroy ordered over his shoulder, already turning back towards the relative warmth of the General's tent. The snow crunched underfoot with each step from the coldness of the air.

General Kierdenan glanced up from his breakfast, as the tent flap rustled. "Cian, m'lord," Vetroy, announced.

"Were ye seen?"

"I do no' believe so, no."

"Good." Kierdenan pushed his plate aside, and regarded Cian

solemnly. His thick brows over his pugilist's nose lowered in a frown, and the scars on his face pulled into new depictions of ruthlessness.

Cian glanced nervously between Kierdenan and Vetroy, and then to the comatose body of General Ryes, who snored loudly under the table from where he had obviously spent the night. A small pool of ale spilled out from an overturned tankard, matting the General's ear to the floor, and it would be a small miracle if he did not awaken frozen to the ground.

Cian returned his attention to General Kierdenan and Lieutenant Vetroy, uneasy with this impromptu audience. Neither man was to be trifled with, and if Cian had somehow gained their enmity he would not leave the meeting alive. He tried to read Kierdenan's face but it was impossible. The General always looked ready to kill. His scars and battered nose masked any other thought.

The General liked to fight. In his early days ruling the Eastern Rebel forces, it had been how he had settled all disputes. He would beat the transgressor to death, and prove his right to rule through the might of his fists. Times had not changed Kierdenan much save that now he delegated his second, Lieutenant Vetroy, to the task of executions, and Vetroy preferred a swift sword to enact his brand of justice.

Kierdenan belched and sucked at a morsel of meat caught in his teeth, picking at it with the nail of his little finger. "General Ryes and I spoke at length last eve, and I am convinced, as is Ryes, that this quest will fail. Cian, ye will no' be going t'

Fennick's Isle. I will no' waste a single man t' Boris' senility."

Cian could not keep his relief hidden at the suspension of the death sentence he had been facing. He had a wife and baby son waiting at home, and he had been heartsick to be leaving them. "Thank ye, General! But…what if the others beat the odds and manage t' retrieve the sword? I thought that ye wanted me along t' stop them from taking it to Commander Boris?"

Kierdenan flicked the bit of meat he had removed from his tooth, sending it sailing towards a corner of the tent. "The quest for the sword is over. The men – and women – will find a place with us, safe from Boris' lunacy. All but one. I want ye t' do what Commander Boris should have had the balls t' do in the first place. Kill this Gralyre fellow. End this farce by the time we veer towards home."

Cian smiled widely, and settled his sword belt more firmly about his hips. He had a score to settle with the lowlanders. "Thank-ye, sir. My pleasure, sir. Do ye want it t' look like an accident, or…?"

Kierdenan slammed his hand to the table, making the discarded plate bounce and clatter. Beneath the table, Ryes' snores suspended with a snort and groan, before taking up once more.

"No more intrigues. Just kill the demon-lover! And be careful. He apparently has some talent with magic."

Cian swallowed. "Yes sir." His blood chilled, for he had no desire to face a sorcerer, lowlander or not. Kierdenan had done him no favour by ending the quest. And as good with a sword as

Gralyre was…!

"Good. Get out."

"Yes sir, thank-you sir."

Kierdenan watched grimly as his man fled. Cian's fear was as it should be, but the man should not have questioned him as he had. "Will he follow through?"

Vetroy lifted the kettle of tea that was steaming over a brazier, and refilled his General's cup. "He will try."

Kierdenan looked up at Vetroy sharply. "Ye do no' think he will succeed." It was a statement, for they had both witnessed Gralyre's prowess during the tournament.

Vetroy shrugged. "He might get lucky, if he attacks from cover, with some o' the men." Vetroy set the kettle back over the coals. "Maybe I should take care o' it myself?"

Kierdenan shook his head. "Gralyre is a swordsman and a sorcerer. I can afford t' lose a minion in a bid t' kill him, but no' ye. I need your help with the muster."

Kierdenan lifted the hot mug, and blew across the surface, squinting against the steam. "Damn Boris t' the darkest hells! The man is no' fit t' lead." It was an old complaint, oft voiced.

Vetroy smiled slyly. "People die on battlefields, my liege. He will no' be in charge for much longer, I think."

A gleam lit a fire in the back of Kierdenan's small brown eyes. "Right ye are, Vetroy. Right ye are."

໕໖

Gralyre's group, smaller and more efficient than General Ryes' and General Kierdenan's men, broke camp and readied their horses quickly, but were then obliged to await the signal to ride. The Generals had yet to make an appearance, so their warriors took their time, gossiping and laughing, as they organized and loaded their packs onto the backs of their horses.

Gralyre yawned, and rubbed the grit from his eyes. It had been a late night, learning how to form Catrian's fireball, and he had not slept well afterwards, for just before she had melted away to return to her body, miles away at the fortress, Catrian had warned him to beware Cian, the Rebel that General Kierdenan had contributed to the quest. Cian was to steal the sword for the Eastern Rebels if it was recovered.

Cian had already announced his enmity at the bonfire the previous night, and Gralyre had little doubt that their relationship would not improve with time. The foreknowledge of the betrayal blackened his mood, and a necessary coldness invaded his soul, as he acquiesced to the knowledge that he would likely have to kill one of his own.

"Good morn, Gralyre."

Trifyn's eyes were also red rimmed, Gralyre noted, though for an altogether different reason. He had heard the lad crying quietly in the deep of the night, but Gralyre found little sympathy to spare. Trifyn was not the only one travelling towards danger and death, and Gralyre had no intention of coddling the unseasoned warrior or he would get them all killed.

In these dark times it was wasteful that a man with Trifyn's archery skills had not yet been battle tested, and Gralyre wondered what influence his mother had had upon that decision.

"Good morn," Gralyre returned curtly. "Go get breakfast."

Rewn, Aneida and Mayvin had sensed Gralyre's foul mood, and had left him be. Trifyn got the message when Gralyre turned his back.

"Alright," Trifyn stuttered, dragging his horse with him a few paces further onwards to where the others had assembled around the morning fire to eat and warm themselves.

Gralyre's gaze was drawn across the compound, and his level of irritation increased tenfold, for there was the other one, Jord, who was as much of a liability as Trifyn, though for opposite reasons. Jord was too independent, too alone in his survival and mistrust. His entire demeanour screamed '*Stay away!*'.

Jord's dark gaze met Gralyre's, and his mouth formed a hard line of challenge. A knife flicked out into his palm then vanished as quickly, and as Gralyre had already perceived, the message was plain. Instead of joining them, Jord looped his horse's reins over a branch, and crouched under a nearby tree. His glare never faltered.

Dotch led his horse out of the morning mist, and gave a friendly wave when he spotted the group, though as he neared, he proved pale and shaky. He massaged his head ruefully, sending his salt and pepper hair into spikes as he arrived. "Sorry I was absent from the fire last evening, lads," he smiled blurrily at Mayvin, "and lassies. I ran into old friends on sentry rotation, and they insisted on giving me a proper send off."

Mayvin's nose wrinkled, as Dotch's words introduced thick alcoholic fumes into the morning air.

Gralyre's mouth twitched, and his bleak mood receded slightly in the face of the man's self-inflicted misery. "Did ye get any sleep?"

Dotch nodded but glared up at the brightly rising sun with bloodshot eyes. "Some."

Aneida grinned, tore a strip of meat from what she was eating, and offered it. "Breakfast?"

Dotch burped, clapped a hand over his mouth, and staggered to a tree where he began to retch.

Rewn shook his head at her ruefully. "Was that really necessary?"

"Absolutely."

Mayvin nodded her concurrence. *Better out than in*, she signed.

Trifyn grabbed a skin of water, and went to Dotch, who accepted it gratefully, rinsing his mouth and spitting before swallowing a few gulps. "Thank-ye, lad," he whispered hoarsely.

The blast of a horn announced that it was finally time to mount up and ride.

ହୁଠଙ

As the sun dropped below a mountain peak, and the temperatures plummeted, they fell from their mounts in exhaustion, with naught to look forward to on the morrow but more of the same hard travel.

Still, sixty men made for light work in setting up camp, some tending to the horses, while axe chopping echoed throughout the glade from the men who were culling deadfalls from the forest, and dragging the wood back to their clearing. Campfires were lighted, and snow was set in pots to melt for water. The last of their fresh meat, gifted by the sentries of the southern pass, was set on skillets to smoke and hiss, as it thawed and charred. The scent of food in the air set their stomachs to rumbling for they had not halted for lunch.

Invisible lines were drawn in the camp, as like drifted to join with like, with General Ryes' pale warriors to one side, General Kierdenan's troops to the other, and the men and women bound for Fennick's Island left on their own, all save Cian who was noticeably ensconced with his comrades, and Jord, who was a camp unto himself.

While Aneida and Trifyn combed the forest for fallen limbs with which to start a fire, Rewn and Dotch dug man-sized hollows in the snow around the firepit that Gralyre was working on lighting, and Mayvin heaved on bowlines to stretch the tarps tautly above them all. It looked to be a clear night, but any cover was better than none to hold the heat from the campfire down at their level. Rewn and Dotch lined the hollows they had dug with stripped evergreen bows to insulate their bedrolls and body heat from the icy ground then finished the task by rolling out the heavy furs into the cozy nests. It was a comfortable division of labor.

"Where's Jord?" Rewn asked. "Should we make him a bed too?"

Mayvin shrugged, and referred a hand towards the darkening woods, where she had seen him disappear earlier in the evening.

"Might as well. He has to join us sometime." Gralyre had pondered how to proceed with Jord, and had decided that it was better to begin how they were going to continue. It was time to start folding these strangers into their midst, for to go into battle divided would be the death of them all.

Trifyn had joined them the first night, and seemed content to remain in their company. Dotch had made things simple by seeking them out, but Jord would bring his own challenges.

As for Cian, Gralyre was content to leave him out of their company. There was no reason the Rebel should die, and Cian would have no opportunity to betray them if he was not permitted to participate in the quest, though when the Eastern Rebels split off to return to their fortress to prepare for war, General Kierdenan would certainly protest the exclusion of his man. But that was a battle for another day.

As though guessing the direction of his thoughts, Rewn asked, "Cian is still travelling with Kierdenan's group?"

Gralyre nodded. "I suspect that he will not want to associate with us until after he bids them farewell."

Gralyre had contemplated confiding in the others about General Kierdenan's secret agenda, but had decided against it for now. There was little gain in divulging his foreknowledge, and giving Kierdenan time to create an alternative plan.

സറ

Aneida savored the peace of the evening woods, enjoying the sensation of stretching her legs after the long day astride a horse, as she dug through the shallow snows beneath larger trees for fallen branches. Trifyn had drifted away from her in their quest for dry wood, but Aneida was not concerned. Privacy was always in short supply, especially as she and Mayvin were the only women in the company. To be able to let her guard down for a moment was a rare luxury.

She had almost amassed enough firewood when she spied a large branch, but as she reached for it – *THUNK* - a knife struck the wood next to her fingertips!

She cried out for Trifyn as she jumped back, her sword springing to her hand, as she spun in search of the origin of the attack.

"Aneida!" Trifyn yelled, dropping his wood, as he ran through the heavy drifts between the trees towards the sound of her cry, his knees pumping high to clear the depth of the snow. With smooth grace born of years of practice he strung his bow, and had nocked an arrow by the time he skidded to a halt at her side.

"What has happened?" Working to slow and control his breathing, Trifyn drew his bow, sighting down the arrow's shaft at the underbrush.

"A knife! Some demon-humping bastard threw it at me!" Aneida snarled in a harsh whisper.

They stood back to back, pivoting slowly, as they scanned the heavy woods for the danger. The familiar tickle of the arrow's fletching brushed the side of Trifyn's cheek, while the warm heat from Aneida at his back was a continual, reassuring presence, as they matched each other's movements in a slow circling dance.

Voices from other firewood parties drifted and echoed throughout the forest, but no one appeared to be nearby. The shadows had lengthened as the sky had darkened, so that there was little to see within the forest murk.

From out of the gloom, another knife thudded into the ground at Trifyn's feet, and his arrow zinged crazily into the woods, as he hopped backwards.

Mocking laughter drifted out of the forest. "I could have killed ye both, and ye would ne'er have seen me!" Jord dropped lithely down from the tree limb from where he had been spying, and planted his feet in challenge.

Aneida sneered at him, straitened from her aggressive crouch, and thrust her sword back into its scabbard with disgust. She turned, deliberately showing her back, as she leaned down to pull the first knife from the fallen limb. "So ye were hiding in a tree, so what." She pivoted, and in a dangerous move, threw the knife back at Jord, sending it tumbling end over end towards his head with deadly accuracy.

Jord smoothly plucked it mid-air, and grinned as he spun it in a flicker of silver around his palm, where it suddenly vanished. Jord showed her his now empty hands.

Aneida's scowl made Jord's smile widen with delight. His eyes sparkled above his generous nose, that was reddened at the tip from the icy temperature.

Trifyn berated himself, and kicked at the snow angrily. He had practiced all his life for a moment such as this, and what had he done? He had rattled, and his first arrow had been spent as harmlessly as a novice's.

He shouldered his bow, and stalked back towards where he had dropped his stack of firewood when Aneida had cried out.

"Someone's missing their mommy," Jord heckled softly, as Trifyn passed. He had obviously listened to the bowman's story the night before, and also to the tears and muffled sobs that had drifted out while everyone else had slept.

Trifyn stiffened and glared. "At least I have someone who gives a fiddler's fart if I live or die, ye big nosed churl! Who would care if ye ne'er came home?"

Jord's eyes narrowed. "No one. I have no home. 'Tis the point. No ties, and no allegiances but t' myself!"

Trifyn grimaced in disgust, and headed back towards camp, leaving his wood behind in his ire.

Jord's knives came out to play, spinning hypnotically in his hands, as he returned his attention to Aneida. "I have been watching ye. Ye and your sister."

"Have ye, now," Aneida grinned brilliantly, and her hand rested on the hilt of her sword, caressing it up and down, crudely suggestive. Her eyes were narrowed dangerously, for if he thought to play her as he had done the bowman, he had a big surprise in store.

Jord's eyes sparkled with interest, before he chuckled self-deprecatingly. "No' like that. Ye make me curious, 'tis all. Ye and your sister are no' like the others, ye are more like me. Ye are survivors. 'Tis all that matters t' ye. No' the honour, and quests, and the horseshit spouted by the bards. So why are ye here?"

Aneida lifted her chin challengingly. "Why are ye?" she threw back.

"My General asked me."

Aneida shrugged. "Same. Besides, war is coming. This way or that, it makes little difference how I die. Just so long as I am spitting in Doaphin's eye when I do."

The merest trace of a smile brushed Jord's lips. "Same." He took a step forward, and halted as Aneida set her feet for balance, shifting subtly in preparation of defense. "Gralyre is a sorcerer, ye know, and General Baldric said he could be a spy for Doaphin."

"I know."

"This does no' concern ye?"

"No. Gralyre does no' have it within him t' betray an allegiance. Ye will see when ye get t' know him. He is no' like us. He is no' like anyone ye have ever met."

Jord frowned, and glared down at the snowy ground, his brows knit together, as he digested Aneida's unexpected defense of Gralyre.

Aneida picked up her firewood, and walked around him. "Trifyn left his pile over there. Bring the rest o' the sticks when ye return t' camp," she ordered as she passed.

໊໋

Jord announced his arrival at their fire by dumping his load of firewood with a clatter.

Gralyre glanced up from where he crouched poking the meat with the end of a knife. "Almost done." He announced to a hungry chorus of murmurs of anticipation. If he was surprised that Jord had sought the group on his own, he did not allow it to show.

Little Wolf watched the meat with famished fixation, and licked his chops noisily.

"'Tis good o' ye t' join us, lad" Dotch clapped a hand to Jord's shoulder.

Jord leaped back, and knives appeared in both hands. "I do no' like t' be touched," he hissed, trembling and blinking with his disquiet.

Dotch waved his empty hands. "Sorry, lad." He pointed a finger towards a pile of furs. "We set ye out a bed there."

Jord nodded, and when his gaze clashed with Aneida's, he dropped his eyes, shamed to have revealed a part of himself that he would have kept hidden. Glowering, he traversed around the firepit, ignoring the bed that Dotch had indicated, in favor of furs that were set up under a tree.

Trifyn straightened in surprise. "That one is my bed."

From where he now sat, Jord glared at him silently, and the ever-present knives spun and glinted in the firelight.

Trifyn sighed anxiously, and plucked at the hem of his shirt. "Ye can use it tonight," he mumbled.

ઈ૭૭૭

Gralyre awoke early, before the sun had yet to rise, though the sky was beginning to lighten as he stood to stretch. Catrian had kept him at his lessons well into the night, yet he felt rejuvenated, for he had slept deeply, and dream free for once.

She was a passionate teacher, filled with patience, and an unexpected humor, as she shared her skills and knowledge with him. With their every encounter, he felt his determination to survive the island grow stronger. Though he knew it to be futile, he had begun to hope that there was a way out for them all, maybe the war could be won, or avoided altogether, maybe Doaphin could be defeated, and humanity saved. It was a fool's dream, yet he clung to it for there could be no victory without hope, even if pointless.

The camp had yet to stir, and except for the men on sentry duty, the Rebel warriors remained sleeping soundly around their smoldering fires beneath the shelter of their tarps, mounds of fur against the white snow - all but Jord, whose bedding was again undisturbed and empty. Gralyre scanned the clearing of sleeping, snoring warriors but could not spot him. The man had a talent for remaining unseen, a skill that must have been useful while working as a spy for the resistance under General Baldric.

Jord had not spoken overly much over supper the night before after dropping off the firewood and appropriating Trifyn's bed, yet Gralyre could see that he was making an effort to know them, and that counted for much.

Jord was uncomfortable to be around, combative and abrasive to everyone, yet Gralyre could see that his skills were an asset to their group. All weapons were needed if they were going to survive. To steal a mystical sword, a thief in the night might be exactly what was needed.

Gralyre drew his sword, and strode a short distance away from the others, swinging the blade's familiar weight to loosen the knots from his shoulders brought on by the long days of riding, and sleeping upon the icy ground. Bringing his attention into the now, and clearing his mind of the past and future, Gralyre breathed deeply of the cold, still air of pre-dawn, and allowed the familiar rhythm to grip him with the power of the sword dance.

He burst into movement, swinging his sword, placing his feet in the familiar patterns, faster and faster, until his chest pumped for breath, and mist evaporated from his sweating body. His blade hummed as it parted the air to the strength of his precision strikes, the music that was set to the beat of his heart, and the acrobatics of the sword dance.

The sun slipped up over the mountainous horizon, and rays of gold slammed heat into Gralyre's flesh, giving rise to the illusion that the sun would never have emerged without his labors. Sometimes, the sword dance seemed to hold that godly power.

The first beams of light reflected off something metallic, the merest flicker to tease the corner of his eye, and his sword leapt to meet it. The silver blur of a knife was batted aside. Three more followed in rapid secession, each one diverted with a flick of Gralyre's wrist to clang harmlessly to the side. His sight widened to include the attacker.

It was Cian.

The tableau held for a moment, before Cian masked his surprise, and sauntered forward casually with a whistle and a false smile. "Impressive. I had heard that ye were good with a blade."

He hissed in surprise, as two of Gralyre's knives smacked the ground next to the toes of both boots, and glanced up in time to see Gralyre's arm drop on the follow-through of a third and fourth knife that shot past either ear, hitting a tree five feet beyond. The impacts quivered the blades that were buried three inches deep into the timber.

Cian touched a small nick on his left ear, his jaw dropping as he stared at the blood, realizing that he was alive only because Gralyre had allowed it to be so. He glanced up and swallowed nervously.

Gralyre's midnight-blue eyes were hard, his cold smile assessing and dominant. "Throw knives at me again, and I will have your head."

Cian nodded jerkily.

"Waken the others," Gralyre ordered. "And fetch my knives." His sword hit its sheath with a rasping hiss, and he stalked away.

Little Wolf greeted him at the edge of the forest where he had been watching over Gralyre's practice, and together they melted into the trees to hunt the wolfdog's breakfast.

The knives had been aimed at his back. What had changed to make Cian try to kill him before they reached the island? Gralyre would have to be doubly wary of the serpent in their midst. If he could discover Kierdenan's new plan, perhaps he could find the path where he would not be forced to kill Cian.

When Gralyre rejoined his group later, the camp had awakened, fires had been stoked, and breakfast was well underway. Rewn met him with a deep yawn. "Where did ye hie off t' last ev'en?" he asked blurrily as he stretched his back.

Gralyre shrugged, oddly reticent to share Catrian's visitations. "Practicing my Sorcery," he compromised with the half-truth.

Rewn handed him four blades, and gestured back over his shoulder. "Cian told me t' give these t' ye."

Gralyre accepted them without a word or expression, quickly secreting them back within his clothes.

"Is this something I should be worried about?"

"No."

"Breakfast," Aneida announced, and they turned to the fire for oats, honey and tea.

Lieutenant Vetroy's heavy hand landed heavily upon Cian's shoulder. "Did we choose the wrong man for the job? Why is Gralyre still alive?"

Cian whirled to confront his lieutenant, distracted from glaring daggers at Gralyre from across the camp – the only knives that he dared throw at the man ever again. Nobody could have reflexes that fast. Nobody! The man had been distracted with his sword practice, and Cian had aimed the knives at Gralyre's back. The man should be dead.

"No sir. I had him in my sights. He got lucky, 'tis all. I will try again!"

"See that ye do," Vetroy warned darkly. "If he is still alive when we take the east trail, ye will no' be."

Cian glanced back at Gralyre. The man would be on his guard now. If Cian was to succeed, he had to strike from the shadows.

Firelight glowed on the trees that surrounded the small clearing where they had halted for the night. In what had become the routine, the Southern and Eastern Rebels chose opposite sides of the clearing in clearly demarcated sides, and left Gralyre's small group to fend for themselves on the fringes.

Because the men and women bound for Fennick's Island were neither a part of one group nor the other, they alternated whose stores they would eat from each evening. Tonight was the Southern Rebels' turn to feed them.

As they erected their tarps and arranged their sleeping pallets, gathered wood and started a fire, Rewn stood in line for their allotment. As a lowlander he was relegated to be the last to receive food, and so was a while before returning with victuals, and portioning out the meager rations to them all. It was cold tack for supper; an oatcake and a few rashers of salted dried venison.

"Is this all there is? 'Tis no' much," Trifyn grumbled hungrily as he accepted his plate from Rewn.

"Ye get used t' it," Jord advised, "This is a feast where I come from." He sank his teeth into the tough salted venison, and tore off a chew.

"Where is that? Verdalan?" Aneida asked antagonistically. She had not forgiven the knife he had thrown at her.

Jord's eyes deadened, as he glanced up from beneath lowered brows, and his hand curled protectively to shield his food, as he swallowed his meat. "Among other places." The flickering firelight lit his face from beneath, casting sinister shadows.

Mayvin glanced between her sister and Jord, and her hands moved gracefully. *You like him.*

"I do no"!" Aneida huffed.

"I did no' quite catch that? What did ye say, Mayvin?" Rewn asked.

"None o' your concern!" Aneida warned while Mayvin smirked at her.

"Here lad," Dotch elbowed Trifyn, who was straining his jaw to chip off a crumb of the stale oatcake, "try dunking it in your water. 'Twill soften it some." Though they had not been given tea they had boiled snowmelt anyway, for the warmth of the water helped ease the chill from the day's ride.

Gralyre cut a third of his venison away, and offered it to Little Wolf, but with a lip curl of disgust, Little Wolf averted his head.

"Everyone stop eating!" Gralyre barked.

Rewn lowered the strip of meat he had been about to stuff into his mouth. "What…?"

"The meat has gone off."

Jord sniffed his salted venison with a frown. "Tastes fine t' me."

Gralyre caressed Little Wolf's ears. "Believe his nose. The meat is tainted."

Mayvin lowered a strip of her ration towards the firelight to examine it, and a flame leapt forward to ignite the preserved meat in a flare of green. Her face contorted, and she threw it into the coals to avoid seared fingers. She looked at Aneida and her hands spoke. *Dipped in Cynamede Salts.*

"Cynamede!" Jord and Aneida both blurted out.

Jord did not know Mayvin's hand language, but the spy for the resistance had recognized the poison for himself. He threw his plate into the fire, where it ignited in shooting bursts of emerald flames, before lurching to his feet, and staggering to the trees. He stuck his fingers down his throat so that in moments he was retching up the food that he had just consumed.

"Did anyone else eat of the meat?" Gralyre demanded.

"No," Trifyn said shakily. "I was soaking it in my hot water t' make a stew taste. I do no' like plain water so much." He glanced towards the moistened oatcake and flung it into the green flames. Whatever had been on the meat, had to have been transferred to the cake. He had been within moments of poisoning himself.

Dotch arose with his tankard of warm water, and jogged to where Jord had finished heaving. "Drink this. Ye have t' flush it from your body!"

Jord grabbed the cup and guzzled, his throat bobbing, as he swallowed all of the contents in one go. His face dewed with sweat and fear, he turned aside, and in moments vomited everything he had just drank.

"Mayvin! More water!" Dotch yelled back over his shoulder, as Jord went into convulsions and fell to his knees, then his side. Dotch moved to support Jord's head, holding him steady as froth began to bubble from between his clenched teeth.

Gralyre stood, and raised his hands for attention. "Everyone! Stop eating! The meat is poisoned!" As his deep voice boomed out over the Rebels, they all paused in their meals.

Gralyre pointed back to the last of the green flames in the campfire, and his suffering man.

Mayvin and Dotch forced more water into Jord, holding him steady, as his legs kicked out in jerky spasms. As he seized, more water was spent into the snow than ended in his stomach.

They rolled him to the side as he began to retch once more.

"What are ye spouting, lowlander?" one of General Kierdenan's Rebels yelled back. The warriors seemed more confused than concerned, as they watched Jord's contortions.

"Heed him, ye fools!" Aneida shouted. "The venison is poisoned with Cynamede Salts!"

Chaos erupted, and Southern Rebels fled to all sides, forcing themselves to vomit their food.

Kierdenan and his men stood by grimly, for they had eaten from their own packs, and so were in no danger.

Gralyre wheeled, and grasped Aneida by her shoulders. "Cynamede. Is it natural or did someone deliberately…?"

"Gralyre, 'tis deliberate. Someone just tried t' kill us."

Gralyre's face went blank of emotion, and Aneida shivered in response, as he gently released her.

"Rewn." Gralyre looked towards his friend. "Who gave you the food?"

Rewn pointed shakily towards General Ryes' side of camp. "'Twas from Ryes. His man, Adifson, dolled out the rations tonight."

"Help Jord!" Gralyre snarled over his shoulder, as he stalked across the camp with Little Wolf hard upon his heels.

Aneida and Rewn exchanged an anxious glance. A wrathful Gralyre was a terrifying force.

General Ryes was regurgitating his meal alongside his men but turned at the last moment, as some instinct warned him of the impending danger.

Gralyre's strides never faltered, as he grabbed the Southern General by the throat, and dragged him backwards until he slammed up against a tree. "Coward! You would use poison to kill us?" His midnight-blue eyes darkened with rage, intent on the gurgling, pale man as he throttled him. In the strength of his anger, Gralyre held Ryes a foot off the ground.

As Ryes' eyes bulged in his purpling face, Gralyre realized that there was a sword point digging into his ribs, as well as two men trying in vain to drag him off their General.

"Let him go! Ye let my father go! He did no' poison ye!" Lieutenant Corr yelled in Gralyre's ear, pressing harder with his sword to get his attention.

Still Gralyre hesitated to release the General. Only a few moments more, and the man would pay for his crime.

"Let him go. If he had known o' the poison, he would no' have been vomiting his meal like the rest o' us. Think man!"

Gralyre grudgingly ceded, but just in case, he bounced the General's head against the frozen bark of the tree one last time before releasing him. Only then did he allow the two men who had been tugging upon his shoulders to drag him from their leader.

Corr dropped his sword, and rushed forward to support his father, as he sagged and coughed, gasping life-giving air.

Little Wolf circled Gralyre's guards, eerily quiet as he slipped in and out of their blind spots, forcing the men to crane their necks to keep both the beast and Gralyre in check.

Ryes' pale moon-face was clammy, as he blinked blurrily.

Corr closed his hand on his arm. "Da! Are ye alright?"

General Ryes patted his son's hand. "Ye a good lad, Corr. I will just lay down for a minute…" Ryes' legs buckled.

A Southern Rebel rushed forward in time to help Corr ease his father to the ground.

Gralyre, now that his temper had cooled to hard reason, fisted his hands at his side. "He ate the meat?"

"We all did!"

Gralyre scanned Rebels who had assembled to watch the drama, but saw that no one else was convulsing. The southerners had all received their rations first yet only Jord had been affected by the poison, which made little sense unless the group bound for Fennick's island had been targeted specifically.

Corr heaved a shaky sigh, and his ashen skin seemed to pale further, as he gently brushed his father's thin blond hair back from his forehead. Seen together, father and son bore an uncanny resemblance. "Take him t' his bed." He gestured to a couple of pallid southern warriors.

"We will. We will take real good care o' him, Lieutenant."

"Thank-ye, lads," Corr whispered, as one man took his fathers shoulders and the other his feet, bearing him off to the tarp under which his bedroll had been set up.

"Gods what am I going t' do? He ate the meat. We all ate the meat." His voice dropped until it was barely audible, and he seemed to shrink in on himself, already grieving. Suddenly, he leapt into action.

"The food must be destroyed! Gods! 'Twas t' have lasted our

journey. We have no time t' hunt. We will be too slow. We will no' reach Fennick's Island afore the Spring Solstice."

"Be calm, Lieutenant Corr," Gralyre interrupted. "If you had been poisoned, your men would already be convulsing. The poison afflicted Jord almost immediately. Let Little Wolf smell the packs. He can tell us which are good and which are not."

"Shut your mouth, ye lowland turd!" One of Gralyre's guards snarled, pressing the point of his sword against Gralyre's throat.

Gralyre knocked the sword away, and backhanded the warrior for his trouble, sending him tumbling into the brush.

"Stop!" Corr ordered his man and Gralyre both. He took a step forward, and his moon-shaped face, so much like his father's, was grave, as he surveyed his men. "Are any of ye feeling ill? Weak?"

A chorus of "Nays," and shaking heads answered, confirming what Gralyre had already deduced.

"Thank the Gods!" Cian sagged with relief. "Let him go!" He ordered the remaining guard.

"But Lieutenant!"

Corr glared at his warrior, who finally sheathed his blade with belligerent compliance.

The guard Gralyre had struck cursed and growled, as he fought his way free of a winter-dead bramble but by the time he had gained his feet, the tide had turned. He wiped the blood from beneath his nose, a brilliant red against the pale skin of his face. His glare promised retribution later, when the lieutenant was not there to intercede on Gralyre's behalf.

Gralyre rolled his shoulders, and set his feet in case he had to defend himself from the Rebel once more.

"Alright. I will allow ye and your wolf t' search the packs." Corr motioned Gralyre to walk a few paces off with him. "Then what?" he asked quietly, his uncertainty in his command blatantly apparent.

Gralyre regarded him gravely. "Your man. The one who was distributing the rations tonight?"

"Adifson?"

Gralyre nodded.

Lieutenant Corr followed the reasoning through to its end. "Where is he!" he shouted at his warriors. "Where is Adifson?"

"Stop your bellowing. I am here," Adifson pushed through the crowd of southern warriors. "Ye canno' believe that I had anything t' do with this!"

"I do no' know what t' believe just yet. Watch him," Corr ordered, and several of his men crowded in to flank their comrade.

Adifson rolled his eyes, and crossed his arms over his barrel chest. "I will want an apology later," he warned defiantly. His whitened skin was translucent to the point that blue veins could be seen pulsing at a rate that gave lie to his air of unconcern.

One by one, Little Wolf sniffed the packs of food thoroughly, and found no further scents of poison.

Gralyre and Corr turned away from the last pack that Little Wolf had been snuffling, to consider the Rebel warrior who had overseen the rationing that evening.

"Well thank the Gods 'twas only the one pack that was bad!" Adifson declared.

Rewn jogged up just then. "Gralyre!"

Gralyre grabbed Rewn's wrist. "Jord - is he alive?"

Rewn shook his head. "Jord has slipped into a coma. Dotch and Aneida are no' sure if he will waken."

"Everyone else is alright?"

"Yes."

"Keep an eye on them, Rewn. Let no one near until we have figured this out."

Rewn nodded, and reversed back to their bivouac.

Corr glanced up at Gralyre, who topped his height by six inches. "It could have been a bad pack that someone slipped into the supplies, and ye were unlucky enough t' receive it," he suggested in a quiet murmur.

Gralyre's lip curled in disdain, as he slowly shook his head.

Lieutenant Corr sighed heavily, unable to keep Gralyre's grim stare, and looked at his boots instead. "Yea, I do no' believe that either."

Corr approached Adifson, nodding to the men flanking him to be wary lest he try to flee. "Did ye leave the food unattended, Adifson, from the time ye unpacked it t' the time ye distributed it?"

"I tell ye it was no' me. I did no' poison the food!"

Gralyre's body shifted slightly, and his eyes narrowed. "You did not answer his question. Did you leave the food unattended?"

Adifson's fingers tangled nervously. He was a big man, but there was something about Gralyre's mien that made his bowels freeze as cold as the icy winter air. "I may have left...taken a piss." His head rose, and his chest puffed defiantly. "But I was no' gone long enough t' make a difference, I tell ye!"

Corr shrugged in confusion, looking back over his shoulder at the looming warrior. "He is no wrong, Gralyre. Ye canno' just sprinkle Cynamede. Ye have t' soak it in. It would have taken a day t' taint the food with enough poison t' cause harm. This took planning. It must have come from the fortress with us."

Gralyre evaluated Adifson once more, and every instinct screamed that the man was hiding something. "Show me the empty pack."

"There, over by that tree." Adifson led the way to a downed forest giant that he had used as a makeshift trestle table to dole out supplies. He picked up an empty oilskin pouch, and threw it at Gralyre's feet. "That is were all o' the meat came from!" he declared.

Gralyre and Corr watched solemnly as Little Wolf sniffed at the pack.

Good food. I am hungry now.

"That is not the source." Gralyre's face blanked of all emotion, and Little Wolf was suddenly stalking towards Adifson. "Do not move," Gralyre warned softly.

Adifson began to sweat. "What? What are ye doing?" He glanced nervously at Corr. "Lieutenant, stop him!"

Corr's mouth turned down at the corners. "What does it

matter if you have nothing t' hide?"

"Who is in charge, him or ye?" Adifson insulted.

Little Wolf's nose wrinkled, and he growled at the pale southerner. The sound rumbled out over the assembled crowd of warriors, who needed no translation. Their own snarls echoed in reply.

Gralyre drew his sword in a long, slow rasp. Corr glanced at the implacable warrior, and mirrored his action.

"No! I did no' do anything! He is lying! Ye canno' trust a lowlander..." Adifson asserted, but one of the men flanking him suddenly reached forward and yanked a loose sack out from within Adifson's heavy winter coat.

"If ye did no' do it, what is this then?" he shook the empty canvas bag.

Little Wolf gave a threatening bark that trailed into a growl.

"That is it," Gralyre confirmed quietly, and the glacier tone laid upon the words condemned the man.

Adifson's face changed from nervousness to cold hate, and he grabbed the short knife from his belt, threatening his own men so that they jumped back, but ringed as he was, there was nowhere to escape to.

Corr shook his head in disgust over the betrayal. "Why? Why did ye do it?"

"I am no' going back t' the Bleak! Ye canno' make me! I will no' live my life in darkness, no' now that I know the touch o' the sun! Just let me go!" Adifson cried out pitiably. "I have t' stay in the light! He promised I could stay in the light...!"

Adifson gurgled, as the tip of an arrow erupted from his throat, pushed through from behind. He dropped to his knees and then fell forward, lifeless, his knife still clutched in his fist.

General Kierdenan passed his bow to Lieutenant Vetroy. "Damn the demon-loving traitor." He spat upon the corpse then glanced at Corr innocently, as if such an expression could ever live on the man's scarred face without artifice. "'Tis the only way t' deal with their ilk."

ဆാ

THE HEATHREN MOUNTAINS – LATE WINTER

Two Demon Rider's perish in a landslide, and join the ranks of the undead Deathren. Only four minions remain now to stoke the daylight fires that foil the ice that would kill Sethreat.

The Deathren are of no use, mindless hunters and feeders that will not survive long in their half-life state. Tonight, the cold mountain temperatures will freeze the creatures solid until the spring thaw, after which they will hunt warm flesh unceasingly until they rot away to nothing.

Clear and cold, the stars shine down, and the moonlight bathes the mountainsides in blue brilliance. Sethreat lifts Its snout to the icy wind. The traitor, Green Crest, is nearer. Only a fortnight ahead now.

Sethreat gains ground on the traitor by vectoring across mountains to shorten the trail between, while Green Crest follows the scent of the Man on long paths through valleys. Still, Green Crest moves quicker, and defeats the cold that keeps Sethreat sluggish and slower than its Demon Riders. How does Green Crest accomplish this feat without the aid of daylight minions? Sethreat barely travels a league in the night, where Green Crest makes several.

The denmate of the traitor, Speckle Tail, mewls. "Hungry."

'Witless hatchling!' Sethreat gestures towards the fresh killed Deathren, of no use except as meat.

Speckle Tail leaps high, clears the distance to a Deathren, and lands upon the creature's shoulders with its talons to drive it into the snow and rocks.

The Deathren does not panic, nor does it struggle. It does not cry out in pain, nor bargain for its life. It feels nothing.

Speckle Tail unhinges its jaw, and bites down, shears off the head down to the torso, and the Deathren's body slackens in final death. The Stalker raises its snout to the moon, its throat works, and its massive head jerks as it swallows. Its next bite takes the torso.

Sethreat appraises the summit of the mountain before It this night. Perhaps the traitor can be seen from the height of the crest.

"To the ridge."

The minions gather near with their torches, for the meager heat banishes some of Sethreat's torpidness for the climb. It longs for the days of spring when such a mountain can be conquered in minutes instead of hours.

Later that night, It sits upon a shelf of stone, and slowly scans the valley on the far side. It awaits movement.

The minions cluster at Its back with their torches, and provide the heat It needs, while Speckle Tail bears the firewood they use up the mountainside. The dull creature is unaware of the insult of being a bearing beast to Sethreat's comfort.

There is no movement in the far valley. The traitor is elusive. No matter. The trail is evident, and It has the scent. The Hunt continues.

৪১৩৪

THE SOUTHERN HEATHREN MOUNTAINS

Jord had not yet awakened, but he had survived to the morning, which boded well. If the poison had not taken him by now, he had a fighting chance of beating it. For once he had remained in his pallet overnight.

General Kierdenan grandly declared a day of rest. However, if Jord had not recovered by the morrow, they would have to abandon him, for he would likely never awaken from the poisoning, and time was a hard mistress.

The morale of all the warriors, especially of those of the south, was grim. They were having trouble fathoming that one of their own had betrayed them.

The Rebel warriors were a rough lot, settling personal disputes with sword and arrow, and as likely to stab you in your back for the shoes on your feet, as welcome you to the fire to share a drink of an evening, but the one code they adhered to was that you never betrayed your unit, for the man at your side was the man you relied upon in battle. Adifson was seen to have tried to murder his comrades, even if Gralyre's man Jord was the only one to have suffered from the poisoning. Such a treasonous act was a low blow to all of the warriors.

General Ryes sported hideous bruises against the white of his throat that silenced his voice to a hoarse, whispering croak, as he set one team of men to chipping through the snow and ice, and another to gathering stones with which to burry Adifson. They could not afford to leave his body uncovered lest it was discovered by their enemies to tell a tale of the Rebels travelling that way.

Gralyre made a point of apologizing to the General for his attack, which Ryes accepted with ill grace. Gralyre knew that he had made no friendships within the southern camp.

Around Gralyre's fire, the mood was even worse. Jord was buried under heaps of furs, as still as death, while Aneida and Mayvin took turns trickling water into his mouth. Their only hope was that the poison would be flushed from his system; so hour-by-hour they bent to the task.

There was little the others could do but watch, keep the fire hot, boil water and a weak gruel, and hope for the best.

"Why did Adifson try t' poison us?" Trifyn finally blurted. He had been leery of voicing the question for the experienced warriors made him feel that he was the only one who did not know, and that by asking he was exposing his ignorance.

"He was bribed," Gralyre answered in disgust. "At the last, Adifson admitted that someone had offered him amnesty should he kill us. Whoever wants us dead is still here, hidden." Across the campsite within the Eastern Rebel ranks, Gralyre's cold gaze locked onto Cian, who glanced away quickly. "From now on, we post a sentry of our own, at night." Gralyre ordered, and the company murmured in accord.

Trifyn gnarled his lower lip between his teeth for a second. "Yea, I know all that, but *why* did he do it?"

Gralyre shrugged. "Dotch, you know of the Bleak... you lived in it for a time?"

Dotch sighed heavily. "Born and bred."

"Adifson said that he would not return, that he would do anything to stay in the light."

Dotch smiled grimly. "The Bleak is the worst place in the realm. Sometimes at night when there is no moon, I feel my nightmares return." He threw a heavy branch into the fire then reached for the flask inside his shirt, taking a long pull, before offering it around to the others. "Adifson made his choice t' betray us, and deserved what he got, but I understand why he did it." Dotch stared across the clearing at the groups of pale-faced southerners who huddled around their fires in subdued silences. "We all do. For the promise t' stay in sunlight, what would any o' us be pushed t' do?"

"Why did Adifson no' just leave like ye did?" Trifyn asked. "How did ye get free o' it?"

Dotch regarded the untried bowman. "T' desert is treason, punishable by death, lad." He accepted the flask back from Rewn, thumped the stopper to ensure it was well sealed, and hid it back in his vest pocket. "When I was a younger man o' about your age, I used t' go raiding in the lowlands for food and supplies for the Southern Fort. It was a privilege for those few o' us whose task it was, for we got t' walk in the sun for weeks at a go. Every time I returned home to the Bleak I vowed it would be the last; that I would leave, and ne'er glance back. Yet they depended so heavily upon the supplies we were able t' scrape together that the obligation would ne'er release me. Over time, I came t' realize that being allowed t' walk in the sun was no privilege, but a curse. If I had ne'er seen the light, I would no' have craved it so, and would likely still be in the Bleak to this day.

"But that is no' how the story goes. I made sure I was always raiding, always in the sunshine, so much so that I even lost my pasty southern skin. One day, I met a lowland lass, named Ella, and married her, and loved her too well t' subject her t' a lifetime o' darkness. So we fled north t' Boris' territory, and waited t' be discovered by a Rebel patrol. I have spent the last ten years pretending t' be a lowlander refugee, lest they send me back south t' face the penalty o' desertion. Until, that is, Catrian approached me about this journey. Somehow, she had learned my secret, and presented me the choice o' going along on the quest, or returning south t' meet my judgment. Either way, it was going t' be the Bleak for me, so I chose the only course that might see my eventual return t' my family."

Rewn frowned, in confusion. "Catrian said that the Bleak is just a fog bank. How bad can it be?"

Dotch shook his head. "'Tis so much worse than fog, lad. Much, much worse. 'Tis the absence o' color and birds, and growing things, and anything good. 'Tis rot and disease. Ye breathe that dark mist in, and it takes root in your bones, and ye feel it bringing the same rot and disease t' your very soul. Day after day, year after year, the rot takes root, and the darkness grows until ye are hollow and empty. Your bones ached with a pain that canno' be soothed. Men and women go mad, and flee into the Bleak, ne'er t' be heard o' again."

The men were silent, as they stared into the fire, each digesting Dotch's description with varying degrees of dismay. No one doubted the sincerity of his words, for that level of repulsion smacked of firsthand experience.

Jord suddenly coughed and gasped, struggling under his furs with grunts of panic.

"Gralyre!" Aneida yelled. "He is awake!" Jord's head rested upon her lap, and she brushed his ragged brown hair back from his forehead. "Hush, rest easy."

Jord's struggles increased. "Do no' touch me!" he slapped at her hands. "Do no' touch me!"

Aneida immediately raised her hands. "There, see, I am no' touching ye. Now settle. We have been that worried about ye. The poison almost had ye, I think."

Jord was not heeding her words; instead he was patting his

hands through his clothes and bedding. "My knives! My…Where ARE THEY!" he bellowed. He tried weakly to rise but the mere weight of the furs was sufficient to keep him pinned to the pallet.

Aneida sniffed righteously. "Ye tried t' stab me with them last night when ye were raving out o' your head, so I disarmed ye."

Trifyn reached to the side, and hefted a heavy burlap sack that clanked and chimed of metal hitting upon metal. He placed it upon Jord's chest. "Here they are. They are all there. Ye sure have a lot o' them."

Jord's agitation eased, and he hugged the bag with relief. "Thank-ye. Thank-ye." He was panting heavily when he opened his eyes to look up at Aneida. "Do no' take my knives. Ne'er that."

"Then do no' try t' stab me with them," she retorted sharply and stood. Jord's head thumped hard into the ground.

He winced and groaned.

Gralyre crouched down and leaned over him. "How are you feeling, Jord?"

"Like I have been poisoned."

Gralyre's lips twitched, and the other men chortled appreciatively at the bravado, and in relief that Jord would recover.

"Rest and recoup your strength. We must ride onwards tomorrow," Gralyre advised.

Rewn bent in with a bowl of weak gruel that had been

stewing in case Jord awoke. "Here Jord, this will help ye."

"Who gave it t' ye?" he asked warily.

"'Twas Kierdenan's turn t'…" Rewn swore, as Jord slapped the wooden bowl from his hands. "What did ye do that for?"

Jord's face purpled, as again he fought with the furs to rise and lost. "I will no' eat any food that comes from those dirty, demon-humping bastards!" His voice tapered to a whisper, as his strength failed him.

"'Tis safe Jord, I promise ye," Rewn reassured. "Little Wolf's nose found the poisoned food, and he has been double checking everything that is given to us. It will no' happen again."

"I will no' eat it, and ye canno' make me!"

Aneida snorted. "Quit acting like a spoiled child."

Gralyre stood. "'Tis alright. Little Wolf and I will take care of this," he shouldered his sword. "We could all use some fresh meat."

"I will come!" Trifyn volunteered enthusiastically.

"Come on then. There are some grouse nesting in the snow just over here," he indicated a nearby hillside. "Let us see how fast you are with that bow when Little Wolf flushes them."

Jord watched them go with a grimace. "Someone should be watching Gralyre. He could be planning t' contact Doaphin or attack us with his magic or anything! How do we know 'twas no' he that poisoned us?"

Rewn shook his head. "Ye have the wrong idea about him, Jord."

"I have t' agree with Rewn," Dotch concurred. "I witnessed

Gralyre attack a General last night, because he only suspected Ryes in your poisoning. Then I watched him move the heavens t' discover the guilty party, and see them punished."

Rewn smiled proudly to hear the words of faith in his beleaguered friend. "Ye should see what he does for people he actually likes," he quipped.

Jord subsided with a frown, as he pondered why Gralyre had risked all to find his poisoner. He was reminded of Aneida's words in the forest when he had asked her about Gralyre, and she had voiced her loyalty.

Could he really be trusted, or was it all an elaborate ruse?

෨෬

Their horses were well rested and ready to run, so that when they began their ride in the morning, they gave their steeds their heads for a time in an effort to reclaim a portion of their lost day.

It was not long after they set out before Gralyre's horse complained of a stabbing pain in its spine.

"Rewn! Something is ailing my horse!" Gralyre yelled to his friend over the pounding sound of hooves, and reined to a stop.

Rewn waved that he had heard, and sent word up the column that they had a horse in trouble.

The column came to a stomping, blowing standstill, and General Kierdenan and General Ryes rode back to see what was amiss.

"What now!" Kierdenan demanded when he saw that it was

Gralyre. "I begin t' suspect that 'tis ye who is sabotaging this mission so that ye can avoid facing Fennick's Isle."

General Ryes said nothing at all, but his hand rose to touch the black and green bruises that shackled his neck, vivid and painful against the whiteness of his skin. His icy glare spoke of rage and injured pride.

Gralyre pulled off his saddle, and his mouth tightened as the damage was revealed. "So you believe it was I who shoved thorns under my saddle blanket?"

"Humph," Kierdenan grunted when presented with the horse's bloodied back. "Fetch a spare!" he ordered Rewn. "And catch up t' us when ye are done. We are no' waiting on ye. We lost enough time with that debacle yesterday!"

"Fine," Gralyre agreed curtly, as he evaluated his horse's wounds.

The animal's back was gouged and bleeding heavily, and some of the clusters of thorns had worked their way into the flesh so deeply, that Gralyre would have to draw them out carefully and slowly, lest they snap and leave a point in the wound to fester.

While Gralyre began to doctor his horse's injuries, Rewn selected a fresh mount from the string of spares that they had brought along for just such emergencies so that their speed of travel would not be impaired.

The rest of the Rebels rode onwards, leaving them behind.

಼ೂಛ

Cian glared over his shoulder, as the column rode away. He could not understand how Gralyre had found the issue so quickly, nor why the horse had not thrown him. At a full gallop the man should have injured himself severely, if not killed himself outright.

Gralyre had the good luck of the Gods on his side. Already he had survived a knife attack, a poisoning, and now this simple accident.

The poisoning had been easy to arrange, the southern warrior ripe for bribing. The fool would have done anything to keep from returning south, but in hindsight it had been a risky plan. If the General had not moved so quickly to end Adifson's words, Cian would have ben implicated in the poisoning, and he doubted that anyone would have believed that the tainted sack of meat had been given to him by Vetroy.

Within a day or two they would be taking the east trail towards home, and he knew that if he had not killed Gralyre by then, that he was a dead man. If he wanted to see his family again, the man had to die, and soon!

But perhaps this latest failure was a blessing in disguise. An idea began to take root, and Cian spurred forward to talk to one of his comrades. He had a plan.

෫෬

As the sound of the column of Rebels faded into the woods, Rewn saddled Gralyre's spare horse, and led him forward.

Gralyre was soothing his injured steed, rubbing a healing balm into the wounds, and praising him for his courage and stamina.

"Still do no' want t' talk about it?" Rewn passed the reins to Gralyre. His eyes went from the embedded thorns to Gralyre's set face. There had been one too many accidents during this journey for them all to be coincidences, and Rewn was nobody's fool.

"No."

Little Wolf bounded into the clearing, cavorting happily with his tongue lolling, and skidded to a halt in front of Gralyre. *She is alone. She should be with her pack. She misses us and follows.*

Gralyre's mouth dropped in surprise. "What? What did you say?"

Rewn glanced between the canine and Gralyre. "What is it? What has happened?"

Gralyre's mouth tightened. "Saliana is following us."

CHAPTER THREE

"What is she thinking?" Rewn yelled over the sound of his horse's hooves. They were galloping down the portion of trail they had only just covered, back towards their camp of the day before, where Little Wolf had said that Saliana had passed only a few minutes behind them after their departure that morn.

Bent low over the neck of his fresh horse, Gralyre forbore to answer. Rewn had been ranting since they had left, and he knew a rhetorical question when he heard one. Gralyre's injured mount cantered in their wake, tethered by nothing more than Gralyre's will that he follow.

Little Wolf fell steadily behind, not quite able to keep pace with the racing horses, but he knew their destination, and soon veered off into the woods to hunt a rabbit that caught his eye, rather than retrace his steps. He would rejoin them when they turned back towards the main body of the Rebel warriors.

Rewn was silent for a moment more, brooding and stewing. "How far now?"

Gralyre looked into the distance, as he sought ahead on the trail with his magic. "She is near," he shouted back to be heard. "She must have caught up with us yesterday when we were not travelling."

"I hope she is alright because I am going t' kill her!" Rewn blustered. They rounded a bend on the trail, and Saliana screamed in surprise to be confronted by the galloping horsemen. Her horse reared, tumbling her off the back to land in a drift of snow.

Rewn and Gralyre were off their horses in a flash, but Rewn was nearest, and reached her side first. "Saliana!" His concern momentarily supplanted his ire, as he cradled her head. "Are ye hurt?"

"No." Saliana struggled to extract herself from the deep snow, and Rewn helped, lifting her up.

Knowing that she was uninjured was all the permission that Rewn needed to allow his anger to slip free. "What do ye think ye are doing? Why are ye here? How are ye here?" His hands closed on her shoulders, and he gave her a rough shake.

Saliana chose to answer his last question first. Her white-blond hair had come loose in her fall, and she could not brush it back because of the grip Rewn held upon her upper arms. "I left ahead o' ye, a day before." Her voice was timid and whisper quiet, and she blinked rapidly to meet his angry gaze. "I waited on the trail for ye t' pass, then followed. I have ne'er been less than a few miles behind since."

Rewn released her and paced away, and then back again. He wagged a finger an inch from her nose. "Ye canno' come with us! Go home."

Saliana shivered but forced herself to straighten from her habitual, protective hunch. "No."

"No…What?" Rewn sputtered.

"I am no' going back, and ye canno' make me." She tucked

her loosened hair behind an ear, and folded her arms stubbornly.

Rewn threw up his hands in disgust, and turned towards Gralyre. "Do ye hear this nonsense?"

Gralyre eyed Rewn carefully. "She is right."

Rewn's bellow echoed through the trees, and Saliana flinched. "Ye are agreeing with her?"

"We cannot force her to leave, nor can we leave her alone to wander the wild, and we have no one to spare to take her back to the Northern Fortress." Gralyre presented his reasoning to his friend. "So yes, she is right, we have to take her with us." His voice flattened, as he glared sternly at Saliana. "For a time, at least. General Kierdenan and his men leave us in a couple of days to return to the Eastern Fortress. She will go with them."

"No! Ye canno' do this! I do no' want t' go t' Kierdenan's fortress!"

Gralyre paced forward, staring down at the fearfully quivering woman until her eyes fluttered anywhere but at his face, and she hunched her shoulders protectively once more, drawing inward like crumpled parchment. "You should have thought of that afore you followed us. What are you doing here, Saliana? Why did you not stay safely back at the Fortress with Dara and Dajin?" The sombre tone demanded the truth.

Saliana cleared her throat, with a sound that was almost a sob.

"What was that? I could no' hear ye?" Rewn sniped, as he stepped into her space in a blatant act of intimidation.

Saliana's spine straightened again, and ire made a soft pink glow come to her cheeks. "Because I chose t', Rewn Wilson!" She shouted, and Rewn and Gralyre both took a step back in surprise.

"All my life I have let others decide my fate. This time I choose. I get t' choose! No' ye Rewn Wilson, and no' ye Gralyre-who-ever-ye-are! And I choose t' go t' Fennick's Island!"

"But…" Rewn began.

"Ye said there was a war coming, that there would be no safety, no' for the ones who stayed behind, and no' for the ones who go! So what difference should I stay or go? At least this is o' my own choosing! At least I will no' die among strangers!" Saliana slapped Rewn, hard, rocking his head from the force of the blow. Then she gasped, and her hand sprang to her mouth.

"I am sorry, I am so sorry!" She shrank away, cringing and hiding her face. "Do no' hurt me, I am sorry."

Gralyre touched her shoulder, and she flinched. "Saliana we would never harm you. You know better."

Her gaze flitted to Rewn's, and her cornflower blue eyes filled with tears when she saw him rubbing his cheek. "I do no' know why I did that. Rewn I am so sorry…"

Rewn's jaw clenched and he turned on his heel and stalked towards his horse.

"Rewn!" Saliana cried out piteously.

"Rewn!" Gralyre shouted for an altogether different reason, as men stepped out of the woods, their crossbows already aiming, as they sprung their ambush.

Gralyre tossed Saliana into a thicket, before diving forward to tackle Rewn to the ground. Rewn's horse, not so lucky, bore the brunt of the initial barrage, taking six arrows to the neck where Rewn had only just been standing. With a harsh scream, it collapsed, dead.

Rewn and Gralyre took advantage of the downed beast's bulk for cover, as more bolts slapped into the snow around them.

""'Tis Kierdenan's Rebels! Do ye want t' talk about it now?" Rewn cried out.

"No!" Gralyre drew his sword, and charged forward. Most of the Eastern Rebels panicked at the unexpected move, and spent their arrows harmlessly before Gralyre was upon them. Those who still had their weapons loaded could not use them or risk hitting one of their own.

Rewn screamed a battle cry, and followed Gralyre into the melee only to find himself face-to-face with Cian. "What are ye doing, man, we are comrades!" Rewn yelled, as he deflected Cian's vicious blow at his midsection.

"Ye are no friend o' mine, lowlander," Cian rejoined with an overhand strike.

Rewn parried easily, and threw Cian back and away. Another Rebel moved in from the side to attack, and it took all of Rewn's training from Gralyre to deal with both men at once.

He ducked another deadly swing from Cian, and drove his sword up as he stood, impaling him under his chin. Rewn did not wait for Cian to fall before he jerked his sword free to block the oncoming attack from the other warrior. Thanks to Gralyre's tutelage, he far outclassed the Rebel in skill, and the bout ended quickly and decisively with Rewn's sword through the Rebel's guts.

Rewn could not meet the Rebel's shocked gaze as he fell. He was shamed that after a week of travel, he did not know the man's name. Perhaps if he had made more of an effort to know Kierdenan's men, he would not have now been facing this man across swords.

Breathing harshly, Rewn glanced up in time to watch the last of the attackers drop at Gralyre's feet, next to a half-dozen more of Kierdenan's slain Rebels.

Gralyre looked over at Rewn, his face spattered with the gore of his attackers. "Are you harmed?"

Rewn shook his head, quivering with the aftershocks. Though he had seen Gralyre fight before, and had been training with him for most of the year, he still found that the man's mastery of the blade bordered upon the supernatural.

"Saliana," Gralyre shouted.

"I am here! I am alright." She stepped daintily over a severed arm, her hand going to cover her mouth. "Who are they? Why did they attack us?"

"They are Eastern Rebels, comrades we have been travelling with for nigh over a week!" Rewn snarled. He turned and kicked Cian, who shuddered and burbled, still alive despite his broken jaw and ruined face. Rewn's thrust had pushed the tip of his sword out of Cian's mouth, instead of ending in his brain stem.

"And these are the men ye were going t' make me leave

with?" Saliana reproached under her breath, not quite brave enough to be heard by the men, despite Gralyre's reassurances that they would never harm her. Life experience had taught her altogether different lessons.

"Now can we talk o' this?" Rewn indicated Cian who was struggling to breath around the blood flooding his mouth and throat.

Gralyre approached with steady strides until he loomed over the fallen man. He placed his bloodied sword against Cian's neck.

"Gralyre?" Rewn prompted.

"He was to accompany us to Fennick's Island, and should we have recovered the Dragon Sword he was to betray us, kill us and return the sword to General Kierdenan."

Cian's eyes widened in horror as Gralyre relayed the entire plot to Rewn. "How!" he managed to gurgle around a mouthful of blood, coughing the word out on a breath.

Gralyre ignored him. "Why try to kill us now? We have not even reached the island yet."

"Kier...Kier...nan. No...quest." Blood sprayed as Cian began to drown.

Rewn frowned, "No quest. Gralyre, what is going on?"

"Do you remember what I promised you, Cian, should you ever attack me again?" Gralyre asked gently.

"My...hea...hed!"

Gralyre's sword sang.

ഇൗന്ദ

It was past sunset when they finally spotted the small fires flickering through the trees that marked where the Rebel's had stopped for the night. There were fewer lights than normal, as a goodly portion of General Kierdenan's man lay dead on the trail behind them.

Gralyre's rage at being forced to kill men who had not been his enemies had grown with every league they had travelled south to rejoin the larger body of Rebels. There had been no time to bury the dead, so Gralyre had called out to predators in the area that there was food to be had. A large pack of wolves had answered the summons, and were even now feasting upon the unexpected boon.

The Rebels had been acting upon their General's orders, and perhaps given the choice, they would not have attacked them. Gralyre would not have treated the remains with this final indignity had he not had to hide their trail from any passing Demon Riders. Getting to the island was his priority, and part of that duty entailed remaining undiscovered on the trail.

Rewn shared Saliana's horse, as his had been killed in the skirmish, while Gralyre's injured steed trailed behind. Saliana straddled the saddle behind Rewn, clasping his waist, and had remained silent since they had left the battle ground.

Little Wolf ranged through the forest around them, sometimes following, sometimes taking point, but always scanning for another ambush. Gralyre was taking no chances that Kierdenan would not try again.

When they trotted into the camp, supper was over, and the men were beginning to bed down for the night.

Dotch waved as they rode in, stepping out from beneath the tarps. "Took ye long enough t' catch up. I thought ye had decided no' t' come!" Though his words were light, there was an air of relief.

Aneida and Mayvin exchanged a look of disbelief when they spotted Saliana on the back of the horse behind Rewn. Aneida's fists came to rest on her hips. "Would ye look at that? What is Saliana doing here?" she murmured to Mayvin.

Mayvin shrugged, but her eyes narrowed.

"Who is that?" Trifyn asked, pointing at the blond woman sitting behind Rewn.

"I will introduce ye later," Aneida stated quietly, as her attention shifted to General Kierdenan, who was rising slowly from his campfire, his eyes scanning the darkness of Gralyre and Rewn's back-trail.

"Mayvin, get the swords. Trifyn, your bow."

"What?"

"Now."

Kierdenan strode forward, and grabbed the bridle of Gralyre's horse, dragging it to a halt, as he demanded, "Where are the others?"

Rewn glanced back over his shoulder at Saliana. "Stay on the horse!" He did not await her nod before his feet hit the ground, and he slapped the animal's rump to move it onwards, and out of the range of the brewing confrontation.

Gralyre smoothly dismounted, and glared at the General coldly, watching with grim disgust, as Kierdenan realized the truth.

"They are dead? All dead? Gods damn ye!" Kierdenan yelled, and threw punch at Gralyre's head with all of his considerable muscle mass behind the blow.

Gralyre ducked smoothly, and drove his fist up into Kierdenan's belly, and as the General folded over the pain, he followed through with an uppercut that snapped Kierdenan's head back.

Gralyre's horse danced away, as Kierdenan stumbled back to keep his balance. Blood welled down his chin from the wound caused when his lips had mashed into his teeth. He grinned, his mouth awash in red, and his scarred face tugged in directions set to give the onlookers nightmares. The General set his balance and raised his fists. "I am going t' enjoy this!" Firelight flickered over his face, shadows and light, as his massive shoulders flexed with strength.

With what seemed the merest flicker of movement, Gralyre's sword left its scabbard. The red light from the campfires glowed along the sharp edge, an omen of violence. "You have had all the enjoyment of me that you will ever have."

"Ye are a coward, afraid t' face me in an honest fight!"

"What do you know of honest fights, and cowardice when you have tried repeatedly to stop this quest, and to kill me and my people from the shadows, with knives and poison and ambushes? There is no fight between us, only justice for the men you sent to their deaths! The only reason that you are not joining your dead is because the Rebels are going to war, and Boris is going to need all of his Generals."

"Boris is an imbecile! This quest is over! Vetroy! A sword!"

Kierdenan's lieutenant responded instantly but a small picket of daggers smacked into the snow around his feet. Jord face was cold with warning, and his arm poised with more knives ready to fly from between interwoven fingers.

For good measure, Rewn stepped up from behind and placed the cold gleam of his steel against Vetroy's throat. "Sheath it!" he hissed.

Vetroy slammed his sword back into its scabbard, his sly gaze canted sideways to meet Rewn's. "Ye had best finish me lowlander, for I will no' forget this!"

Rewn snorted. "Save your threats. We will no' see each other again after this night."

Another Eastern Rebel tried to move forward to lend his blade, but yelped when Trifyn shot it from his hand, the sword ringing as it flew away into the darkness from the impact of the arrow. Aneida, Mayvin and Dotch guarded the rest of the warriors, preventing any further interference.

"Kierdenan, what have ye done!" General Ryes shouted.

Kierdenan growled in frustration, as small tussles erupted throughout the camp, and his men were disarmed. With so many of his warriors dead, there was no contest.

Gralyre glared down the length of his sword at Kierdenan. "I answer to Catrian and no other. She requests the sword, so I will fetch it for her."

"Ye were sent on this fool's errand t' die, and that is precisely what ye will do!" the General retorted, words his only weapons now.

"First there is the Bleak, the endless fog that blocks out the sun, turning day into night. Then there is the sea, cold, choppy, that ye will have t' swim, for the only ferry across t' the Island is guarded by a legion o' Demon Riders. Should ye make it t' the island alive, which is doubtful, ye will then have t' survive until the Solstice, hunted at every turn by Deathren and Stalkers. Then, if ye yet live, ye will have t' steal past at least one Demon Lords, and a couple o' legions o' Demon Riders, all so that ye can challenge a labyrinth that has claimed the lives o' hundreds o' thousands o' Doaphin's own throughout the ages."

Kierdenan sneered at Gralyre, "Ye are no' a man, just a shade that has no' yet passed over t' the realm o' the dead." The General curled his lip and turned away. "I sought t' spare ye with a quick death, and your people with sanctuary away from Boris' insanity. 'Twould be a mercy t' kill ye here, and travel at our leisure the rest o' the way home, rather than ride our horses into the ground only t' deliver ye up t' the Demon Lords on Fennick's Island."

"Try it," Gralyre invited softly.

General Ryes stepped between Gralyre and Kierdenan. "Enough! Kierdenan, ye are skirting dangerously near t' sedition!"

"Ye are a fool, Ryes. Boris does no' care about the south any more than he cares about the sword! Come with me. Save yourselves!"

Ryes' pale face flushed with anger. "I did no' commit t' war lightly, Kierdenan. I did it because I would no' see humanity fade away with a whimper. Boris has ordered the muster, and ye agreed t' it, the same as us all. He ordered these men t' Fennick's Island, and 'tis t' Fennick's Island that I will see them. Ye had no place trying t' stop this. The time t' naysay this plan was at the war council, no' undermining our Commander when ye no longer have t' look him in the eye t' do it! We fight for our lives, and we must leave no weapon in our arsenal. We must try t' reclaim the Dragon Sword. Aye, 'tis pointless… but t' no' at least try? That is a sin." Ryes panted harshly from his tirade, as he pointed at the Eastern General.

"Now, take your remaining men and leave, and be thankful that your position as a General saves ye tonight from a harsher sentence."

Kierdenan glowered and touched his fingers to his bloody lip. "On your own head be it! We will leave on the morrow."

"Ye will leave tonight, or I will finish what Gralyre started."

Gralyre nodded approvingly, and stepped back, at which Ryes motioned for Lieutenant Vetroy to come collect his General.

The last of the Eastern Rebels broke camp and moved out, subdued by the knowledge of the death of their comrades by Kierdenan's betrayal.

Kierdenan's hard, sneering gaze promised retribution for what Gralyre had done, as he walked his horse from the clearing, leading his diminished column of men towards their home.

Gralyre never glanced away until Dotch interrupted by placing a hand on his shoulder. "Well lad, 'tis glad I am that there are no other Generals in camp for ye t' try t' kill. My heart canno' take the excitement." His stare was also following the last of the Eastern Rebels, as they entered the woods.

Gralyre shook his head, unable to make light of what had occurred. "He made me kill comrades, men I broke bread with, travelled with." Little Wolf, a shadow in the darkness faded into the forest in the wake of the Rebels. He would tell Gralyre if Kierdenan attempted to double back for revenge.

Dotch nodded. "Aye. He is a right bastard, that one. The Gods will sever his luck soon enough."

Gralyre's jaw bunched, as he ground his teeth. It had taken everything in him to let the General ride from camp. "The Gods should hurry."

ഇൽരു

"Saliana what are ye doing here?" Aneida asked casually, as she drew a warm, wool blanket over Gralyre's injured horse's back, and secured it in place with a leather buckle.

Saliana placed a feedbag over the nose of her mount, and shrugged, even as her eyes flicked towards Rewn and back again. "I chose no' t' be left behind."

Aneida grabbed her arm roughly, dragging her around to face her. "This is no' a game for a stupid little girl pining after a man!"

Saliana struggled to free her arm of Aneida's grip, but it was too strong to break. "Do ye think I do no' know that? I do no' care if I die."

Aneida bared her teeth. "Do ye care if ye kill us alongside ye, because that is what will happen. Ye are no fighter. At best ye can cook, at worst ye will be a burden that we will die trying t' protect."

This time Saliana did tear her arm free, and Aneida reared back in surprise.

"I am no' a burden!" Saliana asserted fiercely. "I have been learning how t' tend wounds, training t' be a healer. I can help."

Aneida eyed her, considering. "If there is a fight, ye have one job only. Hide. Do no' be a distraction t' our survival. Do ye understand?"

"But…"

Aneida leaned in threateningly. "Or I will kill ye myself right here and now, and leave your body for the wolves."

Saliana gulped and nodded.

Aneida smiled. "Lovely. Come meet the others."

ဆာ

Soon enough, Ryes was calling them to muster, and another day of hard riding began. Followed by another and another, a repetitive blur of endurance, as they raced the Solstice.

In the haste of their passage there was seldom a chance to hunt, and with the poisoner in their midst identified and gone, they were confident in the safety of eating travel rations again; salted, cured meat, and hard oat biscuits greasy with suet. Jord would still not eat a bite of it until Little Wolf had sniffed the food, and declared it safe.

All their resources went to keeping their horses sound, for to lose even one could be the delay that would fail them in the end. They worked in shifts during the hours after they halted for the night, walking their steeds to cool them from their run before feeding them their warm water and oats.

Little Wolf would melt into the dark forest, and return with a bloodied muzzle. He was the only one enjoying fresh food, but Gralyre did not presume upon the wolfdog to bring them his kill. Little Wolf needed the extra energy, for he would not eat from the salted travel rations if he did not have to.

Travelling south through the mountains became treacherous, as the ever-strengthening sun began to soften the snowpack. What appeared to be a solid trail would often collapse beneath them, and the horses would sink up to their bellies, then struggle and lunge to get free of the drifts. Mornings were especially dangerous, for the melt of the day before would freeze overnight and ice the trail. They lost two of their horses to broken legs.

Anxiety, born of time slipping inexorably away, wrapped them in tense bonds, for as they descended from snowy mountain passes into rolling foothills, they moved out of winter, and into early spring where they were surrounded by signs of emerging life.

Daily, the last of the snows were melting under their hooves, as they travelled south through heavily wooded lowlands. Frothy rivers overflowing with ice melt caused delays while they searched for safe crossings. Each hour lost was a setback that they could ill afford.

The frantic pace exhausted them, and tempers grew short, as the food supply dwindled. There was little choice but to ration their supplies, and hope that they lasted to journey's end. If they missed their deadline their chance at the sword would be lost forever.

The hard pace made conversation difficult, and when they stopped to rest they avoided speaking with each other. The evenings around the campfires were bereft of the jocularity and companionship usual to small groups of common cause. Questions were forced and curt, answers were monosyllabic. Chores were completed in enervated silences. They would fall onto their pallets, as soon as possible but their sleep was turbulent with nightmares of dread. They awoke exhausted each morning, and started anew, resolutely miserable.

Gralyre was more fatigued than the others, for the bulk of his evenings were not spent in sleep they were spent with Catrian. The moment the evening meal had finished, and the others were retiring, Gralyre would be pacing in the woods outside of their campsite, impatiently awaiting Catrian's astral arrival.

She was not just his teacher, she was his comfort, his

strength, and his only shining reason to return alive from Fennick's Island. He loved her laugh, and had memorized its joyful ring, he loved the crinkle that appeared between her eyes when she was thinking, and the way her shoulders stiffened when he challenged her.

His lessons progressed well but he grew more despondent with each night's parting. He did not know if it was her despair that was infecting him or his own, for soon he would have passed beyond the reach of her magic, and would not see her again.

හිⓒ⅏

"I just do not understand how it works. If I could see you do it…"

"*Gralyre, you know that I am unable t' show ye in this form,*" Catrian chided. Her shade had grown even more translucent of late, and would soon vanish. Gralyre dreaded that evening like no other.

"Explain it again."

Catrian sighed and placed her palms together only to slowly widen the gap between. "*Think o' a lodestone and how it can either push or pull.*"

"I know how a lodestone works, I just do not know how to duplicate that power! I just cannot grasp it! Why can I not just use my magic to pick up the rock and throw it?"

Catrian bit her lip, and glanced up at him from under her

brows, prompting Gralyre to answer his own question.

"Conservation of Power," he grumbled quietly.

Catrian smiled at his frustration. "*Ye can pick up the stone but ye know that the larger the stone, the more power ye must use t' move it. Better t' alter the stone's Godsmagic t' make it want t' repel the ground, and rise all on its own*," she repeated the core of the lesson once more, "*Then ye can push it anywhere ye want.*"

"Repel" Gralyre repeated, and glared at the small pile of rocks that he had collected, as per her instructions. This was energy that he had not learned of yet in the book, *Aegon's History of Magics in the Kingdom of Lyre,* that Catrian had once given him to study in her tent. He had not made it further than a third of the way through the heavy tome before leaving the Northern Fortress on this quest, and the power of magnetism had not yet been explained. This new Godsmagic was proving stubborn to identify and manipulate.

"*It canno' all come easily t' ye Gralyre. Go now, get some rest, and we will try anew tomorrow.*"

Gralyre watched dolefully, as Catrian hovered through a moonbeam, and her shade faded away to almost nothing, a mere shimmer of an outline with vague shadows for features. "How many tomorrows do you think remain to us?"

"*No' many. We have already continued for far longer than is wise. 'Tis only a matter o' time afore Doaphin's creatures sense ye.*" She moved out of the silvery light, and her form regained enough substance that he could see her sadness.

"I know." Gralyre sat wearily upon the bole of a fallen tree.

"*Gralyre, what is it? Ye are tired and distracted tonight.*"

"'Tis nothing." Gralyre dug up a reassuring smile. "Do not trouble yourself."

"*Gralyre.*" Catrian hovered nearer, and set her fingers to his cheeks, drawing his face upwards so that she could see his eyes.

If Gralyre needed any further proof that her power was waning with distance it was this; there was no tingle from where her ghostly hands touched his skin.

"*Tell me. Share your pain.*"

"Ever since Kierdenan left, things have changed."

"*How so?*"

Gralyre thought for a moment, seeking the words to describe the disquiet in his soul. "We have lost hope."

"*Those o' ye bound for Fennick's Isle?*"

"Aye."

As Fennick's Island had drawn nearer, a thick malady had descended upon the small group chosen to reclaim the sword. They had begun to avoid each other, their attitudes contrastively different than that of Ryes' men who were travelling towards hearth and home.

Gralyre recognized the cloak of melancholy that shrouded them but did not know how to pierce it. If he could not offer them a shard of a promise, he feared that any chance they had of surviving the Island, however slim, would slip away.

Catrian gazed down into his face, feeling his worry, and knowing that his words were as much about the two of them, as about the men and women doomed to perish on Fennick's Island.

"Gralyre, I would give everything if ye were t' return t' me, t' be by my side but we must face the truth that there is little chance o' that," Catrian reminded gently. *"Even if ye somehow survive and return, I may no' be alive, for I go t' war."*

"There is no chance of returning at all, without a will to do so!"

"Then ye must remind them what they are fighting for. Ye must remind them that they have a reason t' live and t' fight." She asked it as much for herself.

"How can I give them that which I have little enough of my own?" Gralyre demanded with heated anguish. He looked into her face, and realized that she had become so translucent that he could see the branches of the trees behind her. His fear was for her, for them both, and for what would never be.

"I have accepted that our deaths are coming, and there is nothing I can do to halt it!" Intense pain blasted through his body, making him quiver with the thwarted need to keep her safe. "But there comes a time, when you realize that you can neither do enough, nor be enough, nor say enough to make up for the fact that you are not going to be there ever again, that you are leaving your loved ones behind to face the world alone!"

"Gralyre!" Catrian protested.

Gralyre stood and walked away from her a couple of paces. His hands came to rest on his hips, as he raised his eyes to the moon.

"Ye are no' leaving me alone, anymore than I am leaving ye. Our lives are no' our own. The Gods have decided that this is t' be our fate."

He sighed heavily, and when he turned to look at her, his eyes were haunted. "Catrian, I am drowning in regrets. 'Tis not just us. I can barely bring myself to look them in the eyes. None of them would be here were it not for me. You sent them with me in the hopes that they would keep me alive, yet now I feel their coming deaths as a heavy weight crushing my soul."

"Gralyre, I do no' know how t' help ye."

Gralyre stepped forward until he was as near as he could be without stepping into her shimmering ghost. He bent his head until their brows would have met had she but been flesh and bone.

They stood that way for a long time, an unsatisfactory embrace compared to the real thing, and when Catrian finally whispered her good-bye and faded away, Gralyre was left bereft.

෩෨

The next evening, soon after they had halted, Gralyre made his way to the General's fire. "General Ryes," Gralyre called out as he neared. "A word." His manner was polite but not subservient. He doubted he could fake submissiveness even were he to try.

"Hurr?" General Ryes grunted in reply from where he sat by his evening fire, drinking strong tea. Gralyre eyed the liquid wryly. His group had not had anything but water to drink of an evening since before Kierdenan had been ousted.

Corr, General Ryes' son, popped open an eye from where he lay on his pallet on the far side of their fire. With a tired sigh he pulled his furs closer, and rolled away from the two men, settling with his back to the light to give them their privacy.

Uninvited, Gralyre sat on a rock, and rested his arms along his bent knees.

The General's face tightened at the presumption. He had not forgiven Gralyre's attack, despite the fact that the misunderstanding had led to the unveiling of the viper in their midst. "What do ye want?"

Gralyre was in no mood for pleasantries either, and got right to the point. "The mood of my group is dismal. If we go into battle with this attitude, we will not live to tell the tale."

"What mood is that?" Ryes asked coldly, slurping noisily from his tea. He did not offer a cup to his visitor.

"Defeated." Gralyre replied after a moment of reflection. "They act as though they are on the gallows, and the rope is already about their necks."

"So what?" the General waved indifferently. "They are right. Ye are all going t' die."

Gralyre's expression froze at the General's flip response to his concerns. "I do not deny that death is a possibility but to go into battle prepared to die is a far different thing than going into battle expecting to die! If something is not done we are already defeated!"

"Ye *are* already defeated!" Ryes threw the dregs of his cup into the fire with a violent flick of his wrist. The fire hissed and smoked from the moisture, throwing demonic, dancing shadows over their faces. "Did ye no' listen t' Kierdenan that night? Nothing he said was no' the truth. Ye will no' be returning with the sword. Ye will no' be returning at all! Your one hope for survival is that we miss the dawning o' the Solstice. And I will ride every horse in our stable into the ground afore I allow that t' happen," he declared cruelly.

"You are missing my point…"

"No! Ye mistake mine," the General pointed a finger. "My one and only concern is t' delivery ye t' the island afore the Solstice. I will no' be wasting any more energy than that on men fated t' die."

"To die… perhaps," Gralyre conceded grimly. "But I would have my men die on their feet, sword in hand, and screaming defiance at the evil they fight, not on their knees with their heads tucked up their arses!" The intensity in his words was not lost to the quietness of his voice.

"Your men?" snarled General Ryes incredulously. "Ye are no' in command o' this expedition! I am!"

"You and your warriors will be joining us on Fennick's Island then?" Gralyre smiled coldly, as bright, sharp rage drew him to his feet.

Ryes flinched back in alarm, his hand rising, as though to protect his throat, but Gralyre merely stalked out of the firelight.

For a moment he hovered on the edge of the light, frustration eating at him. Then his resolve firmed. If the General would do nothing, then it fell to him. Gralyre's indignation shattered the chains of his despair, and he stalked into the trees surrounding the small glade where they had set up their evening campsite.

He could start with finding his group some fresh meat. He was sick and tired of stale and salted trail rations, and nothing could change moral faster than a full belly.

Gralyre called to Little Wolf, who thumped his tail tiredly from across the clearing, then arose with a groan. Gralyre waited just inside the trees for the wolfdog to reach him, before melting into the woods to hunt.

ಬಂಧ

In the morning, the group bound for Fennick's Island awoke to a small feast smoking and spitting over a cheery fire; a rabbit and a pheasant, roasted to perfection.

The General and his men wore sour expressions, as they breakfasted upon the hard biscuits and salted jerky that made up their trail rations, eying the bounty covetously.

Though the pall of hopelessness still hung over the small band, they seemed noticeably more relaxed with their bellies full. It was a beginning, Gralyre acknowledged.

CHAPTER FOUR

In the pre-dawn darkness, Gralyre loomed over the sleeping men and women of his group. Was this the right course of action? He did not know. All he knew was that to do nothing was not an option. Better to do the wrong thing, than nothing at all.

"Wake up." Gralyre shook Rewn roughly before moving over to Dotch. "Get up."

"What? What is it?" Dotch asked in alarm, as he rolled over. "Argh, 'tis no' even daylight," he griped, and flopped back down.

"Gralyre what is the matter?" Rewn asked blurrily.

"Waken the others. Gather your weapons, and meet me in yonder clearing," Gralyre indicated. "'Tis time to train. We are going into the battle of our lives, and I will see us prepared!"

Rewn looked over at Jord's undisturbed bedding. "Where is Jord?"

"Here," Jord called. Already dressed, and at the ready, with his knives flickering around his hands, he stood behind Gralyre with a mulishly, challenging expression.

"Good." Gralyre's smile was all teeth. "You are going to show us how good your are with those knives."

A few minutes later, and the group was assembled in the small clearing outside of camp that Gralyre had indicated.

"Why are we doing this?" Aneida grumbled and swung her sword in long arcs, chopping at the branches of a pine sapling.

Aye, what is the point? Mayvin signed with sharp, abrupt gestures to indicate her ire.

"The point, Mayvin, is that the next full moon is the Solstice, and your battle skills are inept," Gralyre taunted softly.

At the blatant challenge, Mayvin drew her blade and, to her credit, gave everything that she had to draw blood, but Gralyre easily parried every lunge and strike.

"Get him, lass!" Dotch encouraged.

"Cut him!" Jord yelled.

The sharp clanging of the swords drew the attention of the southern warriors who were on sentry duty, but when they saw it was their own travelling companions sparring, they went back to their watches.

"Should we stop this?" Trifyn asked Rewn nervously, as the sharp edges glinted in the rising sun.

Rewn smiled and shrugged. "Keep your eyes open, and mayhap ye will learn something."

Gralyre caught Mayvin's blade on his, and scooped it from her grasp, sending her sword sailing into a bramble patch where it was swallowed by a deep drift of snow that had not yet melted.

Mayvin scowled, shaking her hand to relieve the sting of the impact.

"You." Gralyre pointed his blade at Aneida. "Have you also forgotten everything I taught you this winter, or can you make a better showing than your sister?"

Aneida smiled boldly, and strutted out into the clearing to face him. "I forget nothing, swordsman." With a battle yell, she drew fast, and lunged forward.

Again Gralyre parried every attack Aneida could devise before sending her sword flipping end-over-end into the same bramble bushes that had claimed Mayvin's. "Perhaps you can help your sister find her sword while you seek your own."

Aneida sniffed disdainfully and looked down her nose at him. "Demon-humping bastard," she tossed over her shoulder with a growl, as she walked over to the bushes to help Mayvin search.

"Dotch, you are next."

Dotch spit on both palms, and rubbed them together in anticipation before drawing his steel. Within moments, he watched in confusion, as that same blade was swallowed by the bramble bush next to where the women, on hands and knees, searched in the deep snow for their lost weapons.

"Hey! That was a little too close, Gralyre!" Aneida carped.

Dotch glanced between Gralyre and the bushes. "Really?" he asked wryly.

Gralyre grinned for the first time that morning. Now he was starting to enjoy himself.

Dotch rolled his eyes, and headed towards the sisters.

"Rewn," Gralyre ordered.

"No, thank ye. I like my sword where it is," Rewn chuckled, and patted his scabbard hanging from his hip. He had watched Gralyre play this game before, and had no illusions about where he would be searching when he lost his sword.

"I will have a go," Jord sneered, his knives glimmering in the dawn's sunlight. "But I warn ye, I do no' play games. This is your last chance t' live." His face iced over, and his eyes deadened, rendering him years older.

Rewn tensed at the threat. "Jord, 'tis no' what this is about…"

The smile of lazy enjoyment still played over Gralyre's mouth, as he watched Jord narrowly.

Jord's knives shot towards Gralyre, aiming for his head, his chest, his shoulders. As each one left his fingers, another would appear as though willed into being.

Gralyre parried every one with a silver flicker of his sword, almost too fast for the eye to follow. But they did not finish in the brambles with the other weapons, instead the daggers spiked into a tree to the right, and a tree to the left. When Jord had run out of blades, they were equally divided between the two targets.

Trifyn's mouth gaped. "How the Gods did ye do that?"

"Sorcery," Jord snarled the word accusingly, and spat on the ground.

Gralyre shook his head. "Swordplay," he corrected softly. The light of dawn shone behind him, rimming him in gold, and his imposing presence seemed to swell to fill the small glade, as he pierced each and every one of them through to their soul with his midnight-blue gaze.

"From this day onward," Gralyre pronounced sternly, "there will be no more indolence. We are facing legions of evil, and are laughably outnumbered. But what matters that, if each of you has the skills to kill your share in battle? So when we halt in the evening, we will spar, and when you rise in the morn, ye will train afore we ride. I will give you swords. Trifyn, you will show us the bow. Jord, your knife skills."

Saliana licked her lips nervously. "Gralyre, I am no' a warrior…"

"Too bad." Gralyre denied coldly. "'Twas your choice to be with us. You may not care how or where you die, but by the Gods you will do what is necessary to protect your company." Gralyre's gaze widened to include everyone. "All of you will. Because we can only win our lives back together. By the time we reach the island I will hone you into warriors great enough to lay waste to any evil that challenges us!"

His pledge rang out over the group, and each of them felt a stirring of, if not hope, it was the next closest thing.

"And one last item. Aneida and Mayvin you will teach everyone Mayvin's hand language. The men need to be able to understand her. No more isolation. We stand together, or we fall."

ഇൽൽ

"What do ye think ye are doing, Gralyre?" General Ryes demanded, as Gralyre walked back from the training ground. When Gralyre's steps did not pause, Ryes was obliged to stretch his shorter legs in order to keep pace.

As they walked through camp, fires smoked from the first

wood placed upon newly awakened coals, and quiet conversations drifted on the wind from the southern warriors who had just stirred from their bedrolls.

"I was training my men, General."

Ryes grabbed his arm, and dragged him to a halt. "Do ye think this will make any difference? The Bleak does no' care how fancy your swordplay is! Ye are giving them false hope!"

Gralyre jerked his arm free, and continued walking, leaving the General standing.

"Ye are a fool!" Ryes yelled after him.

Gralyre gritted his teeth and ignored him, praying that his people had not heard the general's words. Their confidence was a fragile and newborn thing. Almost anything could shatter it, and drive them back into the despair that had overtaken them during their travels.

₧₧₧

The training went well, and the company improved daily from the practice, not just in skill, but also in their commitment to each other. Slowly Gralyre was forging them into a unit.

Few were the times that Aneida was not warding off all comers with her *"Attack first and never apologize for it"* strategy, but her boldness was not all for show. The woman was as skilled with a sword as anyone Gralyre had yet met, and on the occasions that he corrected her form, he needed only to show her once and she would remember. Her fire was offset by her sister, Mayvin's cool precision. Where Aneida burned, Mayvin froze, but both women learned with fanatical intensity.

Mayvin was exact in her mimicry of Gralyre's lessons, observing everything that he did, and failing only where strength or flexibility was not yet present.

Even after hunting with the sisters for most of the winter, Gralyre still knew little of Mayvin and Aneida, beyond what he had observed for himself. Aneida wore her bluster as a mask, hiding her true feelings deep where none would discover them, whereas Mayvin showed nothing at all, though there were times when they would sit around the fire at night, and Mayvin would relax enough to laugh silently. At those times, Gralyre could see what a beautiful woman she actually was, although when her face returned to its habitual hardness, all attraction as a woman was lost to her.

Trifyn's expertise with the bow was immense, and as Gralyre encouraged him to teach what he knew, he grew more confident of his place within the group. The privation of travel was beginning to harden him, and he no longer openly grieved for the life he had left behind. He even started to stand up to Jord, who had early on singled him out to bully.

As Trifyn began to fight back, Jord actually began to tease him worse, and Gralyre came to realize that the bullying was a sign of a reluctant, rough affection; Jord fighting against a bond with someone he feared he would lose.

The Gods only knew what Jord had endured to survive, growing up on the streets of Dreisenheld in the shadow of

Doaphin's citadel. He was slow to trust, and that translated into an aggressive need to push them all away, yet at the same time he watched everyone hungrily, yearning for their camaraderie.

To each and every one of them, Gralyre gave all of his strength of will and purpose. The result could be measured in the camaraderie that began to grow around the cook fire nightly, in the little kindnesses that they began to show each other while they travelled, and in the unbreakable bonds of friendship that began to attach them each to the other.

As for Gralyre, he was exhausted. His nights of magical tutelage and hunting were sapping his strength but he counted it well worth the sacrifice to give his group the will to survive.

ഇൽ

Trifyn lifted up a brace of hares. "I shot them while we were riding!" he boasted.

Rewn's brows knit, and a half smile lifted his lips from the solemn furrows that now bracketed his mouth after the months of hard travel. "How did ye retrieve them?" He had not noticed Trifyn stopping during the ride.

Trifyn grinned smugly, and held out an arrow with a thin cord tied below the fletching. "I just reeled them in."

"Good lad!" Rewn praised. "Now Gralyre and Little Wolf need no' go hunting for our dinner."

Trifyn blushed at the praise, but there was pride there too. He knew that the others thought him green. If he could do something for them all, perhaps they would see beyond that.

"Here, Jord," Rewn called out. "Bring those knives o' yours t' come help us skin these hares."

Jord walked up, his knives dancing in the firelight. He glanced from the hares to Trifyn. "What? Ye could no' shoot a bird or two?"

Trifyn rolled his eyes, "Feel free t' starve!" and threw them at Jord's feet before stomping away.

"Gods, Jord, why do ye torment the lad so?" Dotch asked, as he walked over to help with dressing out their dinner.

Jord shrugged and grinned. "What else have we t' do for entertainment?" His razor edged knives made short work slicing through flesh to remove the viscera.

Rewn shook his head. "Ye know one o' these days, he is just going t' shoot ye in the arse with an arrow." Rewn picked up an eviscerated carcass, made some small shallow cuts, and neatly ripped off the pelt. He tossed the meat to Dotch who slid it onto a roasting spit.

Mayvin walked over, and clapped her hands in front of Jord's nose to get his attention. She made a series of signs.

Rewn began to translate. "She wants ye to…mphhh!" his words were cut off when Mayvin slapped her palm over his mouth. Rewn had been mostly fluent in Mayvin's gestures before they had left the Northern Fortress, having hunted with the sisters and Gralyre for the majority of the winter.

He must learn for himself. Let him figure it out, Mayvin ordered. She turned to Jord and patiently repeated her request.

Jord's brow knit in concentration. "Something about water," he decided.

Mayvin nodded encouragingly, then repeated the gestures once more.

"She wants ye to fetch water from the stream!" Dotch crowed triumphantly.

Jord glared at him. "I would have gotten it!"

Mayvin handed Jord a bucket.

"Teach me something else!" Jord demanded, as he followed Mayvin towards the swift moving creek beside which they had made camp.

Dotch laid the full spit onto the forks, suspending the hares evenly over the hot coals of their campfire. Soon the scent of roasting meat teased their senses, prompting the group to gather in anticipation.

There was a ritual to awaiting food from a fire that encouraged conversations, and the sharing of food that built strangers into family. It had ended the isolation wrought by falling into their beds after bolting down cold rations. These nights spent around the fire were fast becoming their comfort, the warmth that banished the cold reality of their future.

Into these warm glows, Dotch would often speak of his wife and sons, sharing his pride and joy with anecdotal stories of life within the Fortress. He was a good storyteller, and had them all gasping in laughter most every night.

Saliana would speak shyly about her desire to become a healer. Trifyn would talk about his mother. Slowly the pall of despair had lifted as, one by one, they had begun to visualize a life after Fennick's Island.

Even Jord had begun to transform. As the days passed, he had become less confrontational, and had even begun to sleep in his own bed, instead of hiding away every night. As a show of trust it was small, yet significant.

"Where is Gralyre?" Trifyn asked. "He is going t' miss dinner again." Gralyre's approval meant much, and Trifyn wanted to see the appreciation in his face when he saw the food.

Rewn glanced at the spot where Gralyre had disappeared, as night had fallen. "He is in the woods again. Practicing his sorcery."

"Why does he do that? Why not practice here?" Trifyn asked.

Aneida grinned. "We should tell ye about the time Gralyre was learning how t' make fire."

Rewn sniggered. "His beard was patchy for weeks!"

Mayvin's mouth opened in silent laughter, as she added, *He almost burned the forest to the ground!*

Saliana grinned, as she lifted her gaze from Mayvin's hands. "I think I got that! Something about trees and fire? He started a forest fire?"

Mayvin patted her on the back approvingly.

Instead of paying attention to the story, Dotch was watching Jord's knives flipping in and out of existence. "Will ye show us how ye do that? I have been wondering for weeks. They are there, and then they are gone. Is it magic?"

Jord shook his head. "No, not magic." He slowed down the

motion so that Dotch could see him palm the blade, and make it appear to vanish.

Aneida watched on with confusion. "But I do no' understand where it goes after it disappears."

Jord leaned forward with a serious expression, and proceeded to pull a knife out from under her fat, red braid next to her ear.

Aneida shouted with laughter, her head thrown back, as her entire body shook. She leaned forward, and slapped Jord on the chest. "Show me how ye did that!" she demanded.

Jord's expression froze, arrested with a flash of disquiet before he shook it off.

Aneida's smile faded. "I am sorry. I forget that ye do no' like t' be touched."

Jord shrugged. "I do no' mind," he said casually, and then affected a leer. "I like it when women touch me."

Aneida grinned maniacally. "Ye best watch yourself, or I will touch ye in all the wrong ways."

Dotch snorted. "Quit flirting."

"We were no'…"

"I was no'…"

Dotch cut through the stutters of denial. "Jord show us one more time, we need t' practice this."

The others drew their daggers, and proceeded to learn the movement, while Jord supervised, and gave minor corrections.

Oddly, it was Saliana who was able to duplicate the trick, much to the hilarity of the group, as Dotch fumbled his knife into the firepit, and Rewn's flew backwards, and was lost in the darkness. Saliana smiled smugly, as she palmed the knife, and made it reappear with almost the skill of Jord.

"I used t' hide eggs from my brothers, back on our farm. Sometimes it was the only food I had t' eat for days," she admitted timidly.

෨໖

Gralyre paced, as he awaited Catrian's arrival. The smell of wood smoke drifted upon rivers of heat within cooler currents of wind. In the distance, through the boles of the large trees, he could just see the flickering lights from the campfires, and hear the soft murmur of voices from the Southern Rebels, as they bedded down for the night. The sound of Aneida's laugh rose above it all for a moment, making Gralyre pause and smile.

The sky bore witness to the turning of the season, indigo, bright with the first stars of the evening. Spring was here.

Soft ferns unfurled against his calves, as he began to pace again, and the scent of crushed mint arose to scent the air.

A darker shadow in the night, Little Wolf lay beneath a tree, his head on his paws, as he watched over Gralyre. His master's anxiousness had infected him this eve so that he was loath to leave on the hunt, as had become his habit. Still, his ears canted back and forth, as he catalogued the soft rustling in the surrounding forest, listening to the sounds of prey creeping from safe lairs to feed. Soon enough, he would find them.

A hush of a whisper reached Gralyre, so faint that at first he thought it a mere rustling of newly budded leaves in the soft breeze.

"*Gralyre.*"

He halted and strained to hear aught else, uncertain.

"*Gralyre.*"

So soft, so distant. She was still trying to reach him. The previous evening her shade had been almost gone, and he had arrived for their rendezvous this night fearing that it was over, that she would be unable to come, and that he would never see her again.

"Catrian!" he called out. He pivoted slowly, trying to spot the shimmering distortion that had become all that remained of her presence.

"*Gralyre….gone…sorry…canno'…*"

"Catrian! No! Catrian? Can you hear me?"

"*…far…canno'…farewell…*"

"No! Not like this! Do not go! Catrian!" Gralyre roared.

This could not be how it ended! If this was good-bye, they deserved more. There had to be more!

Gralyre closed his eyes, and sought her presence with every fiber of his being set to the task, for the merest trace of her, like a sweet perfume left in the air by mountain heather in a storm. '*There!*'

He gathered his magic, feeling the power fusing to his limbs from beyond, as he drew deep of the world's Godsmagic, and stepped forward, out of his body.

The night turned bright with chaotic colors, the brilliant souls of the life that surrounded him; the trees, the grasses, the ferns. But he only had eyes for her. Catrian.

Her eyes widened in surprise, and her hand lifted to cover her mouth. "Gralyre! What…how?"

He glanced behind to see that his body had collapsed into the ferns, and that Little Wolf, glowing brightly with rainbow hues, stood guard above him, his eyes not on Gralyre's body, but on his shade. Gralyre turned back, and reached out for Catrian's hands.

And they touched hers, real touch, and she gasped at the warmth and solidity of the sensation.

Her gaze rose from their clasped fingers to his eyes, and a small tear slipped down her cheek. "How are ye doing this?"

His fingers caught the bright wetness before it could fall, and suddenly she was in his arms, their mouths fused in a frantic embrace that they both knew could not last.

After months of yearning, the luxury of being able to touch her, taste her, overwhelmed Gralyre's senses. He held tight, as if he would never let go, indeed he might not have, had she not pulled away.

"Gralyre I can feel ye!" She whispered brokenly, her hands running up his chest then back down again.

"I know." He cupped her face tilting it so that he could memorize her all over again, as though he was seeing her anew.

She hummed urgently, unable to stop touching him. "No! Ye are no' hearing me. I can feel your magic, all the way north. *I can feel it*! This is too dangerous. We must stop!"

His brow dropped to touch hers, and he savored the hot moistness of her breath against his cheek. "Not yet," he entreated huskily, "please Gods, not yet!"

Catrian groaned. "We must say farewell. Your power will draw every creature from a hundred leagues. Gralyre! Please! We must end this," She entreated, yet her lips clasped his once more, and she whimpered, as the urgency and danger spurred her on. When Gralyre's arms tightened around her waist again, she tore away with a raw sound of agony. This time she held him away with her outstretched hands pressed into his chest.

"Please. I love ye, this it too dangerous. Ye must go." She stared into his widening midnight-blue eyes, not wishing back the words, though they were fruitless, barren things that could do naught but bring more pain at their parting. She watched his eyes, those amazing blue eyes, darken with an emotion so intense, she felt her heart would cease to beat.

Gralyre clasped her hand, and raised it to his lips, turning it over to press a kiss into her palm. "This world, or the next. Know that I love you," he pledged earnestly, and stepped away.

The bright colors drained from his world, and Gralyre opened his eyes, staring dully up at Little Wolf who had guarded him.

෨෬

NORTHERN REBEL FORTRESS

Catrian's spirit reentered her body like a familiar and much loved home, and she convulsed as they fused. Her heart began to beat again, and she drew breath, her first since she had left to meet Gralyre. Her eyes fluttered and opened, and for a moment, she gazed unseeingly up into the softly billowing canvas of her tent, bracing herself for the pain.

When it struck, she curled over onto her side, clasping her knees to her chest as she sobbed. It was over.

℠ℂ

DREISENHELD

"Report!" The Master's order snaps like a whip.

Doaphin maintains his bow, not daring to glance up at the throne. "The magic originated in the foothills of the Heathren Mountains in the far south, and travelled north to where, we know naught. It can only be the Rebels that you are allowing to travel to Fennick's Island, my Master." He cannot quite camouflage his injured whine.

"Why were we not informed that a sorcerer travels south with the Rebels, with Him?"

"We did not know, my Master." Doaphin raises his head, though his body remains bent low. "Surely you will see reason now. We must kill them afore they reach Fennick's Island!"

The Master stares off over Doaphin's head, considering. "No. We will allow them to continue."

"But..." The Master's gaze fixes upon him, and Doaphin

quickly reassesses his contention. "Of course my Master. Your will is all, my Master."

"Leave us."

Doaphin bows from the chamber, waiting for the solid gold doors to boom shut before standing, and turning on a heal. The Master's plan will see him dead if something is not done!

He must stop the Rebels, stop Him, from reaching the island, and triggering the fulfillment of the curse.

But Doaphin cannot speak to the Master's creatures across long distances. For that, he requires a Demon Lord.

What must be done, must be accomplished in secrecy.

∞∞

Doaphin's chambers once belonged to the sorcerer Fennick, once the mage to King Lyre in the days before the empire toppled. The walls are lined with priceless volumes filled with the magic of the ages. The first tier of the library spans from the floor to a height of twenty feet, where a wrought iron walkway circles the large round chamber, providing support for yet another tier of books that soar towards the ceilings. High above, the painted dome depicts the four Gods of Fortune, circling a precious skylight. Fate, Hope, Blessing and Curse roll dice, wagering with the stars in the sky.

Which one of them will be watching his betrayal this night?

The floor is a white marble expanse with golden veins running throughout, of the same origins as that of the throne room. Claiming a small area in front of the massive hearth, a rug of simple weave, mahogany brown, supports several comfortable chairs and low tables that hold discarded books and carafes of golden wine.

The fireplace is carved with fantastical creatures and vines. It burns warmly, throwing heat enough to warm this room, and the one beyond the door in the corner that hides Doaphin's bedchamber, and the slave that warms his sheets. He will make use of both soon enough.

At the polite knock, he bids, "Enter."

"Yes, Lord Commander," the Demon Lord walks in, and bends low in respect. It reeks of evil and power, and self-importance. Its grooming is impeccable, its clothes resplendent.

Doaphin hates the Demon Lords with a passion he can barely contain. He hates their perfection and beauty. Mostly, he hates the Master's love for them.

Once, Doaphin was perfect, and perfectly loved. He hides his withered hand within the slit in his tunic.

"There are battalions to the south, near the Heathren foothills?"

"Yes, Lord Commander."

"Contact your brethren. Have them move north. I have felt the wakening power of a sorcerer."

"I too have felt it, milord."

"The Master's laws must be obeyed. The sorcerer must be destroyed."

"Of course, milord. I will see to it immediately."

The Demon Lord turns smartly and leaves.

Doaphin begins to quiver, and slowly sinks into a chair in front of the fireplace.

Pray the Master never discovers his betrayal.

CHAPTER FIVE

"Ye can no' continue like this."

Rewn's voice jerked Gralyre's head around in surprise to smile faintly at his friend. They were on a wide track, gliding through a dark forest of cedar, the steps of their horses muffled to dull thuds in the soft ferns carpeting the ground. Large granite boulders with green mosses emerging upon their cracked faces, appeared like distorted giants through a mist that undulated in long streamers of filmy silk woven in the spaces between the trees. The air was ripe with the scent of new life.

For once, they had room enough to travel two abreast, and Rewn had taken advantage by bringing his horse even with Gralyre's. As usual, the group of eight rode at the rear of the party, separated from General Ryes and his men by their circumstances.

To keep the horses sound throughout the day, they often alternated gaits. Just now, they were walking their horses, allowing their steeds to regain their wind.

"Continue like what?" Gralyre asked. He suspected that he had been dozing in the saddle, for a light rain had begun to fall, something he had not previously noted. He swiped a hand back over his black hair, slicking moisture away from his face, and was amazed to feel heavy drops dripping from his new grown beard. It had been raining for some time.

"Like ye are responsible for us all. Like we are so fragile that we will shatter if ye do no' look after us."

"I do not know what you are talking about." Gralyre gazed at him steadily.

Rewn made a rude noise, and slanted Gralyre a pointed look.

Gralyre frowned ruefully. "Alright, maybe I have grown overly protective of you all, but we need to be strong when we reach Fennick's Island."

Rewn smiled in triumph, sitting straighter in his saddle, as he faced the path ahead. "My point exactly."

Gralyre glowered at him. "What?"

"Ye think 'tis your fault we are here, and no' back at the camp preparing for war. As if that would see us any safer," Rewn chided.

Gralyre felt a tingling infuse his cheeks with a guilty flush. "'Tis true enough."

Rewn twisted to face his friend. "Is it? Take a good look at your men, Gralyre! Do ye think that any o' us, if given the chance, would turn back from this path? Do ye think that any o' us are no' here o' our own free will? Gods! Even Saliana chose this, and she was ne'er tasked t' come! I was there in the tent with the others when Catrian gave us all the choice. We made it, same as ye did!"

Gralyre rubbed his gritty eyes, and he shook his head. "None of you would be here if it were not for me. You would not even have been asked."

"Ah, yes, I forgot that ye are the loadstone o' the world, and the rest o' us do no' but cling t' ye like iron shavings!" Rewn mocked.

Gralyre's eyes widened, and his fist tightened in the reins, making his horse dance a sidestep. "I have never thought that! 'Tis not what I mean!"

Rewn relented. "What I know is that ye have exhausted yourself with your guilt by needlessly heaping the responsibility for us all upon your shoulders, and 'tis killing ye. And if ye do no' let it go, ye will be no good t' us when we reach the island. 'Twould be a shame t' have t' leave ye behind."

Gralyre was so shocked by the idea that he halted his horse.

Rewn drew rein beside him, and his jaw jutted stubbornly. "I mean it, Gralyre. None here hold ye t' this imaginary account o' yours. Ye had best be letting it go, or by the Gods I swear it, ye will no' be setting a foot on Fennick's Island."

Gralyre glanced away from Rewn's determination, and swallowed hard to dislodge the lump at the back of his throat. A sudden lightness infused him, and he shook his head with a grin, but his reply was stifled by a yell from the head of the column.

General Ryes had rounded a large rock outcropping, and collided with a full contingent of mounted, battle ready Demon Riders travelling from the opposite direction. He drew on his reins so sharply that his horse reared up in protest, pawing at the air, as he and the Demon Rider Commander gaped at each other with matching expressions of staggering disbelief.

Gralyre's exhaustion had made him careless, and he had not sent his senses ahead to scout their path, as he had been wont to do. Now that oversight had placed them all in danger!

He kicked his tired horse into a gallop and, with Little Wolf loping easily alongside his horse, raced up the short column of Rebel warriors to reach the hated enemy. His battle cry, as he drew his sword released the others from their shock. Gralyre heard his small group springing after him into the fray, and the southern warriors were not far behind.

He caught a flash of Ryes' stunned face, as he flew past, and left the severed head of the Demon Rider Commander bouncing underfoot in his wake.

Gralyre cut through the unprepared ranks of the enemy, the quickness of his attack keeping them from forming a defensive line. His sword was a scythe reaping heads, and bodies toppled from horses. Rewn and Aneida were quick to flank him, and at the end of their first charge, eight Demon Riders were dead and several others were mortally wounded, screaming and bleeding out the remainder of their miserable lives in agony.

The battleground was a narrow clearing hemmed by giant boulders and thick forest, and as Gralyre turned his horse for another pass, his heart dropped, as he finally noted the dire number of red-coated Demon Riders that jammed the space, outnumbering their paltry numbers by at least three to one.

Half of the enemy forces turned to face Gralyre, Rewn and Aneida. The other half were too busy with the second charge that came from the Southern Rebel warriors, as General Ryes and his men joined the fight. The light rain, and the pawing, stamping horses soon had the ground churned into bloody muck.

Aneida began to laugh, her call to battle, as she rode out behind Gralyre, and split the head of a 'Rider who got in her way with a brutal strike of her blade. The fierce, scornful sound lifted above the chaos. Except for her sister, there was nothing Aneida loved as well as slaughtering Doaphin's minions.

Dotch, Mayvin and Jord's charge was blocked by the bottleneck of Demon Riders. They were surrounded, unable to press forward or back, and could do nothing but fight to keep the enemy at arm's length. The surging tides of battle drove more and more of the enemy upon them, pushing between their horses, and forcing them to drift apart.

Dotch yelled a warning when he saw Mayvin pulled from her stirrups by a larger opponent. She landed like a cat, a sword in each hand. Her steel was a flickering blur of defense, but she was isolated in a group of several 'Riders, and was sure to be overwhelmed. Dotch flung himself from his horse, beating and bludgeoning at all sides to reach her, but there were too many foes.

Three Demon Riders tackled him into the mud, punching and kicking as they took him down. Dotch lost his grip on his sword, but pulled his dagger, and neatly eviscerated the 'Rider to his left. The blood made the muck even slicker, and neither Dotch nor the other two 'Riders could gain the purchase they needed, as they vied for survival.

Horses and warriors trampled upon all sides, so that Dotch feared he would be crushed if he did not soon gain his feet.

THUNK! THUNK!

Two rapid-fire impacts announced the arrival of a knife between the eyes of each 'Rider, and Dotch spared a glance over his shoulder. Jord saluted him with yet another readied blade, and Dotch nodded, scrabbled to reclaim a sword, and threw himself down the bloody throat of the fighting once more.

At the edge of the melee, tucked into the shadow of a rocky outcropping, Trifyn sat his horse beside Saliana, mindful of Rewn who had ordered him to protect her. He had never been as terrified as he was now.

Saliana stood in her stirrups, and bobbed up and down on her horse, trying to keep sight of Rewn, as a mass of red uniforms briefly occluded him. She was useless, practically helpless in a fight! They were all going to die!

She watched a red-coated Demon Rider eviscerate one of the southern warriors, and rainwater sprayed from the ends of her braids, as she turned her frantic gaze upon Trifyn. "They are dying! What are ye waiting for? Shoot them!" She yelled in his face.

She could not stand to see the others facing death while she did nothing! She drew her dagger, and spurred her horse ahead.

"Saliana! No! Stop!" Trifyn yelled, reaching out too late to grab her.

Saliana barreled into the fight, slashing out with single-minded fear at anything that cut across her path, boring a hole towards where she had last seen Rewn. She feared death, but she feared his more.

With fumbling, shaking hands, Trifyn vaulted from his horse

onto the rock outcropping, slipping and sliding on the wet mossy growths, as he climbed swiftly to gain a vantage point. With expert efficiency, he bent and strung the bow, nocked his first arrow and let fly. He was shaking so badly that the missile went wide of his mark.

Trifyn stared after the lost arrow in horrified surprise, and rubbed a hand over his face to clear his eyes of the rainwater. 'Twas the second time he had rattled under the pressure of battle. He had not missed a target since he was a boy. He vowed that it would not happen again.

Trifyn's mouth compressed into a straight line, and his hands stilled their shaking, as he sighted down the shaft of another arrow. He heard the note the gut made as he released it. The pitch rang true, and he knew that this time he had found his mark. He did not pause to acknowledge the hit, only knocked another arrow and let fly, over and over, until his arm was weak and shaking from the bending of the bow.

Still circling through the skirmish, Saliana searched frantically until she spotted Rewn fighting a loosing battle against two Demon Riders. They were trying to flank him but were proceeding cautiously, for two of their companions already lay dead at their feet.

Saliana's rage engulfed her at the sight of Rewn's danger. Her usually passive, gentle face twisted in a scream of hate, as she drove her horse forward, and launched onto the back of one of the 'Riders.

The creature's knees buckled from the impact, and he

collapsed the rest of the way to the ground, as her knife slashed in and out of his throat.

At the surprise attack, the other Demon Rider paused fatally, and Rewn made quick work of his distraction.

"Get t' safety!" Rewn screamed out between heaving breaths, and lunged forward to engage another enemy.

Saliana stood amid the carnage in her soiled dress, bloodied to her elbows, and watched him race away. She gasped thickly, enduring the tightness in her chest, as she wondered how it was possible for him to look at her, yet never see.

When Trifyn's fingers could not find another arrow in his quiver, he finally absorbed the battlefield as a whole, instead of as a teeming mass of red targets. He tried not to think of how many of the fallen red uniforms bristled with his arrows. He had never killed anything except animals for food. Never had he experienced the wanton destruction of battle.

From atop his boulder he had an unimpeded view of the fight. The noise was thunderous; clangs of weapons, curses and screams of pain, yells of challenge, the howls of the wolfdog, and distressed whickers of the horses all lifted to Trifyn's ears in a deafening cacophony.

And right in the midst of the largest concentration of the enemy, Trifyn spied Gralyre, and his jaw dropped in awe. Never in his wildest dreams had he imagined anything such as this, even after admiring Gralyre's sword skills in the tournament at the fortress, and training with him on the road.

Gralyre had been holding himself in check, hiding his full

abilities, and now Trifyn bore witness to the true master of the sword unleashed.

Gralyre was a blur of movement that never ceased, but flowed with deadly grace from strike to block to lunge. Any 'Rider who challenged him died within three economical blows or less. His face bore a look of utmost concentration, and his guard was impenetrable, as he slaughtered 'Rider after 'Rider. Bodies writhed and died in the muck and blood at his feet, as though he were a vengeful god of war judging the enemy, and pronouncing them unworthy.

Gralyre's sword became stuck fast in the chest of a screaming Demon Rider, as another was attacking from the side with his weapon coiled for a vicious slash. Without pause, Gralyre's body took up the momentum of his previous blow, circling to create a better angle to free his sword, and at the same time placing the wounded 'Rider between himself and his attacker. As he freed his blade, he spun the staggering, injured 'Rider into the path of the oncoming attack, the move hiding the power of Gralyre's unstoppable strike. The advancing 'Rider lost his head, and Gralyre spun with the agility and skill of a dancer to engage in the next battle.

Gralyre fought with only Little Wolf to guard his back now, for Rewn and Aneida had separated from him early on in the fight.

Little Wolf circled behind a 'Rider who was rushing upon Gralyre from the rear. With a vicious howl, the wolfdog sprang, taking the soldier down, and ripping out his throat. Little Wolf shook his head, and blood and mud sprayed from his thick black fur. He leapt from his victim, narrowly avoiding being skewered by the halberd of another Demon Rider, whose thrust went through the dead soldier in the place where the wolfdog had been but moments before.

Mayvin stepped up to the 'Rider, before he could pull his heavy weapon free, and neatly slit his throat, sending him falling onto his dead comrade in a spray of blood. A silent howl of delight radiated from her face as, with a minimum of effort, she blocked the next Demon Rider's wild thrust with one sword and viciously gutted him with the other. As he writhed and screamed, trying to escape her skewering blade, she jerked it free, spun elegantly about and neatly decapitated him with scissor precision, a sword to either side of the his neck. Before the body fell, she spun on guard, and engaged another soldier in lethal combat.

But she did not move quite fast enough, and the 'Rider's blade sank deep into her shoulder. A silent scream of pain and rage contorted her face, as she slashed out, catching the Demon Rider through his throat, and killing him. The 'Rider's sword was still imbedded in her shoulder, as Mayvin's knees buckled, and she fell forward onto the bloodied ground.

From atop his rocky perch, Trifyn watched Mayvin fall, and finally shook himself free of the somnolence brought on by his first shock of battle. He slid down the rain slicked face of the boulder, and stumbled out onto the killing ground, pulling his short sword, and wading through the dead, dying and fighting to reach Mayvin. As more and more of the Demon Riders had fallen the fighting had become sparser, so that Trifyn managed to cross the battlefield unchecked, making it to Mayvin's side quickly.

He rolled her to her back, taking her face out of the muck so that she might breath. Her eyes were closed and she did not respond when he yelled her name. But his shouting drew the attention of the Demon Riders, and he suddenly found himself defending his and Mayvin's lives in the bloodiest battle he could have ever imagined.

Killing from afar with the precision of his arrows was one thing, but being near enough to feel the lifeblood of his enemies splashing hot and thick onto his hands and his face, feeling the pain as they returned blows in a fight to the death, was quite something else.

Gralyre's instruction had been helpful, but Trifyn was a bowman, not a swordsman. He retained just enough presence of mind to raise his blade in defense, as a 'Rider began to hew away at him. Trifyn's fingers went numb from the ringing vibrations, as he blocked the overhead blows.

Trifyn flinched away from the next blow, and the 'Rider hissed, eyes narrowed in enjoyment, as he realized the greenness of the man facing off against him. The 'Rider feinted to the left, and Trifyn moved to block the blow that was not coming.

Off balance and out of his depth, Trifyn never noticed a second 'Rider circling up from behind until a hard arm grabbed him about the throat, raising him six inches off his feet. He dropped his sword to grasp at the choking arm, struggling desperately for air, as the original attacker canted his sword back for a deathblow.

But it never landed. Instead, the arm encircling Trifyn's throat slackened, and the weight at his back fell away. Horror twisted the face of the first 'Rider, and his poised sword tumbled from loosened fingers. Trifyn could not help it. He spun to see what would cause such terror in the black heart of a Demon Rider.

It was Gralyre. He stood tall and fierce, his face wetly painted with the death of his enemies, his bloodied sword ready in his fist, and within his eyes such a powerful certainty of victory that Trifyn's knees sagged in response. Gralyre's black hair hung in a shaggy, bloody, dripping mass to his shoulders, giving him more than a passing similarity to the animal at his side, Little Wolf, whose black fur was matted with gore, and within whose eyes gleamed an intelligence beyond that of a dumb animal. When the Demon Rider broke and ran, Trifyn could not fault him.

With a look, Gralyre sent Little Wolf sprinting after the fleeing 'Rider. Trifyn ducked in reaction, knowing it for foolishness, but unable to stop the primitive terror that consumed him as the wolfdog brushed past after the running soldier, bringing him down within moments to screams, and sprays of blood.

Trifyn slowly uncoiled his arms from where they covered his head, and found himself trapped by Gralyre's blazing midnight-blue eyes.

"See to her!" Gralyre ordered, indicating Mayvin.

Trifyn managed a nod...barely.

Gralyre dropped a heavy hand to the bowman's shoulder, thrusting him at the downed woman, then sprung away after another 'Rider. Little Wolf returned from his kill to join Gralyre, vectoring across the bloody field to meet his master.

Trifyn grabbed Mayvin around her chest, careful of the blade embedded in her shoulder, and dragged her clear of the thick of battle into some sheltering ferns. His fear gave him strength beyond normal, and he managed the feat quickly.

Saliana had left the battle for the cover of the woods, mindful of her promises to Aneida and Rewn to remain free of the fight, lest she cause a fatal distraction. She watched as General Ryes and his men swarmed over the field, creating chaos and a good accounting of themselves, but Saliana had no care for any of them once she spotted more of her friends in trouble.

From across the small glade, Trifyn was beckoning to her frantically, and at his feet Saliana could see a woman's booted legs trailing out of a cluster of ferns. "Mayvin!" she screeched and, thoughtless of the danger and her promises, ran straight across the gory battlefield.

Before she got far, a Demon Rider tackled her to the blood soaked muck, and wrapped his hands around her throat, choking. She kicked and struggled, but could not shift him. Her ears filled with watery mud, as the 'Rider pressed her harder into the earth, muffling her hearing so that the din of battle became a distant thing. Spots were dancing in her vision when one of Ryes' Rebel warriors swung past, and the head of the 'Rider bounced off over the ground. The heavy body collapsed forward crushing Saliana further into the muck.

The Rebel grabbed the shoulder of the corpse, and lifted its heavy weight off her.

"Thank-ye!" Saliana croaked, wiping blood and mud from her eyes, as she stumbled back up to her feet.

"Get clear! Ye are going t' get yourself killed!"

She kept running until she fell into Trifyn's arms.

"'Tis Mayvin! I canno' wake her!"

Saliana dropped to her knees beside Mayvin, and tried to remember all she had ever learned about battlefield injuries. It was not much, for she had not been apprenticed to the healer for long before she left the Northern Fortress, but common sense dictated that the bleeding had to be stopped before aught else. Biting her lip with uncertainty, Saliana got to work.

Across the clearing, Jord and Dotch fought back to back but even that strategy would not work for much longer. The numbers facing them were too formidable. Jord's knives blurred forth, flipping and arcing through the air, and Demon Riders dropped, but for every soldier felled two more seemed to spring into their place. Soon Jord had no more knives to throw, and was left with only two long bladed daggers that he slashed out at any red coated 'Rider that ventured within arm's length.

Where Dotch was able to keep swinging and forcing the 'Riders back, Jord was made vulnerable by the shorter length of his weapons. The 'Riders circling them knew it was only a matter of time before the two men grew fatally tired. So instead of engaging them, the Demon Riders dashed in, one after the other for a brief, aborted attack, hissing their insane laughter. To Jord and Dotch, it seemed they were in the eye of a whirling, deadly, kaleidoscope of red uniforms and sharp lengths of steel.

Both Dotch and Jord were bleeding from numerous cuts, but were they to break their defense to go chasing after one of their tormentors, they would die that much quicker.

With her maniacal laugh, and swinging, fiery braid, Aneida arrived to even the odds. At the unexpected sound of gleeful laughter on the battlefield, the Demon Riders whirled in confusion, not knowing which threat to address, the men facing them or the woman attacking their backs! Their divided attention was the opening the men needed to fight their way clear of the trap.

"Good job, lass!" Dotch praised between rough, panting breaths.

Jord raised his remaining dagger before his cynical, too old face and saluted her. Aneida laughed wildly at him, then ducked, as he suddenly flicked the blade past her shoulder. A Demon Rider dropped with Jord's dagger lodged to the hilt in his throat.

Aneida stepped forward and gripped Jord's hair, pulled him to her, and kissed him recklessly. Then just as quickly pushed him aside, and danced away to find another 'Rider to kill.

Jord staggered a bit and gulped, looking suddenly very young, and turned towards Dotch. "What…?"

Dotch doubled over with laughter, for the expression on

Jord's face, for the end of the battle, and for the joy of still being alive.

General Ryes kicked the dead weight of a Demon Rider from his blade, spinning in search of another foe. But there was no one left.

A lone survivor ran for the trees, but Gralyre motioned his wolfdog, and Little Wolf chased him down. The sound of the 'Riders death heralded the official end of the fight.

From where he stood over the fallen Mayvin, Trifyn raised his bow and empty quiver, and gave voice to a victory yell, shaking his weapon at the skies.

Aneida howled in delight, raising her sword to join the mad celebration of their victory. The others found themselves shouting as well, and Ryes and his men rounded out the choral of triumph; rejoicing in their victory over death, by announcing to the Gods that they yet lived!

For the eight companions, this unexpected battle had rammed home the knowledge that Gralyre had fulfilled his promise to them. They did not have to go to their deaths like prisoners bound for the gallows. They were a formidable threat that would win its way to victory or die trying!

Standing over the women, Trifyn saluted Gralyre with the end of his bow, a wide grin splitting his face. He had seen the number of the enemy felled by Gralyre's sword. With such a warrior at their side, how could they not survive Fennick's Island?

Gralyre lifted his bloody, dripping sword to Trifyn in his own salute of the lad's bow work. And then Ryes' Rebels were surrounding him, pounding him on the back, vowing to follow him into battle anytime.

Gralyre turned his head, and locked eyes with General Ryes, raising a contemptuous eyebrow, as the man's mouth twisted in a curse. Gralyre felt no guilt in usurping his power. There had been a void in the place where a leader should have been, and Gralyre had just stepped up to fill it.

The General turned away, and began shouting orders. "Enough standing around. Corr, get me an account o' our dead and injured. Ye men, there! Behead these bodies! Ye others, see if they have any victuals we can use." He flushed a deep red, and a muscle ticked in his cheek, as his men looked at Gralyre first, awaiting his nod of assent before getting to work. What did it matter to him that his men were hailing Gralyre as the hero? He would be free of him soon enough! If he had wondered why Boris had worked so hard to be rid of the man, he wondered no longer.

Ryes' gaze centered upon the Demon Riders' horses, those that had not fled or been killed during the battle. "And somebody scatter those nags. If we are lucky it will buy us time afore they come looking for their lost men!"

"Belay that!" Gralyre shouted, and his deep ringing voice froze all movement in the bloody glade.

General Ryes sputtered, "Ye dare t' naysay my direct orders!"

"Our horses are spent, and these ones are fresh. Pick out the best of the lot and transfer our goods. We will turn ours loose."

Ryes' mouth closed with a snap, as warriors that he would have sworn were loyal to him, hopped to Gralyre's will. Even...Corr!

Ryes grabbed his son's arm and hauled him back, but Corr pleaded with him, "Da, he is right! The 'Riders' horses are fresh. Ours would no' have lasted much longer. They have near been ridden into the ground with our haste." He shook his arm free, and went to help his men.

Ryes stomped up to Gralyre. "We need those horses for the fight." His arms slashed wildly through the air as he vented his spleen. "That is near forty head o' my horses that ye are suggesting we free!"

Gralyre turned upon him, and leaned near, sparing the General by keeping their conversation as quiet as possible. "And a moment ago you would have loosed over ninety! Take a good look at our mounts, General. We could count ourselves lucky if they lasted out the week. The Solstice or the steeds. Choose."

The Rebels' horses looked sickly when compared to the Demon Rider mounts. They were spare of flesh and their ribs showed from the prolonged hardships of their journey. Even the spares were now footsore, and the pace of their travel had been falling steadily in the past weeks. Whereas the Demon Rider herd was fresh, and fat from a lazy winter.

"The Solstice," Ryes snarled, angered to have his judgment questioned, especially by this man, especially when he was in the wrong and knew it.

Gralyre growled low in his throat, for he needed to work with the General until they reached the Island, and knew he had to throw him a sop. "If you tell me where your fortress is," he suggested through a clenched jaw, "I will instruct our horses, and the rest of the Demon Rider herd, to make their own way there, to be ready for your muster so they will not be lost to you."

"They would ne'er find their way in the Bleak. Leave 'em!" Ryes snapped and stalked away. It gave him shudders to the tips of his toes to think of the powers Gralyre wielded.

When Gralyre established his mind link to the herd, they snorted and jumped for a moment before calming. As he walked away across the gory clearing, the ninety head turned as one to follow docilely after, a mix of the Rebels' spent animals, and the Demon Rider horses that they would not need in order to continue their journey to the island.

"How does he do that?" Corr whispered in awe as he returned to his father's side.

General Ryes glared at his son. "Do no' be idolizing the likes o' him, boy! He is a condemned man, and for good reason, as ye well know!"

Corr's jaw jutted out stubbornly but he nodded his head in agreement with his father.

∞∝

Mayvin finally opened her eyes, and Saliana smiled kindly.

"Ye have a sword lodged t' the bone o' your soldier. I am going t' have t' heat a brand t' seal the wound. Ye just rest easy for a moment, all right? Everything will be fine."

Mayvin nodded tightly, sweating lightly with the pain, but as silent as ever. *Aneida?*

Saliana recognized the hand gesture. "She is fine," she glanced up briefly, and then smiled down at Mayvin, "In fact, here she comes."

Aneida skidded down onto her knees in the moss beside her sister. As she took up Mayvin's hand, her eyes shimmered fiercely but no tears fell. "What, Mayvin! Ye are too reckless. What have ye done?"

Saliana looked up from examining Mayvin's shoulder, and into the anxious face of her sister, Aneida. "The wound is very deep, Aneida. The blow ripped apart her muscle and shattered the bone o' her shoulder. If the break were lower, I would have t' advise amputation o' the arm. But as 'tis so high up, we can bind it flat and hope that it heals. Even so, I fear that her arm may never be right again." Her head swung back to her patient, as Mayvin slammed a fist angrily into the earth. "'Tis the best that I can do, I am so sorry, Mayvin. I am only an apprentice healer after all."

Aneida leaned over her sister. "Do no' worry, Mayvin. One good sword arm is all that ye will need." At her words, Mayvin quieted, and a grim smile curled her lips.

Saliana reared back. "Oh, ye can no' be serious! We must send her with General Ryes when we reach the Island! She can no' come with us in this condition."

Mayvin and Aneida glared at her. "Just bind the wound," Aneida ordered.

"Ye are both mad!" Saliana sighed, as she readied clean bandages from her healer's pouch.

Trifyn pulled the red, glowing iron out of the fire he had hastily built, and passed it to Saliana.

Saliana wrapped a cloth around her fist to protect it from the heat of the brand, and offered Mayvin a stick to bite down on. "I will be as quick as I can but this is going to hurt." She winced in commiseration.

Do it, Mayvin signed. Her face was pale with sweat, and her gaze rose to stare into the eyes of her sister, borrowing Aneida's strength so that she could endure the pain.

Saliana bit her lip, and upended distilled spirits into the wound.

Mayvin's body convulsed from the agony.

"Hold her down! Do no' let her reinjure herself!" Saliana snapped, as all traces of timidness were wiped away.

Trifyn and Aneida splayed across Mayvin's wiry frame, as Saliana slapped the brand into the deep gash. She held the iron steady watching the smoke rising from the searing, until she was certain that the bleeding was stopped.

Mayvin was screaming, but no sound was escaping, in an eerie pantomime that ended abruptly as she lost consciousness.

Saliana shuddered, for as close as she was, she had clearly seen that Mayvin's mouth was scarred inside, and her tongue was a shriveled stump that had been burned away. She had not always been unable to speak.

The wound was closed, but there was nothing Saliana could do about the broken bone, except to bind Mayvin's arm as tight to her chest as possible so that it could not move as it healed.

The bandaging completed, Saliana brushed back a strand of her pale hair, making a face as her fingers slid through a slurry of sweat and Demon Rider blood, wishing she had a moment to clean herself. "Give her water when she awakens," she ordered Aneida as she stood.

"Trifyn. Come with me. Bring the brand." Mayvin was not the only patient that Saliana had need of tending. They had lost ten of the southern warriors, almost half of the company, and she would do her best to ensure that they lost not a man more.

ഇരെ

With fresh horses under them, their speed increased significantly. Only days later, they topped a large rise, and laid out below them, far in the distance past gently folded hills carpeted by dense evergreen forests, rose a massive, undulating wall of black. They had reached the Bleak.

It stretched from horizon to horizon, billowing at its edges, a secret blanket with which to cover the sins of Doaphin. The green forest ended at its borders as though pressed flat by a massive stone. Here and there, spires of dead trunks rose above the blackness, poking out into the sunlight, white from the rot that ate away at the wood. One, perhaps two more seasons and even these would fall away to nothing, for the roiling black clouds would allow no escapees.

General Ryes spat upon the ground. "Fetch Gralyre!" he ordered his son. Word passed down the line of horsemen, and Gralyre rode to the front.

"Behold the enormity o' the Bleak," Ryes announced scathingly, as Gralyre joined him.

Gralyre's keen eyes narrowed, and a frown wrinkled his brow, as he studied the far distant phenomenon.

Ryes turned in his saddle and addressed his men. "Make camp. No fires."

"Aye, General!"

Jingles of harnesses, and creaks of leather followed, as warriors all down the line gratefully left their saddles, and began the evening task of setting up camp.

Gralyre's gaze had not moved from his study, and Ryes smiled unkindly. The only way to truly appreciate the magnitude of Doaphin's magic was from a high, and far vantage point. Then you could understand the danger and the horror, and that once within the Bleak, there would be no respite, no sunlight, and no easy escape.

"It stretches from here t' the sea, a fortnight's ride, and even further out o'er the ocean past Fennick's Island, then west and east for a thousand miles." Ryes was silent for a moment as he considered the distant cumulus mass. "There are people in my lands who have ne'er seen the light o' day."

Gralyre looked at Ryes then, really looked, and realized that what he had taken to be an insipid man, from the paleness of his skin, and lack of lines in his face, was actually a man marked by an unnatural dearth of sunlight. As they had travelled, and Ryes' flesh had darkened, Gralyre could now see the robust General in the man, a match to any of the other leaders he had met at the fortress.

Gralyre's voice softened, in understanding and compassion. "Get me to that island, General. And maybe, just maybe, your people will be able to return to the light."

"An empty promise," Ryes scorned. "There is boldness, and then there is stupidity. Even after seeing that," Ryes gestured widely to the far horizon, "ye still think ye have a chance?"

Gralyre shrugged. "There is always a chance. The only failure is not to try."

Ryes shook his head. "Ye just do no' comprehend, do ye? Boris did no' send ye here t' try, he sent ye here t' die." Ryes bared his teeth challengingly. "Spy." He pronounced.

Gralyre stiffened, and his face went cold and still.

"Aye, I know what ye are. Boris told me all."

"Then you know that there is no proof but the Commander's own paranoia?"

Ryes shrugged. "That matters naught t' me. But best ye get the idea that ye will live out o' your head and accept your fate. Ye are no' coming back from Fennick's Island." Ryes spat on the ground. "No one e'er returns."

ॐ

As usual, the small group ate supper apart from Rye's warriors. This far into enemy territory, a fire simply could not be risked, but the spring evening, though cool, lacked the bitter winds of the mountains. Sitting in a cheerless circle, and chewing unenthusiastically on hard tack and jerky, they watched the sun set over the Bleak. Their first sight of the massive fogbank had rammed home the terrible odds they faced, and they were quiet and grim, as each searched within for the courage to continue. Twilight turned the hilltop blue with lengthening shadows.

Dotch threw down his hardtack with a curse of disgust, and stared off at the darkening horizon that had finally occluded the Bleak from view. He lifted a flask from his pack, pulled the cork, and took a long draw before he passed it to Rewn.

"How are we going t' do this?" Rewn asked, coming directly to the point before upending the flask for a sip of courage.

Gralyre was silent for a long moment, pondering the question. Ryes' taunts were still fresh in his mind, and they filled him more than ever with the determination to live. "We will take it one step at a time, and if the Gods of Fortune smile upon us, we will survive."

Jord snorted derisively. "Sounds like a plan t' me."

Gralyre mouth twitched slightly. Then he set to envisioning a real battle strategy.

"How many of Doaphin's creatures do ye think are in there?"

Aneida asked.

"There is sure t' be Deathren," Saliana whispered.

"And Stalkers," Trifyn warned.

"'Tis the Demon Lords we will have t' truly fear," Jord added. "'Tis been my experience that ye can stay out o' the path o' the Stalkers, and the Deathren are mindless enough t' lead in circles, but the Demon Lords and their magic will always find ye in the end." His gaze dropped and his face blanked of emotion, as he became consumed by a memory.

A hard smile formed on Gralyre's lips, as the kernel of an idea began to take hold. Somehow, the Bleak was the key. If it were stripped away during daylight, how many of Doaphin's creatures would parish? There had to be a way to turn the evil's greatest defense into its greatest vulnerability.

"Dotch," Gralyre asked quietly, "what is your best guess as to what the Bleak is made of?"

There were sniggers from around the circle. "Uh, Magic?" Jord asked sarcastically, as he took his turn with the flask.

Gralyre silenced the laughter with a look that could be felt more than seen in the twilight. "Magic holds it in place, but the bulk of it must be made of something." He well remembered the weeks of study with the book of magic. Conservation of energy was the key, and could be the weakness of the Bleak.

"'Tis like fog, but I have ne'er seen fog so thick. 'Tis like a cloud trapped on the ground, but its boundaries are sharp, like 'tis held inside a box." Dotch demonstrated with his hands as he spoke. "I do no' know what causes the black color."

Dotch stared away into the distance, and his face tightened into a mask of repugnance. "It stinks o' rot and ash and death, and every breath feels like it will choke ye. When ye get used t' it, 'tis even worse." He shivered. "I was a young man when I left. I stole away with my bride, and swore I would no' return. I wanted t' live in the light."

Saliana gasped. "The Southern Fortress is inside the Bleak?" She had not been present to hear the tale that Dotch had told when their journey had begun.

Dotch grimaced. "Aye. The Bleak hides our people away from the creatures. They canno' find us. We canno' find them…" he shrugged, and his eyes became haunted. "Sometimes they find us…"

Gralyre returned to the subject at hand, that they not become derailed from their purpose. Dotch's demons were his own, and there was enough fear in the air tonight without adding to it.

"A box that large would take a terrible amount of energy to sustain, even for Demon Lords," Gralyre mused out loud. "The box must be strong enough to hold mists, but weak enough to allow Doaphin's creatures to pass unhindered through its boundaries."

Gralyre leaned forward, as his plan took shape. "If it is a cloud, it can be blown apart by wind, and if we remove the fog suddenly, when the sun is high, we would destroy most of the Stalkers and the Deathren."

Saliana clapped her hands. "They would burn up! Do ye mean that we would no' have to go into that thing? It would be gone?" Saliana asked with hope in her voice.

"That works for me," Aneida muttered and took a swig from the flask before passing it onwards to Mayvin.

Me too, Mayvin gestured before accepting the drink. She winced, as she tilted her head back to sip, and the movement pulled against her wound. Riding had been torturous, and now that the day was done, she welcomed the heat of the liquor to dull the pain.

Gralyre stared out into the twilight, towards the Bleak and beyond to where the island awaited them. "Twould do the most good if it were dispersed just as we reach Fennick's Island," he mused. "The most formidable defense on the isle would be vanquished, and there would be no time to gather replacements from the garrison of Elevor before the Solstice. We would have no opposition to entering the labyrinth."

"The lady Catrian said that there would be Demon Lords on the island," Trifyn reminded. "What is t' be done about them? They have no fear o' the light."

Rewn nodded. "And I thought that if ye used your magic too near t' them, the Demon Lords would sense ye. Ye would announce our presence on the island, and they would come for us! We would ne'er make it into the labyrinth."

Gralyre rubbed at his bottom lip for a moment, considering options. "Perhaps that is exactly what we want. Maybe while the Demon Lords are chasing me, distracted, they will not see the rest of you steal under their noses."

"Why no' make the storm from here, where they canno' get t'

ye?" Trifyn asked. "Maybe then they will no' sense ye, and ye will no' be sacrificing yourself."

"This near to the Bleak, the size of the storm that I would need to create would overtake us long before we reached the coast. Ryes said that it stretches for a thousand leagues in both directions. And if the storm is too small, what it shifts of the Bleak will just fill in behind it as it passes."

They were all left thinking for a while. The flask made several more passes around the circle before Aneida spoke up. "A rock slide can be started with the movement o' a single pebble at the summit."

"What does that mean?" Jord snorted at her seemingly out of context statement. Aneida tried to glare him down, but Jord held her gaze boldly, smirking.

"It means," Aneida sneered, "that ye men think too much in terms o' brute force instead o' cause and effect! If ye start a pebble rolling, far enough up on the slope, it hits another pebble, which hits a rock, which hits a boulder and by the time the landslide is over, the original pebble is long buried."

"I see what you are getting at," Gralyre murmured, as a new strategy began to form but it all hinged upon the Sorceress. Would Catrian be able to help them? "Catrian would be the only one who could do it, and there are no guarantees that she can or will."

Rewn frowned. "Would the storm even reach us in time from so far away as the Northern Fortress?"

Gralyre shrugged. "A fortnight could be enough time for such a storm to reach us, depending upon its strength and speed. The timing would have to be exact, and the storm would have to be targeted to smite Fennick's Island." Gralyre stood and dusted his hands. "I will attempt to seek council with Catrian, and ask if it can be done, but she is very far away, and magic has its limits. As I use my power it will alert our location to every creature near to us." Gralyre cautioned.

"Just do what ye can, lad," Dotch advised.

Rewn nodded. "If it will give us a chance then 'tis well worth the risk."

Gralyre clapped Dotch on the shoulder, as he walked away. "Give me a few minutes."

"Ye will no' let us down, lad," Dotch said confidently.

Gralyre wished he deserved the faith the others had in him. For a moment, he stood in the darkness, and tried to conceive of another plan. Was there anything else that he could do to create an advantage or an opportunity for their survival? But there was nothing. This was all that he had, and it was a long shot at best, and neutralized naught but one of dozens of threats. The Gods were laughing at him.

Catrian could no longer reach him with her projected shade, but he knew that he was strong enough to use the bond they had formed over the last weeks to stretch out his consciousness to touch her, mind-to-mind. The danger was great this near to the Bleak, but so was their need. He ignored the notion that any excuse would have been sufficient for him to reach out to her one last time.

Girding himself against the eagerness in his heart, he allowed his breathing to slow. Listening to the pulse of his blood, he reached for the calmness of mind and body that would allow him to gather his magic. Ever so slowly he extended his consciousness, searching for the familiar feel of her thoughts, further and further he stretched, feeling his power grow thin with the distance…

His heart leapt as he made contact. *'Catrian.'*

Her first words were scolding. *'Gralyre! How are ye doing this? Have ye learned nothing about conserving your power? Why are ye contacting me? Do ye wish t' be caught afore ye even have a chance at the sword? Are ye mad? Why are ye putting yourself in such danger?'*

'Shh. 'Tis necessary. I need your council,' he gentled her.

'What is it? Gralyre ye must be quick, before they sense ye!'

'I need a storm that will tear away the Bleak, all of it, two thousand miles across. It must strike when the sun is highest to destroy the Deathren and the Stalkers. The origin must seem to be a natural phenomenon, and to come from so far away that the Demon Lords will not sense its approach. The force of wind must be so violent and strike so fast that their magic cannot hold the mists together. And it must reach the island in a fortnight. Can it be done?'

'A fortnight? Gralyre, that is the Solstice, and ye are telling me t' aim such destruction directly at ye!' But as her mind followed his logic, he felt her grudging approval.

'Yes,' Catrian asserted. *'I can do this. But make haste, for ye*

must make the crossing t' the island afore the storm falls upon ye. I canno' guarantee that it will no' be early, and catch ye afore the Solstice. Make camp on the south side o' the island, the far side. Ye will survive the wind better from there. Gralyre, this storm may kill ye. Are ye certain?'

'Aye. There is no other way. Thank-you, Catrian.' Gralyre replied, but that seemed wholly inadequate. His heart filled with longing and grief for what would be their last contact.

'Do no' say another word, I could no' bear it.' She sensed his torment. They had already said their farewells, and this contact, though necessary, was as a knife to her heart, twisting in raw agony so that her next words were brutal and scathing. *''Tis no' possible, ye and I, it never was.''* The subtext was clear. They were both going to their deaths.

'Catrian.' Panic for her safety rolled through him. *'Stay safe, in the war. Do not take chances! Do not sacrifice yourself without cause!'*

Catrian's thoughts were forlorn. *'We leave in a fortnight, on the Solstice, for the muster. We will meet up with Kierdenan's men as we make for the lowlands t' gather north o' Verdalan with Baldric and Laurazan...I should no' be telling ye this.'*

Gralyre's frustration burst through their connection. *'Then do not! I do not want to know! I only want to know that you will stay safe! That you will survive!'* His heart thumped hard. *'You must know, that if the worst happens, my last thoughts will be of you.'*

They would not say the words, but the feelings arcing

between them were undeniable. Grief. Longing. Heartache. It was a language all on its own, wordless, like Mayvin's hand gestures.

'And I ye... Good-bye.' And she was gone.

The contact vanished so abruptly that Gralyre staggered, and fell to his knees. When he slowly opened his eyes to the chilled darkness, his chest felt too tight, and it took several deep inhalations to recover enough to make his way back to the camp.

CHAPTER SIX

NORTHERN REBEL FORTRESS – EARLY SPRING

"They have reached the Bleak, and will arrive at the island in a fortnight, just in time for the Solstice," Catrian informed Boris and Matik the following morning.

"Good! With the Gralyre affair finally put t' rest, mayhap we can concentrate on the real war," Boris clapped his hands, and rubbed them together.

Catrian's face sheeted white, and she glanced down quickly before the two men could see the hurt that her uncle's words had caused. "Matik, how go the preparations?" She managed the casual sounding question, as she smoothed out the map that lay spread upon the wooden table in her quarters. "Are the supply trains well away?" As she leaned over the map, her loosened hair swung forward to further hide her devastation.

"Aye. Our supplies are in place, and ready t' sustain us during the journey out o' the mountains, and our mobilization is on schedule. We will be ready t' break camp on the Solstice," Matik replied. He leaned forward, and placed a finger on the map to the southwest of the Northern Fortress. "It will take us a fortnight to meet up with General Kierdenan, here at Hondor's Pass, and from there," his finger traced the route they would take, "advance down into the lowlands. As ye requested, our march will take us past Verdalan, and much o' our protectorate t' warn as many o' the lowlanders as possible t' flee, afore we rendezvous with the rest o' our forces here," his finger tapped a small dot to the north-east of Verdalan, "at Dapochar on the first day of summer. General Baldric's spy network will be providing us with updates on Doaphin's troop movements, so that we can avoid open battle for as long as possible.

"As we advance on our front," Matik's finger moved south, "Commander Ryes will mobilize his people towards the southeast t' open a mountain pass into the lands o' the Dream Weavers. We expect that they will meet moderate resistance from Doaphin's forces, though we have ne'er pushed in that direction afore, so we hope t' take Doaphin by surprise. Losses should be minimal, and the southerners will hold the ground for the lowlanders escaping the purge that we will send in their direction."

Matik placed a small brass weight on the map to represent their troops. "From Dapochar, we will begin a fighting, controlled retreat back into the mountains t' cover the escape o' the lowlanders through the passes," Matik advised, and placed a second brass weight on the map, "and Laurazon will do the same, heading for the west coast north o' Ghent, where Chartrin's ships will be waiting t' ferry them off the mainland t' the safety o' their island fortress."

Boris leaned over the map to study it once more. "Have we received any word from Baldric as t' where Doaphin is massing?"

Matik shook his head. "No' yet."

"Uncle are ye still certain that dividing our forces is the best course t' take?" Catrian frowned down at the strategy they had devised.

Boris straightened, and his face was stern. "Unless something has changed that will see us t' certain victory, we will only fight when necessary t' protect the refugees. This is the only way t' cover as much territory as possible in the time that remains t' us."

He leaned forward and studied the group of islands off the coast, just west of Dreisenheld, that held the territories of the Western Fortress. "Chartrin is in a good place t' defend his people, and should be able t' hold out for years, barring a magical attack from Doaphin's Demon Lords."

Boris looked t' the blank area of the map that denoted Dream Weaver territory to the east of the mountains, and he stroked a finger at it, longingly. "And if we can just make it through the passes, mayhap we will find allies," he murmured.

Matik nodded. "Either way, Doaphin will be forced t' divide his forces t' chase after us."

"Fine," Catrian agreed shortly. "We leave in a fortnight then."

"Aye," Boris agreed, but unease stiffened his spine. Catrian was distracted. She was still thinking of Gralyre. He sighed gustily, and opened his mouth to remind her once again of where her loyalties and energies should lie.

But she forestalled him. "I will see ye both later. There is something I must do now," Catrian gave them the dismissal.

"For him?" Matik snarled, and then caught himself guiltily. He had picked up on her odd behavior as well.

"As a matter o' fact," Catrian ground out coldly, glaring down her general.

Boris reached out to take her hand in his, but with a jerk she pulled back. He frowned at her rejection but it did not stop him from voicing his opinion. "'Tis always a mistake t' allow emotion t' cloud your judgment in battle. Ye had best end your mooning now! Ye need t' set him aside, and do what needs t' be done!"

Catrian overturned her chair, as she stumbled away from both men, her body made uncharacteristically clumsy, clenched as it was with the need to escape if only for a moment. All was made worse for she knew Boris was right. But she would do this one last thing for Gralyre, as homage for what might have been theirs, and then she would go to her death in the war.

Rage and grief overcame her then, and she lost her hard fought detachment. "Have I no' done all ye have ever asked o' me?" she spat. "I sent him t' his death! Now ye will allow me the time t'..." her mouth worked, as she sought the word she needed, "...grieve!" She drew a deep breath and stepped further away from them.

Boris and Matik exchanged a look. "Catrian!" Boris began, his index finger wagging at her, as though she were an errant child.

Catrian glared at him, daring him to say one more word. She

pointed at her tent flap. "Leave me. Give me the time I need. Ye want my head clear for the war ahead, let me finish what I need t' do!"

Boris' glare was as hot as hers, and a muscle worked in his jaw as his teeth clenched.

Matik drew on his shoulder, trying to move him towards the exit. "Come. Boris, come. Let her be."

Boris blew air through his nose like a wild boar sighting a foe. He could not remember a time that Catrian had ever defied his will, yet these days it seemed all that he received from her. "He is dead," he gritted. "The sooner ye accept the fact the sooner ye can forget him!"

Catrian turned her back, breathing harshly, as she awaited the rustle of the flap to her tent that would herald their departure. She had pledged Boris her life and her powers, for the Resistance and the war, but her heart was her own, and not his to dictate to his will. Boris would have his sorceress back within his fist soon enough, but Catrian's time with Gralyre was hers to treasure, something to keep her strong for the war to come.

ഇൻരു

NEAR DRIESENHELD – EARLY SPRING

Doaphin oversees the muster taking place in the shadow the towering walls of the city of Driesenheld. Hundreds of thousands of Demon Riders, Demon Lords, Stalkers and

Deathren mill over the site, and 'tis Doaphin's task, as Lord Commander, to form the ponderous mass into a cohesive fighting force, as more arrive daily in response to the Master's summons.

For convenience sake, he has had a tent erected so that he can be on hand to deal with the multitude of problems that arise daily from the contentious hordes of evil beings. If he does not provide them with human targets soon, they will turn upon each other.

He pours over the maps spread out on his table, tracing supply routes, and devising battle strategies. But his mind is not on the task. He has just received word that his ambush failed. The Rebels have not been halted, and the latest reports have seen them almost to the Bleak.

The only good news is that the Master remains unaware of this betrayal. Nor the new one he is about to commit.

"You wished to meet with me, Supreme Commander?" The Demon Lord, resplendent in a patterned silk shirt, and striped velvet pantaloons, enters Doaphin's tent. As it shrugs its long cape back over its shoulders, it can be seen that it bears no sword about its narrow hips. It has no need, for it is the weapon. Tall and straight, with neatly coiffed blond hair, and the face of an angel, the Demon Lord exudes pure evil.

Doaphin's eyes narrow as he evaluates his options. He has learned long ago that the best way to prevent death is to disarm an enemy before the fight. Waiting for the Man to take the Dragon Sword is madness, and Doaphin finds that having successfully hidden his first treachery, this next one is much easier to commit.

"The Rebels are trying to reach the Sword. My spies tell me that they will be entering the Bleak soon. They must never reach the island. You will contact your brethren in Elevor, and have the patrols doubled. If the Rebels are found, they are to be eradicated, one and all. And one more safeguard…"

"Yes Supreme Commander?"

"Release the Deathren into the Bleak."

"How many, milord?"

"All of them."

The Demon Lord eyes him slyly. "Is this the Master's will, Supreme Commander? Why is the Master not contacting my brethren directly?"

Doaphin glares down his nose at the arrogant creature. He misses the days of the Stalkers, who always obeyed without question. "I am the Supreme Commander. I always speak with the Master's tongue. Do. As. I. Will." Doaphin lashes out with a whip of magic that flays open the cheek of the Demon Lord's pretty face.

The Demon Lord gathers its magic to retaliate, and Doaphin uses the same whip of air to encircle the creature's throat, and heft it up to dangle and choke. Its serpent's eyes begin to bulge, and its mouth hangs open, gasping at what little air it can obtain while its hands claw at the invisible garrote.

"Your magic is no match for mine. Only the Master is more powerful. Seek to do me harm again, and I will take back that pitiful excuse for life that animates you."

After a brief struggle, the Demon Lord releases its hold upon its magic, and Doaphin relents, watching the Demon Lord tumble back onto the thick, rich rug. The creature is not so pretty anymore.

The Demon Lord rises to hands and knees, and pushes with effort back to its feet before affecting a low bow of respect. "Of course Supreme Commander. As you will, Supreme Commander." The Demon Lord bows its way from the tent.

Doaphin throws himself down into his soft, padded throne of a chair, and raises his withered hand before his face. For a moment he becomes trapped in the far past, and the sounds of troops marching past outside the tent fade away to nothing.

The silence resonates with the prophesy of doom, as though the words have only just been spoken.

Enigma Rise from out of Mist;
Spirit Waken with a Roar;
Dragon Perched on Vengeful fist;
Fell Usurper Rule No More.

ഇറ

NORTHERN REBEL FORTRESS – EARLY SPRING

Catrian braided her loose hair, as she sought to tamp down her ire. She could acknowledge that Boris and Matik only held the interests of the rebellion in mind, but their meddling was noisome. She did not need them to remind her daily of the limitations with which she must shackle herself!

In high dudgeon, she strode from her tent, and across the fortress. All about her, tents had been dismantled, and wagons stacked high with gear, weapons, food, and blankets, as her people mobilized for war.

She must go outside the walls to do what must be done, for such a storm as she envisioned would scour the fortress from the mountain should she birth it here, and it would not do to terrify the folk with her magic, for if they were to see what she was about to do, terrified they would be!

People did not trust magic. Despite the respect they showed now, she knew that it would take very little for them to turn on her. She need only look to what Boris had revealed before Gralyre had left, to tell her that hard fact of life. Catrian was only as safe as she was useful to the Rebels. No more.

Several minutes later, she arrived at the east gates of the palisade, and ordered the two sentries there to raise the bar to let her out.

"But your ladyship," stated one of the two gatemen. "We is no' supposed t' open the gate for anyone." He rubbed a grimy paw down his face, leering disrespectfully at her trim figure in her formfitting buckskins and light cloak. His hand came to rest on his belt, where he gave a heave to pull his pants back up over his hefty paunch.

"That is right," the other guardsman expressed officiously.

"General Matik himself gave me the order! No' t' raise the bar, even for the lady."

Catrian closed her eyes, and sought the patience to deal with the two, before deciding that she had none to spare. She could have explained that she outranked the General, and that it was she who had ordered the gates barred. Instead, with a wave of her hand, she swatted the sentries aside like flies.

Squealing and yelling, the two guardsmen found themselves pinned to the timbers of the wall, fighting the hand of magic that kept them suspended a man's height from the ground. With her fists clenched for control, Catrian barely stopped herself from shattering the gates. Instead, she directed her will and caused the heavy timber crossbar to topple from its perch, and one side of the ponderous gate to yawn open.

Without a backward glance for the two shrieking men, she stormed through, not even pausing to watch the gate slam shut behind her, and the crossbar lift from the ground to drop back into its rightful place. As she strode through the empty practice field, she released the sentries to fall to the ground.

With quick sure feet, she began a steady, ground eating lope, her braid flipping across her back, as she sought the switchback trail down the slope into the valley. For what she wanted to create, she needed a large clearing, and she knew exactly the location. There was an alpine meadow about two leagues away. It would take some time to reach, but it was the only space near enough to the fortress that would meet her needs. She had not taken a horse with her for the destructive magic she was about to unleash would kill most of the wildlife in the vicinity of the meadow. Horses were too precious to the cause to waste on this errand. She would send parties of men to retrieve whatever game was felled by her storm after she returned. Their army could use the fresh meat, as they began their journey.

Her run was easy, for the winter snows were mostly gone now, reduced to slushy spots hidden in the shadows beneath trees, and beside rocks.

The sun had moved well along its course in the sky by the time she finally arrived at the meadow. Though clear of snow from the strengthening sun, the dead grasses rustled in the breeze, yellowed and dry, still awaiting the green shoots that were sure to burst out of the ground within a few days to make it green and lush once more.

Slowing to a walk as she reached the edges of the field, Catrian reached under a tree, and scooped a handful of clean snow into her mouth to suck upon to ease her thirst. There was always a chance that there would be a hunting party in the area, or other Rebels doing duties that had taken them from the fortress. She took a moment to seek through the path of destruction her magic would flow, and was content that no one would be injured from her storm.

She walked out into the field, and halted at the centre of the clearing next to a large boulder. Much of her disquieting ire had bled off during her run, and she now felt in control and ready to unleash her magic. Using cracks and crevasses in the rough granite, she climbed the surface of the stone to sit in the sun and catch her breath.

Catrian reached into her tunic, and removed a sheet of precious paper. After she had spoken to Gralyre, she had spent long hours into the night, consulting her texts and calculating the size and speed that her storm must reach in order to arrive at the island in daylight, before the Solstice, but not so far ahead that it caught Gralyre's party vulnerable in the open. She double-checked the calculations again under the harsh light of the afternoon sun, ensuring that she had allowed for all variables.

Still her heart wavered with uncertainty. She had had to estimate the exact distance to the south coast, and her margin for error was very small. Her best guess could be completely wrong. She had calculated as closely as possible, pouring over maps, and consulting her books, studying everything that she owned that could lend her insights into what she must do but in the end it was the Gods of Fortune who would decide the outcome.

She folded the paper, and put it away in her tunic, before standing, and drawing a deep breath for courage. The boulder raised her high above the surface of the meadow, the perfect platform and vantage from which to launch the storm.

Still she hesitated, closing her eyes and flinging a prayer towards the uncaring Gods. Once she released her tumult, she would be unable to control it or modify its velocity and direction in any way. Without magic to herald the its approach to Fennick's Island, the Demon Lords would be taken unawares, and the wind would strike with such swiftness and force, that they would be unable to turn it from its path, or prevent it from ripping away the Bleak that protected their minions from the sunlight. The tempest would grow in size, enough to assault the entire south coast, more than able to shatter the Bleak from one end to the next. And Gralyre would be right in its destructive path, unprotected on a tiny spit of an island in a barren sea.

'Let it work!' she prayed to the Gods. *'Let him survive!'*

She reached deep, and touched her power, seeking the Godsmagic that spoke to her of movement and force. Then she reached out her consciousness, and touched her Wizard Stone, hidden deep in a quiet pool of glacier water far away in a mountain pass, and drew deeply of its stores, filling her body with air, and movement, rush and power until her skin was afire with needles of static from containing too much energy. Blue arcs of power danced over her flesh, making her muscles quiver and contract.

The breeze that had been playfully teasing the loose strands of her hair stuttered and died, and the air went still and expectant, while she, the lightning rod, stood at the eye of the coming storm.

She held out her left palm, watching the dance of blue static that arced between her fingertips and danced up her arms. It was hypnotically beautiful, and drew her concentration down to the smallest of points. The calculations she had memorized buzzed through her thoughts, telling her exactly the forces she must apply.

Catrian raised her right hand to hover over her left, and an arc of blue lightning snapped to connect her palms. Slowly, holding the connection of energy, she began to circle her fingers, stirring the air. After a moment, Catrian could feel the force of the small whirligig growing upon her left palm.

Concentrating deeply upon the birth of her creation, she tossed the small eddy of wind onto the ground next to the boulder, carefully pushing the velocity of the rotation to grow taller and wider. It gained strength enough to begin sucking loose grass, dirt and pebbles off of the meadow to give itself a dusty form.

She fed it more of her magic, and her hair began to whip as the funnel grew upwards towards the sky, and chunks of sod lifted free of the ground to feed its growing appetite for destruction. It gained a voice, a loud drone begging for release. It was time.

With a scream of effort, Catrian threw out her arms, and her power burst free, a detonation of energy that she poured all of her pain into.

There went her unrealized love for Gralyre, and her grief at his coming death. At her coming death! There went her resentment over her sacrifices for the Resistance, and the impossible task to save the land from the evil that besieged it! Her bone deep hatred for Doaphin! Her rage! *Rage! RAGE!*

Catrian's power surged through her in quantities never felt before, and she screamed in exaltation, as for once she placed no limits upon her strength. This time the Godsmagic could be as it was always meant to be! She could be what she was meant to be! A Sorceress, a wild and elemental creature, free like this wind!

Around her a wild maelstrom sprang from earth to the heavens. Great heaving chunks of meadow, mud and slush ripped upwards into the hungry maw, as it grew larger and larger, wider than the field, tearing up the trees along the edge of the meadow. Soon it would be large enough to consume the entire valley.

And Catrian stood alone and untouched in its eye, allowing the winds to cycle around her. She threw more and more of her magic borne rage into the wind, pushing its momentum, rapidly draining power from the energies stored in her Wizard Stone, until the funnel took on her screaming voice, and the very land rippled in sympathy with her pain.

She used her blue shield to anchor herself and her boulder, to the roots of the earth, to protect herself from the elemental force she had created. With a last explosion of power, she released the wind, targeting the direction of the storm for its journey south, tweaking it slightly to adjust its course to be as precisely targeted for Fennick's Island as possible, though it would be so large when it reached the south coast it would scarcely matter.

Her storm tore a swath of destruction across the face of the mountain, heading south with the roar of an army of screaming banshees. She could hear its voice fading into the distance, and hear the pain of the forest, as great chunks of it were ripped away to appease the maelstrom's lust for devastation. The storm would funnel south, guided by the foothills of the mountain range, and gain in size and speed until it tore apart the Bleak and swept out to sea.

She quivered, as she took gasping breaths, trying to recover from the huge expenditure of magic. Her hair had been pulled free from its plaits by the tearing fingers of the wind, and now lay in tangled disarray about her shoulders, clinging in ropy strands to the perspiration on her face.

The meadow was churned, as though from a plough, and the trees surrounding the clearing were snapped off at their bases. At the end of the meadow a cleared dirt path, wide enough for an army, had appeared, pushing straight as an arrow south through the forest as if a giant had wielded a scythe. If nothing else, she had created a road that would ease their travels to meet up with Kierdenan.

The land and sky tilted around her, as her legs gave way, and she fell to her back, still gasping for air. She had known that the great magic she planned would tire her but had not counted on the incredible weakness she now felt. She could not remember another instance when using her magic had caused her to take faint. Then again, she could never recall releasing as much energy as she just had. Catrian had never come so near to using all of her Godsmagic, though she still retained what she needed to keep her body alive.

She lay still, the stone warm against her back from the heat of the sun, while her breathing slowed, and her heart stopped its thundering. It would take a fortnight to recover, which timed nicely for the rendezvous with Kierdenan at Hondor's Pass.

Despite her weakness, she felt good, released somehow, and fought a drunken giggle that tried to escape. She was smiling as her eyes closed and she feinted.

℘℘℘

"By all the Gods! What is that?" Matik stood atop the wall walk beside the warrior who had summoned him.

The man shook his head, as stunned as his General. "It started from nowhere only a moment ago, and it keeps growing! Are we under attack? Should I sound the alarm?" Against the monstrous cyclone that stretched from the sky, and seemed to span the entire valley, what good would an alarm be?

Matik shook his head. "We are no' under attack. Look! 'Tis moving off."

The storm ripped through the valley, heading south, missing the pass to travel up over the mountain, and soon vanished from sight. A swath of devastation marked its wake, a straight path through the forest that could be easily seen from the height of the walls.

The warrior relaxed with a deep sigh. "Thank the Gods it did no' turn in our direction. What do ye think it was? What caused it?"

Matik's chin lowered, and he played with the patchy beard that was all that had regrown since Gralyre had assaulted him.

℘℘℘

DREISENHELD

The Master steps down off the dais towards the row of Demon Lords that Doaphin has assembled before the throne, paces slowly down the line, pauses to glare into Doaphin's eyes, then turns in a flourish of ermine robes, and stalks back in the opposite direction. The Master's eyes burn with a strength of rage and power belayed by the indolent pace.

"Which one of you failed to realize that there are sorcerers living in the Heathren Mountains? One now travels south with the Rebels, and one remains with their armies to the north." The Master's voice is gentle, reasonable even, in its demand for an accounting.

"My Master…" a Demon Lord begins with a low bow of respect.

The Master waves a negligent finger, and a line of red streaks across the Demon Lord's throat, choking the words.

The Demon Lord scrabbles at its neck for a moment, before its head tips away to topple to the floor, followed by the rest of the body. Blood gushes, soaking the feet of the ones who remain standing. They dare not shift away from the spreading gore.

The Master smiles then. "Who, has failed to recall…" another creature drops in a spray of blood, "…our edict…" the next Demon Lord in line screeches, bursts into flames, and vanishes in thick roiling smoke, "…that no magic…" the last Demon Lord crumples, as though a giant fist has crushed it into the floor, "…may rest in human hands?" The Master halts in front of

Doaphin.

Sweat beads the cheeks of the Supreme Commander, diluting the spatters of blood from the death of the Demon Lords. He reeks of terror.

"Speak!" The Master screams in his face.

Doaphin flinches. "'Twas to be expected, my Master, that the humans would learn to hide their powers eventually, to survive. But both of the sorcerers made fatal mistakes, and announced their presence. Now we can act." His voice trembles.

"And how do you propose we do that?" The Master quivers with the need to kill. What use is keeping such a useless specimen? "We told you that the Rebels are to be allowed safe passage through the Bleak and into the labyrinth. Did! We! Not! Make! Our! Will! Known!" Spittle flies from the Master's lips, the echoes of the screams reverberate through the stone pillars of the throne room.

Doaphin's eyes show the whites, rolling back and forth, as he seeks an excuse or a lie that will allow him to live.

Enough. The small service he provides is not worth the aggravation of his life. The Master gathers power slowly, and watches Doaphin's terror grow apace, as he senses his approaching doom.

"The Stalkers!" He shouts triumphantly.

At the unexpected outburst, the Master pauses. "Continue."

"The Stalkers, my Master, the Stalkers in the Heathren Mountains! Three of them on the trail of the Man. They are near to the location of the human sorcerer. Send the Stalkers! We will eliminate at least one of our threats!"

"And the other?"

Doaphin's smile wavers. "Leave him to aid the Rebels. If the island does not kill him, we will take him when we acquire the Dragon Sword."

An intriguing solution. It buys back his life…for now. "Leave us."

Doaphin scrabbles an exit, bowing across the chamber and through the hammered gold doors.

ॐ

THE NORTHERN HEATHREN MOUNTAINS

Green Crest is exhausted by the magic it takes to keep heat trapped against its scales, and the bitter cold out, but what choice does It have? Nightly, Sethreat gains.

The Stalker lopes over the crest of a mountain, and down the far side, slipping and sliding upon the icy blue glacier that glows in the moonlight.

Reaching the Man first is the only path to survival. Was it madness to betray Sethreat?

Green Crest regrets nothing. When the Master discovers Sethreat's failures, Green Crest will be elevated to stand in glory. It need only win the race.

And there is now triple the reasons to hasten. Not just to escape Sethreat, who gives chase, and to find the Man, who lies ahead, but now also to find a magic wielder. Power has surged, and It has marked the locus. Soon, a sorcerer will feel Green Crest's talons about his neck.

ෂාය

NORTHERN REBEL FORTRESS

When Catrian awoke, the sun had passed low enough in the sky to be lost beyond the peaks of the surrounding mountains, leaving a chill to begin climbing upward from the still thawing ground. Disdaining her exhaustion, she slid down off the boulder, her knees giving way from the impact at the bottom, so that she fell forward onto the ground, catching herself on her hands, as she rested for a moment, and gathered her strength. Using the boulder for support she pulled herself back up to her feet, and began to stagger towards home. The churned ground was uneven and rough, difficult to navigate in the shadows of twilight, as she wove unsteadily back towards the distant lights of the fortress.

Boris would definitely not approve of the power she had just spent helping Gralyre. She was sure to hear of it when she arrived back at her tent. Hopefully, he would be brief, as she needed to rest, to sleep, and replenish her energy.

She had drawn too deeply of her Godsmagic, and was now feeling the aftereffects. More than just exhaustion, she labored to draw breath, and her flesh grew icy from the slowed beat of her heart. She shivered and pulled her cloak tighter. In the shadows of the mountains, the late sunlight did little to warm her. It would be night soon, but the walk would help to heat her flesh. Catrian was bone deep weary, but her soul felt cleansed. 'Twas a good thing that she did not throw temper tantrums often, she smiled to herself.

Her amusement was fleeting, as she remembered the exact purpose that her rage born magic would serve.

'Keep him safe a while longer,' her foolish heart implored of the Gods of Fortune.

੩੦੯੩

HEATHREN MOUNTAINS

"Sethreat, my Stalker, where are you?"

The Mater calls! Sethreat creaks to a knee, stiff from the cold, and lifts Its horned head in adulation. "Master, I await thy words!" It ignores the Demon Rider minions who creep nearer with burning brands to heat Its flesh. Speckle Tail has lagged behind, unable to stand the freezing temperatures. Sethreat hopes it is dead.

"My Stalker, the Man now travels south. You are too slow, and he has escaped you!"

"Apologies, my Master. The cold saps my strength. Shalt I turn south to pursue him?"

"No. You have failed. I have made other arrangements."

Sethreat hangs Its massive head, shamed. "My Master, thou should slaughter this unworthy one."

"I should, yet ye will have an opportunity for redemption."

Sethreat's tail beats the ground like an untried hatchling. The Master is generous. The Master is the bringer of glory. Glory to the Master.

"You have you felt the great magic unleashed only moments ago?"

"Yes, my Master. A great and powerful Sorcerer."

"Kill!"

"Kiiilllll!" It roars in exaltation, and the echoes roll out over the mountains.

The Master's presence leaves as abruptly as it comes, and Sethreat's great joy flags, for it cannot obey. It will not be It who sups upon the flesh of a magic wielder. Green Crest is too far ahead to catch before the sorcerer falls to its talons.

Sethreat turns and seizes a minion, ripping the Demon Rider in twain to soothe Its anguish. It stands amid the steaming blood and entrails, and sneers at the mountainous distance It must still travel to catch the traitor. Green Crest has stolen the kill given to It by the Master.

Yet another reason for Green Crest will die.

෨෮

NORTHERN REBEL FORTRESS

Night caught Catrian less than halfway back to the Rebel fortress. She stopped to cling to a tree, panting to catch her breath. Her effortless jog to the meadow that morning now seemed a lifetime past. Her progress towards home was slow and painful, and she began to give consideration to throwing herself down, and sleeping until morn but she had not brought more than a light cloak with her, and the mountain temperatures could still drop to freezing overnight.

She was too exhausted to continue for the moment so she slid down beneath the tree to catch her breath and message the cramps from her legs. Within moments of stopping, her head nodded forward, and she slipped into a light doze.

She was unsure how much time had passed when the back of her neck suddenly tingled with electricity, jerking her alert.

Magic! She was no longer alone!

Catrian's sluggish heartbeat accelerated, as she dragged herself to her feet, and pivoted to slam her back protectively to the tree, scanning the darkened forest for signs. The rough bark scraped and dragged at her back, as she circled the trunk, inspecting all directions for the source of the danger she sensed.

A twig snapped behind her, and Catrian froze in place, holding her breath. She was on the far side of the tree now. Hopefully whatever was there had not yet spied her! As quietly as she was able, Catrian eased her head around the trunk for a quick glance.

At first she could see nothing in the blackness, though her widened gaze searched frantically from shadow to shadow, bush to bush, seeking movement. Her blood iced in her veins, as a dark shape resolved itself from the gloom, moving in a shuffling gait that belied the powerful speed it was capable of.

A Stalker!

It must have caught her scent when she had created the storm. She had exploded with so much energy that she had drawn it to her like a fly to dung. Fear shivered her flesh, for she had drained so much of her Godsmagic that she could barely lift her legs to walk, let alone defend herself magically!

The Stalker's scaled snout was to the ground, snorting and snuffling at the trail she had left that morning. "Sorcerer, thou art a woman!" It mumbled. "A pretty succulent for my feast!" Its chuckle sounded like chains rasping against stone.

Catrian reached deep within, seeking her residues of Godsmagic. By draining herself of power she would destroy her body's ability to keep her heart beating, and her lungs expanding with air, but she was going to die anyway at the hands of Doaphin's creature!

For Catrian, it was no choice. If she was to perish, then she was going to take the Stalker with her!

She sought a link with her Wizard Stone, even knowing that the magical stores were depleted, for she needed whatever might remain to augment her failing strength.

With a battle cry of effort, she rounded the tree, blasts of energy flowing from her closed fists straight into the Stalker's scaly face.

As the energy slammed into it, it screeched and jumped high into the air to escape Catrian's barrage, but Catrian was relentless in her attack. The fire followed where it went until the Stalker fell to earth and curled into a tight ball, twitching and squealing in pain, as its tough scaly flesh ruptured and split in the heat of the magical flames.

Yelling victoriously, Catrian watched in satisfaction, as her lethal magic slowly overcame the vile beast. But then the unthinkable happened. The energy crackling from her hands sputtered and died, leaving her swaying on wide spread legs for balance.

The Stalker uncurled slowly, and a grinding chuckle issued forth from its ruined face.

Sobs clogged Catrian's throat. She had failed. It yet lived. She had not had the strength remaining to kill it, only to damage it. Her sight darkened, and she slid to the ground, unable to stay on her feet a second longer. The mortally wounded creature still possessed enough life to take hers, but she knew she would not feel the pain when it reached her. Her Godsmagic was spent, and her body was already dying.

The Stalker's horny hide was blackened and smoldering, and its legs and tail were seared through to the bones. It had taken the brunt of her attack upon its back and legs after it had curled away from her. It tried to stand but gave up when its lower body failed to obey its commands.

Its powerful torso was still mostly intact, and it bared its lethal teeth, as it dragged its body around to face her. "Missed...me...Sor...ceressssss," It wheezed and gagged on its own fluids. The nightmare began to crawl towards her.

She shivered with cold, as her heartbeat slowed, growing weaker and weaker. Her eyelids fluttered, watching sporadically, as the Stalker dragged itself nearer. She lacked the strength to move even the tortoise pace necessary to escape the beast's laborious crawl.

She thought of Gralyre, and gave herself over to his memory. The fire and warmth that she had found, momentarily, that had heated her cold life, still warmed her soul now. His name sighed from her lips, and her eyes closed for the last time.

ഇൗങ

"Catrian!"

There was no doubt in Matik's mind that Catrian had been the author of the massive storm, but she had not been seen since she had forced her way out of the gates that morning after their meeting. By late afternoon, Matik had grown concerned enough that he had left through the eastern gate to track her down, and escort her back to the fortress, forcibly if necessary!

"Catrian!" he yelled for the hundredth time, his voice rougher than normal from having called her name so often, and heard naught but the faint echo of his own shout back from the rocks of the mountainside.

All traces of her trail had been eradicated by the wind. Matik had been crisscrossing the area, hoping to happen upon her, but now that night had fallen, he decided to return to the fortress, certain that she had slipped past him, and returned home while he was out wasting his time searching for her.

As he cleared the tree line, and began the long hike back up the switchback road to the fortress, he turned one last time to survey the forest. Arcing blue flames in the distance caught his gaze.

He would recognize Catrian's mage fire anywhere. By its prolonged duration, it could only mean that she was under attack. Though she would be wroth with him for trying to protect her, Matik could not help but break into a run to come to her aid. She was nearby, less than five hundred yards down into the tree line.

"Catrian!" he bellowed. Terrible screams, faint from the distance began to reach his ears as he ran. Reacting purely on instinct Matik loosed his axe, holding the war steel at the ready. He could clearly see little fires sparkling between the trees now, aftermaths of Catrian's magic, but there were no shadows shifting across the flames to indicate that anyone was still moving.

"Catrian!" Matik crashed through the woods. The heavy axe gleamed in his fist, as he leaped a deadfall, and came upon the scene.

The Stalker had finally reached the fallen Sorceress. Its clawed arm was poised above Catrian's vulnerable throat.

Matik shouted in horror, and brought his axe crashing down,

cleaving the Stalker's arm from its shoulder in one brutal stroke. He thanked the Gods that Catrian's fire had weakened its scaly hide, and given him a soft place to aim his blow otherwise his blade would have merely glanced from the creature's tough armoured hide. Without the Dream Weaver wrought Maolar steel, there was no piercing the skin of a Stalker.

The Stalker howled, rolling to its back to confront this new attacker, its one good arm lashing out and narrowly missing bisecting Matik's torso.

The smell of burned flesh was choking, as Matik raised his axe high. The creature's roars stopped abruptly when its head left its shoulders in a gushing fountain of foul, black blood.

Breathing hard from his run, Matik scanned the clearing for any further dangers, surprised to see no other charred remains. How was Catrian taken unawares by the Stalker, and how did she fail to defeat it? She had the power to destroy ten such creatures as this one! What had gone awry?

Dropping to a knee, tears soaked into Matik's beard, as he gently brushed back Catrian's hair with trembling fingers. "My lady? Catrian?" he whispered softly. "Are ye with me, lass?"

Her flesh was cold and waxen, and he did not see movement of breath. "Gods!" he moaned and pressed his ear to her chest. Very faint, very weak, he heard her heart thump out a beat, and under the weight of his head, her chest rose and fell shallowly.

Matik fell back with a gasp of thankfulness. Catrian yet lived!

He sheathed his axe, and gathered her gently up into his arms, carrying her carefully, as he began the hike back up the steep grade towards the Fortress. He thanked the Gods for the instinct that had compelled him to follow after her.

The girl thought that her powers made her invincible, he thought anxiously, as he glanced down into her pale face. He bent and kissed her forehead, something that he would never dare do had she been awake.

"Stay with me, lass! Keep breathing! We are almost home!" He picked up his pace, her slight weight hardly a burden, as he rushed to bring her back to the fortress, to safety. As he ran, Matik prayed to the Gods of Fortune. She must recover...for all their sakes.

CHAPTER SEVEN

THE BLEAK

The fogbank grew larger as they approached, until it towered over them, blocking out all that was green and good in the world, a black horror of seething evil that extended beyond all horizons except for the one behind them. The Bleak.

It was midday when they reached the mists, and as though of a mind, the warriors halted their horses, silent in the face of its enormity. Undulating, shadow wisps, ghostly, curling fingers, reached beyond the borders, and beckoned them to dare to draw nearer to the boundary of the magic. A fitful breeze shifted and stirred the threshold to reveal glimpses of rot and ruin, an entire forest that had been starved of the light unto its death. Each time the wind disturbed the mists, it returned with the foul stench of decay to assault their senses.

In the shadow of the menacing blackness, nobody had much of an appetite, so after only a quick bite to eat, they mounted and turned east, riding parallel to the looming barrier. The Southern Rebels eyed the trees of the forest carefully, and within a couple of hours had found the blazes in the bark of two ancient cedars that marked the trailhead of the safe passage into the Bleak.

All up and down the line, Ryes' warriors reached into their packs, and withdrew long ropes of hemp that they carefully tethered to each horse, forming a chain of safety so that no one would wander away, and become lost within the darkness. Lanterns were distributed, sparked alight, and hung from long poles that were attached to the saddles of the horses with a series of straps.

Winter cloaks, discarded as the sun had grown warmer with spring weather, were donned against the damp chill of a land that had not seen daylight in three hundred years.

Gralyre leashed Little Wolf to his saddle, uncertain of what was to come, but trusting in the precautions being taken by the Southern Rebels, whose lands these were.

It was heartbreaking to see tears rolling down the cheeks of some of the southern warriors, who lifted their faces to accept a last kiss of golden warmth and light.

If 'tis so bad, why do they stay? Mayvin signed, taken by the ritual of the moment.

Aneida shrugged, her usual bold grin hidden away by the trepidation that gripped her.

Little Wolf approached the boundary between light and dark, and his hackles rose, as he pawed at the undulating blackness. He growled, and danced sideways, making a large circle at the limit of his leash to return to Gralyre's side. *'Bad, death, evil. Must our pack live here?'*

'We will not live here, Little Wolf. We will pass through it, and then a wind will come to blow it away,' Gralyre promised.

'We should hunt elsewhere.'

'There is no reason for you to come with me. We go to a bad

place, and we will likely die. You could stay in these woods and live. Safe.' Gralyre had to give his pup the choice. Their fates need not be tied.

Little Wolf glanced back at the Bleak, and then up into Gralyre's face. *'You go. I go. Protect father. Pack.'*

Gralyre nodded, too choked by emotion to bear it. He was humbled by Little Wolf's loyalty and simple courage.

Commander Ryes turned his horse so that his back was to the Bleak, and addressed his men. "Soak up the sun, lads, for the light will protect ye from harm. Hold it in your hearts for the days t' come, and the Bleak will ne'er touch ye. Remember why we choose t' stay. Remember who ye are!"

Ryes' warriors roared their response, their fists pumping in the air.

From atop his horse tied in line in front of Rewn, Dotch made a sound of distress, and pulled his flask from his saddlebag to take a healthy swig before capping it again. His eyes were squinted against his dread.

Rewn watched on with concern. "Are ye alright?" he asked as he moved his horse abreast of Dotch's.

Dotch drew a large breath, and let it escape slowly in a long hiss. "I will let ye know after we enter."

Jord, who was mounted in line ahead of Dotch looked back when he heard his comment, and backed his horse nearer, his clever mind sensing that something was amiss. "We are here with ye, Dotch," he promised, in an uncharacteristic show of support.

Aneida craned her neck to see beyond Mayvin and Jord. "What is happening? Dotch, what is wrong?"

Trifyn's rope jerked as the sisters rode back down the line, prompting him to turn to see what was happening. Noticing the others rallying around Dotch, he released the rope that tied him to the warrior ahead that he might ride back to his group.

"Ye should no' remove it!" the Rebel warned.

"I will return in a moment," Trifyn promised, as he dropped the safety line to the ground.

Saliana, a pale shadow behind Rewn, edged her horse nearer tugging up the slack that lay between her and Gralyre's horse.

Spotting his group clumping together, Gralyre left Little Wolf's side, and walked to the head of Dotch's horse, holding its bridle, as he scratched its neck. His face was full of compassion, for the dread that emanated from Dotch reached out to infect them all.

Dotch never removed his attention from the wall of mist, as though it were a living beast that bore constant watching lest it attack. His face screwed up with disgust, and his warning spat out in a burst of loathing.

"It will pull at your eyes, and ye will see shapes o' things that do no' exist. Ye will hear words whispered in your ear, conversations beside ye, and screams echoing from the air itself. Ye must no' listen. The ghosts o' this place linger, and seek t' entice the living t' their cold bosoms. If ye wander away, ye will be lost t' them forever. The Bleak will stick t' your flesh, and suck the warmth from your soul, cold, so cold, cutting to the bone. And the smell! Like death it is, a stench t' befoul your nose forever. Damp and the rot o' flesh o' Deathren, and burn o' ash from them and Stalkers. But mostly 'tis the darkness that destroys ye. 'Tis unrelenting, until sun and warmth become naught but myth and legend t' the heart o' ye."

Trifyn shivered and rubbed his arms.

Rewn laid a hand upon Dotch's shoulder. "So long as we stick together, we will make it through."

Dotch shrugged out from under his touch. "Just try t' keep your spirits, lad. Just try." He advised bitingly, as he jerked his horse's head around, away from Gralyre's grasp, and walked his steed to the limit of the tie line, to be alone with his melancholy.

Jord's knives appeared in his hands, and began to flip, as he glared stonily at the billowing, black cloud. "How are we t' keep t' the path after we enter?"

Gralyre looked towards the General. "They must have a way," he mused.

They returned to their places in line, and Trifyn tied off the fallen rope to his saddle, securing the group's safety to the rest of the Rebels.

The General was the first to enter the Bleak, keeping his horse to a slow walk forward, while twisted in his saddle for a last, idolizing look at the sunlight upon the lush forest before he disappeared into the blackness. The fog closed behind his horse like a thick curtain, leaving no sign that he had passed save for the rope that hung out into the open, hovering in the air. Even his lantern light had vanished. By then, the next rider, Ryes' son

Corr, was entering, and his light took up the futile battle to hold back the Bleak.

One by one the riders crossed the barrier until finally, as the last in the line, it was Gralyre's turn. Gralyre's horse snorted and tried to pull away, as it entered the cloud, and it took a stern grip upon the reins to keep it calm, as they were engulfed by the Bleak.

A web of clammy, foul moisture instantly adhered to Gralyre's flesh, and his clothing dampened and chilled. He gagged at the reek, and had to swallow hard to quiet his gorge. His breath steamed from his lips in an icy fog, adding even more substance to the thick, tainted air in front of his face.

Little Wolf hesitated upon the threshold of the Bleak, bracing his feet until he would be dragged forward by Gralyre's momentum unless he moved on his own. With a challenging howl, he leapt high, as though clearing a fence, and passed into the mist in the wake of Gralyre's horse.

His dark coat rendered him almost invisible, even within the light of Gralyre's lantern, as he trotted as near to Gralyre's leg as he could.

'Bad-bad-bad!' Mold and mildew sucked at his paws, a gooey sludge that polluted the ground.

Gralyre's eyes began to burn and water, but it was only the mists blurring his sight. The lantern suspended on the stick out over the horse's head created a surrounding globe of dull radiance that actually made it harder to see, for the black fog absorbed the brightness, dispersing the light, and if not quite able to snuff it altogether, muted its power. The encircling lantern light quickly came to resemble the confines of a deep cavern, the weight of the nebulous walls just as crushing and claustrophobic.

Gralyre ducked to avoid solid looking creatures and boulders that drifted past, unable to tell what was real, and what was illusion. Despite the meager light, he could not see the rump of Saliana's horse in front of him, and even the ears of his own steed were indistinct and blurred. Only the tautness of the rope, disappearing beyond the reach of his lantern, told him he was not alone.

They drifted through a rotting forest, once part of the lush lands that lay beyond the borders of the Bleak. Boles of dead trees approached and fled, briefly illuminated before being lost beyond the lantern light, as though they were what moved, and 'twas the horses that stood still.

The perception was inescapable, as the mind tried to make sense of what it saw. Up, down, left and right disappeared, and Gralyre swayed in his saddle, as his senses falsified all direction. Closing his eyes, he allowed his weight to settle in relation to the pull of the ground, so that when he opened them again he was able to fight the vertigo.

Several horses ahead, Aneida stood in her stirrups, peering futilely into the blackness. She blinked and rubbed at her eyes, but the undulating darkness was unrelenting, and her lantern showed naught but mist parting for the passage of her horse in a swirling eddy before closing in behind like the maw of a great predator. "We will ne'er be able t' see an attack!" Her harsh whisper carried past Mayvin and Jord, to Dotch.

Dotch was unimpressed by her fear, too busy dealing with his own. "Ye can smell Deathren and Stalkers coming during the daylight hours. Even as thick as the Bleak is, they are still seared by the faintness o' the sun's light. The stench o' their burning flesh betrays their presence."

Aneida's horse stumbled, and shook its mane with a long, plaintive whinny.

"Keep your horse quiet!" Dotch hissed softly. "Do ye want t' attract every Deathren in the Bleak?"

Sound distorted to the point that Dotch's whisper travelled back to Gralyre, and the disembodied words seemed to be spoken directly into his ear.

The infinitesimal amount of magic it took to quiet the horses was a risk that Gralyre was willing to take. They had not been making much noise, but after that, none of the animals fidgeted, rattled their harness, or made so much as a grunt.

The preternatural silence was disturbing but no one was about to tell Gralyre to reverse his control of their steeds. The darkness screamed of evil, and they felt like mice sneaking beneath the whiskers of a sleeping cat. The few words they spoke were carried by whispers, and they winced with every hoof that fell too loudly.

Trifyn reached out, and trailed his hand over the slimy bark of a passing tree, trying to anchor himself to anything solid and real. With only that soft touch, the forest giant toppled. Dead, its roots long ago rotted away, there was nothing to hold it in place, and the slightest bump was enough to fell it. Four more trees toppled, as it hit others on the way to its final rest upon the infected ground.

"Silence," General Ryes warned them all in a strident whisper. "Be on your guard! There will surely be patrols!"

Saliana pressed a fist to her mouth to hold back her screams when the crashes of the falling trees reached her, for she had no clue what had made the din, and imagined a Stalker reaching out of the Bleak to grab her. No one would ever realize that she had been taken. They would only find her empty saddle when they halted.

She screwed her eyes up tight, and pretended that she was merely riding at night, allowing her horse to be drawn forward by the rope bound to Rewn's. It was better for her flagging courage, for she feared that any more staring into this abyss, and she would break from the line, and gallop back towards the sunlight. It was a fortnight to the coast. How was she ever going to bear it?

Gralyre fought the urge to send his senses outward to scout for Deathren and Stalkers, for even that much magic could betray them to the their enemies. It would have been useless in any case, for there was nothing alive in the Bleak that he could merge with; no small rodents or birds, no stags running free, no wolves. He had to be content that the horses and Little Wolf, whose natural senses were far keener than his own, would alert him to approaching danger.

Over time, Gralyre began to note faint green dots on the ground along their path, and the mystery of how the Rebels navigated the Bleak became clearer to him. Something luminesced to mark their trail, but from horseback, the black fog was too thick to clearly see what it was.

It was impossible to determine how much time had elapsed when the rope ahead slackened, though surely night had fallen in the world of the sun. Gralyre was nose to tail with Saliana's steed before he realized that she had halted with the rest of the line.

The collective might of thirty lanterns congregated together fought back the blackness to a radius of almost twenty feet, and it was a relief to acknowledge that there existed a real, tangible land, peopled with allies. The dull green motes of light that the Rebels had followed had widened into a small ring to mark their first resting place on their journey through the Bleak.

"Roll out the tarps," Ryes murmured the order.

The southern warriors spread out large, heavy canvas ground sheets to protect the sleepers from the odorous muck. Upon the tarp they arranged bedrolls in a tight cluster. There would be no fires, and all but a few of the lamps were doused to save the oil against their need. Their only warmth would come from each other, shared body heat as they slept.

While the Southern Rebels passed around fresh water and hardtack upon which to sup, ever curious, Gralyre took a moment to investigate the mysterious green lights that guided their way. In only a few paces he was beyond the cumulative light, and was once more isolated in the darkness.

As he walked the perimeter of the circle, the dots of luminescence grew brighter as his lamplight approached, and dimmed to darkness soon after he had passed. Bending low, he had difficulty pinpointing the source due to the thick black mist, but he was finally able to perceive an opaque, white stone that fluoresced green within his lantern's light. The bright speck seemed to float above the ground for the mist took away all sense of depth. As he straitened from his crouch, and moved his lantern further away, the glow slowly dimmed. Ryes' speech about keeping to the light was beginning to make sense.

A hovering lantern appeared out of darkness so complete that Gralyre could not see the hand that held it. He raised his own light to cast a larger circle, and was rewarded when Dotch stepped up beside him, their combined lanterns expanding the glow surrounding them both.

"Gralyre, ye should no' wander. 'Tis too easy t' become turned about," Dotch murmured.

Alcoholic fumes joined the miasma, but after this first day of darkness, and more ahead, Gralyre could not fault the man for needing the comfort.

Gralyre lowered his lantern towards the ground, and smiled when the stone glowed brightly again. It was an ingenious solution to navigating the Bleak. "How do ye keep the Stalkers and Deathren from following this path back to your people?"

"We call it lumenstone," Dotch explained quietly, "It glows for only a moment after being exposed to a bit o' light. Stalkers and Deathren do no' use torches, so the stones do no' glow for them. The path remains unseen t' their eyes. We mine it at the Southern Fortress."

A scream resounded out of the Bleak, much too close. A Deathren was prowling.

Gralyre and Dotch doused their lanterns, while in the centre of the clearing all the others did the same. The lumenstone's glow extinguished after a moment longer, leaving the blackness absolute.

Gralyre quietly unsheathed his blade, and heard Dotch's sword scrape gently as he mimicked the action.

He kept his mouth wide to quieten his breath, and used every sense remaining to pinpoint the Deathren's location.

The Deathren screeched again of its need to kill and feed, an unearthly hunger for flesh, and the sound echoed and confused Gralyre's senses. The creature could be a foot in front of them, or a mile away. There was no way to tell.

A shape appeared, undulating in front of him, a phantom created by his mind's need to see, and Gralyre just barely stopped from chopping out at the hallucination. He checked when heavy, dragging footsteps shuffled past, followed by a wake of stench from rotting and burned flesh.

Gralyre made to step out to follow but Dotch, standing shoulder to shoulder with him, felt the motion, and grabbed his arm, holding him back. "Do no' leave the safety o' the lumenstones. Ye will no' find your way back," he breathed into Gralyre's ear.

Soon enough the wailing of the Deathren faded with distance, and after a few tense minutes longer, some of the lanterns were sparked, and activity slowly returned to the camp, though in a more furtive and quiet manner than before.

Gralyre and Dotch reignited their lanterns, and followed the lumenstone path back around the small circle until they spotted the weak glow from where the bedrolls had been spread. For once there was no segregation within the campsite, for the common fear made all of them instinctually band together for protection.

They slept in shifts, half grouped together, huddled in their bedrolls, while the remainder ringed them protectively, hyper alert warriors who sat with their backs to the sleepers to guard in all directions.

Taking his turn to rest, Gralyre lay on his back listening to the muffled breathing and restlessness of the people surrounding him. Few slept this night. The Bleak was eerie enough, but the sound of a Deathren shuffling so near to their small oasis had disturbed everyone. The scent of its seared flesh still clung to the air, mingling with the thick pong of rot and mildew.

Gralyre strained his eyes, yet was unable to see the Rebel Warriors who ringed the sleepers. All lights save one had been doused to conserve lamp oil, and that lantern was but a dim glow at the edge of the circle of lumenstones, marking the trailhead, for if they got turned about overnight, they would have no way of discerning the way forward from the way back.

The lamp was also to aid in an escape if they were attacked, providing a safer path by which to flee. If they panicked, and scattered in different directions, and left behind the glow of the lumenstone trail, they would be lost in the Bleak forever. By fleeing towards the light, they would at least have a chance to navigate an escape.

Gralyre was unaware of the moment that he finally nodded off, only that his world was suddenly filled with past terrors that eclipsed his present ones...

...Warriors scream rage and fear. Sword smashes against sword. Raw grief and despair; lightning falls from the sky, his men morph into black statues. One-by-one. Dead.

He stands alone in a sea of blood; the tide is against him. The wave of evil cannot be stopped. It crashes over him, crushes him, brings him to his knees. A prisoner.

An executioner's sword hangs suspended for a wild moment. Terror! Cannot move! Cannot Escape!

I will not cry out!

The sword bites, and he is wrenched into the swirling blackness. All is pain. The void pulses, the chamber of a giant heart, flaying his soul in a savage rhythm.

I am lost, I am everywhere, I am the universe.

...the void pulses...

I am nothing, I am smaller than the smallest grain of sand.

For brief flickers between he is himself, eroding with every violent cycle to slip away into grinding maw of the voracious darkness.

This then, is death; this then, is my punishment for failure.

Screams of suffering go unheard. Infinity swirls and boils, terrifying, with no eyes to shut against the face of eternity.

Torment and time. A split second is forever. Sanity degenerates into soundless howls and disembodied thrashings...

Gralyre was awakened by a rough shake, and a hard hand pressed over his mouth. "Silence!" the unknown warrior hissed. Gralyre struggled but the Rebel had a knee on his chest, keeping him pinned to the ground.

From his beheading to his torture in the pulsing void, Gralyre was a helpless thrall to the nightmare's power, and within the dark clouds of the Bleak, he saw echoes of the faceless void that tormented him so.

"Ye will bring the Deathren and Stalkers down on us! Stop it! Quiet!"

Gralyre clenched his eyes to block out the disquieting shapes in the mists, and tapped the Rebel's wrist to alert him that he had regained control.

As the Rebel moved away, Gralyre opened his eyes again and glared into the blackness, angrily embarrassed that by crying out in his sleep, he had placed his companions in jeopardy.

But the roiling fog was too similar to the void, and he was suddenly quivering with phobia. Even hard reason could not supplant the notion that, though awake, he was still trapped in his nightmare, and needed to flee. He spent the remainder of his time abed locked in a battle of wills with his paranoia, convincing himself that there was no enemy stalking him from the darkness, and knowing that nothing was further from the truth. For even though the enemies in the Bleak were not the same ones that peopled his night terror, all the horrors of the world were upon them, and a Deathren could stumble into their camp at any moment.

It may or may not have been morning when they broke camp, and followed the circle of lumenstones until they tapered back into a pathway once more.

Unable to discern night from day, they relied upon the trail to tell them when it was time to rest. The lumenstones would widen into a ring, and they would stop, and sleep in shifts for a few hours before riding out once more. Reality drifted away on ships of exhaustion while the unending darkness hollowed out their memories of sunlight.

By day five, reckoned by the number of rest stops they had taken, mold began to grow upon their clothes, and upon the leather of their saddles and reins. Even their food began to mildew though they took pains to keep it sealed in oiled pouches.

When they stopped for their rest, Aneida grabbed Saliana roughly by her arm. "Mayvin is sick. Grab your bag o' herbs!"

Saliana rushed to obey, and was soon kneeling beside Mayvin, feeling the heat that was emanating from her skin. The southern warriors had laid out her pallet for her, that she might rest her injuries, and Mayvin had collapsed, restlessly tossing in her fever. Holding a lantern high, Saliana could see that the woman was only barely conscious.

"Has she eaten anything today?"

"A bit o' ration this morning, but nothing since."

"And water?"

"A bit."

Saliana passed the lantern to Aneida to hold, and carefully drew back Mayvin's tunic to examine her wounded shoulder. She cried out when she saw the black mold growing on the bandages.

Saliana reached into her bag for a small sharp dagger with which to carefully cut the dressing away. As she pulled the cloth free, it broke the scab, and thick puss flowed out of the gash.

Aneida cursed, her voice panicked, and sounding near to tears.

Saliana leaned down and sniffed the injury. The puss did not smell of corruption, at least not yet, but the skin around the wound was puffy and red, extending down Mayvin's arm and chest.

"I need t' clean the wound with spirits. We are going t' need help holding her still. This is going t' hurt."

Afterwards, Saliana left the bandage off, feeling that it was better to leave Mayvin's injury open to the mist, than for her to be blood poisoned by more mildew.

Mayvin's illness excused her from sentry duty, and she was able to sleep uninterrupted the full shift through. When they set out again, she had rallied, though she was still weak.

After two more days of travel, the lands revealed by the

lantern light changed, and the trail took to meandering around steep sided hillocks. The column stopped then, earlier than it seemed it should have, and one-by-one the horses moved up until the Rebels were grouped together. An argument was ensuing between Ryes and his son, Corr.

"We should have come t' it by now!" Gralyre caught only the end of the conversation, as he was the last to arrive.

"What is happening?" he asked Dotch.

Dotch had his flask tipped to his lips, draining it, and as his arm dropped, eddies and swirls of mist churned outwards. His hands were shaking, birthing small, jagged wavelets of vapour that seemed to telegraph his fear, and his skin and eyes looked odd and pasty in the misty, filtered lantern light. Despite the liquid courage, Dotch seemed to be only barely clinging to his mettle. "We have lost the path."

Gralyre felt real fear that almost stole the heart of him, and he peered intently at the ground. "When?" The lumenstone path had been present when they started out that morning, but he had not attended it as they had travelled, his awareness tuned to the animals to keep them quiet, and their senses upon the area, to provide warning of the approach of any of the enemy. However, the glowing path was still visible beside him, and he sagged in relief.

Dotch shook his head. "No' that path. We have come t' the crossroads. One trail leads t' the Southern Fortress, and the other t' the ocean, but both paths have vanished. It all just ends a few feet ahead." Dotch indicated where Ryes and his son conferred.

"How do they even know that we have reached the crossroad?" Rewn wondered nervously. "Mayhap we have no' reached it yet?" The Bleak was depressingly uniform. Except for the large hillocks that they had been winding through for the last hundred yards or so, there was nothing to distinguish their location from any other.

Dotch lifted his head, "Because we are at the burial mounds."

"Graves?" Saliana asked with a quiver in her voice. She peered closer at the hillock that they rested beside. Surfacing out from under the blankets of mold, white skulls screamed, their jaws missing or unhinged, sightless and staring. Thick runnels of mildew adorned rib cages, and skeletal hands, arms and legs that reached beseechingly out of the piles. "Gods!" she whimpered and shifted her horse nearer to Rewn's. The hill was not made of dirt, but of the dead. What they had taken to be merely rotting trees and roots, were the shattered limbs of the fallen.

"This is the battlefield o' Banderlay," Dotch announced with sorrow and reverence. "This is where the peoples o' the south made their last stand, and their bodies were piled by the thousands and left t' rot. There are twenty hills o' death t' mark the crossroads. They guard the way. They show the path," Dotch's words sounded like well remembered scripture.

Corr peered intently at the ground, kicking at the heavy sludge, but being careful to remain in the light.

"'Tis no use, son. 'Tis no' there," Ryes spat in disgust.

Jord's knives flipped in his hands. "Any possibility that the stones were lost t' the muck?"

Dotch shook his head. "There is neither rain, nor wind t' disturb the ground, and the mold will no' touch the stones. They are impervious t' the disease o' this place. The old wives think 'tis the light within the stones that holds back the corruption, a purity that combats the evil o' the Bleak." He shrugged as though unwilling to commit to the tale.

Corr glanced up at his father, and his hands came to rest on his hips. "Someone needs t' scout for the trailhead."

Ryes beckoned one of his men, who dismounted and joined them. He tied a rope around the warrior's waist, passing the loose end to Corr, before giving the man a lantern.

"If ye see the stones, tug twice on the rope, and we will come t' ye," Ryes ordered.

"Good luck, Barl," Corr patted him on the back.

"G'luck, Barl!"

"Ye can do it, Barl," the other Southern Rebels encouraged.

Barl's jaw was clenched tight with fear, and he walked away slowly, glancing back often to watch the cluster of warriors he left behind. At the limit of sight, he glanced back one last time.

"Do no' let go o' the rope, lieutenant!"

"I have ye," Corr promised.

The attending Rebels were silent and tense, and Gralyre realized what a brave act it was to leave the safety of the group, and the lumenstone pathway, with only that thin line for safety. If Barl lost the rope, he would never be seen again.

Barl vanished slowly into the Bleak, armed with naught but his sword and a lantern. Slowly, Corr played out the taut rope that hovered in the air to show Barl's direction.

Gralyre slid into the minds of the horses, but they sensed nothing nearby, yet a prickling warning shivered in the hairs at the back of his neck. Magic was afoot. He drew his sword. "Arm yourselves!" he gritted softly at his group.

Trifyn responded quickly to the order, never questioning what Gralyre sensed. He lifted his bow from his back, and reached into his belt pouch for the string, his eyes scanning the Bleak, though visibility, even with the collective lanterns, was no more than twenty feet. Even from horseback, he easily bent the bow and strung it, drawing an arrow from his quiver to rest at the ready.

Rewn, and Aneida drew their blades, as four more knives appeared in Jord's hands, fanned out and ready to throw.

Dotch cursed, slower to react because of the drink, and fumbled his blade from his scabbard. Even so, he sat his horse, steely eyed and resolute, scanning the mists.

Ryes glanced their way, and his blue eyes seemed to glow bright as lumenstones in the weak lantern light, as he sat up straighter "What is it?"

"If the stones are gone, then they have been moved deliberately! Get your man back! 'Tis a trap!"

As the harsh whisper hung in the fog, General Ryes seemed to sag with the same realization that Gralyre had already come to. The Southern Rebels, following Gralyre's example, began to quietly arm themselves.

"Corr!" General Ryes hissed softly. "Bring Barl back!"

Corr's face was a light oval hovering in the air as he nodded, the rest of his body hidden by a thick hedge of mist drifting past. He tugged twice on the line, then quickly, arm over arm, began to pull in the tether.

"Dotch, stay close to Mayvin," Gralyre ordered.

I can fight, Mayvin's gestures disturbed the fog, and sent corkscrews of vapour outwards.

"With only one arm, you are vulnerable," Gralyre did not mince words, nor seek to give her a false sense of her usefulness. "Saliana, you too. Stay by Dotch and Mayvin."

Saliana nodded. Even wounded as she was, Mayvin was ten times the fighter that she would ever be. As Mayvin awkwardly drew one sword with her good arm, Saliana moved her horse nearer, her dagger in her fist for the little good it might do.

Suddenly the rope balked in Corr's hand, jerking him to his knees as it burned through his fingers, rapidly winding outwards again. "Help me!" Corr cried, and in a flash, five men were off their horses, and had taken up the rope in a massive tug of war with the black mist.

A man's scream echoed out of the murk, followed by the unmistakable wails of Deathren. The warriors holding the line stumbled forward, as the rope went slack.

"Leave it!" Ryes snapped. "Back t' your horses! Prepare for battle! Gather the lights!"

Upon their General's order, the warriors quickly dismantled the horse borne light poles, and dropped their lanterns into a cluster. Barl's riderless horse and the pack animals were herded into a group beside the small collection of lights, and Little Wolf paced a protective circle around them, ears canting backwards and forwards as he listened to the screaming Deathren.

The Rebels fanned their horses out into a tight circle with their backs to the brightness. Gralyre and his group took their places in their number, not questioning the Southerners' tactics. They had had generations to hone their battle strategy within the conditions of the Bleak.

The Rebels stared into the black fog with the light at their backs, that they not be night-blind and unable to see the enemy until it was too late. The lantern light threw giant shadows of armed warriors against the fog, the restless mists infusing false life into the effigies. And then they waited.

The screams of the Deathren continued for a long, heartbreaking moment as they fed on Barl, then abruptly stopped, the quiet made more terrifying, as the darkness and fog hid all from sight. The stench of rot reached them first, strong enough to choke upon. Flakes of ash followed, hovering in the air like dirty snow, and seeming to rest upon the thickness of the fog so as to never reach the ground, further obscuring their vision.

Heavy footfalls raced towards them, echoing from all directions and impossible to pinpoint.

Across the circle behind Gralyre, a horse screamed, as a Deathren launched itself onto its neck. With a yelp of surprise, the Rebel rider stabbed down into the Deathren's brain, and it collapsed like the unstrung puppet of evil it had been, sliding off the horse to shatter its head against a rock on the ground.

The horse whinnied again, a sound of pain and fear, and Gralyre quickly soothed it.

Now came the sounds of hundreds of running feet, drawing nearer, a tattoo of oncoming peril.

A Deathren ran into the light, ragged red uniform flapping like wings. Trifyn's bow twanged, and the Deathren caught an arrow through its eye. It fell back into the shadows and vanished as quickly as it had appeared, as though it had been naught but a phantasm called up from their darkest nightmares.

Trifyn already had another arrow nocked, and was wheezing little moans of terror with each breath, as he shifted his aim towards any misty swirl or eddy. The arrow shaft clattered against his bow.

"Steady, Trifyn. Breath," Gralyre advised tightly.

Saliana screamed, and the sound of a blade cutting through flesh made a dull smack. Gralyre could not look over, as the head of the attacker rolled past, for two more Deathren hurtled out of the mist to attack his horse. His sword flicked powerfully, and two more heads joined the growing collection.

"They are testing us! Testing our defenses!" Rewn shouted.

The sound of footsteps suddenly halted. Everything quieted, nothing stirred, yet the smell of death and burning flesh grew stronger.

Rewn was right, the Deathren had been testing the circle for weakness, and if they had now stopped 'twas because they were being controlled. Gralyre's hand tightened on his sword, as he followed his reasoning through to the end. Somewhere, hidden in the Bleak, a Demon Lord was directing the attack.

"Where are they?" Jord snarled, his hands poised with multiple knifes at the ready.

'Little Wolf? What do your senses tell you?' Gralyre urged.

'Dead ones. Here, there, everywhere. The HILLS!' he warned just as a cacophony of howls shattered the stillness.

"Look to the mounds!" Gralyre shouted over the din, as the full horror was unleashed.

From within each burial mound, skeletons shifted, as Deathren dug their way out into the open. Small avalanches of skulls skidded and slid down the slopes, their eternal rest disturbed by the maggoty flesh of the surfacing creatures.

Jord's hands snapped out, and Deathren after Deathren collapsed in final death with knifepoints buried in their brains, most only half dug from their lairs, now left to join the dead of an age past.

Trifyn's bow sang a song of death, a one-note dirge, killing the creatures outright as they emerged from the grave, or pinning them in place so that they could not join the fight.

But the animated corpses were too numerous to count, and were frenzied with their hunger, churning the black fog, as they charged at the small circle of Rebels.

Trifyn managed one more shot, before the frontrunners of the horde were upon him. Using the stave of his bow, he stove in the head of an emaciated Deathren that clawed up over his horse to reach him, making room to draw his sword. There was no need to worry if he would remember Gralyre's lessons. There was no finesse necessary in this fight, just brute force survival.

The Rebels fought for their lives, as wave after wave of Deathren raced into the light. The creatures had no fear of sword or pain, and only taking their heads would stop them.

Somewhere across the circle, a warrior screamed, as he was pulled from his horse, and disappeared beneath a swarm of rapacious evil.

"Hold the line," General Ryes bellowed.

"Do not let them get behind you!" Gralyre roared, lashing out with great sweeps of his sword. Headless rotting Deathren, still wearing the shredded and mildewed red uniforms from their time as Demon Riders, dropped to amass around him. Survivors clawed over their fallen and each other to rend the warm flesh of the horses and warriors.

Another shriek sounded, as another southern warrior was taken. "Help me! Gods help me...!" his screams ended abruptly.

Little Wolf howled, and attacked a Deathren that had made it past the line of Rebels, and into the circle. He made short work of the rotting flesh of its neck, and its head bounced free before it could harm the horses.

"Form up! Cover the gaps!" Gralyre shouted the order, his arm tireless, as he beat back more and more of the creatures. For every one killed, ten seemed to take its place. They were being overrun by a legion of the dead.

Gralyre cursed at the choice he must make. If they died here, all hope was lost, yet if he used his magic, he would be announcing their presence to every Demon Lord in the Bleak, not to mention whatever lurked in the darkness controlling the Deathren.

Immediate survival won out.

A Deathren vaulted at him over the bodies of the slain, and Gralyre caught it on his sword with such force that he almost bisected the creature. He left his blade lodged in its torso as it fell away, in order to free his hands.

Flames burst from Gralyre's palms, and he flung the fireballs into a seething rush of bodies that were bounding towards him.

WHOMP, WHOPMP! WHOMP-WHOMP!

Hundreds of Deathren ignited, and vanished in consuming heat. Narrowing his eyes against the ash, he threw more of the fire, yet it made barely a dent in the rush of bodies. There were too many. Somewhere across the diminishing circle of Rebels, another warrior screamed in pain.

A green glow painted Gralyre's hands, and prompted him to glance upwards for the source. Out of the mists above a green fireball roared towards them, trailing flames as it fell. Gralyre remembered his lessons, and erected a shield to surround the Rebels just in time.

The plasma ball hit the surface, and blasted fire in all directions, killing hundreds more Deathren, and giving Gralyre an idea.

They needed a barrier that would break the Deathren's attack and protect the few warriors that remained!

Gralyre drew deeply of his Godsmagic, dropped the shield,

and created a line of fire that rushed to encircle the Rebels with a fiery moat of impervious protection. The heat of the flames heated the air, which lifted the ceiling of the Bleak free of the ground to hover like a flat stone above their heads. Within the brilliance of the new light the besieged warriors could now clearly see the magnitude of what they faced, and moans of terror broke from many a throat.

For as far as the eye could see, Deathren swarmed like ants from a kicked nest, some yet digging their way from the burial mounds with rotting hands, and ruined faces. Pure evil, the creature's hunger drove them in their mindless frenzy, as the frontrunners hurtled into the flames, yet trying to reach the warm flesh of horses and men.

Gralyre welcomed their deaths as more fuel for his fire, for holding the flames in place had quickly used up the meager bits of combustibles that had been present. Now he had to keep feeding his magic into the flames to keep the fires bright and hot, for the rot and damp fought the cleansing purity, and were he to relent, the protection would immediately flicker and die.

Some of the Rebels yelled triumphantly, madly, as they watched wave upon wave of Deathren disintegrate in the flames of Gralyre's mage fire, while the few who kept their wits quickly slaughtered the few Deathren who had been trapped within the circle of warriors when the barrier was erected.

Saliana held a shoulder propped beneath Mayvin's good arm, supporting the exhausted women, as she walked her to the centre of the circle to slide into a seated position next to the lanterns.

Both of their horses were dead. Dotch stood protectively over them, his sword soiled with the black, coagulated blood of the Deathren, and his eyes scanning for any further strays to kill.

"How long can Gralyre maintain the fire?" Aneida yelled over the roar of the flaming wall.

"It has t' fall eventually. What will we do then?" Trifyn asked of Rewn, as he pulled an arrow from the quiver on his back and nocked it.

Rewn shook his head, panting harshly from the exhaustion of battle. "Take the reprieve. When that wall comes down, we must be ready!" He groaned, lifting his face in fleeting pleasure. "Gods! 'Tis good t' be warm!"

Jord joined them, for once without his blades, having spent the lot. He was reduced to a single sword. "Deathren! Stinking, rotting…" His battle madness was still upon him, and his eyes rolled aggressively as he turned, keeping a constant watch for another enemy to engage.

The hair on the back of Gralyre's neck shivered, and he knew that somewhere out there, a Demon Lord was gathering its magic for another attack. But what more could he do? When his power failed, the fire would die, and then so would they.

'Conservation o' power, Gralyre. Magic is no' about force, 'tis about finesse!' Catrian's words and lessons came to him, along with an insane notion.

His fire needed more fuel, that he might use less magic. Godsmagic surged through Gralyre, and he threw his arms wide, watching with satisfaction, as his ring of fire raged outwards like a ripple in a pond, a tsunami of flame. It moved so quickly that the air thundered in the wake of its passage. Deathren by the thousands vanished under its white-hot touch, drowning in the heat that roared and crackled over them, and fueling the conflagration that left char and ash in its wake.

He suddenly lost the sense of the Demon Lord's gathering magic. *'Dead!'* he exalted. He had taken it by surprise, and it had succumbed to the flames.

Finally feeling his fire lose the fuel that had fed its greedy appetite, Gralyre allowed the magic to sputter and die, though he watched diligently for any movement within the pluming ash clouds.

The burial mounds crackled and snapped with flames that still fed on the ancient bones. The mound nearest to them settled, and a burst of sparks ascended towards the damp fog ceiling that still hovered above, repelled by the heat of the scoured ground.

General Ryes appeared at Gralyre's side, his face streaked by soot mixed with Deathren blood, his eyes filled with wonder and not a little fear. "By the Gods." He patted Gralyre's back in an awkward show of thanks. "By the Gods," he repeated, his shock absolute.

Gralyre's jaw knotted, as more and more of the Rebels crowded around him, shouting and laughing and sobbing their thanks. Gralyre held his hands up for silence. "Listen to me! Listen!" he shouted for their attention. "We are alive for now, but I used magic. Every Demon Lord in the Bleak has felt it, and they will be sending more creatures to bedevil us!"

"Who cares? Ye are with us!" a warrior shouted loudly, to the cheers of the men.

Rewn met Gralyre's frustrated gaze with a wide grin. "Gralyre!" he roared and raised his sword.

"Gralyre! Gralyre! Gralyre!" the warriors began to chant.

"Enough!" Gralyre yelled around a small smile that he could not contain. The warriors laughed at his effort, but quieted. "We must find the path, and leave this place behind as quickly as possible."

Jord cleared his throat noisily for attention. "I do no' think that will be a problem." He announced loudly, and used the point of his sword to refer back over his shoulder. About a hundred yards out, two clear paths of brilliant green light floated away into the Bleak at right angles to each other, blazing brightly from the prolonged power of Gralyre's mage fire.

"Quick!" General Ryes ordered. "Mark the trails afore they fade!"

The men split into groups and drew small pouches from their belts. Leaning to the side of their horses, they dropped lumenstone pebbles, as they rode towards where the paths began again, renewing the trail markers.

Jord walked out into the scorched field, searching for and collecting his throwing knives.

"Ryes," Gralyre said softly as the men were thus employed. "There was a Demon Lord with them, directing them. Do ye realize what this means?"

The General's eyes widened at the knowledge that Gralyre

had slain an enemy sorcerer, but his heart was heavy with another concern. "They know how we navigate the Bleak."

Gralyre pushed back lank strands of filthy black hair from his brow. "They gathered up as many of the lumenstones as would hold you here, and left an army in your path to ambush you."

Ryes' head turned indecisively from the road that led south towards the ocean, towards the road that led east towards his fortress, his home. "Gralyre, my people! They may already be gone!" His chest rose and fell in a great heave of pain.

Gralyre rested his hand on Ryes' shoulder. "Do not think it, until you see it with your own eyes."

Ryes shook free of Gralyre's touch, and his moon shaped face twisted with bitterness. "The sooner we leave ye upon that beach, the sooner I can discover the fate o' my people!"

℠⁖

DREISENHELD

Doaphin bows low, and keeps his eyes upon the stone of the throne room floor lest the Master read the rage and hate within them. His trap has failed. Again.

There has been an edict in the land for centuries that all humans with a talent for magic be destroyed for left unchecked they might challenge the Master for dominion yet somehow two sorcerers of power have managed to survive to become a threat!

And of the one travelling south with the Rebels? Doaphin has never felt such power, even from the Master. It is as though a God has stepped forth to smite their army unto dust.

The Master sits forward on the gilded and bejeweled throne with words eerily mirroring Doaphin's thoughts. "Have you discovered who the sorcerer is that travels with the Rebels? With Him?"

"I know naught, my Master."

"*I know naught, my Master.*"

Doaphin winces at the jeering taunt. The Master's anger is only loosely in check. Five creatures bore the brunt of the Master's initial outburst, and now lay crushed to jelly in congealing pools of their own blood.

"You are useless to us. What befell the Rebels that they had to use so much magic? Our armies were to have left them be, let them pass! Report!"

"I cannot find the Stalkers or the Demon Lords of the Bleak to demand an accounting, my Master."

"Why?"

Doaphin keeps his breathing as calm as possible, and holds his bow low. "They were destroyed alongside our Deathren."

"The Deathren reserves? How many?"

"All."

"All! Unacceptable! How do you know this when you know nothing else?"

"There was a single Demon Rider survivor."

"We would talk to him!"

"Unfortunately, my Master, the creature succumbed to its

injuries. The enemy sorcerer used mage fire to stop the Deathren attack, and the Stalkers and Demon Lords were caught by surprise in the conflagration. Apparently it was only a chance meeting, unavoidable."

Doaphin had the Demon Rider killed to ensure that his heavily edited account will be the only one to ever reach the Master's ears.

His frustration is immense. He set the ambush carefully, and charged the Demon Lords of the Bleak to personally oversee the massacre. It was a flawless plan that should have annihilated the Rebels. Instead they have advanced nearer to obtaining the Dragon Sword, and fulfilling the curse!

He must be even more cunning in his next attempt to kill them. The Master must never suspect what he did.

"We warned you to not interfere with the reclamation of the sword. Have you betrayed us?"

Doaphin breathes gently, suppressing all emotion save surprise and hurt at the accusation. He dares to raise his head to meet the Master's gaze. "Of course not, my Master. You are my world, I would never subvert your wishes."

ঽৎআ

THE BLEAK

The Rebels were unsure of the exact date, for there was no passage of moon or sun within the Bleak, only the lumenstone path and the circles in which they camped. Yet instinct told them that time grew short. They spent less time at rest within the lumenstone clearings, and more time racing towards the ocean. The southerners were doubly eager to reach the seashore, and leave Gralyre's group behind, so that they could return to discover the fate of their people.

It was a relief when the Bleak began to tease their noses with the scent of brine. Soon the lumenstone path led them to a rocky beach, where the sound of a tide lapped sullenly against a shore. To the best of their reckoning, there were only three days remaining until the Solstice.

"Are ye sure this is the right spot?" Aneida asked. Standing with their feet towards the waves, they could not see the island, only trust that General Ryes had not led them astray.

Dotch nodded, and pointed to three stone cairns that marked the beach. "We will leave from here, and somewhere out there," he waved into the fog, "awaits Fennick's Island."

"If we swim straight, and do no' miss it," Trifyn mumbled.

Jord's daggers flashed in the wan light of the lanterns. "Aye," he agreed with a grimace.

Several feet further along the rocky beach, Gralyre spoke quietly with General Ryes. "What can you tell us of their defenses?" His eyes strained to find a hint of light out over the waves, or even a darker shadow that would reveal the presence of the hidden isle.

"Nothing. No one we have sent t' spy has ever returned," Ryes stated coldly, waiting to see what effect his words would have on the other man's unseemly confidence.

"How do we get across? How far is the crossing?" Gralyre questioned, refusing to play Ryes' game. Time was short, and he needed all the knowledge of the place that he could pull from Ryes' mind.

"Ye could try the ferry at Elevor, but I would no' advise it." A league or so down the coast, the Garrison of Elevor controlled the only ferry across to the Island. Elevor was also the staging ground for Doaphin's troops before they were deployed to the island every spring to attempt to recover the Dragon Sword.

When Gralyre did not rise to the bait, Ryes continued, "We have moved some men across on rafts. They were able to make the swim in about an hour. They lit a signal when they landed. But they never returned. That will be your best chance t' land safely. We have the materials ye need packed away."

"Deathren?" Gralyre asked.

"Aye," said Ryes. "And t' be sure there will be Stalkers and Demon Lords too, although they seldom dirty their hands with actual work."

"Demon Riders?" Gralyre prodded.

"A legion, maybe two. We watch them ferry across each year."

Gralyre snorted with gallows humour. "Let me guess. Even the Demon Riders never return?"

"Welcome t' Fennick's Island." Ryes spat on the rocky shore, as he returned up the beach to where they had left their horses.

The Southerners would not linger now that they had delivered

Gralyre and the others to the beach. There was an urgency driving them to seek out their homes, for they knew naught if their loved ones yet lived, or if their fortress had been destroyed. Also, Catrian's storm was due in a matter of hours, and they wanted to be well away from the coast, and somewhere safe before it struck.

Quietly, the General gave his orders, and his men deposited several packs on the rocky shore.

Gralyre called his group together, and settled his gaze upon Mayvin's feverish face. "Can you continue?" he asked her.

Yes!

Aneida gripped her sister's uninjured shoulder. "Mayvin, ye could go with Ryes, or ye could stay on the beach…"

NO!

Mayvin glared around the circle of concerned faces. *I will not be left behind! We stand together, we die together!* Her gestures were emphatic.

Saliana shook her head. "I do no' think that wise."

My Choice! My Life to give! My death to choose!

Rewn sighed deeply. "Agreed. Together."

"Together," Jord murmured, as though savoring the words, and a flash of panic and pleasure darted through his lonely eyes.

"Together."

"Together," murmured the others, and the pact was made.

One by one, the surviving Rebel warriors came forward, speaking words of good fortune. They had lost five good men at the crossroads, and, were it not for Gralyre, would have perished to the last man. However they knew that they would have no opportunity to repay the life debt, so instead they did the only thing left to them; here a warrior shared a bag of lumenstones, there one gave them a hoarded bit of stale hardtack that had somehow resisted the mildew. Another passed over precious lantern oil, one gave away a length of rope, another a bit of canvas, little treasures and tokens that spoke of their deep regard for the men and women who were about to sacrifice themselves in service to the resistance.

The General mounted, and paused for one last look at the group of eight. He saw the hard resolution in their faces, and in the end, pity stirred for these condemned men and women.

"If it were me, I would no' spend too long camped upon this beach. The 'Riders from Elevor patrol regularly and vigorously. Especially at this time o' year!"

"Thank-you," Gralyre responded simply, as Corr and the Southern Rebels mounted, and fanned out around their General. They had the questers' horses in tow, for they would have no further need of them, unlikely as it was that they would return from Fennick's Island.

Ryes and Gralyre would never be comrades, but since saving the lives of the General and his men at the crossroads, at least the enmity between them had abated.

Ryes raised his arm in farewell, before spurring his horse away, leading his Rebels back into the Bleak via the lumenstone path.

"Good Fortune!" Corr cried, echoed by his men, as they

followed after, clattering off the beach, and over the rise to vanish into the blackness. In their wake, the lumenstone path slowly faded.

"Good," Aneida snarled, kicking at a pebble with the toe of her boot. "I hate long, messy farewells!"

Jord snorted in agreement, and started pulling their belongings together from where Ryes' men had dropped them. Trifyn joined him, helping to section out what would be needed for their crossing and time on the island, and what could be left for their return - if they returned.

Little Wolf sat like a pagan statue, staring out at the occluded ocean, towards where his senses told him the island awaited. A low growl rumbled up from his throat, and his head lowered in challenge.

Gralyre walked to the wolfdog's side, and dropped a hand to rest fondly upon Little Wolf's head.

Little Wolf looked up into Gralyre's face. *'Evil. Everywhere. Over there is worse than here. Can you smell it?'*

'Yes,' Gralyre confirmed.

'We go to the land over the water?' Little Wolf asked.

'We do,' Gralyre confirmed. *'Your senses are greater than mine, Little Wolf. Will you guide us safely through the water to the shore of the island? I am depending on you.'*

Little Wolf was full of pride at the great responsibility that he had been given, and his tail thumped in happiness at Gralyre's faith. *'I will not fail! The water is cold, but clean. A good day to swim!'*

Gralyre rubbed Little Wolf's ears, and grieved the thought of bringing the wolfdog into such danger. He glanced over his shoulder at the others, and realized that his guilt was not just for Little Wolf. Friends new and old would be going with him unto their deaths, but as never before, he acknowledged that he could not do this thing alone. He needed them. They needed each other.

He left Little Wolf on guard, and walked down the beach until the wash of the waves on the rocky shore drowned out the voices of the group. With the ocean at his shoulder, for once he did not fear losing his bearings in the Bleak, and gratefully sought a moment's privacy with his thoughts.

Picking a large, water-smoothed boulder, he sat and drew his cloak about him against the chill in the damp air. For a while, he watched the luminous foam riding in on the dark surf, the only light in this benighted land, and allowed his mind to drift. Inevitably, his thoughts turned to Catrian.

Gralyre's heart ached, and for a moment he lost himself in warm memories. His mind's eye traced every curve of her face, remembered every gesture, and every smile. He recalled her unexpected humour, and her awkward confusion whenever he teased her, as though she had never played before. He yearned to talk to her again, to hear her intelligence and dedication, as she taught him to hone his sorcery.

Finally, he allowed himself to dwell upon the taste of her lips, and the velvet warmth of her skin under his hands.

Gralyre opened his eyes, blinking into the foul darkness, an insult to the beauty of his memories, but knowing it was time to concentrate on the here and now. Out there, somewhere, the island both beckoned and threatened.

His mind drained of pleasant thoughts, and the deadly warrior within glared out at the Bleak with foreboding. Every instinct screamed at him to run from this evil place.

Catrian's tutelage might prove useful but magic was far from instinctual for him yet. He had been very lucky when the Deathren army had attacked at the crossroads, and even luckier that his outlay of power had taken the Demon Lord that directed them by surprise. Yet how had the powerful magic not drawn the rest of the Demon Lords in the Bleak to them?

Although why would they bother? They need only to await their arrival upon the island, for they must guess that he was coming to them.

Gralyre walked back towards the others, ignoring the prickling feeling between his shoulders, as though an arrow were aimed at his back. The crunching of his feet through the wet pebbles of the shore drew the attention of the group as he returned.

They had spent their time creating a leaning shelter of driftwood to block the fretful wind that blew in from across the water, and were now huddling together in a circle, talking quietly, and passing around Dotch's flask to keep warm. They shuffled to make room for Gralyre, as he joined them.

Aneida grunted appreciatively, and shook the flask, listening to the deep slosh of the liquid within. "How is it that this has no' run dry by now? Ye have been sucking upon this like a babe on its mother's teat since we entered the Bleak."

Dotch grinned, amused by her crude taunt. "One o' Ryes' men has a smuggled cask on one o' the pack horses. He will be sore disappointed when he reaches home t' find half o' it drained away."

Soft chuckles passed through the group.

Gralyre took a pull of the fiery liquor, and passed the flask on to Rewn. "We must make the island as soon as possible, or lose what may be our only chance to cross before Catrian's storm arrives. Did you unpack those sheep bladders that Ryes' men left for us?"

"Yea. Disgusting things. What are they for?" Jord muttered.

"For floating!" Dotch hit the younger man in the chest with a heavy fist, eliciting a dirty glare.

Dotch chuckled again. "Here we go Lads and Lassies! The dance is about t' begin! Time t' build those rafts." He scrabbled to his feet in search of the bladders. His mood was much improved now that the inevitable had finally caught up to them.

"Between ye and me, I have had better looking dance partners," Aneida muttered to Saliana, as she stood and dusted her trousers with her hands.

Saliana nodded solemnly, and would have followed but noticed Mayvin struggle and fail to stand. Saliana turned anxiously back to her patient, as the others trailed in Dotch's wake to begin building the rafts.

The travel through the Bleak had been hard on Mayvin. Dark

circles highlighted her glittering, feverish eyes, but Saliana could not tell if the shoulder was septic or not, for Mayvin would not allow her to examine it again. Saliana could only assume that if it were bad then Mayvin would seek her help.

"Can I get ye something for the pain?"

In answer to her concern, Mayvin only glared coldly.

"Alright, alright," Saliana said, holding her hands out soothingly. "At least take this." She passed Mayvin the flask that Dotch had left behind. "Perhaps it will help ye t' get some sleep." She left Mayvin reclining within the driftwood shelter, with Dotch's flask to keep her warm.

It took the better part of two hours to breathe air into the leather bladders. After lashing them closed with strips of rawhide, they sealed the joints with sticky resin, a pot of which had been in the supplies Ryes had left for them.

The rafts were of simple construction. The driftwood they had gathered earlier was lashed together in tight bundles to form four small rafts that would each hold two people, and onto each corner they attached a float. They had contemplated creating a single large raft, but could not devise a means to paddle the heavy craft, and in the end, they realized that their best tactic for remaining undetected during the crossing were the smaller rafts that they could propel with the power of their kicking legs.

They wrapped their packs and weapons tightly in oiled canvas, and lashed these to the driftwood to remain as dry as possible atop the rafts. As with their mode of travel via horseback in the Bleak, each small raft would be bound to another to ensure that no one would drift away and be lost. All of them would follow Little Wolf's lead, so that they did not overshoot the island, missing it altogether or simply become confused by the direction they should take, and end up swimming in circles, lost until they drowned. They were as prepared as they could be for the arduous crossing.

Gralyre took in the exhausted faces, and decided that as tired as they were, they deserved a rest before they began the next leg of their journey.

"Little Wolf will stand guard, so if a patrol from Elevor draws near we will know of it. Get some sleep if you can. We will launch when the tide turns in a couple of hours."

The group was silent, as they watched Gralyre disappear into the mist down the beach.

"Tell me that we are going t' survive this," Trifyn asked tremulously.

"Never speak o' death on the eve o' battle, lad," Dotch advised the green youth kindly.

CHAPTER EIGHT

The chill of the ocean closed slowly around them as they eased into the water. They waded at first, their bare feet feeling for footing in the unseen shallows while they tested the integrity of the small crafts before pushing off with the tide, out into open water.

The two-man rafts they had constructed did little more than keep their torsos above the swells, as they kicked hard with the current, trusting that somewhere in the fog and darkness, Fennick's Island awaited their arrival.

Little Wolf bore the only lantern, tied upon a small float of driftwood pulled in his wake. The group steered their awkward craft by the bobbing light, using it to remain on target, for Little Wolf's black pelt rendered him invisible in the darkness, save for a vee shaped wake displaced by his swim that glimmered faintly, as it dispersed outward.

Gralyre and Rewn propelled their raft after the strongly swimming wolfdog, leading the way for Dotch and Saliana, followed by Mayvin and Aneida, and finally Jord and Trifyn.

The constant churn of the waves shifted the mist to create a narrow space between the water and the fog, making Little Wolf's light shine further than would have been possible on land. There had been much debate over using the light or not, for they were mindful that Ryes' spies had lit a signal fire that was visible from the island to the mainland shore.

Perhaps sentries on the island would spy Little Wolf's lantern, and be awaiting their landing, but Gralyre trusted that the Bleak would work in their favor for once, and that the heavy fog would occlude the small glow over any great distance.

Soon after striking out from the beach, their bodies numbed from the cold, and feeling was lost in their fingers and arms where they clung to their rafts. The darkness created the illusion that they were fixed in place no matter how hard they stroked towards the island. The Bleak, a solid presence above, and the icy water below, entombed them in a claustrophobic space between the two, but no matter their misery they forbore to call out to one another, knowing their voices would carry an unnatural distance across the waves.

Gralyre kicked strongly through the sea, feeling the reassuring tug on the line from the other rafts. Rewn, working beside him, panted lightly from the effort of matching his strokes to Gralyre's.

As they moved further from shore, the swells became steeper, larger, and the chop rougher. A rogue wave broke over their heads, and beside him, Rewn began to cough, faltering as he tried to clear his lungs from the saltwater he had inhaled.

"Are you alright?"

Rewn coughed and nodded. "Yea, keep going." His legs took up the effort again. Gralyre glanced back to see how the other crafts faired, but could only just make out Dotch and Saliana's bobbing raft. The rest of the group were lost in the fog.

Dotch waved that they were okay, and Gralyre fixated upon Little Wolf's bobbling light again. The wolfdog surged powerfully through the swells, keeping a steady pace as he led the way.

After a time, Gralyre could not help asking Little Wolf, *'Are we near?'*

'The evil place is nearer,' Little Wolf concurred.

Gralyre felt the need to curse, but his teeth were clenched tight to stop them chattering. Little Wolf had no conception of either distance or time. To ask him to estimate how near they were was useless. They were nearer could mean anything. They had neared the island the moment they had entered the icy embrace of the ocean. He sought his patience, and concentrated on keeping his numb legs moving. They were beginning to ache from the chill, and he feared developing a cramp if he stopped to rest.

When the pull of the current strengthened, and swells grew ever larger, Gralyre estimated that they had neared the centre of the channel. Waves washed over their heads unexpectedly, pulling and pushing at their small flotilla, spinning the two-man rafts away from each other so that for a time it felt as though they were all kicking in opposite directions. They relied more heavily upon their rafts, as they fought the currents and tired.

"We are getting lower in the water! 'Tis getting harder to move it!" Rewn gasped. The air bladders had begun to lose their buoyancy. With every minute that now passed, their bodies sank deeper, and the frigid wetness invaded further.

Gralyre sensed their progress had slowed, and began to fear that they would slip under the waves from exhaustion before they had a chance to walk into battle upon the island. He lifted his head from his toils, and squinted into the Bleak, trying in vain to spot the dark shore of Fennick's Island, but there was nothing to see except for Little Wolf's lantern hissing and sputtering, as it was almost extinguished from the wash of the waves. They had to be on the last leg of the crossing by now.

Gralyre's attention was caught by a curious, enormous vee shaped wake, moving swiftly towards them before whatever created it disappeared beneath the waves. He blinked, unsure if he had seen anything or if it was merely a trick of the lantern light upon a strange eddy. "Rewn? Did you see…?"

Up ahead, Little Wolf gave a startled yelp, paws flailing in sudden panic before striking out faster than before.

'What is it?' Gralyre demanded.

Little Wolf was too frightened to form a coherent answer, and instead sent an image of something huge and powerful nuzzling past. Almost to the instant the image appeared in Gralyre's mind, something collided with their puny raft, swinging their bodies about in the strong eddy of a massive passage.

"Gralyre!" Rewn shouted, as he lost his grip, his numb hands scrabbling for purchase upon the slick wood, before his body slid away, and floundered in the waves.

Gralyre just managed to snag the nape of Rewn's shirt, and with a grunt of effort, dragged him back up onto the surface of their raft before the strong current could carry him away.

Rewn's hair was slicked tightly to his skull, and he gasped as he blinked the streaming saltwater from his eyes. "What was that? What hit us?" he bellowed, his fear making him careless of the strength of his voice.

"By the Gods of Ill Fortune!" Gralyre cursed. Also uncaring that his voice might carry to the Island, he hollered back at the others. "Swim harder! There is something in the water with us! We must get to shore, now!"

With a powerful stroke, he realigned their craft towards Little Wolf's lantern light. "Swim!" he yelled at Rewn, and the two men began to kick their legs with all the strength left at their command. One corner of their raft dragged lower and lower in the water, and Gralyre realized that the sea creature had punctured one of their floats.

Rewn noticed it at the same time. "Gralyre, we are sinking! If we do not cut the bladder free, it will fill with water and drag us to the bottom!"

"I have it!" Gralyre forced one numb arm to move to his waist to seek for his knife. His grasp was uncertain, and he feared that his numb fingers would loose their grip on his weapon, and send it spiraling to the ocean floor. It was a feat of triumph to pull his arm from the water, prop his elbow up on the raft, and see that the dagger was clutched in his fist.

As quickly as he was able, Gralyre sawed away at the straps that bound the bladder, until the rawhide parted, and the float caught an eddy of current and drifted away across the water. The corner of the raft abruptly dipped lower, but the other three bladders still kept them buoyant.

Gralyre's eyes tracked the float as it left their side, bouncing and deflating as it went. Before it was completely lost to the mists of the Bleak, a large, gapping maw crashed up from beneath the water, and swallowed the discarded bladder in a flurry of snapping teeth and spray. A slick dark body thrashed back into the waves, followed by an eel-like tail that smacked water high into the air from the violence of its return to the sea.

True terror sapped Gralyre's strength at first sight of the massive beast, and his alarmed gaze collided with Rewn's. How could they fight something so large, especially within its own element? Gralyre had never felt so helpless.

A muffled scream dropped their hearts, and had Rewn and Gralyre twisting around to see what had happened to Saliana and Dotch. Gralyre's breath left in a whoosh as he beheld their pale faces through the mist.

"It brushed past my legs!" Saliana's sobbing voice echoed from the darkness. "'Tis going t' eat us!" She shrieked again, as the creature made another exploratory nuzzle from beneath.

"Keep kicking, lass, do no' look back, just keep kicking!" Dotch bade, his voice high and tight with alarm.

Aneida screamed and slapped at the water. "'Tis trying t' reach Mayvin. It smells her blood!"

Jord cursed violently. "Aneida! We are coming! Trifyn swim faster! We need t' get nearer t' Mayvin and Aneida! Maybe the four o' us can fight it off. Harder! Harder!"

"Gralyre! Do something!" Rewn yelled, trying to see over his shoulder to monitor the progress of the rest of the flotilla, and give warning if the creature surfaced, though they both new that the real danger lived below. When it finally came for them, they would not see its attack.

"'Tis toying with us! It could have taken us all with its first pass. What is it waiting for?" Gralyre snarled.

"What are ye waiting for!" he bellowed at the slick hide that surged past their raft, rocking them in the wave of its passage.

Having explored each raft in turn it was now circling them. Gralyre knew in his heart that the real attack would come next. What choice did he have? The Demon Lords on the island would definitely notice when he used his magic, and would be awaiting them when they landed, but 'twas obvious that they would never leave the brine if Gralyre could not devise a way to pen this beast.

Gralyre's consciousness dove deep into an oily, ancient evil, insane with a hunger for destruction and pain. This was no simple beast. *It was aware.*

A roar of rage shuddered through the water, vibrating their bones with the low rumble of its voice. It had felt Gralyre's invasion.

It was a leviathan birthed from the darkest depths of the antediluvian oceans, a nightmare from the ages before mankind. Doaphin had driven it from its lair, and into this channel for the sole purpose of guarding the waters from invasion. The smell of Mayvin's wound seeping blood into the waves had drawn it but Gralyre sensed that it had already been seeking them.

The creature's will was too strong, and too alien for Gralyre to affect a connection! This was no bearing beast used to the rasp of the bridle, or a stag in the forest with simple thoughts that were easily dominated, but a wild, amoral being that had watched silently from its watery tomb as eons passed by on the skin of the world!

Gralyre shuddered and cried out as his mind was almost overwhelmed by the creature's attempt to oust him. He dug deeper into the beast's psyche, anchoring himself within.

The leviathan would not be controlled. Unable to remove Gralyre from its mind, it changed tactics and powered towards their raft instead. One way or another, Gralyre would not pose a threat for much longer.

Consumed by his battle of wills with the sea creature, Gralyre had stopped swimming, and relaxed his grasp. All of his concentration was devoted to averting the oncoming attack.

"Easy, my friend! I have ye!" Rewn swung an arm tightly across Gralyre's back, pinning him to the raft to prevent him from slipping away.

A small corner of Gralyre's mind felt the gesture, and his attention split into two directions. One part of his mind watched from below, through the eyes of the leviathan, as their raft drew nearer, at pale legs churning beneath the rough waves; the other part looked out through his own eyes at the fear contorting his friend's face.

"Rewn!" Gralyre gasped. "I cannot stop it! Its mind is too strong, too evil! Doaphin has placed it here to guard the channel from crossings!"

"Then we must swim faster!" Rewn replied, his voice quivering.

"'Tis here!" Gralyre yelled, and the gapping maw of the leviathan rose before them.

In a mouth large enough to swallow cattle, rows of wickedly sharp teeth curved inwards around the leviathan's massive jaws, perfect for grasping and ripping. Gralyre saw his own fear through the leviathan's eyes, and it let him; let him panic, let him realize his insignificance and contemplate his inevitable death. It could have taken him so easily, but that would have been too quick for the one who had sought to master it.

Gralyre roared, and lashed out with the blade he had used to sever the punctured bladder. A long and deep gash opened alongside the beast's massive jaw, causing enough pain to momentarily turn it from its attack.

Its thunderous howl hammered at their ears before the creature dove deeply, almost taking Rewn and Gralyre down in its wake. The cry continued underwater, making them wince from the sonic pains resonating through their flesh, and for leagues in all directions.

Still connected to its mind, Gralyre saw through the creature's eyes, as it circled in the water, frenzied at the scent of its own blood. It was done toying with them. No one would survive its next attack!

Gralyre's thoughts raced through strategies. He was not strong enough to overcome its will, but perhaps he could work around it. He would have but one chance, for the creature was already rising up from the depths. Through the sea creature's eyes, Gralyre watched their legs, dangling under the dark, mirrored surface of the water, grow nearer, as the beast accelerated upwards.

Gralyre swam deeper into the ancient morass of the leviathan's consciousness, trusting Rewn to keep his body afloat, as he concentrated wholly upon his task. He followed the pathway of energies that allowed him to look through the leviathan's eyes, then delved further into the realm of the instinctual mind than he had ever dared before, far from the conscious will of the beast, and into the wellspring of its life, its great stores of Godsmagic.

It was like a great shimmering lake, stretching as far as the eye could see, shining and verdant. Gralyre waded into the glow, and gasped at the power laid vulnerable to his use. Here he could sense everything the beast could; the rushing passage of the water, the sight of their dangling bodies, the vibrations from their thrashing legs, the scent of Mayvin's blood. Gralyre tapped the lines of energy he found, syphoning off the Godsmagic that allowed the leviathan's senses to function; sight, hearing, taste, touch, smell, and an extra sense that seemed to be able to see through the use of sound, if such a thing was possible, measuring distances and shapes by the return of an echoing click. He gathered it all, and diverted the power away from the creature's use, leaving it helpless and floundering in the ocean. Gralyre felt he would burst from the influx of the creature's

Godsmagic, but held tight, knowing that if he failed, everyone would die. A dark hole opened in the silver lake around his legs, and the leviathan's Godsmagic could not cross the barrier to reconnect its senses.

The leviathan belled in fear and confusion, the underwater sound reverberating around their bodies. It was fighting, trying to force Gralyre out, and it took all of his strength to hold his grip upon its mind, and keep its senses deadened. Minute by minute his control was slipping, as the creature's immense will asserted itself. Just a little longer...he must hold on!

"Gralyre!" Rewn's voice was coming from far away. "We have made it! Can ye hear me? Can ye walk?"

Vaguely, Gralyre felt his body being shaken, then a warm wetness lapping at his face. There was a delay for the sensations to reach him where he clung like a barnacle in the leviathan's pool of Godsmagic. When they did, he released the sea creature, and returned to his shivering body with a long, shuddering gasp.

Far out to sea, a bellow of triumph rose above the crash of waves, as the leviathan's senses returned. It breached the water victoriously before diving deeply to lick its wounds in peace.

Gralyre's eyes fluttered open to discover that he was washed up like flotsam on a hard, pebbled beach. The lantern, set near his head, splashed light up into the concerned faces of his companions who were grouped around him, shivering in their wet clothing. Little Wolf's tail thumped joyfully, as Gralyre's eyes opened, and the wolfdog happily set to licking the salt from Gralyre's face again.

Dotch leaned in to help Gralyre sit up, his salt and pepper hair spiked from the swim, water still rolling off his face. "That must have been some battle, lad." He pressed the ever-present rim of his flask to Gralyre's lips, as the others murmured of their gratitude.

Gralyre drank, thankful for the burn of the liquor that seemed to burst warmth into the pit of his stomach, and settle him fully back into his own skin. "Do not be thanking me," Gralyre warned grimly. "I have alerted every Demon Lord on the Island to our arrival. They must be on their way to intercept us by now."

"Do no' borrow trouble!" Aneida advised with a snort, rising lithely to her feet. "We are still drawing breath thanks t' ye!"

Gralyre sighed his exhaustion, as he pushed upright. Luckily, his toes were still numb from the cold, and could not feel the sharp rocks that he stood upon. "We must away. We cannot rest here!"

Rewn propped a shoulder under Gralyre's arm to steady him, as he limped them both to a large, weathered bolder to sit upon. "First we change into dry clothes." He caught the pack that Jord tossed his way, and rifled within for their boots. "We cannot concern ourselves with Demon Lords yet. We must get t' the far side o' the Island, and find shelter afore Catrian's storm arrives."

Trifyn considered the fog-shrouded landscape. "Do we cut inland? That would be quickest." What little could be seen by the cast of the lantern light showed a rocky terrain, bereft of vegetation. House sized boulders of sandy colored stone lay tossed about like children's blocks. It would not be an easy hike.

"No," Gralyre advised. "There is no lumenstone pathway to guide us here. We follow the shore. 'Twill be longer, but we will not lose our way in the Bleak."

"If we walk in the water, do ye think it will hide our scent from the Deathren?" Aneida asked.

Jord grinned at her. "Worth a try."

"It will slow us down," Saliana fretted.

"And dampen our feet again," Dotch grumbled.

In the end, it was judged worth the effort. So upon cold, stiff legs they set out along the beach, wading in the surf as they could. Once again they relied heavily upon Little Wolf's senses, both to tell them if any patrol approached, and to advise them when they had reached the farthest point around the island from the mainland.

⃠⃞

DREISENHELD

"Have the Rebels arrived?" The Master despises to speak with the Demon Lords of Fennick's Island. Pale beings who have been too long in the darkness of the black cloud, they lack the stunning beauty of the Demon Lords attending court.

"Yes, my Master. They made landing on the morning tide."

"A sorcerer travels with them. A human."

"We have felt his presence, my Master, but did nothing to

impede, as you directed. The Rebels were attacked during their crossing, and he protected them all. He is very powerful."

"Too powerful. We cannot suffer him to live another day. Kill the sorcerer now. Allow the others to enter the labyrinth. If they succeed, bring them to us. Unharmed. With the sword."

"Yes, my Master."

The Master severs the mind link, and leans back on the throne to consider. Has anything been missed?

The enemy sorcerer is the one anomaly. A sorcerer could wield the magic of Fennick's Wizard Stone, and become a force to fear whereas to the rest of the mundane Rebels, to Him, it is merely a fancy blade. It is sensible to eradicate the threat now that the Rebels have reached the island alive.

The Man has proved elusive thus far but destiny cannot be denied, and events will unfold, as they must. There is opportunity to capture the Man with the sword if he emerges victorious from the labyrinth at sunset. A thousand troops under the command of a trusted Demon Lord are held in the garrison of Elevor.

And if they fail to capture Him?

Well, there is always war.

೫ೱ�

FENNICK'S ISLAND

After a few hours of wading through the surf, they found their path blocked by a boulder the size of a small castle that perched half in the water and half upon the beach. Its full height and breadth disappeared into the Bleak. Going around it on the seaward side would be impossible judging by the sound of the crashing surf.

"Little Wolf says we are on the seaward side of the island," Gralyre advised. "Now is as good a time as any to turn inland and seek shelter."

Dotch thumped the rock with his hand. "Well, this would seem a sign from the Gods. I only hope that this is no' the beginning o' a cliff face reaching halfway back t' the far side o' the island."

They trailed their fingers along the stone for guidance, and after about a hundred steps, noted their path curving back around towards the beach.

Trifyn, who was leading the way with their lantern, halted as his fingers encountered an opening in the stone, past which he could not feel the opposite edge. He raised the light, and revealed a lateral crack that split the rock, leaving a gap wide enough for a person to squeeze through.

"I think I found something! A cave maybe." Trifyn called out softly, and the others moved up to join him.

Jord peered into the rift, and a small breeze fluttered his hair, indicating that the split might bisect the rock all the way through to the sea. "If there is a space in there, and another exit out the far side, it will make a good place t' shelter from the storm undiscovered."

He glanced around at his shivering companions, and compassion for their exhaustion softened his mouth. Mayvin was swaying, and only Rewn and Aneida's support was keeping her upright. "I am used t' sliding through close spaces. Wait here. I will go," he offered.

"Here, Jord," Anita bade, as she untied a small sack from her belt and gave it to him, "Take some lumenstones."

Armed with their only lantern, Jord slipped into the crack. The golden light that spilled out through the jagged run in the stone slowly faded away until the group was left shivering in darkness.

Some minutes later, Jord's hand reappeared holding a lumenstone glow, and beckoned them in. With sighs of relief, they squeezed into the crack, and followed the small light of the lumenstones that Jord had dropped to mark their path. The women had an easier time with the passage, slipping quickly through the narrow crevasse. As for the men, their chests and backs scraped with difficulty over the rough granite, though slimy lichen oiled their passage. Little Wolf padded easily through the rift, his lithe lupine form navigating the narrow, twisting path with ease.

After ten paces inward fallen stone blocked their passage, but lantern light glowed from a crawlspace at the top of the rocks, showing them the way. It was steep, but the slope of the slide was sufficient that Little Wolf could climb it with only a slight difficulty. They squeezed through the narrow opening at the top of the tumbled stones, and into a flat surfaced, horizontal rift, that provided them only a body's width of clearance between floor and ceiling.

Their cold and exhausted muscles protested the effort, as they belly-crawled for another ten feet, pushing their packs ahead of them, but it was worth it when they crawled out into a small, scoop-shaped cavern. Shattered boulders from the walls and ceiling had collapsed inward to form a hollow. The cavern tapered back into a crack leading down towards the sea, through which the rhythmic washing of waves echoed and boomed. There was space for them all to stand erect, and more than enough room to spread their beds.

Dotch and Gralyre examined the walls of the crack exiting out to the ocean, measuring the watermarks, and judged that the elevation of the cavern in the massive stone would protect them from any storm surge. They could not have found a more perfect safe haven.

Saliana approached Gralyre, and touched his arm to draw his attention. "I fear for Mayvin. She needs heat and rest. Is there any way to start a fire?"

"Not without magic. I dare not use it or draw the Demon Lords to our hiding place."

Dotch had also heard the request for heat. "There is nothing growing on the island, lass, no wood t' burn," Dotch advised gently, "but Mayvin can have my furs. Just leave me a wool blanket t' sleep under."

They strung skins across the crevice openings to partially block the winds that whistled through, and settled into their damp bedrolls to rest. It was a cold and clammy shelter, but they hoped the tides would hide their scent from the prowling Deathren and Stalkers.

Rewn volunteered for the first watch, as the rest of them dropped where they stood, making themselves as comfortable as possible amongst the fallen stones. Aneida lay down next to her sister, and cuddled Mayvin to keep her warmer.

Gralyre slid easily into sleep, exhausted by the crossing and by his battle with the leviathan. But something disturbed his dreams. It lurked in the shadows at the edge of waking, insignificant, sensed more than felt at first, like a toe dipping into waters at the edge of a still lake, and he the fish, rising to investigate what rippled the stillness. But the tickle vanished as he approached, only to return in a different place.

Gralyre changed direction, and tried to catch whatever it was, but it was quick, and suddenly the tickle was coming from multiple places at once. His dream self became frantic to catch it, an irritant that he had to stop. Then the tickle became a hammer, trying to penetrate forcibly into his thoughts, into his soul...

Rewn shook him awake.

"What?" Gralyre asked groggily, "What is it?" It felt as though he had only just shut his eyes.

"Ye cried out in your sleep," Rewn explained with concern. "Was it your nightmares?"

"No. Not this time." Gralyre's thoughts travelled back to a lake that something had attempted to dive into. Queerly, he could not remember specific details, yet the skin on his neck crawled from a residue of magic. He sat up, dislodging his furs. "I am fine now," Gralyre assured Rewn, though a terrible suspicion filled him with unease.

"Rewn, do you find it strange that the Demon Lords were not waiting for us on shore, and that they have not pursued us?"

Rewn shrugged. "I will do no' but thank the Gods for the luck."

"I do not think it was luck. They know we are here. Why have they not tried to find us? Not a whisper, not a single screaming Deathren. Do you not think it odd?" Gralyre pressed.

Rewn dropped an exhausted hand across his eyes. "Gralyre, this is all odd t' me. There is nothing sane nor safe in this world. I want the sun, and I want t' see my brother smile again. And I want…" his shoulders heaved for a moment, and when his hand passed away from his eyes, they were shimmering with tears. "I want t' live. Just a little longer. If the demons are no' searching for us, good. Pray they stay away a while longer!"

Rewn left Gralyre's side to return to his post near the entrance to their cavern, and for a moment, Gralyre thought about returning to sleep, but a nameless dread warned him off. He pushed stiffly to his feet, working his shoulders to remove a kink from sleeping upon the uneven stones. For a moment he regarded the others, watching them as they slumbered, and sighed as he realized what he must do. He joined Rewn at the rift in the stone.

Little Wolf, always sensitive to Gralyre's movements,

scrabbled to his feet to follow.

"Rewn, I have to see with my own eyes what we face. Keep the others hidden. Safe."

"Ye should take Dotch or Jord with ye, just in case."

Gralyre shook his head. "Little Wolf's senses will keep me from harm. Let them rest."

"There is no time afore the storm, Gralyre, ye should stay."

Gralyre rubbed a knuckle into his gritty eyes. "I cannot. Rewn, I must go."

Rewn's heart skipped a beat, and there was silence between them for a long moment, as they locked gazes. "That was no nightmare, just now. Was it?" he guessed quietly.

Gralyre shook his head, "Not a dream. The Demon Lords know I am here, and are searching for me. If I stay, they will find me, and that will lead them back to you all. I must go afore I betray our location." He cupped the back of Rewn's shoulder, and gave it a little shake of affection. "I am going to ensure the demons stay away a while longer."

"Ye are no' coming back, are ye?" Deep sadness etched Rewn's face, and he blinked to hold back tears. He shook his head in denial. "There must be another way!"

Gralyre sighed tightly. "Rewn, there is none. I do not expect that I will survive until Catrian's storm, but if I do, I will be caught in the open when it strikes."

"Ah, Gods!" Rewn cursed, and embraced Gralyre, thumping his back with a closed fist.

Gralyre thumped him back. "I knew there would be a cost to

fighting the leviathan with magic." Gralyre's voice grew rough with emotion. "You are right. Every moment of life from here on out is a gift! And by doing this, you will all live a little longer."

Gralyre pushed back from the embrace, though he still gripped Rewn's arms. "I will scout the opening to the labyrinth. If I can, I will send Little Wolf back with the location, and he will guide you there after the storm…after I am gone."

Rewn pushed Gralyre away, and shaded his eyes with a trembling hand to hide the tears, while his fist struck against Gralyre's chest. "Gods! I just thought…I really believed that we would make it. That we would get the sword and survive t' tell o' it."

Gralyre took Rewn's clenched fist in both of his hands, as a tear escaped down his cheek. "Me too. Rewn… you must know that your friendship… you… have been as a brother to me." His words were rough with loss and love.

Rewn tried a painful smile. "Ye too. Ye are my best friend, and a better man I have ne'er met." He stepped back, standing straighter, proud and strong in his respect, despite the grief that tightened his features and wet his cheeks. "It has been my honor, Gralyre." He held out his arm.

Gralyre grasped Rewn's arm with his. "The honor was always mine, Rewn. Lead them well. Keep them safe. Get the sword," Gralyre eyed him sternly for his nod of assent. "Survive, whatever it takes! You must survive."

Their arms parted, and Gralyre dropped to his belly to edge into the horizontal passage. "Good-bye, my friend," he murmured and vanished into the darkness.

Rewn's face was a frozen landscape of grief and pain. "Good-bye, Gralyre." His friend. His mentor. Gone.

He would never have suspected that Gralyre would be the first of them to fall, but he knew in his heart that Gralyre would always have chosen to die in protection of his friends. It was who he was.

Little Wolf looked at Rewn and whined a farewell, but ducked when Rewn bent to caress his head. The wolfdog belly crawled forward to enter the crack, and catch up with Gralyre.

80Q8

DREISENHELD

Doaphin glares into his roaring fireplace from his comfortable chair, his face tense as he drains his goblet of the golden wine. He has spent his rage at failure, and is now rapidly descending into despair. The years stretch out behind him, and he wonders how it all went so wrong.

He shrieks, and smashes his goblet into the flames. The rare glass shatters into thousands of glistening, diamond shards.

Somehow the Rebels survived the leviathan, and made the crossing to Fennick's Island, and Doaphin has lost his last opportunity to sabotage the Master's plan.

It is a truth that he has discovered; if one lives long enough, one sees the pattern of history repeat. The players are the same, as if the game has never ended.

Perhaps the Master has been right all along, and He will bring them the sword. Yet Doaphin cannot block the words of the curse that have haunted his sleep for three hundred years.

He gazes into the flames, into the bubbling, ruined face of his chamber slave, whom he has slaughtered in his rage, and weeps pitiably. His doom is upon him.

CHAPTER NINE

FENNICK'S ISLAND

Gralyre and Little Wolf walked through the surf up the rocky beach until they met a shallow stream that emptied into the ocean, and Gralyre stopped to light a lantern now that they had left the cave far behind. The thick mists of the Bleak engulfed them, and Gralyre was glad of the creek to follow inland lest they lose their way. Reason dictated that any stronghold would be near a source of water so following the stream seemed a good choice.

They turned inland, wading in the water to further cover the scent of their trail. The liquid was brackish, and an unwholesome stench arose from the banks. Though an ocean breeze stirred the air, it could do nothing to dissipate the reek, only mix the odor deeper into the black fog. Their footing was treacherous because of a slick glaze of slime that coated the rocks of the streambed.

Little Wolf whined as he leaned down to sniff the water.

"Little Wolf! Do not drink. I think we traverse the open sewers of the Demon Rider garrison."

The wolfdog whimpered, and tried to lift all four paws from the murky liquid at once. He was a very clean beast, and the thought of wading in feces was appalling.

"Just a little further, my friend," Gralyre promised. When he judged they had travelled far enough inland from the others to protect them from chance discovery, they left the midden water, and stopped for a rest.

After rolling ecstatically in the gravel to rub as much of the offal from his fur as possible, Little Wolf lifted his sensitive nose to the air, testing the wind for signs of the enemy. *'Their scent is strong. This is their hunting ground but there are no evil ones near us now,'* was his verdict.

They continued walking inland, following the banks of the open sewer back to its source. The whole island seemed composed of shattered granite, as though an angry giant had smashed his fists down, pulverizing cliffs into rubble. The thick fog made odd shapes of the rocks, making Gralyre tense several times at what turned out to be nothing but stone. Though there was neither covering trees nor vegetation on the island, there were enough cracked and strewn rocks to provide concealment should the need arise.

It was difficult to tell within the Bleak, but by the pull on his legs, Gralyre sensed that the land had begun to slope upwards. The stream began to bounce and fall over stones, following a course it had cut deep into the rock over the centuries, as the noxious fluid drained towards the sea. They had to be nearing the headwater.

The land steepened sharply into a cliff, and the stream became a narrow waterfall that pounded down the face. Little Wolf was unable to climb this grade, and Gralyre was forced to leave him behind.

'Take cover and await me here, Little Wolf,' he commanded, as he attached the lantern to his belt at his side, opposite his sword scabbard.

Little Wolf settled between two stones, becoming just another shape in the darkness, hidden away while he watched Gralyre scale the cliff until he his light was lost to the mists.

Footholds and handholds were easily found. The shattered stones made for an easy climb, despite the moisture of the fog that kept the rock wet and slick. As Gralyre neared the summit, it was the smell that reached him first, a scent so foul it overcame the stench of the open sewer that splashed near his shoulder. The cause revealed itself, as he reached a ledge, and unexpectedly, the summit.

He quickly doused his lantern, and reflexively, though common sense told him that he could not be seen in the heavy fog, ducked until only his eyes were even with the grade. What he had taken for a continuance of the cliff face was in actuality the beginning of a castle's wall jutting out over the precipice.

The Bleak did not creep as thickly near the castle, the dense vapour repelled through some magical warding that created a large, almost mist free, bubble. The result was that Gralyre could clearly survey the fortress, while remaining shrouded in the boundaries of the Bleak, hidden at the cliff edge.

He breathed lightly through his mouth, trying to avoid the stench that was so thick that he could actually taste it. Faint lights shone around the castle, inside and out, allowing him to trace the flow of the open sewer back to its headwaters, to the moat. Its waters had to be replenished by an underground spring, and its overflow was what Gralyre and Little Wolf had followed from the beach.

Taking his time, he carefully studied the fortifications, noting weaknesses. There were many. The centuries of occupiers had whiled away the time by constructing a castle of grandiose proportions, though the structure seemed to have been designed by, and for, the insane. The large building climbed the cliffs behind it, a tortured mass of odd angles, crooked towers, and aborted additions wreathed in snaking coils of the Bleak. Odd rooms and corners jutted out unexpectedly. Whole wings rambled away and stopped, only half completed. Even now, Gralyre could see construction proceeding by torchlight on a preposterous, leaning tower that looked as though a strong wind would blow it down.

And a strong wind was coming! Catrian's storm would wipe this foul blight from upon the earth. Gralyre sank down and turned, resting his back against the cliff face, as he dangled his legs over the edge of the small ledge.

He frowned in thought, as he stared into the emptiness around him. What if the castle guarded the portal to the labyrinth? Should the mass collapse in on itself, there would be no way to reach the sword. Somehow, he had to get within, and try to find the entrance if it was there, but how? There was no way to know how many Demon Lords and other creatures of darkness lurked within.

A rumble reached his ears, and Gralyre shifted to stand again, and peer over the lip of the cliff. He watched as a drawbridge slammed down over the fetid moat, throwing skirls of mist it all directions to eddy around three Demon Lords who marched in step across the heavy timbers.

Gralyre's lip curled in disgust of their unwholesome appearance, as he instinctively crouched lower. Their skin was ashen, their hair white, as with age, and they were dressed in fine robes and jewels. Their albinism was likely the result of hundreds of years spent living in the dark of the Bleak. Evil and power rolled off of them in cascading waves that nearly choked Gralyre with their intensity. He had not forgotten the comportment of the only other Demon Lord he had met, Lord Mallach. Magnified by a factor of three, the malevolence of these Demon Lords was thick enough to strangle upon.

From out of the fortress, following after the ghostly Demon Lords, shambled eight nightmares, and Gralyre recognized that they could only be Stalkers. They were like nothing he could have ever imagined, and he shivered with instinctual terror.

Reptilian in appearance, their flesh was armored in thick, overlapping scales. Double rows of spiked horns marched down their spines, gradually reducing in size, as they tapered onto the thick tails. Long, serrated teeth lifted the flesh of their elongated snouts, and the powerful jaw muscles, disproportionate to the size of their heads, instantly reminded Gralyre of the maw of the ancient leviathan he had fought. Talons to rival the length of Gralyre's dagger, shaped like those of a massive bird-of-prey, tipped their adroit fingers. They shuffled upright on two muscular hind legs that were built for a predator's speed, and enormous clawed feet that kicked chips from the wood of the drawbridge, as they shuffled across to join the Demon Lords. Behind them, their reptilian, scaled tails swayed gently to balance their mass as they walked.

Behind the Stalkers shuffled an army of dead eyed Deathren, vacant, emotionless faces, corpses rotting and dripping, as they staggered towards the Demon Lords. A slight moaning arose from the pack, though for now they were well leashed, and had yet to begin a howling pursuit. The Demon Lords had called their hounds to the hunt at last, and Gralyre knew that he was their prey.

"Comb the beaches. Find where he has landed!" the words of one of the Demon Lords drifted to Gralyre's ears. "Remember! The Master needs only the sorcerer dead. The rest are not to be harmed."

"Thy words are obeyed," one of the Stalkers hissed before turning to the others.

"Brothers! To the hunt!" With a roar, they were off, and the Deathren broke into their tireless run to following after, their screams announcing their coming so that all could hear and despair.

And avoid, Gralyre smirked. The howling cacophony would announce itself in plenty of time to step from its path. For now, they were moving away, which suited him fine. Gralyre followed them with his gaze, as they ran downhill out of the clearing surrounding the castle, and vanished into the Bleak.

A cheering and clanging of metal echoed out of the fog, the noise coming from thousands of throats, and Gralyre realized that the Castle was perched at the lip of a ridge, and that something important was hidden from his eyes in the Bleak below.

"We must ensure that the portal is secure," one of the Demon Lords ordered.

"Idiot. Of course it is secure. The way is closed."

The third sneered. "You do it if you must, but I do not see the danger. He is naught but a Human."

"A Human with magic. He must not be allowed near the cages," the first Demon Lord reminded. He lifted his hands, and Gralyre's skin crawled with the familiar sensation of another's spell casting.

The Bleak parted like the leaves in a book, showing a clear road downhill into a valley. Gralyre had guessed correctly, the castle did indeed sit upon the rim of a large basin, but from where he hid, his angle was not such that he could see what had been hidden, though most of the valley was now visible in the twilight gloom. The basin was a smooth plane of rock, littered with large boulders. Gralyre wondered at the depth of the valley for it seemed to reach below that of sea level.

"See, I told you they were fine. The cages are secure, no one may enter."

Two of the Demon Lords turned away, and walked back into the castle, while the third continued to scan the now visible floor of the valley. Finally, he nodded to himself, and walked back over the bridge, while behind, the Bleak rushed in to fill the gap that had been created. Slowly the chains took up the slack and the drawbridge rattled upwards, securing the castle once more.

Gralyre sighed in relief, and sat back on his ledge, breathing freely for the first time in a while. So the portal to the labyrinth was not hidden within the dark castle, but somewhere in the valley below. He would not have to find a way into the castle of madness after all.

His time grew short now. He must find the Stalkers and their Deathren slaves before they discovered his trail, and lead them away from the others. Gralyre felt an easing that they were now only searching for him, and his group would be safe for now.

But first he would take the opportunity to investigate what lay hidden in the valley below the castle, and confirm that the gate to the labyrinth truly was there.

Watching the fortress for signs of movement, Gralyre topped the ridge, rolling his body over the lip, and crawled to a shattered bolder. When no alarm was raised, he slunk through the thicker fog at the outskirts of the cleared space, making his way quietly from rock to rock, angling towards the road he had spotted. Oddly, there were no sentries posted and activity seemed limited to construction on the castle tower.

He reached the road unchallenged, and burst into a sprint, using the slope to gather speed until he reached the bottom, letting the path guide his steps so that he did not become lost. As the road leveled, he dove behind a large stone, and froze, awaiting sounds of pursuit.

Into the silence, he heard not the expected pounding of footsteps chasing him, but an odd noise, as of a large group of men yelling and fighting. Shifting from cover to cover, he tracked the sound, until the wavering lights from torches overtook the thick fog. He paused, awaiting an alarm, but the noise of fighting was all that he heard. He needed to be closer.

Gralyre darted from shattered boulder to craggy rock, inching towards the torches careful to ensure that he remained invisible, not only to the valley floor, but to the looming castle atop the ridge.

Squinting hard into the occluding black clouds of the Bleak, Gralyre could just discern a massive cage, marked at every corner by a flaming brand. The Bleak had an odd effect on fire, dampening to a pale glow what on a normal night would have been seen for leagues. The torches allowed Gralyre could trace the massive size of the enclosure, but he could not identify what caused the undulating movements within.

Gralyre dropped to his belly, and crawled slowly towards the cage until he could discern individual murmurs and moans, cries of pain and cruel, mad laughter. He slowly peered around the edge of his cover, and saw that the cage swarmed with bodies. Unkempt, and unwashed, Demon Rider troops had been herded together like animals, and were now trapped in iron bound prisons.

And as near as he was now, he could see that there were in fact four pens. Each massive cage had to be holding over a thousand Demon Riders packed so tightly that there was no room to sit or lay, only stand. The odour that had been afflicting Gralyre since he had climbed the cliff, had not been the open sewer after all, but this; sick and dying Demon Riders, stewing in their own filth.

The arrangement of the four rectangular cages, connected at the corners of their short sides, created an enclosed, square plaza in the centre of an iron cross, accessible only from within the cages. A stone arch stood alone there, shimmering with a dull radiance, easily seen, for the mist of the Bleak would not draw near to it. It was roughly the height of three men, with a span of two. Ancient runes scribed on the stone seemed to writhe and move, making the archway difficult to gaze upon. It seemed to glow brighter as Gralyre watched, gathering its power for the Solstice. By its weak radiance, and the dim torches, he could make out the miserable faces of the prisoners.

Looking through the stone arch led not to some mystic, magical maze, but only to the other side of the square and the opposite Demon Rider pens. It would remain nothing more than an empty archway until the Solstice, when the gates of the labyrinth would align.

Gralyre frowned as he studied the cages, finally realizing why the encampment had no sentries, and why he had managed to approach so near without challenge. The Demon Lords of Fennick's Island had no need of guards, for they had perfected their defenses over hundreds of years. By imprisoning their troops within these cages, they had a living wall protecting the entrance to the labyrinth, and it did not matter that their troops were sick and dying within the prison for they were already dead; a sacrifice to Doaphin's paranoia.

For three centuries Doaphin had been sending hundreds of thousands of 'Riders through that innocuous looking stone archway. None had ever returned, and each new crop of Demon Riders had to know this, and likely tried to desert from the moment the ferry from Elevor scraped bottom on the rocky shores of Fennick's Island. Imprisoning them, keeping them penned also served to keep their numbers intact.

The breeze gusted towards him, and Gralyre ducked back behind the rock, as he gagged. The stench was far worse than mere unwashed bodies could make, it smelled like a battlefield in the hot sun, of death. It surrounded him, penetrated his senses even though he tried to breathe shallowly through his mouth. His eyes wandered back to the softly luminous arch, and he suddenly understood where the thick reek originated.

The labyrinth's magic had somehow contained hundreds of thousands of Doaphin's dead. As the gates aligned, the stench of decomposition escaped to warn all others who quested for the sword that they would find only death here.

The idea of countless bodies piled up in a pocket of magic just out of his sight was a sickening testament to Doaphin's insanity. To waste so many lives so cheaply proved Doaphin's madness more eloquently than anything Gralyre had encountered since his awakening.

He contemplated the cages for a long time, searching for a

weakness, a flaw that could be exploited. Though he circled the pens several times, studying them from many angles, he could see no way through the cages to the archway, save past the thousands of prisoners, packed shoulder to shoulder.

There had to be a way! They had not endured and survived so much, only to fail at the eleventh hour! But for now, he had pushed his luck as far as he dared. It was time to lead the Stalkers and Deathren on a chase away from his friends. Frankly, he was amazed he had managed to scout for as long as he had.

Skulking from rock to rock, Gralyre retraced his steps back up the road, skirted the castle, and slid over the cliff edge to climb down the rockface beside the waterfall.

When he reached the bottom, Little Wolf sprang up from his hiding spot to greet him joyfully, and Gralyre spent a long moment with his face buried within the wolfdog's thick fur, grounding himself in something pure and good to erase the vision of the horrors he had left behind. Then together they followed the slimy, mist-shrouded creek back towards the distant ocean.

They were about halfway back, when a scream echoed from far behind.

Gralyre stopped, his body taut and alert, as Little Wolf whined, and glanced back along their trail. There was only one creature that made that inhuman cry.

'Deathren! They have our scent! Into the water!' Gralyre and Little Wolf splashed into the sewage-laden creek, sprinting

downstream as fast as they dared on the uneven and slippery footing.

The baying came again, only this time as a chorus. More had joined the hunt. The screams of the hunters spurred Gralyre and Little Wolf to run faster.

Gralyre thrashed through the water, knowing his effort was wasted. He could not outrun them, and the creek would not hide their trail for long, for the breeze was against them. Blowing in off the ocean, it brushed teasingly through his hair, and straight to the waiting nostrils of the pursuing Deathren.

Gralyre halted, his chest heaving from his brief sprint, and loosened his sword in its scabbard, determined to make his last stand. He would turn and fight, and die with the certainty that he had bought time for his friends. But he could not do battle upon the uneven footing of the diseased flow of water. Sword in hand, he climbed from the muck to the banks of the creek, and set himself for the coming attack.

He pushed away the frightful memory of Hangman's Tor, as another scream sounded, nearer than before, but the mists hid all. Images of the crossroads of the Bleak shivered his spine, and he knew from that experience, that the Deathren would be upon him before he knew it.

'Little Wolf! Go! Go to Rewn!' Gralyre snarled over his shoulder at the wolfdog. *'Lead him to the portal in the valley, as I have described to you!'*

For the first time in his short life, Little Wolf disobeyed. Head lowered in a decidedly wolfish fashion, his ruff stood erect, making him appear twice his normal size. The wolfdog's muzzle lifted in a snarl and his sharp fangs gleamed in the darkness.

Gralyre's gut wrenched in agony at the loyalty Little Wolf showed him, but he wasted no more effort in changing his mind. He swung back to face the approaching death, and let the cold comfort of the sword dance wash away his fear.

Fuelled by the readiness for battle, his sharpened sight spotted the first of the Deathren, naught but a sense of vaporous movement, and his ears identified five more of the creatures through their ceaseless howls. Two, maybe three, he could have survived.

He considered the wisdom of using magic, knowing that if he survived he was inviting attack from the ghastly Demon Lords who ruled Fennick's Island. But perhaps that was exactly what he wanted. The existence of the castle concerned him. Within its depths, the Stalkers and the Deathren had access to permanent darkness, granting them protection from Catrian's storm.

If he could draw them out like puss from an infected wound, and could keep them playing his dangerous cat-and-mouse games until Catrian's storm arrived, then they would be caught in the open and seared by the purity of daylight when the winds ripped away the protection of the Bleak.

Strength flowed into Gralyre, as certain defeat reversed itself into a plan for victory - of sorts - and he summoned his magic. Heat flickered along the length of the blade, gathering and growing in strength until his sword gleamed white-hot.

The first Deathren sprinted out of the swirling darkness with its stiff legged pace, and its arms hanging limply at its sides. Its rotting face proclaimed that its death had not been recent.

Gralyre pointed his sword at the creature, and an arc of lightning spewed from the white-hot tip of the blade. The Deathren burst into flame but kept running. Its jolting steps only ceased when it collapsed into ash just shy of Gralyre's boots. Smoke rose to add density to the fog.

As though the first was the signal to release a flood, Deathren flew out of the Bleak, and all met the same fate as their predecessor. The smell of charred flesh stung Gralyre's nostrils as he unleashed the power of his magic again and again. One after another, the Deathren dropped like moths that flew too near to a candle flame.

Silence ruled the dark once more; as quickly as the attack had commenced, it was over. Gralyre's face was shiny with sweat from the heat, as he allowed the tip of his sword to droop, grounding the blade, and letting the last of the energy discharge into the granite on which he stood.

'Little Wolf, come here,' Gralyre beckoned.

The wolfdog approached, giving the scorched earth and ashes a large berth. He halted and stared expectantly up into Gralyre's face.

'Return to Rewn and stay with him. I am going hunting, but my prey will also be hunting me. You must stay with Rewn, and make sure the evil ones do not get too near to our den.' In the distance, Gralyre faintly heard a Deathren's howl. Time grew

short to make the wolfdog understand and obey.

Little Wolf's ears flickered back and fourth, as he also heard the sound.

Gralyre gave the wolfdog a fond scratch behind his ears. *'You must do this for me, Little Wolf. You are the only one I trust to keep the others safe. After the wind, lead them to the portal, show them where it is.'*

Little Wolf chuffed softly his agreement, nuzzling his face into Gralyre's hand. *'Hunt fierce. Fearless. Do not eat what you kill. They smell bad.'*

Gralyre smiled at the bit of wolfish poetry, "I promise. Farewell Little Wolf," and felt tears spring into his eyes. He had made too many final goodbyes this day.

As Little Wolf loped into the darkness, Gralyre concentrated briefly and eradicated the wolfdog's trail with a small burst of his magic. As he released his spell, he heard the Deathren howl again, much nearer this time. His magic was drawing them like swarming hornets to rotting meat. They moved faster than he expected.

He splashed across the murky creek, and jogged away across the bolder shattered plateau, leading the pursuers from Little Wolf's trail.

Gralyre no longer feared losing his way in the Bleak. Getting lost was exactly his plan.

❧❦

"Gralyre is gone? He has left us?" Trifyn's panic soon roused everyone.

Rewn had just awakened Trifyn for his shift at watch, and had not had time to explain the circumstances of Gralyre's disappearance. "Wait, I have t' tell ye…"

"Gralyre would no' have abandoned us! Something must have happened t' him!" Aneida's concern cut Rewn off. Frustration and worry tinged her voice.

"… 'tis no' what…"

"Maybe he is a spy after all," Jord spat.

The company turned as one and stared at him censoriously. Jord shrugged his shoulders defensively and mumbled. "'Tis what we are all thinking!" Scowling hard at the ground he skittered a loose stone away with a kick from the toe of his boot.

"Gralyre is no spy!" Rewn snapped with certainty. "Last night while ye were all sleeping peacefully, he was attacked by the Demon Lords, and felt that the only way t' keep us safe was t' leave us."

"So he says," Jord sniped.

Rewn sprang from where he sat, and tackled Jord into the rocks. "He is no' a spy!" he yelled, as his fist connected solidly with Jord's jaw.

A knife materialized in Jord's palm, and pressed to Rewn's throat. Rewn reared up off the lighter man, his neck stretching to avoid the sharp edge. "If he is no' a spy, then where is he?" Jord demanded through clenched teeth and bloodied lip.

Rewn's hand was still tightly wound in Jord's shirt, though

he slowly lowered the fist he had raised in a strike. "If Gralyre had wanted us dead, he could have left us t' die in the water! Why would he wait until we reached the island t' betray us?"

"Settle down. All o' ye!" Dotch ordered. With a hefty kick, he sent Rewn sprawling off Jord. When Jord would have mindlessly followed after to continue the fight, Dotch laid his sword at the younger man's throat. "Let it lie, lad," he ordered in a soft voice, as he tapped Jord's cheek with the fat of the blade.

Jord remained tense for a moment before relaxing with a rueful sigh. He opened his hands to show them empty, his knife returned to the hidden pocket from whence it came.

"Your squabbling is pointless!" Dotch declared with an experienced man's pragmatism, as he sheathed his sword. "Save your fight for the 'Riders!"

Rewn sagged against the rough stone he had fetched up against, his hands massaging his ribs where Dotch's stout kick had connected. "Do none o' ye understand?" His voice was low with grief. "He means t' sacrifice himself, t' keep the Demon Lords from finding us afore the storm."

Aneida buckled on her sword with a hiss. "And ye just let him go? Alone?"

Rewn stared into nothing, as tears gathered in his eyes. "'Twas what he wanted."

"Instead o' sitting here with our heads up our arses, I suggest we go look for him. Aneida, ye come with me." Dotch paused to glare at Rewn and Jord. "Try no' t' kill each other afore the 'Riders get the pleasure, eh?"

Trifyn dodged forward to grab Dotch's arm. "But what o' the storm?"

Dotch shook him off. "And Gralyre will be unprotected when it strikes."

An echoing, haunting howl of a Deathren travelled down the rift from outside, and bounced around the rocks of their cave.

Aneida drew her sword, staring into the crack where she and Dotch had been but moments away from entering. Had they left the safety of the cavern, they would have exited into the path of the monsters.

Jord's face and eyes went dead cold. "They are hunting. They have caught the scent of prey."

"'Tis Gralyre." Trifyn whispered in anguished certainty. "Who else would they be hunting?"

"Well..." Jord started then trailed off, not knowing what to say. He shook his head numbly, wandered towards the back of the shelter, and squatted to stare into the passage leading out towards the sea to evaluate a possible escape route.

"Is there naught we can do for Gralyre?" Trifyn demanded.

"No lad," Dotch stated with harsh certainty. "We canno' go after him now, and if he is no' dead yet, he will be afore we can reach him. I only hope that he took the time t' cover his trail, and they do no' track him back t' us!"

"That would have been the first thing he did," Rewn whispered past his tight throat.

They all flinched, as more howls set the stones of their shelter to reverberating.

As suddenly as it had begun, the screams ceased, leaving a silence that was somehow worse for its finality.

"He is dead. Gralyre is dead!" Saliana's eyes were full of compassion and sorrow as they met Rewn's, before she buried her face in her arm to muffle her sobs. She knew naught if she cried for Gralyre's certain fate or for the pain she had just seen contort Rewn's face.

Aneida straightened from where she had been leaning despondently against the rough stone of the giant boulders that made up the floor of their cave. "Yaaaaa!" She grasped a heavy stone, and heaved it at the cavern wall, the smack of impact accompanying her pained scream.

Trifyn hesitated then placed a sympathetic hand on Aneida's shoulder. With a violent move, she batted his gesture away, stalking to the side of her prone sister, and flopping down beside her.

Mayvin clasped Aneida's hand in fevered strength, as their gazes fused in shared grief. The tableau held as they all sunk into their despair.

"Listen!" Trifyn broke the silence with a hoarse whisper, as though to speak any louder would surely lead the Deathren back to them, though the pounding of the waves muffled any small noises that the group might make. He crept nearer to the horizontal crack, a hand raised for silence.

"What do ye hear?" Dotch cocked his head.

"It sounded like...Wait! There it is again! There is something in the passage," he whispered urgently.

There was a hissing rasp as swords were drawn in readiness. The sound of claws scraping off rock reached their ears over the sound of the booming surf.

"We will no' be escaping out the seaward side. The tide is in, and the waves are too high and strong now," Jord advised tightly. He did not look at the others, as he delivered the bad news.

"We are trapped in here!" Trifyn breathed in horror.

"Steady..." Rewn breathed, warning them all to stillness.

"Ye can no' outrun Deathren anyway, Trifyn," Jord advised coldly. "They are tireless. Better t' stay here, with our backs t' the wall. With only this one opening they canno' swarm us. We can hold them off until the storm strikes."

"He is right," Rewn shuddered as memories of his latest brush with the relentless creatures flooded his mind. "If we flee, the Deathren will run us t' ground, and rip us t' shreds!"

Trifyn nodded and strung his bow, selecting an arrow and setting it to the string.

"'Tis here!" Saliana pointed towards the dark opening in the stone.

Grumbling with effort, two black paws appeared, as Little Wolf materialized from the passage, crawling on his belly as he left the rift.

"Ah!" Trifyn yelled, startled as the wolfdog appeared, and relaxed his bow to aim downward.

Little Wolf trotted into their midst with lupine disregard for their panic. He padded directly to Rewn's side, circled once, and then lay at his feet. He let out a high keening sigh, staring beseechingly towards the entrance of the cave.

Rewn raised his blank face to follow the wolfdog's gaze. "That is it then." He mused quietly, the shock of it all seeping into his voice. His sword slowly lowered until the point grated upon the rocks. "He really is gone."

ৰূল্ড

Gralyre sprinted until his legs quivered with fatigue before he turned and fought, leading the Deathren as far from the shoreline refuge of the group as possible. He used his sorcery sparingly, and only as a last resort if the Deathren came at him in a rapacious pack, for with every burst of power, he could feel the Demon Lords honing in on his position.

His sorcery was far from instinctual, and he needed time and space to gather and release his magic. Sooner or later the Demon Lords would send a stronger evil against him, or come themselves, so he did his best to conserve his strength against that happenstance.

The Deathren were mindless instruments of evil whose hunger drove them relentlessly and predictably. Once Gralyre discovered how to conceal his scent from them, with small bursts of his magic that swept the dust from his footprints, they were no more hazardous than a runaway cart. Dangerous if he were to stand in their path, but since they were unable to recognize the strategies he employed against them, it became a simple matter of giving them a false trail to follow, and stepping out of their way.

He could hear them coming for leagues, and their wails announced their numbers and locations so effectively, that many times he was able to track around them, and come at them in an ambush from behind. In this way, the Bleak worked as much to his advantage as to theirs.

He kept his lantern burning as low as possible, both to hide the light, and to preserve the oil, for when the fuel ran dry, and he lost his light, he would be left blind and vulnerable to his enemies.

Gralyre lost track of how many Deathren he destroyed. His life narrowed to a blur of battles and retreats, of stalking the Deathren by their shrieks, choking on the ash and the stench of their burning flesh, and feeling his sword hacking through their bloodless, dead flesh.

Eventually, the running and fighting took its toll, and he found himself reeling with exhaustion after destroying a particularly large herd of the creatures. He was not sure how much time had passed since he had left Little Wolf, but instinct told him that Catrian's storm must be near.

Clearly able to hear another company of Deathren baying off on one of his false trails, Gralyre crawled into a hollow under a large boulder and collapsed in exhaustion. He was as safe as he could be for now, and took advantage of the respite for some much needed rest. He placed his lantern where he could easily find it again when he awoke, and blew out the wick to conserve the oil.

The darkness was absolute, and cold enough that he began to shiver now that he had stopped moving. Gradually, his body relaxed, but his mind was given no such relief. Almost to the second that he fell asleep, Gralyre was bombarded by the Demon Lords, their attacks coming hard and fast, as they sought his location, but Gralyre had spent the last months learning how to shield his thoughts from Catrian, and was able to resist their incursions, at least for now.

After a time, he was startled from his soldier's nap by the eerie silence of the perpetual night. The Deathren had ceased their screaming, and some nameless dread had seized the darkness, the amoral intelligence of a dangerous evil.

Gralyre scrabbled up to crouch down behind the rocks in which he had slept, too terrified by the unknown to dare to light the lantern, but trusting, by the way his skin crawled, that somewhere in the darkness a Stalker hunted him. Quietly, he picked up the lantern and tied it back to his belt, lest he lose it when he fled.

Gralyre supposed he should feel triumphant that he had finally manipulated the dangerous predators into the open, vulnerable to the coming storm, but all he felt was fear. He had never faced a Stalker in battle, and did not know if he had the skill or power to destroy one.

If only he had the sun's protection! How long before the storm struck? Gralyre was disoriented, and could not mark the passage of time. One day or many? Who was to say? Time was a foreigner to the Bleak.

Moment by moment, as nothing happened, Gralyre grew dubious that there was anything awaiting him in the darkness. Perhaps he had awoken from a nightmare? There was only one way to be certain.

Gralyre reached out with his magic, trying to sense the threat more clearly, and immediately realized his mistake, as he felt power snaking towards him, fast, an unstoppable force of evil. He had revealed his position to the enemy!

Gralyre covered his head with his arms in an instinctual move to stop a blow, which was no deterrent to the powerful magic. The force wrapped him in stinging, choking bonds, knocking him backwards several feet to land hard amongst the rocks.

Gralyre gasped and gagged at the oily feel of evil oozing around his body, encapsulating him, as he convulsed and contorted in an effort to escape.

He sought anything within his limited arsenal of knowledge that could help him combat this attack, but this was a manifestation of power that Catrian had never spoken of.

Then as suddenly as it had assailed him, it was gone, retreating back towards its sender. The magic had not been meant to kill, only to disable and hold him in place to be collected, Gralyre recognized, as he pushed feverishly up from the ground, staggering a few paces, before he bent at the waist, and retched up the scant food he had left in his stomach.

Some distance away, there was a thunderous roar, unlike anything he had every heard, a voice that speared such instinctual terror into the heart of him, that before he was aware, he had gained traction with his fear-leaden legs, and sprinted into the darkness of the Bleak, his whole being consumed with the need for escape!

Animal grunts panted from his lips, as he mindlessly pushed his body to greater speed to leave behind the residue of evil that had briefly stroked his soul. It was a nightmare flight for, unable to see, it seemed he was running in place even though his legs were churning as fast as they could.

He stubbed his foot against an unseen rock, and went sprawling. Only the thick calluses on his palms saved him from gashing his flesh open upon the rough stones, as he rolled to a stop. The fall was like a slap to his face, snapping him back from the debilitating hysteria that had briefly owned him. Gralyre stayed on his hands and knees for a moment, sucking in large gulps of air while his brain began to function once more.

The bellowing roar sounded again, so much nearer, and Gralyre shuddered, as he estimated the rate of its travel. There was no time!

He scrabbled off his knees into a surging sprint. Moments later the sounds of shifting, disturbed rocks smacking off each other made him turn his head reflexively, though the Bleak would ensure he would never see the nightmare about to overtake him.

The ground suddenly dropped out from under his running feet, and he was falling. Hidden in the dark fog, he had missed the edge of a cliff.

Gralyre twisted mid-air, and flung himself against the slope, hands and legs scrabbling to slow his fall. His clothing shredded, and then his flesh took punishment from the sandpaper texture of the rocks, until finally, his feet caught on a ledge, bringing his slide to a jarring halt.

Gralyre gasped and coughed in pain, as he clung to the cliff face, and his mind flew through his options. If he climbed back up, it would take time, and the Stalker would be awaiting his arrival at the top. The same outcome occurred if he were to stay put. The only option was down. He could climb, or… A familiar sound reached his ears.

Surf!

He connected his Godsmagic to the stones that he clung to, and revealed the shape and height of the cliff to his mind's eye. Close below the ledge upon where he had halted, a deep inlet thrashed water against the cliffs.

Gralyre leapt high, pushing out and away from the slope of the cliff with all his might to avoid being ground upon the rocks below in the surging waves. Unable to see into the Bleak, he trusted to his magic and his luck to guide him safely the rest of the way down into the water.

Wind whistled past his ears as he dropped, long enough to send a bolt of panic through him at the thought that he may have miscalculated. Without warning he plunged into the ebb of a receding wave and fought his way to the surface of the water. Gasping and thankful, he struck out for the far side of the small inlet with powerful strokes. The cold water stole his breath but he was thankful to it nonetheless. Perhaps the water would occlude his trail to the Stalker for long enough that he could think of an escape.

Gralyre berated himself as he swam, ashamed that he had allowed the Stalker to stampede him into mindless flight. He might just as well fall on his sword now, and save himself the epic struggles to come. The salt water burned into the scrapes on his face, arms and chest, a welcome penance to atone for his lack of discipline.

His feet struck bottom, and he dragged himself up on the opposite shore. The night air felt warm compared to the cold of the water he had just left, and his shivers abated quickly.

There was only one person who could give him the knowledge that he needed to fight a Stalker. He had vowed not to contact Catrian again, but his need now overtook his caution. He had well and truly announced his presence on the island, and contacting her now would not place him in any more danger than he was already in. Gralyre had brief respite afore the Stalker found him again. He had to act quickly.

He closed his eyes, calming his mind with the rhythmic ebb and push of the tide. When he was ready, Gralyre reached out for her.

'Catrian.' He called her name like a supplicant in need of his goddess's benediction.

ഓരു

THE NORTHER REBEL FORTRESS

"When will she awaken, Boris? It has been days since the attack!" Matik's harsh whisper of concern was almost lost within his thick beard, as he hovered over Catrian's still form, and patted her cold fingers awkwardly.

The two men stood at Catrian's bedside in her tent, where Matik had brought her so many days ago. Her chest continued to pump air, and her heart to beat, but day-by-day both grew slower, weaker, as she started to die. She had never awoken from her coma.

"She drew too deeply o' her magic t' conjure that storm, and then fight off the Stalker. She may never revive," Boris stated sadly. "I ne'er told her anything, Matik. She will die thinking that I do no' love her! My poor, poor lass!"

Matik sighed deeply as he scanned Catrian's sunken cheeks and eyes, her colorless lips. "What was she thinking? What are we t' do without her magic beside us?" Matik asked the same questions every time he visited Catrian, unable to reconcile her sacrifice. With another heavy sigh, he slipped her clammy hand back under the thick covering of furs.

Boris tugged Matik's shoulder, and guided him out through the filmy curtain that separated Catrian's quarters to the table, and to the tankards of ale and rolled maps that awaited their study. Boris had appropriated Catrian's tent to be nearer and to tend her, his having already been packed and stored for the march to the lowlands.

"We canno' await her recovery, Matik. We will leave in two days, as planned, t' meet Kierdenan, and join with the others in the offensive," Boris muttered, pushing aside the maps with a weary sigh.

Matik wiped the foam of ale away from his mouth and beard with the back of his fist. "That is no' our greatest concern."

Boris leaned forward to listen.

"Rumours are flying that Catrian is dead. That even if she lives, she is too crippled t' help us in the war. The men fear t' fight without her power. They fear that without her help, they will all die."

Boris rubbed a hand over his short, grey stubble, and rocked backwards in his chair. A disgusted snarl twisted his lips. "'Tis all we need. She could have considered this afore she spent herself!"

Matik frowned impatiently. "Ye must handle the situation delicately. T' them she is no' just a leader, she is a talisman o' good fortune."

Boris' eyes dropped to his tankard, studying the swirling bubbles in the ale, as he thoughtfully rotated the mug within his large, scarred hands. "Maybe they are right. This is a magical battle we fight, against the most powerful sorcerer ever born." Boris lifted his gaze; troubled and uncertain for the first time that Matik had ever known him. "What hope do we have without some sort o' sorcery at our side?"

Matik swallowed heavily, feeling as if he had been stabbed in his guts. Boris was the Commander, the voice of surety and strength. But suddenly he seemed a broken old man facing the specter of mortality, and flinching away for the first time. Matik glanced from his Commander's face, unable to brave the haunted soul staring out at him from Boris' eyes. He feared the expression was mirrored in his own countenance. Forbearing an answer, he raised his mug to quaff more ale.

"Gralyre!"

At the sound of Catrian's cry, the two men leapt to their feet. Chairs crashed over, and spilt ale was left in pools to gradually drip from the table, and soak into the maps, as they sprinted across the tent, and through the curtain that separated her bed from the rest of her quarters.

Catrian lay where they had left her but had flung off her coverings. Her head tossed back and forth, her body arching as though under attack. Sweat stood out in beads upon her forehead.

"Hold her down!" Boris ordered, throwing himself across her thrashing legs.

Matik flung himself across Catrian's torso, striving with all his might to restrain her struggles. His eyes met Boris' across the convulsing sorceress. "She spoke his name. Is he attacking her?"

"How should I know?" Boris growled.

"Gralyre!" Catrian wailed, body heaving from some nightmare vision. 'Ye must no'…must no'!'

ഉറര

Catrian floated where nothing could touch her. She vaguely wondered if this was death but found the concept unimportant. Instead, she felt curiosity towards a sense of urgency that was pulling her attention back towards a place she had dreamed of once; a place of strife, fear, uncertainty, and hate.

So many hurtful feelings, though now she was no longer subject to their dominion, and the pull of life was easily ignored.

Then someone called her name. There was emotion there, and a face, a man, and something stirred in her becalmed soul. It was a voice she knew she would follow to the ends of time. She remembered the honesty of his soul, found deep in the places that could tell no lies. Regret touched her for what she would never know, for what was truly gone. She had sent him to die.

Catrian reached out to touch the voice, trying to remember more, trying to remember a name. It came with great difficulty.

'Gralyre.'

Once, she had wanted nothing more than to be his. Would they be together in death what they could never be in life?

'Gralyre, Ye must no' let go! Ye must no' lose me!'

Twisting and crying out she tried to maintain her grip upon him, tried to follow his voice back to her life. For a moment she was back in her body. Her eyes were open but her vision was blurry and fogged, as she strained to find Gralyre's face, but the two men hovering above her were strangers, and she retreated back to her safe place where nothing could reach her. Only one thought came with her.

Gralyre was dead. She had sent him away to Fennick's Island

to die. 'Twas not he who had called to her.

There was nothing left for her here. This life was too hard, too painful. With a quiet sigh, she stopped struggling to return to the living world. She released her grip on the lifeline that she had briefly clung to, and her soul drifted away on memories, back into the cool serenity of her Wizard Stone.

ဢဢ

FENNICK'S ISLAND

Gralyre's eyes snapped open, and he surged to his feet, maddened by grief, and unable to contain the horror that was overwhelming him.

"Catrian!"

The thunder of his cry was lost to the roar of the tide.

'Gone! No! Impossible!'

Catrian had not answered his summons at first, no matter how he had strained with his magic. He had thought that she was ignoring him, doubled his efforts, and been briefly rewarded when he had felt her weak touch. He had clung to the wispy trace of her soul, trying to grasp it, imploring her to stay, but she had evaporated away from him.

Gralyre hung his head and cursed, his chest heaving with unspent tears. What had happened? She was soon to be marching to the front. Had Doaphin attacked her? Killed her?

Gralyre's hands tightened into fists, and he shook his head in denial.

'No! She is not dead! She cannot be dead! I reached her! I must try again!'

Calming his breath and his mind, he sought Catrian once more. For a moment he brushed against her soul but she slipped away from him again, her thoughts vanishing from his like water from a hot stone.

Gralyre's eyes snapped open. The dark, fog shrouded landscape with its phantom shapes was blurred further by his pain. If only his magic were stronger, he would be able to hold on to her, save her! She had answered his summons once, he knew that he could reach her again, but he needed more power to bring her back.

'The Dragon Sword.'

Gralyre's harsh breaths suspended, as the thought erupted in his mind.

During their briefing in Catrian's tent before they had begun their journey, she had read from a book penned by a Dream Weaver seer, who had posited that the Dragon Sword of Lyre was also the Wizard Stone of Fennick. If this was so, then the sum of the ancient sorcerer's power might be captured within the blade, ready to impart its wisdom to whomsoever possessed it. With that sword, he could save Catrian!

Gralyre raised his chin, and stared blindly into the darkness, as his mind's eye saw the portal to the labyrinth, unreachable at the centre of five thousand caged Demon Riders. The Dragon Sword was Catrian's only hope of life, and Gralyre no longer had the luxury of sacrificing himself for the group. He had to survive the Deathren, and Stalkers and Demon Lords, then Catrian's Storm. The Gods of Fortune had just raised the stakes of this game.

A shower of stones and boulders rained down into the opposite side of the inlet, followed by the heavy splash down of a body.

'The Stalker!'

In the face of his greater fear for Catrian's life, Gralyre lost all fear for his own. His jaw flexed with determination. Nothing was more important now than getting to the Dragon Sword, and no creature of Doaphin's was going to stand in his path!

The Stalker was moving fast through the water, powerful strokes churning it towards Gralyre, where he stood on the opposite shore.

Gralyre would not wait meekly for it to kill him, and the Stalker would never be as vulnerable as it was right now! He waded boldly into the shallows, and plunged his hands into the sea, sucking the residual warmth from the water until it began to freeze around the Stalker, slowing and then halting the beast, as the ice thickened and deepened, suspending it in place.

The ice would not hold it for long. Already the hairs on the back of Gralyre's neck were vibrating, as the Stalker amassed its magic, and began to smash great cracks into the solid surface, shattering a channel in the ice.

But the trick had slowed it enough to allow Gralyre time to seek the minds of the creatures that inhabited the waters of the inlet. There were large schools of fish, sharks and eels, and creatures to which he had no name. He overthrew all their minds, and heightened their hunger to a terrible degree. With a voraciousness that far surpassed their natures, Gralyre turned them all into sawtooth mouths with fins.

The sea creatures converged upon the Stalker, surrounding it in a boiling froth, and Gralyre witnessed the attack through thousands of eyes.

But it was through his human ears that Gralyre heard the Stalker roar, as pieces of its flesh were flayed from its body. The attack was inescapable and relentless. Gralyre drove his aquatic army into every gap in the Stalker's armor plating, and once within, they ate their way deeper and deeper. Within minutes there was nothing left of the beast but a sinking skeleton with tattered flesh clinging to its bones, and even these were being plucked clean by the relentless hunger of the fish.

Gralyre released the minds of his aquatic army, and gasped as his consciousness returned from a thousand divisions, and slammed back into his own body. He struggled to hold himself free of feinting forward into the water that he still crouched above with his arms buried to the elbow.

He stumbled from the surf, dropped to his knees, and then rolled onto his side, fighting to regain his sense of self. He had almost become lost, spread too thin within the thoughts of so many.

Is this what had happened to Catrian? Had she drawn too deeply of her magic and lost herself? Had it happened when she had created the storm?

Gralyre shuddered, and his guts clenched at the thought that she might have injured herself for him. But no, she knew her importance to the resistance was too great to risk herself in such a manner. Something else must have occurred. Surely the only power in the land strong enough to challenge her was Doaphin himself? Had the evil one learned of the Rebel's plans, and sent his magic against her?

Gralyre slammed his fist against the rock, welcoming the small pain, letting it distract him from the greater wound in his heart. He would retrieve the Dragon Sword and save Catrian. And then no force in the land would stop him from destroying Doaphin, and anyone else who may have harmed her!

Gralyre reached out into the night, searching for the pool of evil that would betray the presence of another Stalker. But all was quiet. He was safe for the moment. His luck was holding, as only one Stalker had attacked, with the others likely splitting up to cover more territory, as they searched for him on the island. After that outlay of magic they would all be speeding their way to his location. He had to move.

The Demon Lords were being strategically wise. They knew that he was after the sword, and that they need only await him at the portal to the labyrinth. Meanwhile, he would be run to exhaustion by their minions, and be that much weaker when he finally faced them. They would not have much further to push him, Gralyre acknowledge with a grimace of fatigue. Just as long as they were all out in the open waiting for him to arrive when the storm struck!

He forced himself to sit up, and took a moment to spark the wick on his lamp, thankful that the salt water had not penetrated too deeply into the reservoir and fouled the oil during his swim across the small inlet. The tin of the reservoir was deeply dented from his fall, but thankfully had not ruptured.

Wearily, he climbed the rocky slope off the beach, and headed in an exhausted shuffle towards the seaward shore of the island. He did not know how much time he had left but instinct told him that he needed to find shelter quickly. A hard wind had started to push against his back, and seen by the soft light of the lantern, the shifting fog had begun to stream past like a river.

The storm was coming.

Rewn awoke groggily, disoriented in the weak lantern light, and uncertain of how long he had achieved his fitful slumber. For a moment, as he stared up at the roof of the cave, he wondered if the sun still shone elsewhere, or if the light had been extinguished throughout the world. Would he die, never feeling the warm caress of sunlight again? He stuck his chilled hands under his armpits to warm up his fingers, and walked over the shattered boulders to the front of the cavern to relieve Dotch's watch. If he was ever blessed enough to see daylight again, he would never take the sunshine for granted.

Dotch did not turn at his approach, his eyes ceaselessly

trained upon the crack near the floor of their cavern, almost as if he expected Gralyre to reappear. "They have stopped," he muttered.

"Who?" Rewn asked on a yawn, as he stretched upward trying to remove the kinks from sleeping on a stony bed.

"The Deathren."

With those two words, all lingering sleep fled from Rewn's body. "What do ye make o' it?"

Dotch just shrugged, and gave up his post to the younger man. What could he answer that they both did not guess? "I am going t' eat some breakfast, then get some sleep."

Rewn touched Dotch's shoulder to detain him. "We should go easy on the supplies, there is no' much left."

Dotch stared levelly into Rewn's eyes. "In a day or two, lad, it will no' matter if we have victuals or no'." He patted Rewn's hand where it gripped his shoulder as he turned away, and headed towards the packs.

Rewn eased down on a boulder next to the rift and settled his sword at his side with a sigh. Dotch was right, yet it was strange how alive Rewn felt even now, for the labyrinth and his certain death seemed surreal. Perhaps that denial of the inevitable was the nature of man.

Little gasps of fear caused Rewn to glance towards where the others were still rolled tightly in their sleeping furs. Saliana was having another nightmare. In their dark lair, awaiting the storm to destroy Doaphin's demons, no one slept undisturbed.

Since Gralyre's death, the vitality had drained away from

them all. Once there had been hope of victory, or at least the hope of spitting in the eye of danger, and every one of them had felt as formidable as epic heroes. Gralyre had given them that, had kept ferocity and hope alive within all their hearts. With Gralyre gone now, they just felt...common, and their pathos consumed them. They spent their time eating or sleeping, with little conversation between them.

Gralyre had seen it, and had galvanized them once during their journey. What would it take to rouse them again? What could Rewn do to help them when he was as afflicted as they? He sighed heavily, and sagged forward to hang his head.

At that precise moment, Little Wolf sprang up from where he had been sleeping, and loosed a howl of alarm that reverberated in the small space, vibrating their bones.

Jord exploded from sleep with a throwing knife in each hand, just as Aneida rolled to her feet with her bare blade pulled from beneath the pack she had slept on.

"Demons take ye, ye stupid mutt!" yelled Trifyn. He scrambled to the back of the cave to distance himself from the keening dog. His blond hair stuck up in strange directions giving him the appearance of deranged surprise.

"Make him stop!" Saliana begged with her hands clasped to her ears.

"Yeah, what is he on about?" Jord demanded in a surly voice, as he put his knifes away.

Rewn shrugged. "How should I know?"

Aneida returned her sword to its scabbard, and bent to check on Mayvin. Her sister's eyes were sunk deep from the illness that racked her frame. "Keep the furs around ye," she fussed, as she wrapped Mayvin's shoulders in warmth.

With fingers trembling from her fever, Mayvin pointed at the wolfdog, and signed. *What is he staring at?*

With everyone now awake, Little Wolf stopped howling, and cocked his head at the crack leading out of the little cave. Everyone froze, as they tracked the wolfdog's attention to the slit in the rocks. Into the sudden silence in the wake of the wolfdog's howls, the pound of surf and dripping water sounded eerily loud.

Little Wolf's head lowered wolfishly, and he turned away from the crack to meet each of their eyes with his urgent, intelligent gaze, snapping and barking, advancing forward, and forcing the others to fall back towards the seaward side of their shelter.

"What is it, Little Wolf?" Rewn whispered, taking several paces back into the cavern. "Is it a Deathren?"

It was fortuitous that he had moved away from the opening, for at the precise moment, Catrian's storm shattered the Bleak. The force of the wind blew Rewn across the cavern, fetching up next to Trifyn on the back wall.

Rewn grunted in agony, as the bodies of Dotch, Aneida, Saliana, Jord, Mayvin, one fearfully scrabbling wolfdog, and their packs, respectively, followed after. The tarps they had strung across the entrances to keep out the sea breezes, folded neatly, and were sucked out the seaward crack. The ground shook and tilted, as the massive boulder rocked to the side, and stones shifted and rained down from the ceiling of their little cave. The roar of the wind was deafening, as it screamed through the throat of the crack. Spume from the ocean whipped through the opening, soaking them where they were pinned by the force of the wind.

"We must anchor ourselves!" Rewn yelled with difficulty, as the wind caught in his mouth, vibrating his cheeks, and he began to slide towards the seaward crack. He had visions of folding as neatly as their tarps had, and being sucked out the opening.

"Here!" Aneida screamed, struggling to hold a length of rope she had worked from a pack that was pinned against her chest. "Tie this around yourselves!" Her words could scarce be heard over the shriek of the wind. With difficulty, Aneida looped one end of the rope over the boulder she clung to, catching herself and her sister in the coils, before stretching the free end towards Jord. As he reached for the rope, it tore free from her grasp, whipping and snapping with the force of the wind.

It cracked across Jord's face, flaying open his cheek in a spray of blood. He ducked, cursing, as it made another pass, raising a welt on his arm. The flailing cord vibrated too fast for him to catch hold of.

Dotch and Rewn both made a grab for the rope and missed. It moved like a striking snake, almost too fast to see. Gritting his teeth against the pain, Jord thrust his arm into its path, accepting the bite of the lash, as he brought it under control. Struggling against the pull of the airstream, Jord looped himself to Saliana, while she dragged Little Wolf towards her across the rockface, and caught him in a coil or two before the loose end snapped from her grasp, and whipped against Dotch's chest.

The wind grew stronger, sucking them towards the seaward crack, as they were caught in a riptide of the wind's current. Still unanchored, Rewn and Trifyn slid further away.

Dotch formed a loop and tossed it over Rewn's head, wincing in sympathy as it tautened at Rewn's neck.

Rewn choked and struggled, and managed to get a hand through the coil, and push it down under his arms, as Dotch released the free end to his control. As Trifyn continued to slide away, Rewn scissored out with his legs, and caught Trifyn around the waist. Quickly, he tied him off, and then bound the free end of the rope around an anchoring boulder.

The rope held fast, and they cursed and cried with pain, as they were beat against the rough walls by the push and pull of the gale. Their packs slid away across the wall, and stuck fast against the seaward crack, while clothing and bedding whisked away, and out to sea. The wind tore at the packs until they burst, and food, weapons, and the last of their supplies vanished into the maw of the storm.

The tempest raged for what felt like an eternity, then as abruptly as it had struck, it vanished, hurling itself out across the ocean. Released from the pressure of the wind, the group slid down the rough wall and collapsed in a heap.

"Is it over?" Saliana whispered fearfully.

"Aye," Rewn answered shakily. "Is everyone alright?"

"Mayvin!" Aneida's strident panic brought everyone to her. "Wake up!" Her fearful gaze met Saliana's. "Help me!"

Saliana struggled against the ropes until Jord severed the tangled bindings for her, and she dropped to her knees. Dotch grabbed her arm, and helped her the rest of the way to Aneida's side.

Saliana laid a hand against Mayvin's lips, feeling for breath, and then bent her head to press her ear to Mayvin's chest. "Aneida, 'tis all right," she reassured as she sat upright. "She has lost consciousness." Saliana looked at Trifyn, and held out her hand for the waterskin at his waist. "Water!" she snapped the order, and Trifyn hastened to obey.

After a quick inventory, everyone agreed that they had survived, albeit not without some scrapes and bruises. All bore deep rope burns from the violent pull of the wind upon their bindings, though Jord's wounds from the lashes he had taken trying to capture the rope were the most sever.

Their supplies were gone. All that was left was what they had managed to tie to their bodies, and a pack containing Saliana's medicines that had fortuitously been pinned down by some fallen rocks.

Little Wolf trotted to the opening of their cave, now running vertically instead of horizontally due to the rolling of the huge rock, and raised his snout to the air. Satisfied, he trotted back to the group. He danced excitedly before them, whining urgently.

"Grab what weapons are left t' ye," Rewn jerked his sword scabbard from some the rocks where the wind had lodged it.

"'Tis time."

"No' without Mayvin!" Aneida snarled defiantly.

I am fine now. The wind knocked me out.

Saliana, still crouched beside her, looked at Mayvin sternly. "Ye should stay here and recover. 'Tis safe. Ye need no' come with us. Ye have done enough."

Rewn knelt at her other side. "Listen t' Saliana, Mayvin."

Quit treating me as an invalid! Mayvin's hands slashed violently through the air, registering her ire, before she pushed to her feet. *Are ye coming or not?* She glared down at them both.

Aneida nodded approvingly. "Tell me if ye need rest!"

Saliana dusted off her hands, as she stood and shouldered her medical bag with a disapproving sigh. "Ye are both crazy."

They crawled out of their shelter, and into a world transformed. Like newly created beings emerging from a womb, they blinked blurrily, in awe of the beautiful, golden sunshine that Catrian's storm had left in its wake. The night-blighted island steamed in the new warmth, as it began to evaporate the cold, dank water that had pooled for centuries within the stones.

Saliana lifted her arms, and did a small jig, letting the daylight wash over her, and sobbed a laugh. The sound broke the tethers on all their emotions, and within seconds they were all hugging and laughing, bouncing and jumping wildly with joy. The long night was over. The Bleak was no more.

CHAPTER TEN

They followed Little Wolf in a ragged line, gaping at the destruction wrought by Catrian's storm. They had to pick their footing carefully as they trekked through shattered boulders, for steam from evaporating water cloaked the ground in undulating pools of mist - a thin remainder of the deep fog of the Bleak. The rising humidity made breathing difficult, and they were soon stripping their woolens, as sweat burst forth on brows, and dampened shirts.

Trifyn chortled as he pulled off his heavy overcoat, and left it in a mildewed heap on the ground behind as they walked on. "Did ye e'er believe ye would be warm again?"

Dotch looked back at the coat, an island in a pond of white mist, and then at Trifyn. "Ye should no' be so quick t' leave that behind. The night may be chill, and ye will be thankful enough for its heat then."

The young bowman frowned, and then jogged back to retrieve it.

The island was eerie and still, no bird song, no insects, and no movement from creatures great or small other than themselves. The quiet clank of weapons, and their scuffing footfalls, disturbed the perfect silence, and had them on high alert, unable to believe that they were the only beings to have survived the storm.

"How can we be sure that all the Deathren are dead?" Aneida whispered.

"We can no'," Dotch answered her grimly. "But they will no' show themselves in daylight, so we are safe enough for now. We follow Little Wolf t' the portal o' the labyrinth, and the Gods willing, we have no' missed our opportunity, for truly, do any o' us know the exact day?" Shrugs answered him from all around.

Little Wolf, who had been ranging ahead of them, crossing back and forth across their trail to pick up any stray scents, halted. His head lowered aggressively, and his ruff rose high, as a dirty growl escaped his throat. Slowly, step-by-step, he stalked forward, his nose pointing at a danger only he could sense.

Quietly drawing his sword, Rewn nodded to the others to do the same.

Fingering his throwing knives, Jord crept after Little Wolf on quiet feet. "Whatever it is, the Wolf does no' like it!" he mouthed.

"Could be a Stalker or a Deathren. They dig themselves a hole and crawl into it when they get caught in sunlight," Dotch whispered. "This one may have already been napping when the storm arrived."

"Spread out and ring Little Wolf. We will attack on all sides!" Rewn hissed.

As quietly as possible, they spread out in a half ring, and converged on the spot Little Wolf growled at. The ground could not be seen clearly because of the shifting vapors from the evaporation of water. The creature's lair could be anywhere.

Little Wolf's hackles rose higher. His growl became loud and harsh, as he gathered himself for a lunge.

"Stupid animal!" Aneida bit out fearfully between gritted teeth. "There is nothing there!" She adjusted the grip on her sword with her sweating hands.

"There is something." Rewn promised. He had been around the wolfdog enough to trust its instincts implicitly.

His eyes swung back and forth, as he scanned the ground in front of them. "There!" Rewn whispered as the fog eddied to reveal a large shape. Wildly thrusting out with his blade, he winced at the sound of metal ringing off of rock. It was only a large boulder.

"Maybe 'tis under that rock?" Dotch swiped at the sweat dripping into his eyes. The perspiration was equal parts fear, heat and humidity. "Here!" Dotch motioned to the men. "Help me shift it."

The men put their backs to the stone and with one grunting heave, rolled the boulder away.

Little Wolf yelped as the rock bounced towards him, and bounded back several steps, before circling forward on cautions paws. His head bobbed in agitation, as he growled and whined with fearful urgency at a spot on the ground now revealed by the moved stone.

"Is it dead?" Saliana whispered hopefully.

"No," Jord muttered. "It has dug deeply." He took a prudent step back.

Trifyn stomped his foot on the place where the boulder had

lain. "Feels like loose gravel. Something definitely dug this up recently."

"I do no' think ye should do that," Rewn cautioned.

Trifyn scuffed his boots across the dirt once more. "Why no'? I thought we wanted it t' come out o' its hole." He squinted cockily in the bright sunlight.

"Do no' be a fool, lad!" Dotch growled, grabbed the younger man by the shoulders, and hauled him back out of the shallow depression left by the boulder.

Just as Dotch pulled Trifyn back, a virulent green ball of fire burst from the ground, sending them all scattering for cover. More fireballs followed, raining down upon their hiding places, seeking them out through the power of the Stalker's magic. The ground shook from the force of the explosions, and thunder roared in their ears. Deadly shrapnel from shattered stones blew through the air, as they scrambled back and fourth in a lethal game of hide and seek that they could not ultimately win.

"Dotch!" Trifyn gasped contritely. "I am so sorry! What have I unleashed upon us?"

"It was no' ye, lad! Watch out!" Dotch yelled, as they sprang away from their cover, narrowly avoiding the deadly barrage of magic. "It knew we were here all along! It but awaited its opportunity t' attack!"

"Retreat!" Aneida shouted.

"No!" Rewn countered with a roar of his own. "If we do no' take care o' it here and now, we will only have it on our arses tonight when the advantage will be all its own!"

"How do we kill it?" Trifyn yelled.

"I do no' know!" Rewn dove behind a rock. "Dotch?" he bellowed, his mouth muffled by dirt.

"Do no' look t' me! I have no' a fiddler's fart o' an idea!"

"Well somebody better think o' something fast!" Saliana squealed, slapping at her cloak where it had caught on fire from a near miss.

The fireballs abruptly ceased to belch forth from the ground, as a wind dervish arose from nowhere, and settled neatly over the entombed Stalker. Dirt and rocks sucked upwards into the vortex, whirling tighter and tighter, as the wind churned away the Stalker's protection. The ground mist and debris gave the small funnel a ghostly appearance.

Huddled behind their rocks, the company held still with fear, certain that this was a new magic from the Stalker, readying to destroy them. But as suddenly as it had appeared, the wind moved off a pace or two and dissolved, showering the ground with the rocks and sand that it had collected.

The Stalker loosed a terrible, blood-curdling scream from the exposed pit, and there was a loud detonation, as it caught fire. The flames roared high into the air, then vanished, leaving a thick oily stench wafting away with the breeze from the ocean.

"What the Gods was that?" Trifyn gulped, as he stood up from behind his boulder. Caution shadowed his every move, lest this be a trick of the Stalker's.

"Stay where ye are!" Rewn motioned the others back, as they uncurled from their various hiding spots. "I will look." He received no arguments from his companions.

The hole was burnt black around the edges, and thick smoldering smoke still billowed from within. Swallowing heavily, keeping his body as far from the pit as possible, Rewn craned his neck and took a peek, flinching back before his eyes had even registered that the danger was over.

"You looked as though you could use some help," an amused voice commented.

Rewn recoiled, scattering tiny pebbles in all directions before he got control of his heartbeat. Then he grinned and laughed out loud, as he turned to greet his friend with a tight hug. "Ye are late, Gralyre!"

The others cried out in welcome, as they emerged from hiding, circling Gralyre and thumping him on the back.

Little Wolf galloped up, and threw himself at Gralyre's chest. With a grunt Gralyre withstood the assault, unable to stop laughing as, with paws on his shoulders, Little Wolf began to lick him under the chin.

Gralyre dug his hands deep in the wolfdog's ruff, shaking Little Wolf back and forth with mock fierceness.

Little Wolf keened, and panted contentedly before dropping to all fours, leaning his body solidly against Gralyre's legs, determined to stay near.

"Where have ye been?" Rewn laughed in delight. "We all thought ye dead!"

Aneida's voice held a note of remembered pain. "We heard the Deathren, night after night and then they stopped!"

Gralyre's face sobered. "The Demon Lords have a castle overlooking the valley of the portal. I could not take the chance that any of Doaphin's creatures would be able to take shelter there from the storm, so I made as much magical noise as I could to draw them out. It worked!"

"But they howled for days! How were ye able t' evade them?" Saliana questioned shyly.

Gralyre's mouth quirked. "Strategy, sword and sorcery," he answered mysteriously, and hugged her tightly.

For once Saliana did not shy away from the attention. "I am glad ye are safe!" she hugged him back fiercely.

Trifyn touched his arm. "What o' the Demon Lords? Were they in their castle?"

Gralyre grinned. "We need not worry about them. The storm took care of that for us."

"Ye did the right thing, lad," Dotch pronounced approvingly, "But I for one would like t' know how ye survived the storm!"

Gralyre grimaced at the reminder of what it had cost Catrian, and his levity fell from him like a discarded cloak. His friendly charm disappeared and he became the hard warrior, fixated upon the task ahead. "I will tell you all when we reach the portal. Come then! We have a sword to collect! The Solstice is almost upon us."

෨ඁ

No longer fearing to meet Stalkers or Deathren, Gralyre lead them directly to the main road that ran from the beachhead for the ferry from Elevor, to the Demon Rider cages that protected the portal, and beyond to the far side of the valley and the Demon Lord castle.

Soon after finding the road from the rocky beach, they entered a winding narrow pass in a cliff, just wide enough for two carts to pass. The red rock walls hemmed the road on both sides, prompting Jord to whistle, and suggest, "'Twould make a great spot for an ambush." The offhand comment had them all sneaking glances upwards thereafter, searching for movement within the rocks at the top of the canyon.

After almost a mile the road exited the narrow pass, and the world and sky expanded outwards over the valley of the portal. The circular depression was at least a quarter of a mile across, and at the exact centre stood the entrance to the labyrinth. "There it is," Gralyre murmured to himself, as much as to the others.

Mayvin tapped Aneida in her excitement. *Look! The Portal to the labyrinth! We did it!*

Glowing and sparkling in the sunlight, the gate stood miraculously untouched at the center of the iron cages, scoured clean of centuries of grime by Catrian's storm. It was a bright point of pure radiance amid the ugly metal prisons.

Gralyre grinned at their expressions, as they gaped at their first view of the cages, the glowing portal, and the ruins of the Demon Lord castle across the valley from them, now little more than a pile of rubble strewn across the basin.

"What o' the Demon Lords?" Dotch asked, his eyes busy searching for threats amid the ruins.

Gralyre surveyed the destruction with hands on his hips, and his legs spread wide in challenge. "I have sensed no magic at work since the storm ceased. As near as I can tell, all three Demon Lords were crushed when the castle fell. As I said before, the Demon Lords no longer present a problem."

Smiles began to emerge, and an almost giddy excitement gripped them, as they truly began to believe that they could accomplish what no man had in three hundred years.

As one, they started down the hill into the basin. Massive red cliffs, like the one they had just exited, ringed the circular depression, walls of stone that had been folded upwards and shoved away from the center by some cataclysmic impact of ages past. Striations ran from summit to ground, as though ancient dragons had sharpened their claws there, leaving deep furrows in the rock faces.

From their vantage point, as they walked down the hill, they could clearly see the cross pattern in which the immense cages were set, and the glowing portal at the centre that they protected.

"Are ye sure that is the entrance? Where is the labyrinth? That archway leads t' nowhere!" A note of betrayal clouded Jord's voice. "What if the real portal is actually inside the castle, and 'tis now buried?"

Aneida slapped him lightly across the chest with the back of her hand. "Calm down," she advised when Jord glared her way. "Ye know that the way is only open one day a year. Wait 'til the

Solstice, then ye will see our labyrinth!"

Jord's knives flipped out then vanished. "How do we know we have no' already missed the date?"

"We did not miss it," Gralyre reassured, "otherwise the cages would be empty of Demon Riders. They would already be in the labyrinth searching for the sword."

The cages, crammed full of 'Riders only days ago, were now mostly vacant. Packed together, shoulder to shoulder, they had been left to rot until they were released into the labyrinth on the day of the Solstice. Almost half of the prisoners had already turned Deathren due to the horrendous conditions that they had been subjected to. These Deathren had been obliterated in the killing rays of the sun upon the passing of the destructive maelstrom. Only a few hundred 'Riders wandered aimlessly around their pens now, survivors who had not been killed by Catrian's storm,

The group walked down onto the flat of the basin, and it was only a few hundred yards further on to the stinking pens. The ground-mists had finally burned off in the growing heat of the spring day, and they could clearly see the challenge that they now faced.

Saliana gagged and clapped a hand over her nose, pinching her nostrils. "Gods! That smell. It canno' all be them," she referred to the cages.

Gralyre shook his head. "No. 'Tis coming from the labyrinth, I think."

"There is no labyrinth," Rewn reasoned, breathing through

his mouth. "No' yet."

Dotch eyed the terrain. "Three hundred years o' failure... All those dead 'Riders have t' be somewhere. Think o' it. Millions o' bodies, just out o' sight."

Saliana made another gagging sound.

Rewn cleared his throat. "How are we t' reach the portal with those cages o' 'Riders guarding the way?"

"And where should we make camp?" Dotch added.

"We solve both problems at once," Gralyre decided grimly. "We will camp in the square bound by the cages, next to the portal. I want no more obstacles to our entrance!"

"In this stench?" Aneida protested.

"Ye will get use t' it," Jord advised. "Just breath through your mouth, and it will no' be so bad."

'Tis strong enough to taste, Mayvin signed, as her face scrunched in disgust.

"We can fight our way through the emptiest cage," Dotch suggested. "That one!" he advised after a moment's study.

He pointed at the cage nearest to them then motioned Trifyn forward. "Ready your bow, lad. Best t' shoot them from afar rather than risk ourselves without cause."

Trifyn licked lips gone dry. "Can we no' just climb over the top o' the cage, or better yet why no' just climb where the corners meet? 'Twould be faster."

Dotch shook his head. "We would ne'er reach the centre, no' with their long pikes poking us in the guts as we tried."

The Demon Riders had a surplus of weaponry to choose

from, left behind by those who had perished in flames upon the exposure to the sunlight. The one thing they did not have were bows, probably to keep them from trying to kill their Demon Lord jailers.

"We would have t' kill two cages then, to climb the corners." Rewn's eyes were narrowed against the sun as he considered the prisoners who had armed themselves at their approach.

"But it will be a slaughter!" Trifyn protested.

"That is the idea!" Jord grabbed Trifyn impatiently by the scruff and propelled him into position. "They would do worse t' us," he reminded harshly. He stepped back, one of his knives appearing magically in his hand. "They are lucky we do no' have time t' play!" Jord bared his teeth in a feral smile.

Trifyn shuddered, and reluctantly pulled his bow from his back, fumbling to string it with shaking hands, when the group knew that he could do it quicker on the darkest night with his eyes shut.

Trifyn had killed before - in battle, and to protect his friends, but never as a wholesale slaughter of penned prisoners.

Gralyre recognized that Trifyn was wavering, and placed a hand on the lad's shoulder, halting his preparations with his bow. "What do you think they will do to us if we enter that cage with the odds as they are now? Two or three hundred, to our eight?" Gralyre asked firmly. "We must defeat them all to win through to the portal."

"I know," Trifyn whispered, sweat breaking upon his brow.

Aneida's face tightened, and she turned away. Rewn

swallowed hard, and became interested in a loose thread upon his sleeve. They well remembered the day their innocence was stripped, and replaced with the hardened will to survive at all costs. This was a journey that Trifyn needed to make on his own, and it was painful to watch.

Gralyre squeezed Trifyn's shoulder encouragingly. "This is a war, Trifyn, one such has never been fought. There are no treaties to be made, no flags of truce. These creatures exist only to kill us, to kill mankind. We are fighting for the very survival of our species!"

Gralyre roughly turned Trifyn to face the cages. "Do you see them, Trifyn?" he asked harshly. "Look at them!"

Trifyn quivered from the stress of the moment. "Of course I can see them," he mumbled.

"War is ugly and cruel, and there is nothing noble or heroic about it. There is only survival. When you see an opportunity to attack, you take it! Then you thank the Gods of Fortune if any of your own still live!"

Trifyn ducked out from under Gralyre's touch, turning away and passing a hand over his eyes. "But they are just helpless in there. I... I do no' think that I can do this!

Jord snorted, a sound of infinite disgust.

Gralyre's mouth compressed, and he silenced Jord with a hard glare before addressing Trifyn once more. "If it helps, think of yourself as the first charge, Trifyn. Because we are so few, we must act with the courage and resolve of many."

"Then why do ye no' use your magic! If we need t' attack

from afar why must it be by my bow? Where is your magic now?" Trifyn was backed into a corner, and lashed out at the injustice of it.

Gralyre stared at the younger man, not angered by his outburst for he could well understand what Trifyn was going through. His calm midnight-blue gaze fixed the lad in place. "I doubt I have enough magic left in me to move a grain of sand."

For the first time, the others noticed the pallor under the grime of Gralyre's face, and that his wide legged stance had more to do with balance than swagger. Even as they watched he seemed to sag.

"Gralyre! I am a fool! I did no' see," Rewn berated himself, taking Gralyre's arm to steady him towards a boulder to sit.

"All I need is a good night's sleep," Gralyre replied, gently shaking Rewn's arm away. Gralyre's attention returned to Trifyn. "And so it falls to you." Gralyre may have been exhausted but that did not diminish his commanding presence.

Trifyn nodded, shamed by Gralyre's courage and devotion to the group that had pitted him alone for days against roving bands of Stalkers and Deathren. Trifyn could make no less of a sacrifice than that.

His quivering jaw firmed, as he accepted the truth of Gralyre's words. This was no heroic bard's tale of old battles, this was real, it was ugly, and there was no honour in it. The caged 'Riders had to be put to death in order for them to reach the portal. To not take the opportunity to even the odds was to put his companions at risk, and destroy the best chance to get the sword that men had had in centuries!

He wiped his sweating palms against his tunic, then unshouldered his quiver and removed the arrows, stabbing them point first into the ground for easy accessibility. He had not many left, for the maelstrom had stolen most of them away. "Ten. That is no' enough, we will still be too outnumbered t' fight our way through."

Dotch rubbed his hands together. "Everyone spread out. See if ye can find what is left o' the armoury of the castle. We need more arrows."

Within the hour, Trifyn had eight full reams of arrows at his feet, giving him two hundred targets to seek. Muffling his conscience for what he must do, he plucked an arrow from the ground, fit it to the string, and sighted down the shaft. He had chosen a location near the cages so he would not need much elevation for his arrows to hit their marks, which would make it easier to shoot between the bars. His concentration narrowed, and he adjusted his aim to the slight buffeting of the now tame breeze.

With a deep-throated note of death, the string thrummed and the arrow released. Without waiting to see it hit its mark, Trifyn notched another arrow and let fly, then another. Three arrows were in flight before the first slipped between the iron bars, and buried itself in a red-coated chest. The small group watched as a Demon Rider fell.

"Nice shot," Jord murmured.

The Demon Riders in the cage did not notice the first of the deaths, still disoriented by the sudden sunlight after months in the dark. But when two others dropped with wooden shafts protruding from their hearts, howling pandemonium erupted. The 'Riders began to run, around and back and forth within the cages, trying to escape the lethal barrage raining down upon them. One by one, they perished.

Trifyn did not stop, until all of the arrows had been spent. Then he hung his head, breathing harshly, as he massaged the aching muscles of his drawing arm. No one commented on the wetness of tears on his face.

"That leaves...twenty or so," Gralyre quickly counted the remaining enemy. With a harsh scrape, his sword left its sheath. Like a deadly echo, the others did likewise.

"Good job, Trifyn," Jord approached the bowman, flipping a knife expertly and hypnotically over and over in his hands. "Now we have a chance!" Jord slapped him on the back.

Trifyn shied away, "Do no' touch me!" he snarled. He staggered to a stone and retched until nothing more would come.

Saliana pressed a water skin into his hands when he was finished.

Trifyn took a deep swig, and when he finally turned to face the group, they were shocked at the change to his face. The happy-go-lucky youth had disappeared into the hard, cynical eyes of a warrior.

Trifyn considered his bow, as if it were a serpent, as if it had only now revealed its true and lethal purpose - where before his skills had been just a proud game. He shivered once, as though fevered, then with quick, efficient motions, unstrung his bow and placed it back in its special sheath across his back. He drew his short sword. "I am ready," he announced.

Gralyre lead them through the rubble of the destroyed castle towards the Demon Rider cage, where two hundred of the enemy now rotted in the sunlight.

৪৩৫৪

NORTHERN REBEL FORTRESS

"Boris!" Matik called out, as he lifted the flap and entered Catrian's tent.

Boris jerked in his chair, set near the hot brazier, startled out of his nap by Matik's sudden arrival, and rubbed a tired hand over his blurry eyes. "What is it," he asked quietly, glancing pointedly towards the curtained partition that hid the comatose Sorceress from their view.

Obligingly, Matik lowered his voice. "Boris," his hoarse whisper was only slightly quieter than his usual booming voice. "Huntsmen who have returned from the forest say that something is amiss. The woods are too quiet, and the game has fled!" Disquiet had been snaking up Matik's spine for some days, ever since Catrian had fallen to the Stalker. The return of the Huntsmen had only confirmed his instincts. Something was amiss, something much worse than just Catrian's illness.

Boris nodded to the chair set opposite to his own, and Matik flung himself down, and leaned forward urgently with his arms resting along his thighs. "Men who have been scouting these forests since their birth are afraid t' leave the palisade walls, and three hunting parties have no' returned."

"Deserters?"

Matik shrugged. "Perhaps... but the outposts have no' reported men attempting t' flee the valley through the passes." Matik's gaze lowered to where his hands clasped. "The Huntsmen believe the missing men are dead."

Boris was silent for a long considering moment. "Do ye trust these Huntsmen? Is their judgment sound?"

"They are no' men prone t' the irrational. If they say there is something dangerous in the forest, I believe them. I would no' have bothered ye otherwise. And there is something..."

"What is it, my friend? Do no' hold back. Tell me what ye sense."

"I am no' sure. The fortress feels different. Perhaps 'tis only the eve o' war, but men cease t' speak upon my approach, and scatter. And something else is bothering me."

"What?"

"How did the Stalker that attacked Catrian enter the valley without destroying the sentry posts and raising an alarm?"

Boris was silent for a moment. "Perhaps it came o'er the mountains, and no' through the passes?"

Matik patted his beard thoughtfully, "Mayhap." His mind chewed on the problem with slavish tenacity. He could only remember a handful of times in the past that he had ever felt this disquieting premonition.

Boris leaned back in his chair. "Do ye believe that there is another Stalker in the valley? Is that what killed the missing Huntsmen?"

Matik shrugged. "Could be." It still did not quite fit.

"What word from the sentries at the passes?"

"All clear, as o' this morning."

"Did the runners get away?"

"Yes," Matik stated. "I saw them off this morning."

The runners made for the lowland rendezvous at Dapochar to inform the Generals of Catrian's illness. Boris had awaited Catrian's recovery for as long as he dared, but now time had run out, and they marched at dawn to meet Kierdenan to whom Boris would bring word of her illness personally. Catrian would remain behind with a healer, and a small contingent of men for protection, to recover or die as by the will of the Gods.

On the eve of war, the Commander would not see his people demoralized by a threat of danger. "Ensure that the gates are still sealed. Double the men along the walls. Tell them t' keep their eyes and swords sharp!" Boris snapped out the orders.

Matik pushed up from his chair, saluted his commander, and strode out into the drizzle that had begun the day. It was good to see a glimpse of the decisive old Boris. Since Catrian's illness, he had been looking too tired, too defeated. The men needed to see Boris strong for 'twas his courage that would augment their own.

It was not enough to see the fortress secure. Matik could not dispel the sense of something worse in the wind. Going on instinct, he began to send warriors scurrying. "Get those children t' the centre o' the camp!" he ordered at an old warrior who was walking past with a load of firewood with several grandchildren cavorting about his legs.

"I want ten more warriors guarding these wagons. Twenty more at the gate! Check the fire buckets are ready!" Within a remarkably short space of time, Matik had people running back and forth across the fortress in controlled chaos.

As warriors arrived at their assigned posts, an air of tension gripped them, and not a little confusion. Were they not to march in the morning, and here they were preparing to defend against an attack?

For the remainder of the day they waited while nothing happened. Matik paced the walk around the top of the walls, goaded by his sense of impending doom, while the men muttered their discontent, as he passed from range of hearing.

Then finally, a shout came from the walls. "Someone is coming! To the eastern gate!"

The message relayed itself quickly to Matik's ears. He sent a runner for Boris, as he jogged around the wall walk to the watchtower of the east gate.

"There sir," a young lookout pointed. Just inside the tree line at the bottom of the ravine stood a man, carrying the white flag of messenger.

"Has he parlayed his dispatch yet?" Matik snapped.

"No, sir. He has just been standing there!"

Boris appeared beside them atop the wall. "What is it?"

"A messenger!" Matik murmured. "But why does he no' approach?" Even as he asked the question, the messenger hoisted his flag and walked into the open. It took him a short time to wind up the switchback trail to reach shouting distance of the gates. The man had obviously been awaiting the Commander's appearance.

"He is staying low o' bow-range," Boris pointed out grimly. Before the messenger began to speak, Boris already suspected what was to come.

"Speak and be heard!" Matik yelled the customary greeting. "No harm will come t' ye."

"I speak with General Kierdenan's voice. Harken! Boris Kinsel, I have decided that ye are no longer fit t' lead. I give fair notice as an honourable man, that I will engage ye in battle tomorrow for the right t' the leadership o' the resistance, and the right t' control the sorceress, the lady Catrian!" Having delivered his declaration of war, the herald fled back down the trail, and into the woods.

Boris and Matik's gazes clashed. "Kierdenan would no' be brave enough t' try this..." Matik began.

"...unless he knew that Catrian was no' a threat!" Boris finished Matik's sentence.

"How could he have known Catrian was ill? He canno' be here! He should be travelling t' meet with us at Hondor's Pass!"

Boris gazed steadily after the departed herald. "Because the demon-humping bastard was already here! He intercepted our runners. Our outposts have fallen. That is why there was no word o' the Stalker passing into our valley."

Matik turned woodenly, and followed Boris down off the wall walk. The enormity of the betrayal held him silent in shock.

"Likely he had intended to ambush us as we marched from the valley tomorrow," Boris snarled out over his shoulder, "and news of Catrian's illness has now made him bold."

"If Kierdenan has captured or killed all o' our runners, it means that the other Generals will no' know o' Catrian's illness. If we are late to the lowland rendezvous, they will think we have deserted them. What can we do?" Matik asked, lengthening his stride to match his commander's.

"One problem at a time, General." Commander Boris spared him a sideways glance, his face florid with rage. "Prepare for battle!"

CHAPTER ELEVEN

FENNICK'S ISLAND

Pikes stabbed out from within the cage, as Gralyre grabbed the padlock on the iron door and rattled it to see if he could snap the catch open.

Jord's knifes flipped between the bars, and three 'Riders dropped. The others scurried back, no longer eager to challenge the men and women about to storm their prison. Rewn, Dotch and Aneida took up flanking positions to ensure that no other Demon Rider neared as they worked to open the cage.

Rewn threw his weight against the gate experimentally to try to spring the hasp. Some scale flaked off, but the metal was strongly forged and fastened. They could not open it without a key and, no doubt, the only key to the lock was owned by the resident Demon Lords, now buried beneath tons of rock in the collapsed fortress. "Now what?" he asked over the screaming cacophony from the inhabitants of the other three cages. Offal and rocks pelted down amongst them, but the angle was difficult for the throwers and the missiles were easily avoided.

Gralyre breathed out heavily, swaying from the expenditure of strength that he did not have, and grasped the bars of the cage for support.

"Gralyre!" Rewn banded an arm about Gralyre's waist to

keep him from slumping further.

"I have not slept in while," Gralyre shrugged, as he allowed Rewn to prop him against the bars to rest. "Can anyone pick a lock?" He joked tiredly, as he scanned the faces of the group.

Jord walked forward, and peered at the padlock. "I could open this on a dark night with my eyes closed," he snorted derisively.

Aneida rolled her eyes. "How did I just know ye would be the one?"

Jord grinned at her taunt, and pulled a sliver-thin dagger from within his jerkin. His eyes took on a faraway glaze, as he slid it into the keyhole, and probed delicately. With a squeal of rusted disuse, the padlock opened, and Jord pulled it free of the hasp, swinging the door open with a flourish and a bow.

The Demon Riders rushed the door, more interested in freedom than stopping the company from invading. The skirmish was fierce and bloody but quickly finished, for the 'Riders were weak and diseased from their time of captivity.

Gralyre felt no pity for the creatures, only fierce gladness that they were dead and his people were safe. Now that the way was clear, they needed only to pass through the second gate at the back of the cage to reach the central square, and the portal to the labyrinth.

"Gralyre, should we behead the corpses?" Aneida asked as she prodded a bloodied red uniform with the toe of her boot.

Save your arm. Let the sun take them in the morning, Mayvin advised.

Gralyre nodded his concurrence. "Mayvin is right. Let them turn, then let them burn," he advised coldly. "Jord, reattach the lock so the Deathren cannot escape onto the island tonight."

Jord retrieved the lock, and snapped it closed at the gate they had just passed through, locking them in.

Gralyre passed a hand over his eyes to erase the grit of exhaustion. When he reopened them, Saliana had joined him.

She handed him the water skin. "I would offer ye food, for I suspect ye have no' eaten since ye left us, but the storm took the supplies. This is all we have."

"Thank-you." Gralyre tipped the skin to his mouth, allowing only a trickle, as there was little water sloshing within.

"Look out!"

Precious water spilled down his chin, as he spun to confront the attack. A 'Rider had risen alive from the heaps of the dead, and was rushing them. Gralyre thrust Saliana behind him, but had no time to draw his sword. His reactions were sluggish from exhaustion.

A breeze slapped his cheek, as an arrow passed by, and thudded into the creature's chest, the force throwing it back to lie dead amongst the other corpses. Gralyre glanced over his shoulder at a white faced Trifyn holding his released bow, the string of which was still quivering.

Gralyre nodded to the bowman. "Thank-you." He turned back to the others. "Be careful, there could be more." After the near miss, the group picked their way more carefully through the masses of dead to investigate how they were to exit the far side of the cage.

The exit door to the centre square was as securely padlocked as the outside gate had been. Gralyre imagined that a key would be thrown to the starving troops, allowing them to exit into the centre square, and from there into the labyrinth, perhaps with a promise of food if they returned victorious with the sword in the evening.

The others waited expectantly, as Jord produced his lock-pick. Holding it skillfully within his forefingers, he probed gently at the padlock. "Ah!" He smiled in triumph, as there came a loud click. With a strong twist of his wrist, and a rasp of rusted metal, the lock fell free, making a sucking sound, as it struck the muck and offal of the cage's floor.

"Nice touch," Aneida complemented him, as she and Saliana helped Mayvin through the open gate.

Jord flipped his knife in a snazzy display, and it vanished magically back up his sleeve. "Locks are no' the only things I am good at opening," he flashed her a dazzling, meaningful smile.

Aneida's eyes narrowed to slits, and her free hand dropped to caress her sword pommel. "Thieves are like t' end up with their hands lopped off," she murmured with lazy menace, as she walked past with Mayvin draped between her and Saliana.

Jord heard a loud snicker, and turned to glare at Dotch, Trifyn and Rewn, trying to pinpoint who had made the jesting noise. While Rewn and Trifyn tried valiantly to suppress their mirth, Dotch, older and wiser, ushered them quickly past the fuming knifeman.

Jord turned his glare on the only one remaining. Gralyre returned the look flatly but something in the back of his eyes danced with hilarity.

"Ye got something ye want t' say?" Jord muttered, hostility straining the muscles of his neck.

"No. Not a thing," Gralyre promised, utterly deadpan. Little Wolf sneezed from the filthy muck of the cage, and danced past the two men into the cleaner square containing the archway. Gralyre followed after, a smile twitching about his mouth that he dared not allow the prickly Jord to witness.

The square was empty save for the softly glowing archway. It was an eerie site; a doorframe leading to nowhere that seemed to collect the sunlight and reflect it back threefold.

Gralyre approached the portal, and trailed his hand across the surface of the left side jamb. Unlike the stones that made up the valley, the doorway was carved from a single block of white alabaster. Every surface was etched with the runes of an ancient language that Gralyre was unable to decipher, but as he touched the figures they writhed under his fingertips, warm as though alive. Light moved beneath the surface of the stone, circling and swirling around the runes.

Rewn joined him with a low whistle. "Now is that no' something t' see?" He clapped Gralyre on the back with a grin. "We did it. We are here. We made it!"

Gralyre nodded with a grim smile. "Now for the hard part," he joked darkly.

Rewn snorted, and looked through the portal at the full cages of Demon Riders that were screaming and taunting them. "Should we kill the rest, put them out of their misery?"

Gralyre shrugged tiredly. "'Tis a pointless waste of effort to risk our lives further when they pose no threat. They have no arrows, and no ability to reach us. The Demon Lords built their cages well. Starving the way they are, they would have escaped long before now, had it been possible."

The storm's fury had killed many 'Riders, whose corpses had served to alleviate the rapacious appetites of the rest. Still the prisoners eyed the small band, as they would a sumptuous feast. Many threw taunts and insults, as well as litter and debris from the cage floors, trying to lure the humans near enough to the bars to grab.

Eventually, their sickness and weakness caused them to tire of the game, leaving them glaring sullenly at the small troop that had won its way through to the archway. There were only sporadic outbursts after that, a way to alleviate boredom more than to incite a fight.

Night fell gently over the island, and for once the darkness did not herald the familiar oppression, for the beloved stars twinkled down from far above.

The constellation called the Eyes of the Gods of Fortune reminded Gralyre of a night long ago, after he had awakened as a stranger to himself. Since then, he had worked to carve a life with the Rebels, but in the end he had failed, and it had only led here, to an impossible quest for a sword that had belonged to a

Prince.

However difficult it had been to win a path through to the entrance to Fennick's labyrinth, Gralyre could not escape the knowledge that in three hundred years, not one of the millions of troops that Doaphin had sent through this portal had ever returned.

If they failed in their quest there would be no one to tell the tale, and the world would never know how near they had come to success, that they had made it all the way to the portal, and had not perished in the Bleak under the talons of a Stalker. And should this be humanity's last gasp of life, as Doaphin began the war to end all wars, then there would also be no one left behind to hear of it. It was a disquieting notion.

They camped in darkness except for the gentle radiance emanating from the archway. The night was not chill, but the hideous odour of the Demon Rider cages, and rotting graveyard hidden away beyond the empty portal, the shrill screams of the newly animated Deathren, and the sporadic catcalls and threats from the three occupied cages, kept them all far from the land of restful dreams.

Awake and tense, they sat in a tight circle for a time, and discussed their plans for the morrow in hushed voices that would not carry to the three cages that still held living prisoners.

"Will it be tomorrow do ye think," Trifyn asked, "or the day after?"

Jord's knives flipped out and back, moving restlessly. "It had better be tomorrow, for we are out o' food, and those 'Riders do no' look edible."

"Pray that tomorow is the Solstice," Gralyre corrected sternly. "The high waves from the storm will keep the ferry from Elevor from crossing to the island tonight but by tomorrow that will have changed. We can expect reinforcements to arrive."

"They will be too late," Trifyn replied. "We will already be in the labyrinth."

"Maybe," Rewn cautioned. "If tomorrow is the Solstice."

"It will no' matter. Inside the labyrinth or no', they will surely be awaiting us when we emerge," Dotch predicted.

"If we emerge," Jord muttered under his breath. The others pretended not to hear.

"Any force will have t' come through the cages just as we did, through the locked gates," Aneida calculated.

"What if they have the keys?" Trifyn asked nervously. "They would have all the troops they needed by emptying the cages at us!"

"Opening the locks takes time, even with a key." Aneida mused. "Ye will be able t' shoot the 'Riders as they try. Plus, a couple o' people could hold the door t' the labyrinth against many if the Demon Riders try t' follow us through the portal," Aneida exchanged a long look with Mayvin. "Look at how wide it is. No more than two at a time could come at us, no matter how many were backed up behind them."

Mayvin's fevered eyes glittered hungrily at the thought of killing Demon Riders. She nodded her head, as her hands wove vigorously in agreement. *I will not be able to move quickly in the labyrinth. Better that I should stay here, and guard our retreat.*

"Mayvin and I shall stay outside the labyrinth to protect our retreat," Aneida corrected, holding her sister's hand. "Together," she reminded Mayvin.

Gralyre nodded in agreement, and then added, "Trifyn, you will stay behind with Mayvin and Aneida."

At a note of dissension from the young bowman, Gralyre stated in a tone that did not allow for dispute, "Retrieving the sword will be of no consequence if we cannot win free of this island with it! Your bow will make all the difference against a force attacking through the cages, and no difference at all to the outcome within the labyrinth. You will be their only protection if a Demon Lord joins the battle! He will throw his magic at you from outside the cages, and not risk his neck. Your bow will even out the odds."

"What of me?" Saliana asked, speaking up and surprising all. She was usually so silent that at times her presence was forgotten. But the thought of being parted from Rewn, made her voice quiver with panic. After tomorrow, she might never see him again.

"You have a patient that you must see to," Gralyre reminded her gently.

Saliana's jaw jutted out mulishly. She did not argue, though her eyes strayed fretfully to Rewn time and again after that.

Trifyn threw a small stone into the centre of their circle, his face tense. "Are ye that sure that there will be a retreat? No one has ever returned."

All eyes turned to Gralyre, and he realized that their thoughts had been wheels turning in the same ruts as his, dragging along a cartload of uncertainty.

Gralyre sat straighter and smiled, cold and hard, projecting as much confidence as he was able. "I am sure. None of those who have entered Fennick's labyrinth were human. A wily old sorcerer would ensure that the no creature of Doaphin's would ever reach the prize."

Jord made a rude noise, clinging stubbornly to his pessimism. "Legend says only the Prince can reclaim the Dragon Sword."

Rewn looked up with bright eyes. "Who is t' say that Gralyre is no' the Prince?"

"Rewn..." Gralyre gave a dismissive wave, not wanting a lie to stand between him and the others.

"No," Rewn countered. "I have travelled with ye for almost a year, and o' only one thing am I certain. Ye are no ordinary man."

The others murmured their concurrence.

"I canno' say for certain if ye be good or evil, a prince or a serf, but ye are no' just a man. Ye have greatness within ye. If this is t' be done, ye are the one who will do it."

"We will reach the sword together," Gralyre vowed, touched and humbled by Rewn's faith in him.

By the easing of the faces around the circle, Rewn's faith had infected everyone with some degree of optimism.

Dotch sighed and squinted up at the starry sky. "Whatever tomorrow brings, we need t' rest. We may no' be able t' sleep, but we should at least lie down and try. We do no' want t' challenge the labyrinth exhausted."

After that, they all fell silent. There was nothing left to say, and thoughts of the morning consumed each of them.

Gralyre drifted away from the group to stand beside the glowing pillars of the empty portal. Gently, he traced the runes running through the rockface, unreadable, ancient etchings that moved under his fingertips, assuming new cryptic messages from moment to moment. It painted his face with shifting light as of sunbeams reflected from restless waters.

All that had gone before meant nothing if they did not win the sword. Should he fail, Catrian would be lost forever, locked away in the cold, magical prison of her Wizard Stone. Even were he to recover the sword, it might already be too late to save her.

He dropped down, and propped his back against one of the glowing pillars of the empty archway, finally allowing his exhaustion to rule.

Was she still alive? Would she survive until he could return with the sword? He resisted the urge to reach out with his consciousness for some sense of her, for fear that there would be nothing to find.

Gralyre glanced across the small clearing at his group. Saliana was tending Mayvin's shoulder while Aneida whispered to her sister, distracting her from the pain. Dotch was running a whetstone up the blade of his sword with the rasping regular strokes of a cat cleaning its fur. Jord and Rewn were dicing, and Trifyn was waxing the strings of his bow to prevent them from stiffening in the humidity left in the wake of the storm. Good people. They had come far and endured much; he had to believe they would succeed. They must succeed. For Catrian's sake.

Gralyre stretched out across the threshold of the portal. He closed his eyes, awaiting sunrise with equal parts hope and dread in his heart but sleep was a stranger, despite his exhaustion.

ഇൗരു

NORTHERN REBEL FORTRESS

Boris and Matik walked the wooden planks atop the walls of the Rebel fortress, ensuring that the defenses were ready to withstand Kierdenan's attack in the morning.

"How did it come t' this?" Matik snarled. "Kierdenan has always been ambitious but I would have staked my life that he was a loyal man!"

"The question is, loyal t' whom?" Boris mused grimly.

"What do ye mean? Do ye think that he has crossed over t' Doaphin's camp?" Matik demanded in a startled voice. "Surely, Catrian would have sensed it at the war council."

Boris stopped, and leaned his elbows on the top of the wooden wall between the crenellations, staring into the darkness at the glittering array of lights in the distance that heralded the presence of the enemy they had once called friend.

"Catrian is a person o' her own free will, no' a trained dog t' be leashed and taught tricks," Boris snorted, "as I am more aware o' than most. So I put it t' ye, what does Kierdenan think he will achieve by taking her?"

"He seeks t' become the Commander o' the Rebels. With Catrian gone, and ye gone, there will be none t' naysay him," Matik suggested, as his eyes darted back and forth in time to his thoughts.

"Mayhap..." Boris mused slowly, "...but then why seek t' capture her?" He turned back to the night, the faint light from the stars barely illuminating his profile. "She is ill, defenseless. If he sought her death, now would be the time t' do so! But he does no' want her dead, he wants her for himself. T' what purpose?"

Matik shrugged helplessly. "Maybe he seeks a wife? He has pressed his suit afore."

Boris snorted. "I pity any man foolish enough t' try t' force that woman t' bed or wed." His hands tightened upon the top log of the wall. "And Kierdenan is many things, but a fool? Never. '...the right t' control the pet sorceress.' Those were the herald's exact words!"

Matik growled through his thick beard, "He would no' be able to control her any more than he could control an avalanche or a thunderstorm!"

Boris nodded his agreement, and was silent for so long, that Matik nervously begin to stroke his beard. He could sense that something was brewing in the old man's brain. Whatever it was, he could tell that he was not going to like it.

Boris sighed heavily, his eyes haunted at the betrayal. "I think he hopes t' use her, t' trade her against the lives o' his own people. Instead o' going t' war, and saving as many o' the lowlanders as possible, he seeks t' buy his own skin!"

Matik almost gagged at the thought. "Does he no' realize that Doaphin will make no deals. That Kierdenan, his people, Catrian; they will all die, along with what is left o' our last chance at freedom!"

Boris swung back around to gaze at the amassed campfires flickering in the darkness below the tree line. "I doubt that he has thought the whole matter through, Matik. Kierdenan formed his plan on the march. He has given himself no time for second thoughts."

Boris settled his shoulders before he began to pace along the wall walk again, inspecting the men who stood ready for battle. "We have lost our way, my friend," he threw back over his shoulder at Matik who trailed in his wake. "It used t' be so clear t' us, who was evil and who was good."

Matik had been walking several paces behind the Commander. He glanced up to comment on Boris' bitter words, and spotted movement in the darkness, the glint of a blade. "Boris! Look t' your sword!" Matik gave warning.

Boris spun to face forward, but was not in time to prevent the assassin's knife from piercing his chest. He could vaguely hear Matik's battle roar, as everything went black, and he pitched forward onto the rough planks of the walkway.

As Matik sprang forward to help Boris, several men who had been lounging at their posts moved to block his path. He watched in anguish as his old friend fell.

Then Matik was fighting for his life. "Traitors! Assassins!" He yelled, struggling for room amongst the attacking warriors to draw his axe.

The man who had stabbed Boris gave the Commander's body a hefty kick off the wall walk, sending it soaring into space to drop the twenty feet to the ground.

Matik could see men approaching from across the battlements, but he did not know if they were loyal fortress warriors, or more of Kierdenan's agents. It would not matter, either way. They would not reach him in time. He and Boris had been well and truly ambushed!

Matik was never able to draw his axe. Three men wrestled him to his knees, and he felt the chill of steel pressed to his throat before the hot slice of the blade. As he fell, he could hear across the compound the sounds of battle. Kierdenan had not awaited morning to launch his treacherous attack.

ഇൽ

Dajin and Dara huddled within stacked firewood peering through chinks in the logs, watching soldiers rampage past their hiding place, as neighbour turned upon neighbour. It was madness! An enemy could be wearing the face of your closest friend. Chaos had erupted when General Kierdenan had breached the gates with the aid of his spies.

From somewhere, Dajin could not remember in the kaleidoscope of battle, he thought he had heard someone yell that Commander Boris was dead, and Matik as well. Dajin had quivered with fear, for if such warriors as they could fall, what possible chance did he have to survive? So he had grabbed Dara, to hide away from the fighting as best as they were able.

Though he had promised Rewn that he would keep Dara safe at all costs, the more he thought on it, the more convinced Dajin became that protecting his twin was a coward's choice. A true warrior would not be cowering with a woman, Dajin thought tearfully, he would be in the thick of the fighting!

For a moment, his gaze was drawn back to Dara who cringed beside him, whimpering her fear. She clutched the dagger that Rewn had given to her against her chest, and the whites of her eyes flashed, as she strained to spy what was happening outside.

Dajin listened to the clash of swords, and the screams of bravery without before turning his ears to within. The contrast was deafening; frightened pants of air, whimpers of fear, from Dara *and* from himself.

His terror dissipated like mist in the heat of his vainglorious ego. He was missing it all! Soon it would be over, and he would not have had a chance at the glory! What would be the tale of his brave deeds? That he cowered in a pile of firewood? He knew that if Rewn and Gralyre were here, they would be smiting the enemy. Not hiding! Not they!

Dajin recalled the scorn and disappointment on Rewn's face in the wake of their father's death. His brother had called him a coward when Dajin had told him he wished that Saliana had died upon the slope. Rewn had condemned him again in the ice cave when Dajin had tried to protect the unarmed Matik from Gralyre's traitorous attack.

The disappointment in his brother's eyes haunted Dajin still. Rewn believed Dajin to be a coward, and nothing Dajin could do would ever change that now. Rewn had gone to his death, never having seen his brother in a different light. Dajin ground his teeth to hold back his tears of self-pity.

Well that was not going to happen this time, Dajin vowed. He was through cowering in the shadows while others beat him to the triumph. But what could he do to redeem himself? What would Matik do?

The answer came quickly enough. Matik would protect the Sorceress, especially now when she was too sick to protect herself!

Dajin's sly smile was not pretty. Not only would he win acclaim for a brave act but he would also be well away from the fighting as he did it! In his naïveté, he thought that protecting the Sorceress would be no different than protecting Dara, huddled here in a woodpile.

"I am going!" Dajin decided aloud.

"What? What are ye talking about?" Dara shot back at her twin, breathing in harsh frightened sobs, flinching, as clashing swords sounded nearby. "Going where?"

"I am going t' go get the Sorceress! She is sick, and with Matik and Boris both gone, nobody is going t' look out for her!"

Dara grabbed his arm. "Do no'! 'Tis too dangerous! Stay here with me!"

Here was another who thought him incompetent! Were they all against him? Face twisting in contempt, Dajin threw off Dara's arm. "I can take care o' myself! Besides," he continued, "'tis no' as if I will be fighting! I am just going t' collect her, and bring her back here t' hide with us." He peered outside to be sure that the way was clear.

"Dajin! No! Do no' leave me alone!" Dara begged, as Dajin clambered his way from the pile of wood, dislodging the logs that they had hurriedly stacked around themselves.

"They will no' just let ye walk through the length o' the fortress with the Sorceress slung over your shoulder, and do no' a thing t' stop ye!" Dara yelled at his retreating back, as she frantically reassembled the hidden shelter.

Dajin ignored her. Dodging from shadow to shadow, he crept towards the central square where the tent of the Sorceress was located. Most of the fighting was still concentrated at the east gate where the invading forces had entered, so the journey proved uneventful and anticlimactic to the vainglorious warrior.

Dajin had thought that he could get to Catrian, and return unseen but he arrived to a cluster of fiercely battling men blocking his path into her tent. Dajin faltered in his determination, and ducked behind an overturned cart.

There was no way in without fighting his way through. His hope for acclaim fizzled, and he became what he truly was; a scared young man who never thought of the consequences before he acted.

A battle yell challenged Dajin from behind, as one of

Kierdenan's warriors happened upon him.

Dajin flinched but though he was crouched low, got his sword up to block the attacker's blow from reaching his neck. Unable to stand and fight because of his proximity to the cart, Dajin dropped and rolled instead, taking the warrior by surprise. Tumbling the under the length of the cart, he gained his feet in time to meet his foe's renewed onslaught.

The man outweighed him, and was obviously a veteran of many battles, but a master had taught Dajin to fight. Though he despised Gralyre, he had not been fool enough to disregard the man's lessons. Dajin feinted right, and then left. Seeing the warrior's sword anticipate his next move and twitch right, Dajin went left again, slipped his thrust past the man's surprise, and felt the sickening give of flesh around his sword.

Dajin froze, staring into the warrior's eyes, and watching as the realization that he had been given a deathblow came over him. Horror, rage and grief chased across the warrior's face amid tears of pain that rolled down his cheeks.

Dajin trembled at the realization of what he had done. Taking a life had never seemed to be that big of a deal. He had killed before, killed Demon Riders, and other minions of Doaphin, but this was different in a fundamental way that he had never known before. This was a man. Not an evil man, just a man who's General had thrown him into a fight against his own kind.

With a panicked yowl, Dajin tried to pull his sword free, but it was stuck fast. The warrior screamed in pain, lashing out with the weapon that he still held. Dajin could do nothing but take the blow, but the warrior was weak, and his sword had shifted in his bloody grasp so that it was the flat of the blade that struck Dajin's face, cracking open the skin across his cheek but doing little other damage. His foe drew back for another try.

In a fit of fear born strength, Dajin reared back, and kicked Kierdenan's warrior off his blade. Lifting his sword on high, he brought it down hard, splitting the man's skull. Rattled by the experience, Dajin continued to chop down on the warrior, over and over until his arm ached from exertion, and the man's face was mashed to a bloodied pulp down to his neck.

When Dajin regained his wits, he was horrified by what he had done, but his ego came to his aid as always.

He had vanquished his foe, as was right and proper! His chest puffed proudly, as he turned his back to the corpse, and smiled when he saw that the fight had carried them towards the back of Catrian's pavilion.

While the group of warriors continued to do battle at the front of the tent, Dajin would steal the Sorceress from out the back. He glanced about warily to be certain he was unobserved before hacking an opening in the canvas, and pushing through the slit.

His improvised doorway had led him into Catrian's bedchamber, and there she lay on her cot, sweat soaked and shrunken from her ordeal.

As Dajin strode forward to scoop her up, Dara's words came back to haunt him. She had been right. There was no way to get Catrian across the compound unseen and unchallenged. Not unless he disguised her!

His boots ground blood and muck into Catrian's woven grass mats, as he spun on his heel, scanning the tent's interior for something, anything. Dajin's eyes lit upon a thick fleece that had slipped from the bed to pool on the floor, and an idea blossomed.

He tugged Catrian off the bed and onto the skin, then with one push, he rolled her up, saying a quick prayer to the Gods of Fortune that she would not suffocate afore he had made his claim for bravery! With a mighty heave, he slung her across his shoulder. If all went well he would appear to any watchers to be running to save his belongings.

Bent sideways by the weight, Dajin shuffled through the slit in the canvas, and teetered his way back across the compound. The warriors still fighting at the entrance to Catrian's tent were none the wiser that he had stolen their prize!

The journey back to the woodpile was proving dangerous in the extreme. The fighting had grown worse now, and he seemed to be moving against a tide of fleeing women and children.

Kierdenan's troops had set the fortress ablaze, and the glow from the fires lit up the night sky, creating fearful, dancing shadows in which anything could be hiding! Dajin hesitated, coughing slightly from the thickening smoke, as he rested against the split rail of a paddock. The animals within had long since been herded away by their keepers, and for the moment he was alone in the flickering shadows.

If he returned for Dara, and then turned around to flee with the rest of the survivors, he would have to carry the Sorceress in both directions. He should just get Catrian to safety now, and trust that Dara was smart enough to do the same. He was, after all, now responsible for Catrian's safety, he reminded himself pompously.

But Dajin felt a twinge of unwelcome shame at the thought of deserting his sister, and the image of Dara, huddled flat in the woodpile, panting with fear, skirted across his mind's eye. He cursed in his indecision, and wiped a clammy hand over his sweating face, but even his over-blown ego could not justify abandoning his twin.

But what to do with the Sorceress? It made no sense to take her with him to collect Dara. She would only slow him down, and instead of saving his sister and the Sorceress, they would likely all perish!

He glared at the bundle at his feet, and nudged it roughly with the toe of his boot. If he stashed her, he could get Dara then collect the Sorceress on his way back, but he was loath to leave Catrian for fear of someone finding her before he could return. All of the dangers he had faced to rescue her from her tent could be for naught! Someone else could steal Dajin's glory. Again.

He had to hide her well.

Dajin roughly dragged Catrian in her wrappings to an empty water trough, and tipped it over to cover her. He stood back to evaluate the job, and was satisfied that no one would spot his hidden treasure. But he must not leave her for long, for the fire was spreading, and it would reach her eventually.

Drawing his sword, Dajin began a quick, careful jog back to where he had left Dara, cursing his sister all the way for forcing him to put his future at risk to come to her aid!

⁗⁖

It has long journeyed into the mountains following the stinking trail of Green Crest, only to discover the burnt dust of the traitorous one in the valley below a Rebel stronghold. Sethreat howls with pleasure that the betrayer is dead! The roars echo back from the mountains, and birds take wing, and animals large and small, predators and prey, take flight.

Speckle Tail whimpers, and Sethreat disdains to acknowledge the sound. A Stalker never grieves, not even for a denmate.

It is just the two of them left now. The last of the Demon Rider minions have perished on the trail days ago, but they are no longer needed. Spring has come and the nights grow warm.

Sethreat breathes deeply of the painful last moments of Green Crest's death, savors the scents of anguish, and discovers the faint fragrance of the one who killed it.

Magic! Powerful Magic! A woman! Sethreat purrs with great joy. The betrayer has not usurped the Master's gift!

Three gifts in one night! The death of Green Crest, the Hunt of a Sorceress, and a bloody battle in the fortress above!

The humans fight amongst themselves! War is ever the breeding ground of chaos, and It thrives on that state. Sethreat will kill and maim and feed! There is but one taint.

"Thou art not welcome to kill with me." Sethreat raises the crests of bony plates upon Its back and yawns Its jaws wide to aggressively show the size of Its dagger teeth.

Speckle Tail has been well schooled to obey during their Hunt. It hisses, tail thrashes, and talons hold wide and unthreatening.

Resplendent submission!

"Keep thou away from my kills, lest thou become one!"

Sethreat quivers in anticipation, and ground-eating leaps carry It up the slope of the mountain, disdaining the switchback road, towards the sounds of deaths, and the glows of fires. Vaguely, It is aware of Speckle Tail vectoring away towards the east wall, but the fantasy of what It shall do to the magical one consumes Its mind, and spurs Its speed.

Smoke, blood and terror burns Its nostrils; a hedonistic brew. Its powerful hind legs easily vault It to the top of the protective wooden wall, and It lands in the midst of glorious battle. Sides mean nothing to It, as It wades through ranks of soldiers with impunity. Kills at will! They are all Human, all chattel upon which It feeds! But first comes the raptures of the deaths!

The warring Humans slowly become aware that a larger danger than the swords of their foes moves through their numbers. Sethreat howls at the confusion It causes, as Humans stop attacking each other in order to flee.

Some of the brave stand and fight, but It laughs, as the swords of the Humans bounce off its horned hide. They lack the weapons to harm It! Only the magical Dream Weaver forged metal of Maolar can pierce Its scales, and Maolar has long since vanished from the lands! Sethreat crushes skulls in its talons, uses its spiked tail to maim any who attack from behind. It moves constantly, never still, in magnificent debauchery of death!

It is reminded of the early days of the Master's reign, as It twists the head from a fleeing warrior, and baths in the shower of blood. It urinates on the carcass in excitement, claiming the kill, before It dashes through the embattled fortress, killing everything that comes within Its grasp.

In the excitement of the moment, It forgets Itself and Its armoured plates lift in joyful abandonment. A Human warrior strikes from behind, and his battle-axe finds the space between Its scales and bites deep.

Pain!

Sethreat roars and backhands the warrior to the ground. Slashes, pulls, tears, until naught but a fleshy stain soaks into the ground. It pulls the axe from Its shoulder, and spikes it into the mutilated carcass. The Human's death does little to ease the hurt.

Careful of the wound, It locks Its scales back down for protection. It sniffs briefly at the axe, tasting the scent of Its own blood mingled with that of the dead Human. The axe is not forged Maolar.

It has been too long since It has seen real battle, and It forgets that mundane weapons can harm if the armored ridge on Its shoulders lift in aggression or pleasure, and leaves softer flesh exposed.

Its delight in killing tarnishes. Sethreat slaughters a Human who seeks to skewer It with a pike, but Its heart is no longer in the carnage.

Sanity returns. It seeks the Sorceress. Its stomachs clench with hunger when It recalls the Magic Wielder. Sethreat inhales deeply of the smoke laden breeze, and seeks the perfume of the Sorceress. The strongest concentration lies towards the centre of the fortress.

~ ~ ~

Though the south and east sides of the fortress were in disarray, friend and foe alike fleeing for their lives in the wake of Stalker attacks, the rest of the stronghold was still at war, unaware that Doaphin's creatures were loosed amongst them.

Kierdenan had finally managed to push his warriors through to the centre of the fort, unto the very threshold of the Sorceress' tent.

The General exulted in the ease of his successful coup. The courier had told the truth! Catrian was ill, must be ill, for her to have allowed so deep an incursion into her territory. The battle had been fought, as battles ought to be! Between mortal men with cold steel, and no magic to taint their valor! The General grinned in fierce triumph, shouting at his men to rally forward.

There had been a risk that Boris' couriers had lied, despite Vetroy putting them to the question, which was why Kierdenan had attacked prematurely, at night, making certain the first casualties included the Commander and General Matik.

Kierdenan spared not a moment's regret for Boris and

Matik's deaths for their views were unrealistic and antiquated, and would have seen the destruction of the Rebel forces. Boris and Catrian's plan had been madness. They would have decimated their fighting force to protect people who had no right to demand protection after failing to fight for themselves! There was no way for the disadvantaged rebellion to win in open conflict with Doaphin.

But by their deaths and the capture of Catrian, Kierdenan would become the undisputed leader of the Resistance, and when he sold the Sorceress to Doaphin, it would buy his people a place of privilege within the regime; safety and peace at long last.

What cared he for the lowland cowards that Doaphin and his minions fed upon? They were nothing to him, and not worth the life of his people. The lowlanders treated the Rebels with less respect than they gave the Demon Riders. When the Rebel forces demanded supplies in return for protection, the lowlanders were insolent and hostile, preferring to be left alone for fear that Doaphin would hear that the Rebels had come calling. They did not want help. They were content under Doaphin's tyrannical rule. Kierdenan would see to it that their wish was granted!

General Kierdenan was certain that Doaphin would not kill off all the lowlanders. Had that been his intention, he would have exterminated the lot of them centuries ago! Catrian had been manipulative in her scrying, for the sorcerer folk were ever a sly and calculating lot, and not to be trusted!

Kierdenan had fought his last battle in defense of the

lowlands. It was time for a new Reaver King to replace the Sorceress Queen!

⧽⧼

It had taken all of Dajin's stealth to return to Dara. He had been forced to hide time and again, as the tide of the battle had overtaken him. Now he was behind enemy lines, and the danger had increased tenfold! If he were not quick in retrieving Dara, he would not make it back to where he had left the Sorceress! They would be trapped!

"Gods! No!" Dajin yelled. The woodpile he had left Dara within was afire. Dajin stumbled forward, screaming his sister's name, his arm raised before his face to block the intense heat. Was there a chance that she was still alive, hidden inside?

Dajin kicked through the burning wood. Empty! His relief turned to rage, and he hurled a burning log into a nearby tent with a curse. He had made the return journey for nothing! Dara had already fled! He stumbled back, as the tent ignited in a burst of heat and flames.

A hand touched his shoulder, and he spun with a spasm of fear to find his sister, white and shaken, her dagger bright with blood. Dajin did not pause to ask her what had happened for her torn dress, and seasoned knife spoke for her.

"Come on," he growled, grabbed her hand, and towed her away. Dajin was disgusted at her listless responses, her shocked features. It was not as though she were the only one to have had to kill this night! He neatly suppressed the remembrance of his own reaction when forced to kill Kierdenan's soldier at Catrian's tent.

They wove through pockets of flame-flickering darkness, choking on the smoke, holding in their coughs fearfully when they heard the shouts of battling soldiers, until they finally arrived at the spot where Dajin had hidden Catrian.

"Help me!" He hissed, as he dragged the heavily wrapped body of the Sorceress out from under the overturned trough. "Take her feet! We will be able t' move faster!"

Dara complied woodenly.

Crouching low, they made for the south gate, hoping that their escape had not been cut off, and that the gate was not yet under Kierdenan's control. The sounds of battle grew distant, and South Sector appeared oddly deserted. The battling soldiers who were in evidence elsewhere were absent here.

Dara stifled a scream, and Dajin's half of the burden increased suddenly, as she dropped Catrian's feet. "What?" he griped.

Both of Dara's hands covered her mouth to stifle the whimpers of terror crowding her throat. She pointed at a corpse, her outstretched arm trembling fiercely. "Stalker!" She moaned with fear.

"'Tis no Stalker!" Dajin jeered. "'Tis just a dead soldier. One o' Kierdenan's t' judge by his colours!"

"I know that he is no' a Stalker!" Dara cried hysterically. "Look at him!" She turned slightly. "And him, and them, and her..." She pointed to more and more corpses that littered the area.

Suddenly Dajin saw what had been readily apparent to Dara, and a jolt of terror blasted him so strongly, he thought for a moment that he would soil himself! No sword or spear had caused the wounds of these men! No soldier would have stopped to feed! He licked fear dry lips. "Maybe it was Deathren?"

"We would have heard their howls!" Dara reminded him. "We must leave! Now!" Dara tried to run, but Dajin caught her arm.

"Wait! The Sorceress!" Dajin yelled to halt Dara's flight. There was no way that he was leaving his prize behind, not when his reward was within his grasp.

Dara looked from Dajin to Catrian's limp form. Biting her lip to quell her panic, she returned to pick up her end of the fleece wrapped Sorceress.

Forbearing all stealth they rushed for the gates, no longer fearing opposition for there was a killer loose within the fortress. The gates were smashed open, and unguarded by all but the mutilated dead.

Gasping from their exertions, they scuttled through the wall, and onto the switchback path that wound down the mountainside towards the thick trees, glancing back often for any signs of a pursuing nightmare.

სოღპ

Sethreat tracks the scent of the Sorceress to this tent, that men fight a last, bitter battle to defend, and knows that Its hunt has ended. Its triumphant roar stops warriors in mid-clash. It wades into the thick of them; razor talons sever and slice, barbed tail crushes a path to the entrance of the pavilion.

Men flee. Others try to fight, but inferior weapons bounce uselessly from Its scales. It views the puny efforts with disdain, and sticks a scrabbling Human into Its mouth. Sethreat closes Its eyes to savour the sensation of shattering the Human's skull in Its powerful jaws, and sucks free the sweet, juicy morsel of the brain. Forbearing the rest of the carcass, It spits out the corpse amongst the survivors, scattering them from Its path. It laughs at the spectacle.

A nice appetizer, for the main course. Its anticipation builds, as It brushes aside the puny barrier of the tent flap. In Its wake, Sethreat hears the survivors screaming their retreat.

ഇരു

"Kierdenan is dead! Fall back! Fall Back!" Lieutenant Vetroy ordered hysterically. His men fell in behind, as Vetroy lead the retreat at a run.

As word of the withdrawal spread, and others joined the flight, someone asked, "What is it? Why are we running? We were winning!"

"The Sorceress called up a Stalker t' protect herself! She is in league with Doaphin!" Someone else answered.

The hysteria infected the warriors quickly. Soon, even Commander Boris' men, who moments ago the Eastern Rebels had been clashing with, were running for their lives in their midst. All animosity was forgotten in greater peril. The fighting ceased, as word of the retreat and the presence of the Stalker spread.

Vetroy was shocked to the depths of his soul by what he had seen this night. Until his dying day, he would remember the sight of Kierdenan being consumed by the creature of darkness.

CR

Sethreat stands in the empty tent, and keens with impatience.

It cannot be! It must not be! The magical one escapes!

It flicks Its forked tongue out to test the residual warmth of the bedding. "Yesss. Thou art ill, and unable to defend thyself!"

It groans with need, and loses Itself in the scent of her sickness. For long, perfect moments, Sethreat fantasizes about the kill. *First the soft flesh of the body, slowly, to keep her alive while It feeds...*

It breathes deeply once more. There is a fleeting scent in the air of Human male and blood. The disturbed bedding has a bloody handprint smeared upon the ticking. Here is the answer to the mystery of the Sorceress' disappearance! An accomplice carries her to safety. And there is where he made his escape with Sethreat's prey!

It rends the slit at the back of the tent to widen it for its bulk, and gains an even stronger scent of the culprit. It bounds across the compound, doing what It does best.

ഔരു

"She is too heavy! I have t' rest!" Dara beseeched her brother. When he refused to slow, she dropped her end of Catrian in protest. Thus halted by the heavy drag of the Sorceress' body, Dajin turned on his sister.

"What are ye doing?" he hissed. "Do ye want us t' be killed by a Stalker?"

"No!" Dara wailed. They were deep within the forest by this time, and she thought it unlikely that a Stalker was near enough to hear them. "But I have t' rest. Besides, what makes ye think that it would be hunting us anyway?" Her gaze fell to the still form within the roll of fleece. "Oh," she mumbled dejectedly. Her face was white when she turned it back towards Dajin.

"Dajin," she whispered, "We have t' leave her behind. We can no' outrun a Stalker. No' and take her with us!"

Dara's fear was contagious, and for just a moment Dajin recognized the sanity of her suggestion, before his ambition reasserted itself. "No!" he shouted the denial, making a chopping motion with his hand. "We have t' take her with us!" He puffed up his chest. "She is too important t' the Resistance t' leave behind t' certain death!"

Dara made a rude sound in her throat. "There is no Resistance, ye dolt! There never was. All the stories Da told us were falsehoods, though he knew it naught! The Rebels have been hiding safe in the mountains, disdaining those o' us who suffer under Doaphin's yoke, raiding and feeding off o' us, as surely as the Demon Riders themselves! Only three people kept the dream o' rebellion alive. Two were slaughtered back at the fortress, and the last lies dying at our feet. We must think of saving ourselves!"

Dajin's gaze darted from the fleecy bundle to his sister's face. "But if we can reach one o' the Generals with her…"

"And ye know where the rendezvous is? General Matik confided all t' ye, did he?" she asked snidely. "How long do ye think it will be once the war starts, and the killing and the dying, afore the Generals turn on Catrian, just as Kierdenan did?"

Tears marked tracks through the soot on her cheeks. Dara was wounded to the quick at the thought of abandoning Catrian to die, but she could see no other path to survival. "I do no' want t' leave her… but… she is so ill, she may already dead." Defeat infected her voice, as she slumped against a tree.

Dajin was at Catrian's side in a flash, unwrapping her swaddling, and leaning close to feel for breath. "No! She yet lives!" he claimed in relief.

Dara's eyes narrowed suspiciously at his frantic reaction. "What is the real reason ye are risking our lives for her, Dajin?" This sudden altruism was not in his character, and she doubted the motives behind his sudden chivalry.

Dajin had always been able to lie to his father and Rewn but he could never fool Dara. His twin knew him too well. She had born the brunt of too many cruel sibling tricks to believe the best of him. He sighed, rubbing his hand over his face in unconscious mimicry of Rewn. He glared at Dara, as one clever lie after another chased across his brain. Judging by the mutinous, cynical look on her face, he knew that nothing short of the truth would move her. But then the truth could always be slanted to his advantage…

"If ye must know," Dajin attempted to portray wounded dignity, "by rescuing her, I will put an end t' the label o' coward that Rewn and Gralyre have given me!"

"Do no' be an arse!" Dara fluttered her hands dismissively. "They do no' think that, Dajin!"

"And our family will have an easier time o' it. The Rebels spit on us because we are lowland born, but if we rescue one o' their most important leaders, then we will be accepted as one o' them. Given positions o' power, even!" Dajin's eyes narrowed cunningly. "Ye o' all people know the dangers o' being a lowlander in the camps!" He ruthlessly stuck his verbal knife where his sister was most vulnerable.

Dara blanched at the low reminder, and her fists clenched, as she stared at her brother for a long moment. In the end she bent and picked up Catrian's feet.

Keeping his grin of triumph hidden, Dajin hoisted his end of the sorceress, and they began their stumbling flight once more.

ೞೞ

"Who art thou Hunting, Brother? Hast thou also scented the Magic Wielder escaping into this forest?"

Sethreat grinds Its teeth, a sound like the shattering of rocks. The youngling, Speckle Tail, blocks Its path, and It considers Its options. Kill Speckle Tail. Kill the Sorceress. There is no time for both, for dawn approaches.

It flexes cruel talons, but recalls the Master's edict. It cannot kill Speckle Tail. It quivers with suppressed need to rend the head from the young one's body, and anoint the night with the hot splash of blood. But that is too quick, and there is no time afore sunrise to satiate dark urges. When Sethreat kills Speckle Tail, the torture will last for days, not minutes.

Soon.

Kill the Sorceress! It will not forego another night afore feeding upon the Sorceress and her magic.

Sethreat's wound burns like fire. Pain. A sensation seldom felt in three hundred years. If the other suspects the injury it will attack. A show of strength is required.

Sethreat bares Its teeth to establish dominance over the youngling. Its horned scales rise along the ridge of Its back, an evil threat that makes the other tense and step back. "We seek two humans, young one. A Sorceress, and the one who seeks to bear her to safety!"

The lesser Stalker lowers its eyes in obeisance, bows its massive head to show its subservience, and thrashes its tail like a hatchling.

Sethreat watches the lie dispassionately. It knows that at the first opportunity the lesser Stalker will betray It, and struggles to suppress the need to slaughter it.

The Master's will is all. The will must be obeyed.

"What of the Man, brother? Hast thou found him?" The lesser Stalker's question is insolent, an insult to Sethreat's prowess.

Sethreat backhands Speckle Tail. It flies backward, and snaps off the trunk of a sapling with the force of the impact. It whimpers, and Sethreat barely holds in check, and salivates as, in Its imagination, It tears and rips the throat of the youngling. "The scent is old. The Hunt continues. The Master knows all."

It hates to allow this lower creature a share of the kill, but short of binding it and leaving it for sunrise, Sethreat has no choice but to allow it to attend the feast. "Whilst thou hunt with me, brother?" Sethreat offers grudgingly.

දැඥ

They were crossing a small clearing when the sound finally became noticeable. "What is that?" Dara hissed in a loud whisper, trying to stop but pulled along by Dajin's momentum. "Whist! Dajin! Stop! There is something out there!"

"I do no' hear anything!" Dajin grunted over his shoulder, almost losing his grip on the Sorceress, as Dara dug in her heels again. Forced to stop, he finally heard the faint rustling, surrounding them and creeping nearer, a tightening ring of quietly stirring leaves. He gurgled in fear, as his slackened muscles dropped his end of the Sorceress to the ground. Dara had already loosed her own hold.

"The Stalker has found us!" she moaned in chill terror. She backed away from her frozen brother, and the unconscious Sorceress. Turning in place she tried to detect a direction that was not blocked by the whispering leaves. "Dajin!" she cried. "Do something! Draw your sword!"

Dajin was incapable of movement beyond involuntary shivers. He was fighting just to breathe, as all his blood drained to his feet. He could no longer feel his heart pumping! He was going to die! He gasped air, trying to make his muscles move to defend himself and his sister, but his body refused to obey.

It was the same cowardly affliction that had overtaken him at Hangman's Tor, when he had watched, as though in a dream, as his father died, as Rewn and Gralyre fought to defend themselves from the Deathren. Their screams still rang in his ears. No, wait. This time it was Dara who was screaming at him to help her. Mute with terror, Dajin stared through her, as his mind fled his immovable body.

Seeing that Dajin would be of no help, Dara pulled her short dagger from her belt. She stared at its pitiful length, sobbing with the knowledge that she would have to get that close to a Stalker just to wound it. She was going to die!

As she avoided Dajin's fear contorted face, something deep inside released a burst of strength to bolster her faltering courage, and Dara's hand tightened convulsively on the hilt. If she perished this night, she would die standing and fighting not cringing in fear! Her days of cowering were over!

She averted her eyes from Dajin's gasping, quivering form, and slowly circled her brother, waiting for the attack, wondering from which direction it would come! The suspense proved too great.

"Show yourself, coward! Bring yourself t' my knife!" she screamed.

The bushes parted like waves smashing against rocks.

ଛୀଔ

The scent is strong now. Sethreat will soon reach the prey! Earlier a woman joins the trail. Its tail slams the ground in anticipation, as It leaps along the forest trail, ripping deep gouges in the loam. Three now to kill. It will give the youngling the two humans, a sop, and keep the Sorceress for Itself! A long string of saliva drips from Its jaws, as the first sounds of fleeing footsteps reach Its ears. For just a moment, Its concentration leaves the one who follows.

"Thou hast hunted well, brother," the lesser Stalker snarls, and makes a quick motion with its talons.

Magic slams into Sethreat, seizes limbs, smashes It into the forest floor. It can neither move nor roar.

Helpless!

Sethreat has never suspected the youngling to possess so potent a magic. It underestimates Its opponent, and now It pays with Its life.

Speckle Tail gloats, circles Sethreat in the dirt. Its forked tongue flicks forth to test the scents of the night. "Thine blood seeps darkly. Thou hast allowed thyself to be injured by a Human! Thou art pitiful and undeserving of The Master's favour!"

The spell the lesser Stalker weaves is strong, but not insurmountable. Sethreat will escape at length, but by then the youngling will have killed It. Or the sunrise.

Speckle Tail leaps upon Sethreat, kicking and gouging, tearing great runnels in flesh with its powerful talons. Sethreat feels nothing, for the youngling's spell numbs all pain. At length it stops, and stabs talons into Sethreat's jaw to lift Its head.

"Thine death hast come, brother, but thou must await mine pleasure."

What is this?

Can the youngling be so witless as to leave It living?

"Thou must dwell upon thy death, and abide in the knowledge that the Master shalt reward me greatly for the slaughter of the Sorceress. Thou shalt feel the burn of the hated sun afore thine life is done!" It hisses the laughter of its kind and releases Sethreat. Then the youngling's claws dig deep, kicking back divots of earth, rocks and twigs, as it bounds after the fleeing Humans.

Betrayed but alive. Sethreat smiles fiercely, as Its counter spell begins to take effect, and tingling returns slowly to Its limbs. It will not catch Speckle Tail before it feasts upon the Sorceress, but It will not be lying like a trussed pig when the sun defeats the night! It will live to take Its revenge! The young one will die for this betrayal. The Master will approve.

಄಄಄

The Stalker roared out of the bushes, snapping a small sapling in twain with the momentum of its passage. Dara's scream froze in her throat. There was no time to think. The creature moved too swiftly. She threw her arms up in defense, as the Stalker hit her, knocking her spinning into the ground.

It did not pause to kill her but headed straight at the unmoving Sorceress and Dajin. Dara rolled over painfully in time to watch the Stalker hurl her brother against a tree. Dajin fell to the ground in a tangle like a broken and discarded doll.

The creature bent to delicately unwrap the fleece-clad figure of Catrian, crooning a sound almost like a purr.

Pure, undiluted rage swept away Dara's fear, giving her a strength she had never known. She had retained her grip on the hilt of her dagger, and now scooped up a large rock in her other hand, something that in a regular instance she would have had trouble lifting with two arms. Her face contorted with no small amount of madness, as she heaved herself to her feet. "No! You canno' have her!" She hurled the heavy rock at the beast, and it bounced heavily off its back.

She did not stop to reason that she had been more than willing to abandon the Sorceress to the Stalker a short distance back down the path. She did not stop to reason that she was forfeiting her life, for she knew that the Stalker was to kill her anyway.

"It is folly to challenge me thus, puny female!" The Stalker bared its impressive array of double-rowed, serrated teeth. The scales along its back flared upwards, their razor edges catching the weak starlight. "If thou runs, thou might yet live come sunrise!" It taunted, and hissed its strange laughter. As though Dara was of no consequence, it turned back to its task, taking its time to relish every moment of the kill.

Dara's outrage overflowed, and wrung tears from her eyes. She had been persecuted all her life! A victim of the Women Tithe! A victim of the men of the Rebel fortress! She was not about to die a victim of a Stalker! Oh, it would kill her, of that she had no doubt, but she would choose the manner of her death, not this evil minion of Doaphin! And she would not die groveling or running! The Stalker would not feed on Catrian while Dara watched on!

"Doaphin's Dog," she whistled mockingly and patted her leg. "Are ye fearful o' my puny female knife?" she taunted.

೫೦೧೩

Speckle Tail rears back in surprise. In all its days in this realm of man, it has never once had to deal with insults. Men fear it, or run from it, or die screaming under its talons, but they never taunt it! Never!

It leaves off from its feast preparations, and makes an aborted leap at the Human female. It skids to a stop, confused, when she does not flinch, but steps forth to meet its attack! It falls back in confusion, for the female would not be so confident unless she can hurt it. There must be something that it misses! It stretches as tall as it can to test the air. There is something! What is that scent?

৪০৫৪

Dara gloried in the Stalker's hesitancy, and threw herself forward in attack, just as the Stalker suddenly sprouted quills. From the surrounding bushes, arrows flew in a terrible buzzing rain, and the Stalker staggered to and fro from the impacts. Maddened by its crippling wounds it charged at Dara, its talons poised to rip and rend. Its eyes glowed red, malevolent and evil.

With anger born strength and speed, Dara dodged to the side and rammed her dagger to the hilt into the Stalker's baleful, serpent eye as it passed. So near did it miss her that she felt the abrasion from its scales, like sandpaper against her cheek and shoulder, the slight impact knocking her to the ground.

The Stalker crashed to the earth, driving a long sliding furrow from the weight of its momentum, thrashing and kicking, mortally wounded. Arrow shafts snapped and impaled deeper as it contorted. Briefly Dara thought of striking again, but decided that she would rather watch it suffer than draw near enough to end its misery.

She watched numbly, waiting until the last of its death throes had passed. Only when she was certain it was dead, did she finally come to the realization of what she had done.

'I live!'

The thought blew into Dara's mind, obliterating all other sensation, sound or feeling. She spied her dagger protruding from the Stalker's eye, and her breath sounded harsh in the sudden silence of the clearing. Even with the clear evidence before her, she could not quite believe that she had managed the feat.

Stalkers were invincible. She had always been told that only magic, Maolar or sunlight could kill them, and none of these things did she have in her possession.

At last her mind noted the arrows, and she frowned as it finally occurred to her to wonder where they had come from. Leery of removing her gaze from the body lest it spring to life once more, she slowly glanced up.

They ringed the clearing, tall, strong warriors, with long bows hanging from their shoulders. The shafts of arrows in the quivers upon their backs stuck up high above their heads. In the shifting light of the night and stars, the arrows looked like branches sprouting from their shoulders, making her wonder if spirits of the trees had come to life, and taken the shape of men.

Only magic could kill a Stalker, so the magic to kill this one must have come from them. It was the only explanation, for surely one weak woman could not have struck the deathblow!

The bowmen parted, and from their midst a wizened old man materialized, and walked towards her. He stopped to kick the Stalker, then grunted in approval. "Well struck, woman." He spoke with an odd accent.

"I did nothing," she murmured dazedly, wavering on her feet, as her adrenaline seeped away to leave her weakened. "'Twas your magic arrows did the deed!"

"We did naught but weaken it. 'Twas you struck it in the right spot." He bent and retrieved her dagger, wiped the blood off with a quick motion of his hand, and passed the blade back, haft first.

Dara accepted the dagger numbly, her mind reeling from the knowledge that she had really done it. She had killed a Stalker! And with no more than a dagger! Wait until Dajin heard! He would turn sick with envy.

A hard lump formed in her throat at the thought of her brother. "Dajin!" she cried out, turning away from the strange old man, and running to where her brother lay crumpled at the base of the tree. She pulled Dajin's head into her lap, bending to feel his breath upon her cheek. He yet lived!

"Dajin! Dajin! Can ye hear me?" Dara pleaded, shaking him slightly. She felt his body flinch, as she jostled him. He moaned but his eyes remained closed.

The old man crouched beside her, and ran his hands lightly over Dajin, feeling and probing. He glanced up, and his eyes crinkled in a kindly way. "A couple of broken ribs. He will live."

Dara's eyes shut in thankfulness, as the old man moved away, and opened them again to find him gently unwrapping the Sorceress, finishing what the Stalker had begun. He cupped his hand over Catrian's forehead and bent in concentration.

Whatever he was doing seemed to cause him great effort for he released her suddenly with a gasp.

When his gaze snapped Dara's way his face was fierce, and no kindness lived within. "How long has she been like this?"

"I...I...do no' know," she stammered. "For maybe a seven-day? Or a fortnight?" Uncertainty caused her voice to tremble.

A howling roar echoed from the forest. Dara let out a frightened yelp. She had heard that sound one too many times this evening to mistake it. "Another Stalker!" she keened, hugging her brother protectively. "'Tis another Stalker!" What courage she had found, left her in a rush. She had borne too much this night.

The old man jumped nimbly to his feet. "Treg-la-meck," he ordered calmly, but his men were already moving to form a guard around the fallen.

One of the warriors separated from the others, giving commands in a strong, deep voice. Their language was incomprehensible to Dara, but their actions were not. The men formed two lines, bowmen to the rear, and pikemen in the front. In the universal language of war, that required no interpretation, arrows were nocked, and with a mighty creak, the wood of the bows bent under the power of the steady armed bowmen. The commander raised his arm in readiness of the signal to fire. They waited.

ഔർഇൽ

Sethreat crashes through the underbrush, forgoing stealth for speed, and relishes the destruction It leaves in Its path, as It anticipates the devastation that lies ahead. Speckle Tail will die screaming and choking on its own blood! Sethreat will not suffer it to live a moment longer. The Master would approve.

An unusual scent slows Its impetuous rush. Many men. And blood. Not a Human's. A Stalker's! Speckle Tail is slain, and what kills one Stalker will kill another!

Sethreat scratches deep furrows into the ground, as It skids to reverse direction.

THRUM! TWANG! WHISTLE!

Arrows snap through the trees as Sethreat retreats, strikes Its upper arm, pierces scales, bites deep into soft flesh.

How can this be?

There is but one metal sharp enough to harm It, and it has not been seen in the lands for centuries. Arrows tipped in Maolar can mean only one thing - the Dream Weavers return!

The magical metal burns, and the sickness of light poisons Its perfect darkness. It jerks the arrows free as It flees, whimpers in alarm at the sight of Its own blood. The arrow wounds throb a counterpoint with the axe gash in Its shoulder, and the long talon slashes from Speckle Tail's attack.

And It has failed to kill the Sorceress, or capture the Man. Sethreat moans in fear of the Master's coming displeasure.

It will tell the Master tomorrow night, for the dawn is upon It, and Its injuries, grievous. Cowardice decides the matter.

CHAPTER TWELVE

FENNICK'S ISLAND

The darkness was embracing a pale mauve glow on the horizon when the dawning of the Solstice sun triggered the magic of the labyrinth, and the portals began to align.

The company was startled awake by a rumbling and rocking of the ground that bounced them over the hard packed stones. Unable to gain their feet, they crawled towards each other, or clung tightly to larger boulders in an attempt to anchor against the heaving earth. The portal began to glow brighter, casting harsh shadows among them.

"What is happening?" Saliana screamed, as she clutched at Rewn's outstretched hands.

"'Tis the portal, the Solstice is upon us!" Rewn yelled, as he pulled her protectively into his chest. He kicked out with a foot, bracing to keep a rocking boulder from rolling over them both. It was still dark enough that it was impossible to spot the others. "Aneida! Mayvin!"

"Here! We are here!" The sisters were curled against each other in an open spot between several boulders where they had bedded down the night before. Mayvin's face contorted in a silent wail of pain as her shoulder was jostled and smacked against the undulating earth while Aneida did her best to cushion her against the upheaval.

"Gralyre!" Rewn called out.

Gralyre shouted back, "Dotch, Trifyn and Jord are with me!"

"I have Saliana!" Rewn shouted back.

The imprisoned Demon Riders fought the earthquake and each other in panicked surges over the length and breadth of their cages. Those unlucky enough to be on the edges were crushed against the iron bars from the weight of the bodies, and the ones who fell were trampled to death underfoot in the panic.

The Deathren, who had never stopped their obsessive ululations of hunger throughout the night, began to smoke from the eminent dawn's light. Even as they overbalanced and fell from the shaking of the earth, their blank faces and clouded eyes remained fixed rapaciously upon the humans.

The ground heaved and quaked with more and more violence. Large boulders on the surrounding ridges broke free, and tumbled down to join the wreckage of the once rambling castle fortress of the Demon Lords.

The first rays of sunlight crested the high slopes that guarded the valley, and the Deathren howls were silenced in bursts of flame. Then, as suddenly as the quake had begun, it stopped. The portal's glow continued to intensify.

Breathing harshly, the small company raised their heads, and cautiously began to stand, and find each other. The imprisoned Demon Riders clung to the iron bars of their cages, and screamed hostility at the humans who had done the impossible by taking the portal.

"Is that it?" asked a shaky Trifyn. "Is the doorway open?" The radiance of the portal kept increasing in intensity, giving every object a second shadow, competing for brilliance with the rising sun.

Little Wolf let out a loud yowl, shaking his head and scratching at his sensitive ears with his paws. He turned tail and ran towards the empty cage that still drifted with dust and ash from the spent fires that had consumed the Deathren, putting as much space as possible between himself and the glowing archway. Unable to retreat further, he writhed against the bars, yelping and crying.

"Little Wolf!" Gralyre rushed forward.

The Demon Riders in their cages fell to the ground, clawing at their heads and gnashing their teeth, as they shrieked in agony. The combined howls sent chills of fear up the spines of the waiting group.

"What is wrong with them, Gralyre?" Rewn demanded loudly over the cacophony.

But Gralyre was incapable of answering. His hands were clamped to his ears against a sound that brought him to his knees. He had entered Little Wolf's mind, and been smote by the same supersonic screech that was getting louder by the moment.

"Arrgh! What is that?" Saliana wailed, clapping her hands over her ears, as the sound of the aligning gateways reached a frequency that all could now hear. She fell to her knees and then to her side, curling tightly against the pain.

One by one they succumbed to the power of the sound. It

blasted through their bodies, vibrating through them despite their hands blocking their ears.

"Get away...!" yelled Gralyre. "Get away from the arch!" The others could barely hear him, but they followed his lead, crawling towards the now empty cage. The sound became louder and louder, and added torturous frequencies and harmonies that made them twitch and flop, as they lost control of their functions. It was like rusted metal and breaking bones. It shattered through their bodies, thrumming their innards like a demonic harpist. Blood from ruptured vessels burst from eyes, ears and nose, blinding them, choking them.

The sonic dissonance reached a crashing crescendo, and then stopped. The sudden silence was as loud as the screech of a moment ago. Their ears rang in sympathy, blocking all small noises but the sound of their own pounding heartbeats.

Gralyre attempted to stand, but stumbled, off balance from the injury done to his ears, and crashed to his knees. He wiped the blood off his face with his sleeve, and looked around for the others. They had made it about three quarters of the way back to the empty cage before the intensity of the shrill sound had flattened them. No one was moving now, and a chill wind of fear blew through him that they might not have survived the onslaught.

Gralyre crawled doggedly to Rewn's side and shook him until his eyes opened, bloody and red from burst vessels.

"Hemmy mish?" Rewn garbled, as he tried and failed to sit upright.

Gralyre sagged in relief, and pressed Rewn flat with a weighted hand to his chest. "Wait here, I will check the others." Gralyre could not hear his own words, and suspected that he was shouting, but Rewn nodded, and his head dropped weakly back to thump against the ground.

Gralyre left Rewn's side, and crawled to Dotch who was already awake, but was staring at the portal, blinking like a pigeon that had been knocked from the sky by a rock, and yawning as though trying to unblock his ears. He pointed and yelled something that Gralyre could not understand.

Mayvin's hand language came to their rescue, as Gralyre signed, *Dotch, are you all right?*

The portal. It is not done yet!

Gralyre glanced back at the portal, and became arrested by the brilliant light emanating from the runes carved into the stones. Sparks of electricity ran over the figures, and snapped across the empty space between the jambs. Booming claps of thunder assaulted their already damaged ears, as the lightening bolts lengthened their arcs, striking the ground further and further from the radiant portal, drawing dangerously nearer to where the company lay in the dirt.

'Little Wolf lie flat, get away from the metal cage!' Gralyre ordered. The dog lay down on his side, panting heavily with fear.

Several feet away, Gralyre saw Jord stumbling to his feet, using the cage to pull himself erect, and shaking his head to clear the dizziness. He was unaware of the danger.

"Get Down!" Gralyre yelled. But Jord could not hear him. Gralyre took a running leap, and tackled him to the ground. Where Jord had stood, lightening spat, grounding against the metal bars.

Everyone lay down! Gralyre signaled urgently.

The group flattened themselves in the dirt, making as small a target as possible for the seeking tongues of lightning. In this task, the surrounding iron pens actually aided them, drawing the electricity to the path of least resistance. Miraculously, none of them were hit.

Within the cages it was another story. Demon Riders still incapacitated by the horrific noise, were leaning against the metal bars when the lightening struck. They were blown across their enclosures by the force of the current, dead before they hit the other side of their prison. Like the ravening beasts they were, the starving 'Riders pounced upon their fallen, and began to feast.

The lightening bolts gradually subsided until the crackle of electricity no longer shot forth from the glowing doorway. The sun had cleared the horizon now, and bathed the inhabitants of the valley in the rich golden glow of the first light of spring. The portal settled into a buzzing hum like a maddened hornet's hive.

"Look!" Gralyre pointed. Where before there had been naught but the other side of the square seen through the opening between the standing stones, the jambs now framed a shimmering mirror. The reflection undulated like the surface of water as seen from beneath.

The reflection of their grimy, bloody visages greeted them as they approached slowly, noticeably reluctant to take the final steps through the portal. Their doom was upon them.

Gralyre finally broke the tableau, shouldering his sword and striding forward. Unwilling to be left behind, even in the face of this fearful magic, Little Wolf came to heel.

"Gralyre, wait!" Rewn yelled, his arm outstretched, as though to pull him back. Their hearing had recovered save for a slight ringing.

"We have only until sunset! There is no time to lose!" For Gralyre there was no choice. His only pathway back to Catrian lay on the other side of this remarkable doorway.

Gralyre stopped in front of the portal, facing his greatest hope and greatest fear, facing his own shimmering image. A tall, hard faced warrior, black of hair, and beard, with runnels of blood leaching down the side of his cheeks from his bleeding ears, eyes and nose, stared back at him with grim, willful determination. Gralyre reached out his hand towards the reflective surface, suppressing his misgivings and doubt. Reaching the sword was Catrian's only hope of survival, and that was all the incentive he needed to find his courage.

His fingers touched their mirror image but there was no surface to feel only a faint pressure as of a current of water that swirled against his palm. Hardening his jaw, Gralyre pushed forward, and as his hand cleaved through its own reflection, it replaced the image, reaching away as it should, as though he had plunged his arm into clear water. Conversely, it was disorienting to see the rest of his body still reflected upon the shimmering surface.

Gralyre looked back at Rewn, Dotch and Jord. "See you all on the other side," he promised. He drew a deep breath and held it, as though about to dive into a pool, and stepped through his reflection.

With no hesitation Little Wolf sprang after, sparing a snarl for the Wolf that rose up at him from the mirror. He landed lightly at Gralyre's side, grumbling and growling. His ruff was raised high in distress but he was too loyal to return to the outside.

Gralyre dropped his hand to Little Wolf's head, soothing the animal as best he was able when he himself was trembling and gaping with discord. Nothing was as it should be. As far as the eye could see was verdant lush meadow such as he had never seen during his travels within the decimated landscape of Doaphin's occupation. He had been expecting something sinister, a twisted path of stone and iron and magic, or more of the same shattered boulders and cliffs of granite that made up the rest of the island. Not this. This was far more frightening for its unexpectedness.

For all its lush beauty, this grassland was completely devoid of life. No birds. No bees. Neither stinging insects, nor chirping crickets were to be seen, heard or felt. The sun was high in the sky, as it would be at noon, though morning had just barely dawned.

His neck prickled from residues of magic that eddied

throughout the lands before him, and every ounce of his body screamed at him to flee.

He glanced behind at the shimmering glow that hung in the air, and swallowed thickly to moisten his dry mouth. He could not see through it to his companions. Once more all he saw was his own shimmering reflection.

౪౸ౚ

Saliana began to gulp for air, fright tightening its grip upon her heart, not for herself, but for her brave Rewn, who boldly approached the portal in Gralyre's wake. She lifted her hand to call out to him but her words were strangled in her throat. He did not see her, and he did not look back as he stepped through.

౪౸ౚ

THE LABYRINTH

With a battle whoop, Rewn erupted from the mirror, coming to a running, panting halt beside Gralyre. Close on his heels came Dotch and Jord.

Dotch forced a grin. "T' the demons with the thing!" he grunted between gulps of air.

Jord thumped Dotch on the back. "I second that."

Gralyre gave them a moment to orient themselves, watching on in silence, as they exclaimed at the landscape before he spoke.

"We do not know in which direction the sword lies. With so little time 'tis best that we split up, and each take a point of the compass. All that is important is that one of us reaches the sword, so if you win through the next gate, spare no thought for each other. Continue moving forward with all haste."

They all nodded their agreement to the plan, and with wishes of "Good Fortune," headed off in their quartered directions. Gralyre, with Little Wolf at his side, quickened their long, steady strides to the right of the gate. Dotch gave a friendly wave over his shoulder from the left before they were all out of sight of each other. Jord rounded the shimmering portal and, broke into a ground-eating jog, disappearing quickly over the horizon without a glance back. And Rewn trotted straight, the entrance at his back, shouldering his sword with nervous, sweat-slicked hands.

෨ඏ

There were no changes to the landscape, as Gralyre and Little Wolf loped easily through the grassland. It was an endless, emerald meadow, unbroken by hillocks or rocks, or by any blemish in coloring to the verdant grasses. There were no landmarks to point them in any one direction, nor to tell them how far they had already travelled, though the light sweat Gralyre had raised, and the small movement of the sun bespoke at least a solid hour of running.

Gralyre glanced back, and was surprised to see that their passage had not disturbed the grasses, and there was no trail to mark their direction back to the entrance of the labyrinth. Exasperated by the facelessness of the landscape, Gralyre halted. *'This is pointless!'* he growled at Little Wolf.

Panting lightly, Little Wolf flopped noisily down on the grass at Gralyre's feet. His muzzle wrinkled in distaste and he immediately jumped up again. *'It smells bad here,'* the wolfdog complained.

'I do not doubt it, with all of the Demon Riders who have perished here over the ages!' Gralyre commiserated. Once again he scanned the verdant, but strangely empty fields. "This is all wrong..." Gralyre mused aloud, to shatter the eerie silence. He turned in place, scanning all directions for something, anything that would point him towards the sword.

"Help!"

Little Wolf's ears pricked and swung about, cupping in opposite directions. He suspended his panting momentarily to pinpoint the plea.

Gralyre reeled back to the direction that they had been moving. Where there had been naught but featureless grassland, now stood a heavily wooded gulch. The hairs on the back of his neck stood on high, as the plea sounded again.

"Help! Please! Anyone! Help me!"

It was a cry so faint that Gralyre was certain that the sound of his own footsteps would have drowned it out, had he still been walking. He approached the gully warily, disturbed by this sudden manifestation in the hitherto featureless prairie. With a gesture he sent Little Wolf to circle to the side, lest it prove a trap.

"Please hurry! I cannot hold on for much longer! I beg you! Help me!"

The sobbing cry was so pitiable, so urgent, that it drove Gralyre forward at a faster pace than caution dictated. He threw himself to his belly, as he reached the gulch, and poked his head out over the edge. Directly below him, grasping an exposed root, and dangling out into space, a young woman twisted and scrabbled, trying desperately to find a foothold.

"Gods!" Gralyre cursed in surprise, and reached down to catch her hand in a strong grip. With a flex of his powerful arms he lifted her up over the edge to safety.

Sobbing, she collapsed against him, holding him tight and whispering how grateful she was. Her form was warm and womanly and despite himself, Gralyre felt his body stir. With a rueful smile for his libido, he carefully peeled her clinging body away, and for the first time, saw her face.

She was stunningly beautiful. Curling golden locks streamed down her back, framing the perfect oval of her face, luminous blue eyes gazed into his with adoring intensity, and lush, red lips revealed a hint of pearly teeth, as she smiled shyly at him. Her dress was luminous white, cut low off her shoulders, shaping her rounded breasts in a heart shaped line, clinging softly to the gentle curve of her waist, and from beneath its hem, delicate legs curled beneath her.

Gralyre cleared his throat to cover the sudden stutter of his heart. "Are you harmed?" he asked gently, his voice husky with the sudden need to protect.

"Yes. I am fine now, thanks to you." She gazed up at him, touching his face lightly with her small delicate hand, her polished nails combing through his short beard, the slight scratch of them electrifying. "What would I have done had you not been here? How can I ever repay you?" she breathed suggestively. Her blue eyes were tiny pieces of sky, just as deep and pure, luring him to fall forever.

Gralyre struggled mightily to push away the carnal images that suddenly crowded his imaginings. "Your safety is payment enough," he offered gallantly, and almost winced at the banal old saw.

But his momentary disquiet brought him back to the moment, of where he was, and he remembered to be suspicious of her appearance in the heretofore featureless landscape. "How did you come to be hanging by that root?

She sighed heavily, blue eyes narrowing ruefully. Her low cut bodice slipped further down her pale shoulders with her deep, shuddering breath, exposing even more velvet skin. Gralyre sternly pulled his eyes away from her cleavage, and sweat broke upon his upper lip.

"'Tis the nature of this place," she explained. "'Tis ever so dangerous. One moment you are walking along picking wildflowers, and the next the ground opens beneath your feet." She shrugged delicately, and her dress gave up its fight and slipped artfully down one beautifully curved shoulder. Only the softly rounded curves of her breasts now kept the gossamer fabric in place. "I do not know what I would have done if you had not been nearby." She quivered, and touched his chest with the tips of her fingers, a grazing caress that left burning fire in its wake.

Gralyre's mind blanked of any thought but of her beauty, and his suspicions evaporated, for surely such an exquisite creature did not have a deceitful bone in her body? Accepting her explanation with no more questions, Gralyre reached out and plucked a bunch of pretty weeds that were growing in a clump beside where they sat. He presented them with a flourish. "Your lost flowers, m' lady," he smiled charmingly.

She giggled enchantingly, her eyes dancing with pleasure, as she took the flowers from him, and she buried her nose in the posy. "Thank-you kind sir!" She stood and curtsied to him, then, suddenly off balance, she fell against him.

Gralyre caught her around the middle, and pulled her against his chest, as he allowed her momentum to carry them both back into the soft meadow grasses.

"Are you alright?" he breathed huskily with concern, as he rolled to ease her to her back. He felt flushed, feverish, as he loomed over her soft body. All he could see were her red lips, so close to his...so close, he wanted to taste, had to taste! The smell of crushed wildflowers rose to engulf his senses, and he gasped a great lungful of air.

'Keep your mind on the sword!' he ordered himself

desperately, amazed by his uncharacteristic lack of control. His arms began to tremble with the effort of holding himself away, and his manhood strained and pounded to be set free.

"I am fine, now that you are here," she whispered throatily.

Her arms were suddenly around his neck, drawing his lips down to her sweet waiting mouth. Gralyre tried one last time to lift away but she was stronger than she looked, and his will was not in it. After the second kiss, he no longer wanted to escape. His arms stopped trying to push her away and instead, wrapped themselves tightly around her graceful back, straining her to him. He groaned deeply in his throat. Berries, she tasted of ripe strawberries, the exact colour of her lips.

′′′

Jord halted. What had he heard? It came again. A cry for help, desperate, pleading. One of his many knives appeared in his hand. In such a place as this, nothing could be taken at face value.

With a scream of fear, a beautiful woman, dressed in warrior garb, brown braids streaming behind, came running over the crest of a hill. Moments later, two mounted Demon Riders followed after, chasing her to ground, shouting and laughing, as they herded her along for the sport of it.

Jord frowned. He had not noticed a hill there before. His suspicious thoughts flew from him as the woman cried out again, and tripped in the tall grass. In moments, the Demon Riders were off their steeds, surrounding her. A second knife appeared in Jord's free hand, as he instinctually sprinted to her aid.

She was back on her feet, pulling her sword and standing to do battle, but she was too winded to fight. With a couple of quick moves, the 'Riders had her disarmed. She backed away, shivering and screaming, as the 'Riders advanced with their bared steel touching her throat.

The Demon Riders, intent on their prey, did not hear Jord's approaching footfalls muffled by the tall grasses. Not wanting to give them an opportunity to cry out, perhaps alerting more of their kind, Jord's knives shot away with flicks of his wrists, and impaled the 'Riders at the base of their skulls. As he had intended, the creatures folded quietly to the ground.

He jerked his knives free of their necks, and cleaned his blades on their red shirts before placing them back in their hidden sheaths. Only then did he train his attention onto the woman who had watched it all in silence.

She stood proudly before him, breathing heavily from exhaustion, and Jord could not help but stare at her. She was the most beautiful woman he had ever seen. Her leather tunic outlined her lush body while her short, warrior's kilt revealed the longest, most slender legs he had ever seen. Jord licked his lips, as thoughts of the quest flitted away from his thoughts.

"Ye saved my life!" She gave Jord a look that made him blush at its boldness. In a society where women were scarce, and beautiful women even scarcer, Jord had never had a woman give him such a glance before.

He cleared his throat, and could not help leering. "Ye can owe me one." His eyes narrowed with pleasure at the sight of her beautiful long legs, her strong thighs, and her hips. He rubbed his sweating palms against the stomach of his shirt, unconsciously miming Mayvin's gesture for hungry.

"I like t' pay my debts immediately," she purred. Her hands went to the laces of her leather jerkin, undoing them slowly, playfully.

Jord's breath panted with expectation. This could not be happening, was she really going to…?

In a graceful, animal move, she pulled the tunic off, and cast it carelessly to the ground. In the hot sun, her bare breasts glistened with perspiration from her run from the Demon Riders.

For the space of a heartbeat, Jord was held immobile with lust. Then with a growl, he crossed the short space between them, and grabbed her in a rough embrace, inexperienced and awkward in his fervor, but felt her return his passion in kind. She fit against him perfectly! She was perfect!

He pushed her to the ground, moaning in pleasure, as her hands went to the buttons on his pants. He had to have her. Now!

&ɔσ

Rewn ran forward, certain this was the direction the cry for help had come from. He craned his head, scanning the featureless prairie for any sign.

"Oh, help me!" the pitiable, and desperate cry came again.

And suddenly Rewn saw her. Chained in a crow's cage, she was swinging in the slight breeze.

'Where did that come from,' Rewn pondered suspiciously.

When she spotted him, she reached out between the bars of the cage. "Please, kind sir! Help me! If no' t' release me than at least give me water! Please! Mercy! I beg o' ye! Mercy!" She sobbed. "The Demon Riders caught me, and locked me in here t' die!" She strained her arms further between the bars, setting the cage to a wild swing. "Please help me!"

Angered at yet another injustice at the hands of the Demon Riders, Rewn strode forward and drew his sword. "Get back now," he cautioned. With one hard blow, he shattered the lock on the cage, stepping back, as the woman tumbled free. As she sobbed her gratitude, Rewn bent to offer her his water. She turned her tear-drenched face up to his, and Rewn found himself drowning in the most lustrous brown eyes he had ever seen.

"Water?" he managed to choke out past his dry mouth.

She smiled tearfully at him, taking the water skin from his hands. She tilted back her head, and sent a stream of liquid from the skin into her mouth. It overflowed her lips, spilling down her rounded chin, soaking the bodice of her simple dress.

Rewn's eyes followed the path of the water greedily, lost to the moment.

When she offered the water skin back to him, Rewn mindlessly tipped it to his own lips, sputtering on the sudden, unregulated stream. "Ye spilled some," she murmured, her liquid brown eyes teasing.

Beguiled, Rewn held still, as she brushed the water from his bearded chin. "So did ye." It seemed the most natural thing to brush the water free from her lips, and suddenly they were on his, and the world and all its urgencies faded away.

Duty, the quest, the danger, all of it paled when compared to the warmth of her mouth on his.

His first kiss.

Moaning with pleasure, they sank beneath the shade of the crow's cage.

ഇരു

"I am so grateful that ye rescued me!" the beautiful woman smiled at Dotch. "If ye had no' happened by, I would surely have perished in that river!" She threw herself into his arms, hugging him tightly, rubbing and chafing her taut body against him, clad in nothing more than a thin, wet fabric that hid nothing of her form.

Dotch patted her awkwardly upon her shoulder. "There, there. It was no trouble at all," he mumbled.

He was hosting thoughts that an experienced man like himself knew better of. He had been too long on this quest, he decided. Dotch's mind travelled back to his wife and two sons. They were his world and he suddenly missed them so fiercely that he could scarcely stand it. He had told his wife he would come back to her, knowing full well that he was telling his first lie in their long and happy union.

The group had made it further than he had ever dared to dream, and had sacrificed much for the sake of the Prince's sword. But not this! Dotch would not undermine his beloved wife's memory!

He sighed heavily, as he grabbed the young lady by the shoulders, and set her firmly away from him.

"What is wrong?" she pouted. "Do ye no' think that I am pretty?"

Dotch ignored the question, old enough to spot a honey trap when he saw one. He bent and looked into her face. "Do ye really want t' repay me for helping ye?"

She nodded vigorously, smiling happily. She stepped back from him and began to lift her sodden skirt.

"No!" Dotch yelled throwing out his hands, before smiling at his own overreaction, "No, lass. That is no' what I meant!" Before she could work up her cute pout once more he quickly clarified. "I am searching for a sword. Do ye know which way I need t' go t' find it?"

She danced away from him, laughing. Concerned, Dotch began to follow until he realized that something remarkable was happening. The woman opened up her arms and stretching them high above her head and a bright aura of light surrounded her. It reached an intensity that Dotch could no longer look upon, and he threw up his arms to protect his eyes. After a moment, he realized the light had subsided. Lowering his arms cautiously, he saw that the beautiful young temptress had turned into the next portal. He had passed the first trial of the labyrinth.

His breath caught in wonder, as he walked to the shimmering archway, noting that it was a duplicate of the first but for the stone of the pillars made of finest jade. Briefly, Dotch spared a thought for his companions, wondering how the younger men had fared against this test of devotion. But time was running out like water through a sieve.

As promised, he would continue forward and spare no further thought for the fates of the others. Steadying his courage, Dotch stepped through the portal and into the second circle of the labyrinth.

ॐ

'It smells bad here, and I am thirsty,' Little Wolf whined in disgruntlement.

The wolfdog's complaining, impatient thought interrupted Gralyre's mindless nirvana, shattering the spell that had been at work upon his senses.

He levered himself away from the woman's delectable body, and rolled to his back, breathing heavily, as he berated himself.

'How could I have forgotten Catrian, even for a moment?'

The woman followed after him, draping herself over his heaving chest, and fitting her mouth to his once more, but her allure had waned, and Gralyre's lust had evaporated, nothing more than magic and illusion.

Finding his strength, he pulled her arms from around his neck, setting her firmly away, though her lips clung to his with surprising strength. When she made to return to his embrace, he halted her with a firm, "No!"

She gasped of hurt, and her lips quivered, as one perfect, shining tear clung to her delicate lashes. Gralyre watched the display dispassionately. Now that her succubus magic was shattered, her beauty seemed diminished. He no longer felt the insane pull of desire that had gripped him mere moments ago. Perhaps at one time, this wounded dove would have moved him, but now he found her tears exasperating. He much preferred a strong woman who would stand at his side to fight for him and fight with him, not one who would use calculated manipulations.

Catrian.

His yearning for the Sorceress rippled through the emptiness of his heart, banishing the lingering cobwebs of desire that had clouded his judgment.

"I am sorry," he sought to ease his rejection, "but I have no time for dallying this day. No matter how beautiful the enchantress," Gralyre finished courteously, gently lifting her chin, and brushing her tears away with his fingers, hoping that the lady would not be too offended by his rebuke to aid him.

She gave him a watery smile.

Encouraged, he asked, "I search for a sword. Can you help me?"

She rose gracefully, and backed away from him, a mysterious smile curving her lips. She spread her arms wide, lifting them high above her head. There was a blinding flash of light, and in her place stood the second portal. Similar to the first in every way, save that it appeared to have been carved from a single slab of jade. Lights writhed deep within the stones, playing over the runes like the shimmering scales of fish swimming in a deep pool.

Insight into the nature of the labyrinth curved Gralyre's mouth with triumph. He had passed the test to his devotion. He only hoped that his next trial would prove as pleasant as this one had been. Then he sobered, for there was nothing to celebrate here.

If not for Little Wolf's interference, he most likely would have failed this test of his faithfulness and honour. Had the others been equally tried? Had they passed? What would happen to them if they failed? Gralyre refused to entertain the thoughts further.

Calling Little Wolf to his side, Gralyre passed through his reflection in the shimmering portal of the second gate, seeking out the next test that would win him the sword, and perhaps, Catrian's life.

ഇ⊃രു

"That was incredible!" Jord growled contentedly, as he pulled the warrior woman tight to his side. Sweat slicked his skin, and he gloried in the quivers of pleasure that still shocked through his flesh. "I could stay here forever!"

She pulled away from him, jumping lithely to her feet. Jord watched from his back, arms behind his head, as his smile faded, made uneasy by her sudden withdrawal.

"Where are ye going? Do ye no' feel the same?" Uncertainty crowded the pleasure from his voice. He sat up in confusion, and ran a hand through his rumpled hair, as a scowl replaced his bliss. He did not like his vulnerable tone, it was not like him - none of this was like him. Jord never forgot the dangers surrounding him! Never! Yet for the entirety of this rapturous interlude he had forgotten all. Certainly she was beautiful, but not half so striking as other women he had met, and she could not hold a candle to the flame of a certain warrior woman's tresses. He scanned the area for danger, and realized that the bodies of the slain 'Riders had vanished.

"Where...?"

A wind sprang from nowhere, scything across the meadow in an invisible wave, and hitting his face with a blast of stench so foul that he gagged. "What is happening?" He watched in horror, as the landscape melted away, feathering off in the wind like sand being blown from a paving stone.

"Wait!" Jord tried to gain his feet and stumbled over his discarded clothes, falling to a knee. The wind roared, blowing his hair into his eyes, carrying with it the smell of rotting corpses. The meadow evaporated like mist and the woman with it.

"No!" Jord shouted, running towards where she had been standing. He tripped and sprawled into brittle bones, and the partially decomposed bodies of the hundreds of thousands of Demon Riders who had died within the labyrinth over the last three hundred years.

Jord leapt up with a yell of disgust, searching for ground not covered with vile remains, as his bare feet strived for balance within the unstable layers of bone. There was nowhere to go. Horizon to horizon was carpeted with bodies in various states of decomposition. Their rotting stench rose up to choke him, as he staggered across the mounds of flesh and bones searching for, and finding his discarded clothes.

His hands were shaking, as he pulled up his pants, and stamped his feet into his boots. The day had turned grey as a winter storm, and the chill raised a noxious fog from the bloated bodies, wreathing fleshless bones in phantom tissue.

And he was trapped in this hell until his death released him to become yet another rotting corpse. "No!" he screamed angrily. Then more quietly, "No," he whispered in despair.

Deep within, a fire of defiance began to burn, growing brighter and hotter, stiffening his spine. Jord glared at the corpse-strewn landscape with a sneer twisting his lips. This was nothing compared to the horrors that he had endured in Dreisenheld! He had gotten careless, but he was not dead yet. If there were a way out of this hell then he would find it. After all, that was who Jord was, a survivor and an escape artist, and no prison, not even this one, would ever hold him. He need only find his exit before sunset.

CHAPTER THIRTEEN

Gralyre stepped from the jade archway into a nightmare world of fire and brimstone. Sulfurous gases rose from a bubbling mire to choke him, expelled by bursts of flames that shot twenty feet into the air. He stumbled back, using his arm to shield his face from the blasts of heat. Sparks danced in the air with every belch of fire, and slowly settled to smolder upon the narrow bridge of land that bisected the fiery bog, leading in a curving path away from the portal. Blackened, baked clay lay in shattered plates atop the pathway, curled at the edges to teeter underfoot.

Little Wolf grumbled at the sharp odours and devastating heat. He hid behind Gralyre's legs in an effort to shield himself from the columns of flame.

Gralyre forced his steps forward, easing carefully along the narrow bridge of land, lest he fall into the infernos to either side of the path. Every breath seared his throat, choking him, burning his lungs.

'Hot fires burn, wolf feet yearn, for cool snow and clean air.'

Gralyre spared a grin for Little Wolf's poetry. *'Keep your wolf feet on the solid land. We must find our next portal quickly. We cannot bear this heat for long.'*

Testing his footing with each step, Gralyre slowly led Little Wolf through the burning fen, but the labyrinth's trial did not present itself. Was the test merely one of endurance, a challenge to their strength?

After a half hour of trekking through the swamp, a burst of flame caught Gralyre unawares, setting the sleeve of his shirt afire. He beat it out, scorching his fingers, but saving his arm from harm. He flexed his singed hand, thankful that the burn was not too severe.

A wave of dizziness caught him unawares, and he stumbled a step. Hot. It was too hot. He drew his water skin and cupped the liquid in his palm, parceling out some for Little Wolf, before he took a long swallow for himself. Gralyre shook the skin gently, recognizing by the swish of liquid that it was almost empty. They would perish in this heat without water.

He pulled off his shirt in an effort to cool off, and discovered that it was soaked through with his sweat. He had sought the added protection it afforded him from the flames, but what was the point? The heat was broiling him inside his own skin. The narrow path blurred in front of his eyes, tilting to a crazed angle. But it was not the path moving, he realized, it was he who was swaying like a blind drunk, from a combination of sweltering heat and the brimstone fumes.

Beside him, Little Wolf keened in distress, and collapsed to the ground.

"No!" Gralyre yelled. He leaned down to lift the wolfdog back to his feet, and almost joined the animal on the ground. "Do not lay down! We must keep moving!" he bade as Little Wolf collapsed again. He whipped his loose shirt around the wolfdog's underbelly, and hefted him up, supporting the pup's weight while Little Wolf's paws beat weakly against the ground in an effort to walk.

"Why bother? You know you cannot reach the sword! You will fall, and all the world will burn for your failure!"

"Who said that?" Gralyre challenged with a bellow. The tails of his shirt loosened in his grasp, and Little Wolf slipped back to the ground. Gralyre reeled, lost his balance and stumbled, catching himself at the last moment, as he sought the speaker.

A shimmering flame danced in the air less than a foot in front of his eyes. Gralyre raised his arm to fend off its heat, as the flame addressed him once more.

"You are pitiful! Look at you! You think that you will be the one to reach the sword, when Doaphin and all his creatures could not? Who are you? You are nothing! A man with no past. A man with a stolen name!" The flame expanded and contracted to the cadence of its taunts.

"You are wrong!" Gralyre slurred dizzily. "I will reach the sword! I have to!" he finished with a challenging shout. The heat and fumes had driven him mad. He was arguing with a phantasm.

The flame danced merrily with laughter. "Of course you must reach the sword, to save your own worthless hide!"

"No!" Gralyre shook his head in denial, almost sending himself spinning to the ground. "That is not the reason! I have to save Catrian! The sword is her only hope!"

"Ah yes," the flame sputtered. "The Sorceress. You seek to

impress her with your worthiness so that she will forget you are evil. 'Tis a smart ploy for a spy."

"I am not Doaphin's spy! Catrian knows I am an honourable man!" Gralyre's legs sagged, as a feeling of intense melancholy swept through him. "She knows who I am!" he whispered insistently, as his knees hit the hard baked clay of the path, but a tinge of uncertainty coloured his words. What did either of them know of the dark places in his mind? What secrets were hiding, and what would it mean to them all if those secrets were ever revealed?

The flame, it seemed, had heard his thoughts. "Which is why she sent you to your death! Not that it matters. The Sorceress is dead! Just like everyone you meet. You are poison! First the pups, then Wil, and now Catrian. Is there anyone you have befriended, and not killed?"

Gralyre's trembling hand cupped over his mouth to hold back his soul deep grief, as the agony of accumulated loss suddenly swept through him. He shook his head. "No... No... No..." Tears welled from his eyes, and a sob shook his powerful frame as his heart broke. He looked at Little Wolf, and saw that the wolfdog's eyes had shut. Had he killed him as well?

"How like you to fail her. Catrian would be alive right now, were it not for you," the flame twisted the knife.

'Dead? No!'

He refused to accept that she was gone! He would not allow it, not while he still had breath in his body! Impelled by this faith, Gralyre drew his sword, and surged back to his feet.

"Catrian is not dead!" He wiped his arm roughly across his eyes to stem the tears.

"What difference does it make? Even did she yet live she would still be lost to you! She can never be yours! You are nothing! If she were alive, she would laugh her scorn into your face!"

"No! She cared...She cares for me!" He corrected, as he shook his head against the sucking pool of grief, and his free hand made a chopping motion of negation. "She is not dead!" He refused to think of her in the past tense. He must reach the sword!

"Fool!" the flame chortled. "She only pretended to love you to control and manipulate you. Why else would she send you, a nobody and a spy, upon this quest? You do not even have a name! You are a man without a past! Doaphin's spy!"

Gralyre slashed clumsily at the mocking flame, cleaving it in twain. The momentum of the sword pulled Gralyre off balance and he stumbled to regain his footing before he plunged into the burning, sulfurous bog. The fires danced merrily and laughed, two now, where only one had been. He had merely doubled his torment.

"You have no name!" The first flame taunted.

"No Name! No Name!" The second flame chirped, as it circled Gralyre's head, racing around and around, dizzyingly. "No Name! No Name!"

"My name is Gralyre!"

The first flame giggled and jittered with amusement. "A fairy tale name you stole to cover up your worthlessness!"

"No Name! No Name!" went the second flame, revolving around Gralyre's head, faster and faster until it seemed a solid halo of fire.

"If you were to die no one would miss you! Certainly not your dead Sorceress!"

"My name is Gralyre!" he roared. But was it? Was it really? Doubt consumed him. Gralyre drew deep upon his inner fortitude, searching for a truth with which to fight this battle.

"No Name! No Name!"

He sought the place that was the core of his willpower and identity. The well from which he drew the pride and courage to face the world as a king, when he had less place within it than a beggar! His eyes snapped open as he found his integrity.

"No Name! No Name, No Name, No Name!"

"Why do you not sit here and die! No one will grieve your passing! They will rejoice! You have a sword, use it!" ordered the flame.

"My name is Gralyre," Gralyre stated with quiet authority, and absolute belief. He might not be a prince, but he knew who he was; honourable, strong, a leader and protector, a good man, a warrior, a sorcerer, and the women he loved was relying upon him to be all of this in order to save her life.

No longer fearing the flames of self-doubt that assaulted him, he strode forward, sword held before him in challenge, and the flame receded, dwindling in size, as his confidence reasserted itself. "I will not fail Catrian."

The second flame that had buzzed around his head like an angry wasp gave one more chorus of its taunt. Gralyre smacked it with the flat of his sword, and it snuffed out with a little pop. His attention returned to the first hovering tormentor.

"My name is Gralyre, and you have no idea of what I am capable. I will not fail to save Catrian! I. Will. Not. Fail!"

At his words, the flame blew backwards, and struck the ground, detonating with enough force to knock Gralyre onto his backside next to Little Wolf. From out of the inferno grew an amber portal, the shimmering escape from this fiery ring of the labyrinth into the next.

Gralyre sheathed his sword, and bent weakly to haul the inert Little Wolf into his arms. With a shout of effort, he hurtled them both through the gateway.

₧₧

A league of carnage passed Jord by, as he hiked doggedly forward, and he became numb to it all. Even the smell faded to his nose, as he placed one foot in front of the other, keeping his head down to avoid the panoramic testimony to the futility of escape. There was a strata of corpses, skeletons hundreds of years old overlaid by generations of death, with the last season's Demon Riders still rotting on the top layer.

So it was that Jord nearly walked right past the huddled man, until the sobbing caught his attention, and stopped his steps. At first he could not pinpoint the sound of quiet despair. The acres of corpses stretched unbroken. When the wailing sounded once more, his eyes sought to isolate the moldering remains of Demon Riders from what had made the noise, and he finally spotted the hunched and shaking figure. The slight movement was all that differentiated him from the decomposing remains he squatted amongst.

Slowly, holding his breath least he draw attention to himself, Jord stooped and picked up a long leg bone, the bony foot still clinging to the opposite end. As quietly as possible within the brittle landscape, he stalked the sobbing man. In this accursed place nothing was to be taken for granted; he had learned that the hard way. This could all be another trap, one that would send him to a worse plane than this.

When he drew near, recognition made him sag in relief. "Rewn!" he dropped the bones, and rushed to crouch by his friend's side. "What happened?" He clapped the quietly sobbing man on the shoulders. "No' that I am no' glad t' see ye!"

Something was wrong. Rewn was not responding. "Rewn?" Jord shook his shoulder, rocking him to gain his attention.

Rewn finally looked up, and his tear stained face crumpled, as another sob tore through him. "Keep away from me!" he begged. "I am bad luck t' all I meet."

Jord snorted derisively at Rewn's pathetic statement. "Like I am no'?" he quipped. When Rewn did not even try to aid Jord's attempt at levity, real concern began to tighten Jord's vitals. Looking into Rewn's eyes was like looking into the eyes of the Dreisenheld palace slaves. They were dead, without hope, without joy, even fear had been stricken from them. Despair so consumed Rewn that there was no room left for any other emotion. What had happened to change this strong, courageous man into this quivering mess?

Jord grabbed Rewn's face in his hands, keeping the other man from turning away. "Rewn. What has happened man?" With Rewn to help him, Jord's chances of finding a way out of the bone yard would double, but not if Rewn became his burden.

"The flame was right! My father is dead because o' me. If I were any kind o' a son, it would have been me who died, no' him! And my brother's wickedness is all because o' me. If I had paid more attention t' him, he would no' have gone astray. My sister was raped because I was no' there t' protect her. And now I have failed every man, woman and child in the world. I have failed t' reach the sword, and now everyone will die because o' me! 'Tis all my fault!" Rewn sobbed. "'Tis all my..."

SMACK!

Jord's hand stung, as he struck Rewn across the face, rocking back his head. It was better than listening to a litany of self-pity and blame.

"Your brother is no' evil, he is young and trying t' prove himself! Your father's death was a valiant one, t' save ye all from the Deathren, so do no' cheapen his selflessness with your false woe! Who has filled your head with such lies?" Jord shook Rewn roughly. Were Rewn's eyes more aware? The slight pain of the cuff seemed to have broken though his despair.

"It was the flame. It was inside my head. It knew all my

secrets, all my innermost sins..."

"This flame was just the labyrinth's trial," Jord guessed. "It did its job well, for here ye are, come t' the same pass as I!" He glared angrily at the mist-shrouded bone yard.

Rewn coughed on a sob, and wiped a grimy palm across his tear stained face, shaking his head, as though coming awake from a nightmare. "But it was so real!" he argued, still unwilling to release his grip upon his misery.

Jord flopped down beside Rewn, grimacing as age-fragile bones snapped beneath his weight. He rested his arms against his bent knees, as a knife casually appeared in each hand, and began to flip. "At least ye made it farther than I." The knives disappeared then appeared. "My lust landed me here." A self-deprecating grin pulled at his lips. "I could no' resist such a siren as she."

Rewn sniffed, and a small grin played upon his mouth, as he gave a small laugh. "I managed t' resist, but barely."

Jord grinned, glad to see Rewn returning from his ennui. "How? Ye are no' a man t' prefer other men, are ye?"

Now Rewn did laugh. "No. 'Twas the crow's cage I rescued her from. It reminded me of a place..." he stopped talking and his face twisted once more with misery. "...the place my father died."

Rewn watched Jord's knives as though hypnotized. Appearing. Disappearing. "'Twas my self-doubt that was my downfall," Rewn mused painfully, fully aware now of the test he had failed. The anguish of his guilt lived within him, where it had been all along, though it had taken the flame to bring it to the surface. In all the instances where he held himself accountable, there had been no way to prevent the inevitable. The Gods of Fortune had thrown the bones, and all had been lost. He was not to blame. A little of Rewn's old spirit returned, for logic told him that if he had born this burden all along, then he could carry it once again.

He shuddered slightly at the thought of his fate had Jord not found him, and brought him back from the edge. Rewn would have sat here amongst Doaphin's dead, and allowed himself to die. He tore his gaze from Jord's hypnotically dancing blades. "So what do we do now?"

The knives disappeared a final time, and Jord leapt to his feet. "Now we have less than a day t' find a way out or we become one o' them." He kicked a skull and sent it skittering across the landscape where it shattered on a ribcage.

CHAPTER FOURTEEN

Gralyre stumbled through the amber gate, and into the midst of a battle. He dropped the now struggling Little Wolf, and drew his sword for protection.

Men fought to either side of him, slashing and gouging, screaming and dying. Barely recovered from the ordeal of the last test, Gralyre blocked the thrust of a screaming swordsman. Beside him, Little Wolf came alive, growling with intent, and throwing himself in front of his master.

"Retreat!" The scream came from the back of the melee. Horns blared, drums boomed out the signal, and the armies parted, leaving their dead and dying crumpled upon the ruined field of battle.

Gralyre stood in the centre of the newly created space, his chest heaving from the surprise of it all. He had forgotten his shirt in the fire swamp, and his torso glistened with sweat from the heat he had just left. The labyrinth's greatest trap was to disorient the traveller. Thrown rapidly from one situation to the next, those who did not adapt, those who did not solve the obscure riddle posed, were doomed to failure. What new bedevilment did the labyrinth have in store for him now?

The armies reformed on opposing sides of the churned fields. To the left of him, were men wearing colours of black and gold and to the right the opposing warriors wore purple and gold.

Here he was, stuck in the middle, and it was too late to try to mingle into one of the armies, though without the proper uniform he was sure to have been discovered anyway.

He remained in his challenging battle stance, sword at the ready, awaiting what would come. Perhaps he would have to defeat these armies to reveal the next gate? It was not an encouraging thought, but whatever the trial was to be, it would be best to hurry it along. Time was not his ally, and in his disorientation, he could not tell how much had elapsed since entering the labyrinth that morning.

In this place, the sky was grey and threatening of rain, and a sharp, cool wind blew from the east, ruffling the pennants of both armies into angry snaps, as they unfurled. Gralyre fought a shiver, as the wind dried the sweat on his flesh, and glared challengingly at the commanders who were prominently displayed on opposite sides under billowing striped awnings that flaunted their colours.

Still growling from the alarm of awakening in the midst of battle, Little Wolf took up position beside Gralyre. His lips drew back over his teeth, as he bared his fangs with threat. The thick black fur along his shoulders ruffled, adding to his menacing presence.

'Be calm, Little Wolf,' Gralyre soothed the wolfdog, *'until we know what it is we face.'*

There was a rustle of unease from amongst the armies, as they glanced back and forth from Gralyre and Little Wolf to their commanders. Finally a man of black and gold rode out from the ranks. No sooner had he departed, then a man of the purple and gold also set forth.

They arrived at Gralyre's side simultaneously, and were already shouting their messages to be the first to deliver them. "The Lord Archivald demands to know what you are doing upon his lands!" Black and Gold demanded.

"Ha!" The purple and gold herald spat, as he arrived in a flurry of dust and hooves. "Archivald is a foul midden heap! The Lord Chretias demands to know what you are doing upon his lands!"

"Sniveling coward!" yelled Black and Gold, his face purpling with anger. "How dare you speak my lord's name?"

"Coward? COWARD!" screeched Lord Chretias' messenger. "It was not my army that fled the field, moments ago!"

As the insults grew ever more heated, Gralyre realized he had been forgotten in their lust for each other's blood. He did not have time for this! Every moment he delayed, the sword slipped further from reach! He sent a thought to each of the horses, who promptly dumped their obnoxious burdens into the muck of the field and ran off bucking with joy at their freedom.

Still not distracted from their fight, the men attacked each other. As their swords crossed in the first exchange, Gralyre smashed his sword onto theirs. Black and Gold lost his weapon with a curse. Gralyre caught it on the fly, and planted his boot into the man's chest, sending him tumbling back to the ground. Turning fluidly from the kick, Gralyre batted aside the second herald's blade, and dug the sharpened tip of his sword into the man's neck. "Drop. Your. Weapon," he ordered, biting off each word and letting it drop like a stone in a well.

As Purple and Gold twitched his sword up to attack, Gralyre shifted his grip, drawing a fine bead of blood upon the man's throat. He raised an eyebrow ever so slowly. Purple and Gold swallowed heavily, reading his eminent death in Gralyre's cold midnight-blue eyes. His sword fell from loosened fingers.

"Ha!" From the battle-churned ground, Black and Gold scrabbled forward on his belly to grab his enemy's fallen blade, and found the point of his own sword inches from his right eyeball. He too froze.

Panting heavily, Little Wolf walked over to the fallen sword, and planted a heavy paw upon the hilt, pinning it to the ground. He fixed Black and Gold with his intense gaze, and a low rumbling growl boiled from between his teeth while his muzzle peeled back threateningly.

Black and Gold made a small strangled sound in the back of his throat, and slowly withdrew his arm from its reach for the weapon.

Confident that neither man posed further threat, Gralyre addressed the Purple and Gold Herald. "Tell me why you make war!" he ordered.

"Because they are ignorant peasants, who dare to pass themselves off as the rightful lords of...achhhhh!" he came to an abrupt halt as Gralyre increased the pressure of his sword point on the man's throat.

"Tell me why you make war!" he commanded once again.

This time, his voice was rimed with the cold of a grave, his patience at an end. Little Wolf growled his counterpart.

Purple and Gold's explanation rushed from his lips, "Lord Archivald is a filthy trickster! He fixed a horse race so that he would not lose his prize stallion. Lord Chretias declared the wager to be in bad faith. So we went to war."

Gralyre turned his cold glare upon the man in Black and Gold, who was humbled upon the muddy turf. "Is this a true account?" he demanded.

Black and Gold wet his dry lips. "Yes! Every word is truth!" The man's crossed eyes did not stray from the steady point of the sword that hovered steadily a lash length from his pupil. "L-l-lord Chretias made a bet with Lord Archivald on a horse race, and refused to give up his prized vineyards when he lost."

Gralyre gazed thoughtfully at the field upon which they stood, where blackened, twisted vines lay trampled into the muck. Barely recognizable rows of broken stalks peeked through amongst the fallen dead of both armies. Gralyre's lips twisted into a sneer. "You will return to your Lords, and tell them that they may each pick a champion. When that is done, I will fight these champions, and if I defeat them, the vineyard is mine, the horse is mine, and this war is over. Go! Now!" he ordered, stepping away, and lowering the weapons.

"They will never agree to your terms!" stammered a much humbled Black and Gold, as he inched to his feet, fearful that any sudden movement would set the Wolf at his throat.

"They will meet with my conditions!" Gralyre shouted

making the men in front of him flinch. His booming voice carried well to both of the waiting armies. "Or prove themselves cowards, as well as dolts!"

The two men scampered back to their respective sides, and presented themselves to their commanders. After a brief and heated consultation, the two leaders rode forth to meet Gralyre's challenge.

The purple and gold ranks parted for four men carrying a gaily-decorated litter. Purple and gold striped the awning under which stacked pillows supported the massive bulk of Lord Chretias.

From the black and gold ranks came a man dressed in ornate silver armour upon a showy, white charger of great beauty and massive stature. A bemused smile curled Gralyre's lips. Surely they did not think to challenge him themselves?

"How dare you...!" sputtered Lord Chretias, as his litter bearers puffed to a halt. Red wine sloshed over the edge of his jewel-encrusted goblet, staining a purple and gold pillow. "Be careful!" he spat at his slaves, striking one across the shoulders with a short quirt.

"A thousand pardons, master," the slave whispered, straining to level off his corner of the weight of the litter.

"What is the meaning of this?" interrupted Lord Archivald, who arrived upon his flashy steed. Its pale mane blew in the wind, and gold jingled from the black leather saddle, as it pranced and showed off. "You are interfering with our war! Begone knave!" The weak, wintery light glinted off the ornate, polished armour that had never so much as received a scratch from the nick of a dagger.

Gralyre stared levelly at the two pompous idiots. *'Run off the litter bearers!'*

Little Wolf turned into a fanged monster, lunging at the men bent under the weight of the litter. The bearer unlucky enough to receive the brunt of the attack grabbed his torn thigh, and screamed with pain, as he let his end drop. The off-balance litter fell heavily onto its side, as the bearers turned and fled rather than face Little Wolf's teeth. They left their master sprawled in the muck in a flurry of purple and gold silk, liberally stained with the red wine he had so recently enjoyed.

Little Wolf pursued the bearers a few loping paces to make sure they kept running. Licking his bloodied snout, he returned to where Gralyre was collecting the reins of the quivering stomping stallion that had just unseated its illustrious rider.

Lord Archivald lay in the dirt like a turtle on his back, unable to lift himself against the weight of his armour, arms and legs spinning, as he spit and yelled.

Lord Chretias fought his way free of the collapsed wood and fabric that had been his regal litter, almost as helpless under the massive weight of his body.

Upon the defeat of their lords, the armies charged forward to defend their commanders. "If you do not call them off, I will allow the wolf to rip out your throats!" Gralyre's growled words had the lords yelling to their men.

"Fall back!"

"Stay Back!"

The armies subsided, though they had drawn near enough to clearly hear all that now transpired.

"What do you want?" stammered Lord Chretias. "I will give you anything!" His pudgy, cunning face worked its way into what he must have thought was an ingratiating smile.

"Do not believe him!" sneered the stocky Lord Archivald, as he rubbed at a scratch in his fine silver armour, with a grimace of regret. "It was such a promise that started this war!" Lord Archivald thrust out his chest like a rooster, angling his head just so for the full effect of his words to stun his audience. "I always keep my promises," he boasted, "and I will give you anything!"

"Ha!" snorted an indignant Lord Chretias. "He would keep his promises, except he cheats so that he will never have to!!"

"Welsher!" sneered Lord Archivald.

"Swindler!" spat Lord Chretias.

Gralyre's eyes narrowed. The armies could well hear the words for the bowl-like shape of the field aided in the acoustics, a natural amphitheater. "I have two Lords who have promised me anything in return for their lives!" He shouted to be sure all heard his words.

Gralyre pointed his sword at Lord Chretias. "I want your vineyard," Gralyre waited for Lord Chretias' gasp of indignation to fade, and for Lord Archivald's smirk of superiority before he continued, shifting the point of his blade towards the armor-clad fop. "And I want your horse." The armies murmured, and from somewhere, someone clapped spontaneously, and was quickly hushed.

"I will never give up my horse!" yelled Lord Archivald with great theatrics. "He is of the finest lineage, a king among horses, and no fit mount for a churl such as yourself!"

"I will die before you get my vineyard!" howled Lord Chretias.

Gralyre turned his back on both lords to face the entrenched armies. "By their own words, these two Lords are forsaking their vows. By their own words they both are branded liars and cheats!" Gralyre yelled, playing openly to the crowd of warriors. If he did not get them on his side, all would be for naught.

"You!" he pointed at the purple and gold clad warriors, "and you!" he spun to confront the black and gold banners, "have been fighting and dying for what? Leaving your own fields to die of neglect for what? Leaving your families to starve, and your wife and children to fend for themselves from marauders for what?" he fired the questions rapidly at the troops.

Gralyre bent and yanked a trampled bush from the ground. "A vine!" he yelled. Gralyre infused his voice with as much scorn as he could. "A horse!" He whipped the ruined plant hard against the snowy white rump of the stallion. It whinnied in fright and galloped away across the field, aided by an implanted fear from Gralyre. Its glossy coat was marred by black dirt on its hindquarters.

Hardened warriors on both sides blushed and lowered their heads to scuff their boots like chastened lads. An ugly murmur began to swell as the men considered his words.

"You have been fighting to defend the honour and glory of your Lords!" Now Gralyre's demeanor assumed a note of sadness. Slowly he turned back to face the furious Lords of which he spoke. "But both of them are bereft of such noble qualities. You have been dying for a Cheat and a Liar."

Gralyre's face iced into its most formidable lines, as he addressed the Lords directly. "Your vineyard has been destroyed by your war!" he stated disdainfully to Lord Chretias. "And your horse has fled, never to be seen again," Gralyre taunted Lord Archivald. "The reasons for your discord are gone! Upon whom will you make war now?" he mocked, pushing them just a little further.

"We will make war upon you!" screeched Lord Chretias.

"Yes!" yelled Lord Archivald. "We shall grind you into meal for this humiliation!" he swatted Lord Chretias lightly on the chest. United in their anger towards Gralyre, their own animosity was gone. "Come Chretias! Ready your troops!"

"Yes!" Lord Chretias waggled his head in agreement. "And you ready yours, and we shall destroy this insolent peasant!"

Gralyre's swords came up, pinning the Lords in place. Terror chased shock across their faces at the threat. "I did not grant you your leave of my presence!" Gralyre gritted out imperiously.

He waited for the knowledge that they were not in control of the situation to penetrate their small minds. "The vineyard and horse are mine or you both die. Say it."

Triumph and satisfaction flickered across Gralyre's face, as he saw what was occurring in the ranks of the opposing armies.

They were leaving. Despite the danger that Chretias and Archivald were facing, they were walking away, and returning home. The war was over, whether the Lords caved to his demands or not!

With the desertion of their armies, Chretias and Archivald seemed to deflate. Three chins quivering within the folds of his purple and gold robes, Chretias' voice was querulous, "I deed you my precious vineyard, in perpetuity."

Sweating within his ornate armour from the unaccustomed fear, Archivald ceded his stallion. "Take it, if you can find it." His face was surly and annoyed.

The familiar buzz started vibrating against Gralyre's skull, and grew louder as a golden gate materialized in the air, and the trampled vineyard and armies melted away as if a curtain had been pulled back to reveal the truth of the world.

Gralyre called Little Wolf to his side and stepped through the portal.

৪৩০৪

FENNICK'S ISLAND

The men had been gone for several hours, and the sun stood high in the sky, blasting the dry, rocky stones of the square with intense heat. Little breeze reached them here, in the bottom of the bowl shaped valley, and the boulders seemed to draw in the sun's warmth and magnify it back a thousandfold. The portal continued to glow and buzz, the silvery reflection throwing back images of ugly, iron prisons.

From where she lay, fever wracked, upon the ground, Mayvin drew her sword awkwardly from its sheath. Her glassy gaze caressed the length of steel lovingly even as her fingers began to polish the length of the blade with the cloth of the blanket that covered her. Mayvin's condition had worsened throughout the day. Her wound poisoned her body, and her attention wavered in and out of reality.

Saliana drew Aneida aside so that they could talk without being overheard. "Aneida, I am sorry. I do no' think…" Saliana bit her lip, and placed a comforting hand on Aneida's shoulder. "I fear Mayvin will no' survive the day."

"Shut up! Just…!" Aneida's gut clenched at the news, but she had already known. Anyone looking at her sister could tell that her death was upon her. Aneida's eyes watered from the pain in her heart. "I doubt any o' us will see the night, healer," she sneered, as she spun away from Saliana's compassionate gaze.

Aneida knelt by Mayvin's side, holding her clammy hand in one of her own, halting her from compulsively cleaning her sword. She could not stand the thought of Mayvin's coming death. She was the last of her kin. Now, as Aneida looked into her sister's pale face, she saw no fear, only a sadness that her life was to end.

Mayvin gripped Aneida's hand tightly, looking intently into her eyes, then shook free so that she could sign, *Carry on. Finish it. Promise me.*

Aneida swallowed hard. "I promise."

When Mayvin heard this, she subsided against the pack she pillowed her head against. She smiled and nodded. *Good.*

Aneida smiled back through her grief. "Just rest now. Save your strength." As her sister's eyes drifted shut, reclaimed by the fever that racked her, Aneida left her side, and looked to the top of the ridge that Trifyn had climbed.

Trifyn had left the women soon after the men had passed through the portal. The way through the empty cage was still sealed with padlocks, and without Jord's skill at picking locks, Trifyn had been obliged to climb over the bars. He had hiked the road to the top of the ridge, and then scaled the canyon wall. From the height of this lookout, he could watch for the ferry's arrival, as it carried reinforcements across the short channel from the mainland garrison at Elevor.

"Trifyn!" Aneida yelled with her hands cupped around her mouth to see that the call made the distance needed. From within the cages, the Demon Riders mocked her with several choruses of *'Tri-fyn!'* in sibilant falsettos of their own.

From atop the canyon, where Trifyn had taken up a lookout position, came the flash of his sword. Aneida drew in a long steadying breath.

Saliana moved to stand next to the warrior woman. "Was that the signal?"

Aneida nodded. The Demon Riders from the garrison at Elevor were on their way. "Stay with Mayvin. I want t' see for myself what we are facing."

ഇരു

After signaling to the women, Trifyn resumed staring out across the bright blue water. The height and position of this ridge made it a simple matter to view all approaching crafts from the mainland. Having spent most of the morning gazing across the water in search of the ferry, he had not considered how the enemy would approach after landing on the island. But now he looked for a vantage place where his bow could do the most damage.

His gaze traced the path from the far distant quay, following the road from the beach into the narrow canyon that cut through the ridge and past his position, and into the valley of the portal. And then he saw them.

Trifyn's heart leapt, and he scrabbled down from his perch, sprinting along the dangerous, rocky path to meet Aneida, as she began her climb up the steep embankment. "We are saved!" he crowed, as he skidded to a halt. "I think we are saved! If they are what I think they are!" he was rocking from foot to foot in his excitement. "Come on! Come and see!"

Spurred on by Trifyn's eagerness, Aneida trotted after him, as he led the way back up to where he had stood lookout all that morning. From there, Aneida stared out over the rocky terrain, following Trifyn's pointing finger.

"There, and there and there! There must be more o' them! If they have no' been damaged by the storm, we can hold the whole o' the army here!" Trifyn chortled.

Aneida's smile was chillingly predatory. "Those lazy bastards!" she murmured appreciatively. Deadfalls and traps peppered the top of the narrow canyon throughout its length, still waiting to be triggered. The approaching army would be crushed before they ever had a chance to fight! "Jord said it would be a good place for an ambush!"

"I do no' understand this," Trifyn grinned. "Why would the Demon Lords build these defenses when they could wipe out an army with a wave o' their hand?"

"Because magic is tiring, no matter how powerful the sorcerer. When ye become too tired t' fight, ye must have some other, more mundane, defense t' fall back upon. Since they put all o' their soldiers into the cages, they had t' be able t' hold this pass against an invading force with only a few men."

Trifyn's eyes shone with hope. Their mission had been one of valiant sacrifice, now they stood a chance of taking the Demon Riders with them!

⁊

THE LABYRINTH

Gralyre and Little Wolf entered a realm of darkness and stood still, waiting for their eyes to adjust. Stars spattered across the sky in unfamiliar constellations, and the thinnest sliver of an oddly malformed moon peeked through the scudding clouds. The weak moonshine set the foam of an unnamed sea to glowing with a faint luminescence, as the waves lapped gently at the shore. The small stones of the beach chimed, as the ebb and flow of the tide shifted through them.

Gralyre's heart sank for if it was night then he had failed. For Catrian's sake, he prayed that it was yet another disorienting trick of the labyrinth, and that time still remained to claim the sword and escape.

Little Wolf growled viciously. His hackles rose, and he glared at the gently lapping water.

Trusting the wolfdog's keen sense of danger, Gralyre assumed an aggressive battle stance. One thing that the labyrinth had proven was to expect the unexpected. He spared a thought for his companions, wondering how they faired, then thrust them from his mind. To win through to the sword, he needed to concentrate upon the task at hand. These trials left no room for error.

The labyrinth was insidious, and well designed to eliminate Doaphin's minions, and prevent them from advancing to find the sword. But what of men? Would any human be able to win through, or was it as Jord had predicted, that only the Lost Prince could reclaim the Dragon Sword?

The wavelets washing gently against the shore suddenly increased in violence and volume until a huge wake rushed up the rocky slope of the beach, wetting the tips of Gralyre's boots.

Little Wolf jumped back from the rushing foam, whining urgently. Then he chased after it, as it receded once more into the gentle lapping of the midnight ocean. *'Run, run, run! I will attack, and you run!'*

With a command, Gralyre brought Little Wolf back to his side. *'What is it? What do you sense?'* He tried to penetrate the darkness that lay out over the water but the night hid all from his sight. Whatever had caused the wake was very large.

'Big. Evil.'

Gralyre could feel Little Wolf's confusion. The wolfdog had no vocabulary to describe what he was seeing. Gralyre's sense of unease grew, as droplets of water began to rain down upon him, and he glanced up. A giant, clawed reptilian foot that was rapidly descending upon where he and Little Wolf stood blotted out the stars.

"Yaaaaaah!" Gralyre threw himself sideways to avoid being crushed. Little Wolf moved even faster, the canine reflexes that much quicker than a man's. They were both well out of harm's way when the gargantuan claws dug deep into the gravely shore where they had stood mere moments before.

Gralyre hit the beach with his shoulder, rolled and came up in a battle stance, sword at the ready. His mind reeled at the enormity of that giant foot, the claws of which stood as high as his eyes, and his stomach turned to ice. His gaze travelled slowly up the iridescent scales of a leg of unbelievable proportions, and up ever higher to where the moonlight shimmered along the razor sharp edges of the larger, boney plates protecting the torso of the beast. Up even higher, the head and shoulders of the creature were hidden in the depths of the night sky.

Gralyre drew a gasping, shuddering breath, his first for

several long moments he suspected. If his test was to slay this vast beast, there was no way in which he might succeed. *'Not without my magic!'*

Gathering his scattered wits, he concentrated furiously upon the end of his sword, and a fireball sparked into being, wreathing the tip of his blade. Pulling back his arms, he slung the magic skyward with all his might, at an angle he hoped would intercept with the creature's head. As the flaming ball of light roared upwards, he turned away to protect his night vision, for the sudden glare on so dark a night left afterglows on his eyes. As the light travelled higher, it illuminated more and more of the creature. It was this circle of softer light reflecting off rainbow hued scales, that he watched instead.

From out of the reaches of the sky, a massive, clawed hand snatched the glowing fireball from the sky like a child capturing a spark-bug. The glow of the light dimmed but was not extinguished. The creature held the fireball easily, seemingly impervious to the flames and heat.

"Very resourceful, human!" boomed a voice so deep it made the thunder of the most violent surf puny in comparison. With the voice came a horrific stench of decaying fish. Gralyre fought and failed to control a gag.

The fireball, still burning furiously within the trapped cage of the clawed hand, was raised further, revealing a face from out of a nightmare. Gralyre's mind blanked, either from fright or his amnesia, and he could not fit a name to the creature. He fell back several steps in spite of himself. "What are you?" His own voice, which he had always taken for granted as deep and commanding, now sounded pitiful and hollow to his ears.

The horned, scaled head dropped, coming nearer. The eyes with their elongated pupils, shone eerily in the weak glow of the muted light. The mouth opened to reveal wickedly curved teeth of aged yellow as it spoke. "I am, what I am," it chuffed, blowing more of its foul breath in an unwholesome wind at Gralyre, and sending his hair into a whipping frenzy. "I need no name. I am forever. I am."

Valiantly, Gralyre stood his ground, and held his breath until he judged that the effects of the rotting breath had passed. He took a gulp of air, and fought back his gorge. He had misjudged. The air was so permeated by the odour, that he could taste it.

'What have you been eating,' he wondered in disbelief, as he blinked frantically, to get his watering eyes to focus on the awesome beast.

'Better to ask what I have in my other hand, Human!' The thought boomed just as viscously into Gralyre's mind, as its voice had thundered into his ears.

Gralyre staggered, and fell to the ground. His ears rang and black spots clouded his vision. His equilibrium returned quickly but not without a price, for when he brushed at wetness on his upper lip his hand came away bloody. He hacked and spit to remove the blood from his nosebleed that had drained into his throat, and lay still upon his back for a moment, shivering with aftershocks. He had lost his sword but did not concern himself with it. There was no way that his puny blade could harm such a creature as this!

The titan waited patiently for him to recover. Its snout seemed set in a sneer, showing off wicked fangs, each gleaming as large around as a tall oak.

Gralyre lifted his back from the rocks, and rested his arms on the tops of his legs, as he regained his breath. Then flinging his head back he shouted up at the beast, "What do you have in your other hand?" Whatever it was, it must be the key to the next portal. The sooner he got free of this level of the labyrinth, the better!

Instead of answering with word or thought, the creature slowly lowered its hidden fist until it was held suspended just before Gralyre's gaze. Held delicately within the mesh of claws, Dotch struggled futilely against the huge fingers. His fear was writ large across his face, as he reached out to Gralyre with panicked arms. "Gralyre! Gods, help me!" he begged. Then with great sacrifice he changed his plea. "No! Get free, lad! Quick! Afore the beast gets ye as well!"

Dotch's contradictory babble barely registered through Gralyre's fright for his friend. "Dotch!" He ran forward jumping high, trying desperately to reach him, but the claw was raised swiftly out of sight, disappearing with its struggling burden back up into the depths of the night sky. The cries faded as the beast's fist vanished.

Gralyre skidded to a halt, chest heaving, staring skyward for any sign of his imprisoned friend.

Little Wolf arrived at Gralyre's side accompanied by a

clanging, grating sound.

Gralyre glanced down, and saw that Little Wolf had retrieved his sword. *'Good lad!'* he praised, as he accepted the weapon's hilt from the wolfdog's mouth.

"What do you want?" Gralyre slashed his sword viciously at the air, impotent in his challenge and knowing it, as his eyes scanning the night sky for any sign of Dotch.

"Your friend's life for yours!" boomed the titanic creature. The gale force wind of its foul breath washed over Gralyre, and sent him staggering again. "I would feed off your power! You must give yourself, and your Godsmagic willingly to me. In return, I will spare your friend's life."

Gralyre's ears rang, from the explosion of sound that was the creature's voice, and from the shock and fear for Dotch's life. His brain raced to find a way out of the no win bargain. If he turned himself over to the beast he would die! Catrian would die!

But if released unharmed, there was a chance that Dotch might still win through, and retrieve the sword in his place. If there were no exchange, the massive creature would simply kill them both. "What assurance do I have that you will allow Dotch to live after I have taken his place?" Gralyre demanded.

The beast lifted its snout high, and roared angrily at Gralyre's words.

Again, his sword slipped his grasp, as Gralyre trapped his ears with his hands, and fell to his knees, bowed to the earth by the power of the titan's voice. The volume of before had been a mere whisper compared to this assault.

"I have seen a thousand sunrises, human! My kind soared through clouds ere man dreamed its first dream! Your kind is as a beetle to me! You would have me pledge to a beetle?" It bellowed. "What assurance do I have that you will honour your promise should I let my prisoner go?"

Gralyre gazed thoughtfully at the beast. Had the creature been evil through and through, it would have simply made the promise with no intention of keeping it. But instead it had shown pride and scorn. Had it been human, Gralyre would have sworn it was insulted.

Gralyre planted the tip of his sword hard into the rocky soil of the beach, driving it deep enough to stand freely. He steadied himself on a knee, keeping his gaze fixed aloft upon the two baleful orbs glittering by the trapped light of the fireball. "My name is Gralyre," he stated in his strong voice. "I have no memory of who I am, or from whence I come. I have no memory of my life, if I was an evil man or good. I can only say who I am now. I am Gralyre, and I will keep my promise to you." He took a deep breath, praying to the Gods of Fortune that his sacrifice would see Dotch successful in claiming the sword. "If you allow Dotch and Little Wolf through the next gate, I will submit to your will." He vowed, then stood, crossed his arms over his chest, and stared up at the beast that had grown so still that it seemed to have been turned to glittering stone.

Slowly, it lowered the fist that held the struggling Dotch. Bringing its massive claws to rest in the lapping shallows, it uncurled its fingers, allowing Dotch to stumble free.

"Come on, lad! If we run we can get free!" Dotch's face was drenched in hysteria.

Gralyre gripped him by the shoulders, steadying his friend. "I made a vow that I must now fulfill, Dotch."

"No!" Dotch yelled. "Ye need no' keep a promise made t' a creature o' evil!"

"Dotch," Gralyre stated softly. "A vow is never made to a foe. 'Tis made to yourself. Would you have me break faith with myself?"

Dotch's shoulders slumped in Gralyre's grasp. "Dotch," Gralyre murmured, bringing his friend's gaze back to his. "Take Little Wolf. Find the sword. Take it to Catrian." he swallowed hard before continuing. "Promise me. You must do this for me."

Dotch's chin went up a notch. "I vow t' retrieve the sword, if my strength does no' desert me, and see it safely back t' Catrian."

Gralyre's mouth quirked in a small smile of gratitude. "Then I know it will be so. Thank-you." He dropped his hands from Dotch's shoulders, crouching down to bring his face to the eye level of Little Wolf's.

'Stay with Dotch!' He ran a hand over the wolfdog's silken black head one last time, and then stood.

'No! I must stay with you! You are my pack!' Little Wolf howled, an anguished sound that carried out over the gently lapping waves.

'I am sorry, Little Wolf. I lead the pack. I must challenge this

creature, not you. 'Tis not your place, nor Dotch's. Stay with him, protect him as you would me.'

Little Wolf began to keen softly, his whimpers sounding more of the young pup he still was, than the adult wolf he would soon be.

"Keep safe, Dotch!" Gralyre bade by way of farewell. "May the Gods of Fortune favour your quest for the sword!"

Dotch's face contorted. "Good-bye lad. I…Gods! Thank ye for my life!"

Gralyre nodded, and jerked his sword free from the beach, sheathing it as he walked towards the waiting claws of the beast. Whatever fate awaited him now, at least he could be sure that his friends were one gate nearer to winning the prize.

Intent as he now was on his coming death, he failed to heed Little Wolf, as he sniffed at Dotch and backed away, growling. Gralyre bravely stepped through the massive claws onto the waiting hand of the beast, and felt the world around him shift. He staggered and fell, expecting to feel scales but instead his hands sank deeply into a cushion of fragrant moss. When he lifted his head to confront the baleful eyes of the titanic creature, the brilliant orbs of two suns blinded him instead, shining through the high bows of old trees.

He had passed through another gate! Triumphantly, he got to his feet, and dusted himself off, but stiffened in sudden, soul crushing panic! *'Little Wolf!'* He spun frantically in place, seeking the portal he had come through, but it was gone! Little Wolf was trapped in the last circle of the labyrinth with the beast!

"Dotch!" he screamed. "Little Wolf?" But the verdant forest that surrounded him muffled his voice, and not even the chirp of a bird or buzz of an insect answered his frantic calls.

Gralyre threw his mind wide, seeking any trace of Little Wolf but he felt no familiar contact from the wolfdog. The labyrinth had claimed him. And what of Dotch? Had he also become trapped, or had he found his own gate to continue onwards? Was it possible that Little Wolf was with Dotch now?

His head and shoulders bowed beneath a weight that seemed too heavy to carry, and a guttural sound of pain escaped through his tight clenched teeth. Not Little Wolf! Gods! He could have borne anything but this! Breathing in deep gasps of air, he waited for the first wave of pain to ease, and for numbness to take its place. His pathway was clear. The fates of everyone in the world that he held dear hinged upon his ability to persevere. He forced himself to stumble foreword.

This was no time for grief. His pup may yet be alive, and the sword might have the power to release him. And what of the others? Had they also been defeated and trapped by the labyrinth? Had that truly been Dotch he had met, or was he, even now, wallowing in the flaming bog? Was Rewn trapped forever between the two attacking armies of Lord Chretias and Lord Archivald?

Gralyre thrust away the disquieting imaginings, and picked up his pace through the trees. He could not allow the sacrifices of his friends to come to naught. He had no idea how long he had been battling the labyrinth, but deep within he sensed that time grew short. He broke into a run.

ಬೊಂ

FENNICK'S ISLAND

The barges would soon arrive from the mainland, which left Aneida and Trifyn little time to familiarize themselves with the deadfalls, and other lethal devices that the Demon Lords had maintained to foil an invasion when they were at their most vulnerable. Though there was not enough time to discover all the traps that had been created, they managed to rough out a battle plan. If they were very lucky, their initial attacks would appear to be accidents caused by the havoc of the recent storm.

Aneida and Trifyn parted ways to take up their first positions, hidden opposite to each other within the upper cliffs of the narrow canyon. From there, they watched the barges' final approaches to the rocky shores of Fennick's Island.

The Demon Riders would have to hasten if they were to arrive at the portal in time to make either a bid for the sword themselves, or to capture whoever might emerge from the labyrinth with the prize. So unless they wanted to march for the remainder of the afternoon to get around the cliffs to the ruined castle at the far side of the valley, they were committed to travelling through the narrow canyon that lead a direct path to the valley. Aneida and Trifyn were gambling all that the Demon

Riders would take the road of least resistance.

Aneida crouched in position, squinting against the hot, bright sunlight, watching as the four barges from the mainland surged in the surf, pushed the final distance to the shore by the high tide that still boomed and roared from the violence of the storm. Oars plied the waves to the sound of a beating drum.

She turned the blade of her sword against the light, flashing a signal back to Trifyn's position on the opposite side of the canyon. She was on point, telling him when to trigger the first trap.

The two short flashes she had just signaled meant *'Stand Ready'*. One long flash would be the signal to release the trap upon the unsuspecting reinforcements. When Trifyn released his device, she would run up the canyon path to ready her own ambush, and he would then act as the lookout for her. So they would harry the 'Riders, frog-leaping to stay ahead of them while decimating their numbers along the way.

Her breath quickened, as the barges ground onto the beach. They were large, flat-bottomed ferries designed specifically to relocate troops the short distance across the water from Elevor. The oars came to a rest as the sound of a drum ceased, and wide planks banged down. Demon Riders spilled forth, forming three columns. They were afoot, horses having been left behind for space to pack more 'Riders onto the decks.

Aneida made a quick headcount. They were facing almost four hundred 'Riders. She grinned fiercely as the creatures marched up the beach, taking the path towards the narrow canyon, and directly into the killing field. Though she knew they could not possibly see her, she dropped to her belly as they entered the canyon, and passed below her hidden position. Her quickened breath puffed dust away from her lips, as she watched, eyes narrowed like a hungry mountain lion, as they marched past her towards Trifyn's first ambush.

Fierce relief roared through her when she realized that no Demon Lord accompanied the 'Riders. Perhaps Doaphin had called all Demon Lords to him in preparation for the war, or mayhap they had all been stationed here, upon Fennick's Island, when the storm had blown their castle to rubble. Whatever the reason for the lack, these troops would pay for the oversight.

The many booted feet walking in step, kicked a haze of dust into the air that boiled up over the top of the canyon to be teased away by a stiff seaward breeze. Coiled and ready, Aneida sought patience, as the marching Demon Riders seemed to take forever the finish winding into the canyon and passing by her position. She raised her sword in preparation of the signal. For just a moment, the sound of the marching feet teased memories of terror and helplessness from her heart, of a dark night, long ago, and unspeakable loss. She blinked fiercely, and her lips pulled back from her teeth in a feral grin, as battle readiness overtook all emotion, and honed it into her bloodthirsty need to destroy as many of them as possible! For her dead family! For her dying sister! For the men in the labyrinth who might be the salvation of them all, and the instrument of Doaphin's destruction! This was her silent battle cry! She flashed her signal in one long burst of light towards where Trifyn waited.

Trifyn saw Aneida's signal, though he was unable to see the passing troops from where his trap was situated, and with a grunt of effort he put his back into pulling the ripcord that yanked the block of wood free, the block that held a keystone in place that in turn held a pile of rocks suspended over the narrow canyon.

As the block popped out, Trifyn stumbled and fell forward to his knees at the resultant release of tension on the rope. He looked back over his shoulder expectantly, but nothing moved. The trap was a dud.

He fought back a curse, and was just pushing to his feet when the keystone suddenly dropped.

The resulting avalanche of stone gathered in force and fury as it rained down. Screams drifted up through the endless roar of falling stones, dust billowed, and Trifyn hid his face in his arms, clinging to the narrow path when it felt like the entire canyon was collapsing around him.

After the rumble of falling death ceased, Trifyn peeked over the ledge to view the damage. Across from him, he could see Aneida's broad grin flash, as she raised a fist in victory.

The rear of the Demon Rider columns had vanished under the avalanche of stone, and the survivors were, even now, dusting themselves off, and putting their injured to the sword. Screams of pain abruptly ceased as the wounded were killed. Trifyn grimaced as he watched, although he supposed the strategy was sound for the creatures; no injured to slow them down, and a host of newly dead Deathren to swell their numbers come the sunset.

With their retreat blocked, the reinforcements no longer had the choice of doubling back to the beach, and taking the longer, safer route around to the far side of the island. They had no choice now but to continue up the canyon. The 'Riders seemed unaware that the rockslide had been anything other than an accident of fate, as the 'Riders collected themselves, and began their forward march once more.

Trifyn caught movement on far side of the canyon, a flash of brilliant red hair in the sunlight, as Aneida ran to stay ahead of the column, and beat it to the next deadfall. Trifyn took up his point position as spotter for Aneida's trap, and flashed two long bursts of light against his sword.

Stand ready.

With the luck of the Gods, no Demon Rider would make it out of this canyon alive.

ഇരൻ

THE LABYRINTH

After an eternity of crunching monotonously through the silent bone yard of the labyrinth, the sound of howling in the far distance made both Rewn and Jord stumble to a halt.

"What was that?" whispered Jord. In the eerie, grey realm of this endless graveyard it was difficult to pinpoint the location of the cry. His head swiveled violently, as the eerie howl sounded again. "Deathren?"

"No!" Rewn cut him off sharply, "'Tis daylight!"

"How can ye tell?" Jord muttered. This was the labyrinth and anything was possible. The fog-shrouded land seemed timeless, no day, no night, an endless purgatory that they would wander until they perished.

Rewn held up his hand for silence, and cocked his head to listen more closely. "It sounds more like a wolf t' me."

Rewn and Jord's gazes locked, as the same thought occurred. They took off at a run towards where the howl seemed to have originated. Slipping and sliding over the uneven landscape, they made so much noise that in the end it was Little Wolf who found them.

"Look!" Jord panted, halting at the sight of the black wolfdog loping easily towards them. He laughed in relief, and slapped his knees, as he bent double to catch his breath.

"Is Gralyre with him?" Rewn craned his head to scan the horizon that in this flattened landscape seemed dishearteningly far away.

Jord stood upright again, his eyes narrowed. "No 'tis just the wolf. Gralyre must still be in the game."

Little Wolf danced up to them, whining excitedly. Rewn put out his hand for the wolfdog to sniff in greeting. After verifying his identity, Little Wolf turned to Jord.

Jord had never warmed to the wolfdog, mistrusting of Gralyre's constant companion, and the secret communication the two shared. He tried to back away, caught his foot in a ribcage, stumbled over a skull, and landed flat on his back. Little Wolf happily thrust his muzzle into the startled man's face. Then, mission accomplished, he moved off.

Jord wiped a grimy sleeve across the wet mark on his face. "Erg!" he stated with disgust, as he got to his feet. "I am never sure if the wolf will no' consume us all without Gralyre here t' control him!"

"Do no' be a baby!" Rewn chortled, his spirits revived at the sight of Little Wolf. "With his nose, we might be able t' track our way t' the sword from this side o' the veil, and win free o' this accursed place afore sunset!"

Little Wolf gambled away, then stopped, turned to face the men, and barked urgently.

"Oh sure," Jord mumbled pessimistically. "And when the wolf has led us so far astray that we may never find our way back, he can feed off us, as he starts t' starve!" But with no better plan to be had, and with one direction of the graveyard dishearteningly similar to the next, following the wolfdog seemed less absurd than it should have.

Little Wolf set a punishing pace that the men did not quibble with as they followed after. They were racing time for their lives, and it mattered naught if they were exhausted at the end of the long day so long as the sword was in their possession, and they were free of this abattoir.

"Do ye think he knows were he is going?" Jord asked after a time, wondering how Little Wolf could keep his nose flat to the bones while at a full lope.

Rewn shrugged his answer, too winded to speak, but even he began to question how Little Wolf could discern any scent other than that of the putrid rotting corpses.

৪৩০৪

FENNICK'S ISLAND

Saliana paced within the confines of the empty square surrounding the portal of the labyrinth, careful to keep her distance from the occupied iron cages. She had learned the hard way that when she got too near, offal would be thrown at her, but even that was preferable to the empty cage, for in the midday heat, the many bodies of the 'Riders, the ones who had not turned Deathren overnight to be consumed by the dawning sunlight, were now rotting in the midday heat, and the stench of death unsettled her stomach. The Demon Riders had been eating their own for some time, and these bodies were the slain that would never turn into Deathren. So they remained. And rotted. And stank.

Another rumbling boom rolled out of the distance, and Saliana shielded her eyes against the burning rays of the Solstice sun to try to see what it could be, but whatever it was remained out of sight in the high cliffs surrounding the valley. The crash echoed for few moments more before fading away.

She glanced back at her patient in time to see Mayvin struggle to her feet. "Mayvin! Ye must lie still! Your injury!"

Saliana's fretting protests did naught to stop her. "Where do ye think ye are going? Are ye trying t' kill yourself?" Saliana demanded, and ran to support Mayvin, as she almost fell.

Mayvin's face was bright with fever, and she seemed to be gasping in her air, as though breathing had become a chore only sustained through strength of will. Mayvin pointed to the lookout rock where Trifyn had spent the morning watching for the barges.

"Ye will ne'er make it!" Saliana insisted. "Lay still now. Rest. Conserve your strength."

Mayvin turned anguished eyes her way, seemingly unable to muster the strength to even sign her words.

Saliana suddenly realized what it was costing Mayvin to stay behind while her sister went into battle. Saliana bit her lip in indecision, for 'twas the same way she had felt this morning, watching Rewn enter the labyrinth without her. She could not fight them both, and gave a frustrated stomp of her foot, knowing before she said it that she would help Mayvin to reach the summit. "Alright! I will help ye! But we are going t' walk very slowly!"

Saliana helped Mayvin to climb over the empty cage, step by step traversing the squares of metal that made up the bars, and then down the far side.

Mayvin smiled, and weakly drew her sword, stabbing it point down in the earth for use as a crutch. Periodically, more booms and crashes echoed from the cliffs, as they made their slow way up the rocky slope that lead to the lookout. Mayvin's face was wan with sweat, and she gasped her air in shallow bursts. Saliana wondered how she had summoned the strength for the climb.

At length when they arrived at the lookout, Saliana sat Mayvin down, and forced the water skin on her, making sure she drank her fill, though Mayvin tried to refuse. Fussing over her patient, Saliana did not realize the reason Mayvin was slapping her hands away, until Mayvin finally grabbed Saliana's chin, and pointed it towards the mainland.

Up the canyon that folded its way towards the distant beach, Saliana could see where Aneida and Trifyn hid in the cliffs, and the column of soldiers mincing along the canyon floor. Then her eyes travelled further, and she saw what had caused Mayvin's disquiet. Six more barges were just now landing on the beach by the empty four that had carried the first wave of Demon Riders to the island!

"Oh.... Oh no!" Saliana whispered. She watched as they disembarked, but quickly lost count. "There are hundreds! What shall we do?"

Mayvin pinched her shoulder for attention and held up six fingers. By Mayvin's count there were six hundred 'Riders landing on the beach.

Together they watched in dismay, as the new arrivals quick-marched into the head of the narrow canyon. They were slowed somewhat by having to clamber over a large rock slide blocking the entrance, but once over, they moved with greater speed. They were only slightly hindered by the other rock slides and debris that had already killed so many of the advance unit. There was nothing to impede their progress now that all of the deadfalls had been triggered. Mayvin and Saliana watched in horror as Aneida and Trifyn released yet another rockslide onto the Demon Rider vanguard, blissfully unaware of the approaching danger.

ဆာလ

Time was passing, and still this circle of the labyrinth had not revealed its trial to Gralyre. He picked up his pace, jogging easily through the park-like setting. There was no particular trail to follow, just the large gaps between trees that were overgrown with leafy mosses and ferns. If time had not been a concern, 'twas a place that Gralyre would have enjoyed resting within, perhaps napping in the warm beams of the two suns that filtered through the giant heights of the old behemoths, giving light and shadow a chance to dapple the forest floor.

Gralyre had long since ceased to worry about the direction he chose. He knew that the labyrinth would launch its attack on his senses regardless, and it felt better to be moving than standing still. He loped through the trees, scanning the territory for signs of the trial but as the miles passed, still nothing presented itself.

Hard fear curdled Gralyre's stomach, as the playful suns turned cool, and began their evening descent, creating long, double shadows behind each tree. Had he really run out of time, or were these suns moving on their own illusory courses, independent of the world outside. How long did he have afore true sunset?

Gralyre halted beside a tree that looked the same as every other he had passed by on his run. Too much time had elapsed with no hint of the trial he was to face. Something was amiss.

He unstoppered his water skin, and drank the last of it, taking long pulls of liquid until the vessel ran dry. He slowly pivoted in place, as he considered the forest, his chest billowing, as he caught his breath. He had run for miles, much time had passed, and the labyrinth had not besieged him with a dragon or a maiden in distress. There had to be something at work other than what he had seen thus far. But what? Perhaps direction was the answer to this test?

He discarded the water skin, as there was no sense burdening himself with its empty weight, and chose a different direction to jog in. After a few moments, he spied something up ahead, and grinned in relief, experience having taught him that when the landscape changed, the test had begun. But as he approached the spot, it turned out to be a water skin, similar to what he had discarded. He picked it up in confusion and shook it, but it was empty, save for a few drops, and a horrible suspicion blackened his thoughts.

Gralyre pulled his dagger, and hacked a chunk from a tree. The raw spot in the dark bark stood out, pink and oozing sap. Gralyre sheathed his knife and jogged away. Within moments, he saw a flash of pink approaching through the trees. He cursed virulently, as he came to a stop and saw the mark he had created, and left behind mere moments ago.

To be certain that there was no mistake, he drove his dagger hilt deep into the tree, and chose another random direction. Within the same span of time, he was back where he had started, looking at the hilt of his knife.

It was a trap. No matter how far he had run, the magic of the labyrinth had been transporting him back to the beginning, over and over again since he had arrived, and he had never noticed. He had run for hours, and covered no more ground than the same fifty or so paces.

Gralyre jerked his dagger from the tree, and stared up at the sky. How much time had he wasted?

Conditions within the labyrinth were odd, changing from midnight to noon within the passage of a portal, and leaving him bewildered as to the passage of the day, but intuition warned him that he had wasted precious hours trapped in this magical forest, unaware that the insidious trial had already been at work.

Winded and confused, Gralyre flopped to the ground beneath the marked tree to catch his breath, and try to understand the nature of the trial that was before him. 'Twas obvious that he could wander forever, and never move more than a stones' throw in any one direction. This then was a true maze. Of all the paths in this forest that he could choose, one must lead out of this enchanted grove. But how was he to find it?

He ripped the bottoms of both breeches away, up to the knees, and used his dagger to cut tiny squares of the cloth. When he had collected a goodly amount, he walked forward slowly, counting his steps, and leaving a sliver of fabric with every stride. Within thirty paces, he stepped onto the first piece of cloth he had dropped.

Gralyre's clever mind raced for a solution. There had to be a point at which he was magically transported back to the beginning. Was that the solution to the test? If he could move past that barrier, would the portal then appear? The trail of fabric he had dropped would have to cease at the place where the magic reset him upon his path.

He shimmied up a tree, and gazed out over the forest grove. The dark fabric was difficult to spot, as the light of the lowing suns waned, but he finally determined that it abruptly halted after about twenty paces, and began again fifteen paces from his tree - but from the opposite direction.

He climbed down from the branches, and braced himself with determination, tamping down the panic that demanded he hurry. Keeping his eyes on the blaze marked tree, Gralyre walked backwards through the foliage. Perhaps he could confound the magic of this forest if his eyes never lost site of his point of origin?

However, when his foot stepped back across an invisible threshold, there was a blur of movement, and he was suddenly staring out at the forest that was behind his marked tree. Spinning on his heel, his jaw hardened for he could clearly see his pack lying on the ground fifteen paces away. Walking backwards had gained him nothing.

'Think! There must be a solution!'

Gralyre returned to his pack, and sat beside it, crossing a

hand over his eyes. There was an answer. There was a way out! He took a deep breath, and tried to get his mind working, but all he could see was Catrian's face, all he could feel was the sense of his own failure at her coming death.

'Reason it through. Figure it out.'

He picked up his discarded dagger to idly flip, as he thought. Every direction led back to the place where he began. This place felt less like a test and more like a trap. He could try to use his sorcery, but he had no clue what to use to confound this trial.

His gaze was caught by the glitter of his blade, as it spun in the air, before the hilt smacked down firmly into his hand. With a flick of his wrist, he flipped it again. Around and around, the spinning blade of the dagger caught the light, and flashed it into his eyes. The sun was setting quickly.

If the nature of the test was a trap, then there had to be a way out, a direction he had yet to try. Would there be a signpost of some kind, like a unique tree, that would lead to the portal? But he already knew that the forest was utterly uniform. The dagger blade flashed as it spun.

He was circling the solution, he could feel it, but he needed more time! The dagger flashed again, blinding him. He caught the handle by instinct, halting its motion. The sun was setting; he had no more time. If he did not discover the solution all was lost. His friends, the fate of all mankind under the evil boot of Doaphin! And Catrian...

Gralyre raised his head, and swallowed thickly, as he gazed forlornly out at the late day suns. It could not end like this! He would not allow it! He flipped the knife once more, and was rewarded by the flashing blade. He stared across at the setting suns. More time! He just needed more time!

Flash. The blade's reflected brilliance once more caught his attention.

'The SUNS!'

Awareness slammed into him like a heavy punch to his guts, halting his breath, and he missed his catch, fumbling and losing the dagger. It speared the ground with a force that left its hilt quivering. The flat of the blade faced him, shinning brilliantly.

If the suns were in his face, then what light was the blade reflecting? He spun his head to look back, but there was naught behind him but more dappled forest and ferns.

Hardly daring to hope, Gralyre pulled the knife free of the dirt, and lifted the dagger before his eyes, angled to reflect the unknown light. There, distorted by the polished metal of the blade was the shimmering gate! He looked over his shoulder but could still see only the forest.

How was he to reach it? He had already walked backwards once, and had been unsuccessful, but, he grinned, he had walked backwards in the wrong direction, and had been gazing elsewhere. Perhaps, he was required to keep his gaze upon the reflection at his back?

Gralyre fixated upon the image of the shimmering portal in the blade, fearing it would vanish if he looked away. He took a long step back, then another, suppressing his awareness of the surrounding forest until he stood upon the gate's threshold.

It was there! It was right there!

He turned his head until the portal should have been visible from the corner of his eye but he still could not see it. The forest surrounded him, but clearly in the mirror of the blade, he could see that he was mere inches away from his own shimmering reflection in the liquid surface of an amber coloured portal. The runes pulsed and glowed beckoningly.

Holding his breath and praying to the Gods of Fortune for success, he took the final step backward, and could have yelled in victory, as the shimmering light of the next gate engulfed him.

₨₩

"Why did he stop?" a breathless Jord asked a panting Rewn.

"How...should...I know?" Rewn snapped while trying to catch his breath.

The two men glared at Little Wolf, as the wolfdog wandered in ever contracting circles with his nose to the ground. Seeming to have found what he was looking for, Little Wolf sat. His panting tongue stopped its locomotion, and his ears cocked forward, as he stared intently at a point in the air. Jord and Rewn looked at each other, then back at the spot, as a shimmer rippled through the space that Little Wolf was fixated upon.

The air ripped open like a curtain had been parted, and within a flash of light, Dotch tumbled out into the rotting corpses, fetching up in the embrace of a whitened skeleton. He heaved himself to his feet, doing a little dance as he tried to remove rotting 'Rider corpse from his arms and chest. "Demon humping, inescapable, enchanted forests!" he cursed.

Despite their predicament, Rewn and Jord found themselves laughing.

Dotch glanced up in surprise. "Lads!" he yelled with a grin, and then lost it as he considered the ramifications. All of them had failed. "Gralyre?" he asked.

Jord shook his head. "No sign yet."

Rewn smiled. "He will do it. He will get the sword." It was a statement of absolute faith in his friend.

Dotch nodded, his eyes narrowed in concern. "I hope ye are right, lad, because I reckon that our time is almost up."

೫෦ଓ

Gralyre exited backwards through the portal, and caught a brief glimpse of his undulating reflection in the surface of the mirror before the gateway faded away, leaving an unimpeded view of what seemed to be the apex of a high mountain plateau.

His image had shocked him, for it was a roadmap of what he had endured this day, from the dried runnels of blood that still flaked beneath his ears, to the ash and mud that smeared his body, to the snaking streams of sweat that had cut deep channels through the filth of his chest and face during his run in the forest. Even the wafting scent of rotting fish lingered in the air about him. But it was his face that remained trapped within his mind's eye, ragged, filthy, and set in hard lines of desperation, as he wondered what challenge he must endure next.

Open air, and the clouds of the heavens surrounded him on all sides, and he drew in a large lungful of the fresh air, crisp with the scent of altitude and ozone, as he got his bearings and braced himself for the next trial. The flattened granite of the plateau was littered with boulders, some as large as small cottages, some rocks smaller than his fist, and was roughly circular in shape with a diameter of about fifty paces. He walked towards the edge of the expanse, and stopped with a queasy lurch when he realized that this was no mountain peak. The plateau was suspended in the air! Beneath him was naught but clouds! As he stumbled back from the drop-off, his boot rolled off one of the smaller rocks, and he had a momentary quaver at the thought of falling.

As he steadied his footing, the air manifested a voice, as deep and ancient as the rocks upon which he stood. "Which is stronger within you? Choose and prove your worth!"

The voice was in his head, it was echoed from within the rocks, it vibrated inside his chest, and compressed his lungs and his heart. It brooked no dissension.

"Choose? Choose what? I do not understand!" Gralyre yelled back, for he had lost all patience with disembodied voices.

"Choose who you would be! Choose the light, or choose the dark! CHOOSE!"

To Gralyre, the choice was not a choice at all. "I choose the light!"

"So be it," the voice rumbled ominously, setting the smaller stones of the plateau to bouncing, as they resonated in concert.

Gralyre felt a stabbing deep in his being, a tearing of the very fabric of his soul, and flung his head back, screaming, as something essential was sundered and wrenched away from him, created from him.

Black vapour streamed from his eyes, nose and mouth, choking off his breath, as it churned into itself, coalescing into something solid, something menacing, an entity that reeked of pure evil. Bolts of angry red lightning shot through the length of the thing and collected into sparking red holes where eyes would be. Limbs extended, and the hovering torso settled upon misty black legs.

Gralyre collapsed onto one knee, wheezing and gagging the last of the foulness from his lips. As the remnants of black vapour left him, he finally gained a gasping breath of the clean air, and felt himself suddenly lightened of all burdens.

His heartbeat settled, and his breathing steadied, and for no reason at all, a smile of pure happiness shot across his face, and he laughed. For the first time since he had awakened without his memories, he felt himself content and happy, free of all doubts, guilts and hatreds.

He grinned up at the shadowy presence forming above him, and realized what had just happened. The power of the labyrinth had cleaved him into two beings, one of light and one of shadow. By choosing sides, the evil of his soul had been made manifest in this shadow man.

Gralyre was deeply disturbed by the amount of darkness he

had carried within him. But no more! A peaceful smile spread across his face for he was released from all chains, and it was a beautiful day to be alive!

The Shadowman flexed its empty hand, and an obsidian sword grew out from its misty palm. It turned the midnight blade before its angrily sparking eyes, as though admiring it, before its glowing, red gaze fixated upon Gralyre, who was still kneeling at its feet.

Gralyre felt no fear as he stood, only a vague curiosity at the shadow's actions. Then he recalled the disembodied voice's words.

'Choose and prove your worth.'

Was he meant to fight this creature? He felt no ill will or need of conflict, but the Shadowman had armed itself so it would only be prudent were Gralyre to do so as well. He loved to sword dance in any case, and here in the crisp air the exercise would be exhilarating.

With a chuckle of pure joy and anticipation, his blade leapt into his hand, swinging up just in time to protect his neck from a severing blow, as the Shadowman attacked.

But Gralyre returned no strike of his own, for the very thought of harming his shadow self was abhorrent, and as the attacks came faster, harder, he did naught but match his opponent move for move, doing only what was required to protect himself from harm.

For the first time in memory he was able to employ all of his considerable skill against an opponent, and the powerful beauty of his mastery was a wondrous experience that thrilled him. But as the battle continued, one sided in aggression but equally matched of skills, Gralyre recognized that something was amiss.

All of his expertise with the sword was present, but it held no vibrancy, and seemed of no more consequence to him than the sweeping of a broom would be. The pulse of the dance was missing, and with it the sharpness of his senses. The battle rage that made any deed permissible in the name of survival was absent, and Gralyre felt nothing but compassion for the creature that sought his death with such mindless ferocity. He was content and happy, almost fatalistic, for the fear of death that made life a priority was missing. Were he to die here, so be it.

By contrast, the Shadowman's pain and rage manifested in crackling lightning bursts along the surface of the churning black fog of its body, illuminating contorted features in the brief strobes of light, as it slashed and thrust with its blackened sword. Gralyre was repulsed by the rough parody of his own face, wondering if this was how he appeared to foes upon whom he made war.

They fought across the granite platform, Gralyre always giving ground to his shadow, until the dark warrior forced him to the brink of the plateau, where nothing lay beneath but slowly drifting clouds.

Gralyre, sweating now from his exertions, realized that he would die. Though he felt no need for self-preservation over the life of his shadow, he knew an obligation to his friends, and to the woman he loved. They needed him to live, so he tried to step to the side, to move away from the precipice, but his dark self was there to block his retreat.

The Shadowman hammered at Gralyre's blade, forcing him ever closer to the brink.

'Catrian,' Gralyre's heart sang. Their fates were inextricably entwined, and by his death would he cause hers.

He stumbled on a stone, and fell to his back, his head hanging out into space. Lightning flashed in the shadowy face above him, revealing a chilling smile of triumph.

But Gralyre had finally found a talisman to fight for. Pure, undiluted love filled his being at the memory of his Sorceress. A fierce protectiveness steadied his arm, and surged new strength through his muscles. He rolled out from under the descending black blade, and gained his feet, spinning to meet the oncoming attack, as his dark shadow recovered from the miss, and lashed out with a roar.

Gralyre would do anything to protect Catrian, and surmount any obstacle to save her! He would even fight the greatest darkness within himself! Suddenly the beat of the dance was upon him, returned to him, as he found the part of himself that had been missing from the fight.

His awareness of the Shadowman, of what it represented, burst upon him with perfect clarity, and he knew exactly how to defeat it. For the first time Gralyre brought the attack to the entity, and the misty being stumbled back, as Gralyre forced the fight away from the drop-off.

This darkness had always been a part of him, and he had

always tempered its power with his honour, conscience, and intent. It was human nature to always undergo the struggle to do good and not evil. He had thought them evenly matched, but now he knew that the light in him was stronger than the dark. It had always been stronger.

Gralyre's sword began to glow with a white light, and when next he slashed at the Shadowman, his weapon passed through its obsidian blade, as though it were of no substance, chopping deeply into the misty torso, and straight into the shadow's heart. There it held, impaled. The doppelganger's essence roiled and hissed like the steam from a kettle around his puncturing sword, and Gralyre was forced to release the blade to shake out his frost burned fingers.

The Shadowman threw back its head, and screamed its rage and pain at the heavens, and its voice was Gralyre's voice. Then it began to fade, until Gralyre could spy the surface of the plateau through its body, but it was not quite defeated. The Shadowman's black sword dissolved from its grasp, and it grabbed ahold of Gralyre's face.

Images of battles exploded into Gralyre's mind, endless parades of slaughters he had perpetrated, and men he had killed. He staggered backwards, his light side unable to reconcile the carnage. Gralyre's impaling sword fell through the misty torso to clang harmlessly to the ground, as the Shadowman darkened again, gaining strength, as the Gralyre of Light faltered.

Then Gralyre remembered why he had fought, why he had killed. He had been fighting evil, and injustice. He had been fighting for the side of righteousness, protecting the innocent so that the horrors of Doaphin would not prevail.

Once more the Shadow fell back, fainter than ever, as the Gralyre of Light reclaimed strength. Almost nothing remained when it launched its final attack, throwing the loss of the pups, the loss of Wil, and all of Gralyre's failures into his mind's eye.

Gralyre's pain and guilt crashed over him, and nearly stole away his hard won victory, but he had already fought this particular battle today, and he now knew how to defeat his guilt forever. "I forgive you," he whispered hoarsely to his shadow. With an anticlimactic *POP*, the Shadowman vanished.

Gralyre staggered dizzily, and when his faintness passed he felt himself made whole once more. He spared a moment's regret for the passing of the creature of pure light that he could never be, but would always strive to become. Sometimes dark deeds were necessary to combat evil and save the innocent, but it was only through the guidance of the light that he was able to determine those times. By tempering his inner darkness, he could trust that, though he might not always make the right decisions, he would make them for the right reasons.

Be his memories hidden from him or no, he no longer feared whom he would be revealed to be when, or if, they ever returned for he had proven to himself that he had more good within him than evil. It was enough.

Sheathing his sword with a rasping flick, he entered the humming gate that had appeared, and set off to do battle with the last challenge.

CHAPTER FIFTEEN

Gralyre stepped through the seventh and final gate, onto a road of uneven, slate paver stones that were cracked and buckled, as though the earth beneath were a snake trying to shed old scales. Wisps of mist wreathed the ground, slinking coyly around fallen columns that lay like the bolls of great, toppled trees to either side of the stone pathway, and whose shattered stumps were as broken and worn as the teeth of an old man. The sky was a dull grey, giving no indication of the lateness of the hour, but then he needed naught but his own inner timepiece to know that the day was waning. In the far distance, he could barely see a circle of columns upon a small rise, and his heart raced with excitement, for this must surely be where the sword lay. He had made it!

He need only step forward to claim his prize yet the labyrinth had taught him caution, so that though he wanted to run, he tested each step forward. Unable to see his footing clearly in the low lying mists, he cautiously followed the ancient, uneven road delineated by the shattered columns to either side, unwilling to trust the apparent ease of this, the final test.

Despite his vigilance, he stumbled upon an uplifted stone, grunting as he caught his balance against one of the massive, collapsed columns. Walking upon the buckled pavers was taking too long, but there were other pathways he could make use of.

Gralyre leapt to the top of the fallen column, clear of the ground-hugging mist, and trod nimbly down its length before leaping the gap over to the next.

In this way, he quickly covered the distance towards the distant hillock, and when he reached the end of the last of the toppled columns, he paused to evaluate what it was he faced.

Less than fifty feet ahead, rising like an island in the mists was a small hillock, humped like the back of a turtle. Though the space from the end of Gralyre's column to the hill was hidden in swirling fog he could clearly see the ancient road leading into the open temple at the crest. Sixteen columns that had somehow remained erect over the ages formed a circular honor guard for a stone sarcophagus.

Gralyre leapt down off the column and back to the buckled pathway, but the curling mist made it troublesome to judge the ground level. He landed awkwardly, and a paver stone beneath his boot wobbled, making him work to recover his balance. As he windmilled his arms, and stepped back to steady his footing, the flat stone skittered forward out from under his boot, and splashed into liquid. The fog was hiding something.

Gralyre inched forward, and then faltered to a halt for where the paver had splashed in, the liquid bubbled and boiled, as it hungrily digested the stone offering. The resultant upheaval stirred the mists away, and showed his path to the hill to be blocked by a wide moat.

Gralyre hastily stepped backwards, as the boiling liquid geysered and spat. Even so, he was not quick enough, and it splashed onto his sword sheath. Immediately, it began to smoke and burn, eating quickly through the tough leather.

'Not water! Acid!'

"Gods!" Gralyre cursed, and unbuckled the scabbard, letting it drop to the ground, where the droplets of acid finish eating the sheath, and began to pit the blade within. It happened so quickly that there was no way for him to save his sword.

Gralyre took several further prudent steps back from the edge, checking his body for any other spatter, but he had been fortunate that only his scabbard had been touched by the splash.

Hands on hips, he took a moment to study the landscape, squinting his eyes as he tried to measure the curvature of the moat's path against the dimensions of the hillock in the center, attempting to estimate the distance across, but the blanketing fog hid the shores of the far bank from his keen sight. Gralyre was forced to acknowledge that it was too far to vault, and the thought of his fate should he fall short, and land in the acid moat finished that idea.

The grave-like stillness was shattered by the burble and boil of the caustic moat as the acid finished consuming the paver stone.

He stared yearningly across at the low hill, where the crypt was centred in its ring of columns. It had to be the resting place of the Dragon Sword, and perhaps also the tomb of the Lost Prince, the answer to the riddle of what had befallen the ancient hero. There had to be a way across, a bridge somewhere, and it would only be sensible if it was located where the road met the moat.

Now that the acid had settled, Gralyre cautiously inched forward again to the edge of the stone path, and crouched down, waving his hands to stir away the thick vapour. Triumph made him smile grimly, as he revealed the ancient, acid-pitted, mortared stones of a bridge landing, however, the mist frustratingly kept the far side of the moat hidden from his gaze, giving no clues as to the nature of the draw bridge that must be suspended on the far side.

There had to be a way to extend the bridge, a trigger mechanism of some kind, otherwise, there really was no way to reach the sword, and the labyrinth was naught but an elaborate trap. As though in answer to his disheartening thought, the mist eddied away, revealing a man-sized obelisk of black marble set to the right of the path.

It had definitely not been there a moment ago, but illusion was king in the labyrinth. Adjacent to the obelisk was the raised stone masonry of an ancient well, and several feet away from both, on the banks of the caustic moat, rested a wooden platform with a weight and pulley contraption hooked onto it.

Well used to the labyrinth's tricks by now, Gralyre did not question why he had not previously noticed the structures, only allowed himself a moment of relief that the trial had finally manifested. He made his way towards the apparatus that could only be the controls to the much-needed drawbridge.

Ragged, age-worn hemp ropes disappeared into gaps in the stones at his feet, while several suspended iron weights delicately counterbalanced a small hovering platform. He rubbed a hand over his bearded chin, as he bent to examine it, to understand the mechanism at work, and realized that the drawbridge would only extend upon the correct amount of pressure upon the platform, an exact weight that would trigger the device. Too much or too little would throw the counterbalance off, and destroy the machinery, severing all access across the moat. Carved into the wood of the platform were four slashes. | | | |

He turned to examine the timeworn well. A waist high wall of stacked stones circled the well to protect the liquid within. Two crystal decanters, one large and one small, balanced upon the wide lip of the rounded wall, but he avoided touching them as he examined the artifacts closely, for the labyrinth had taught him a healthy respect for its challenges; they were never quite what they seemed.

Leaving the well be for the moment, Gralyre walked to the man-sized, black obelisk, and saw that it was boldly inscribed with deeply carved symbols.

In the upper left corner were three deep slashes, and in the upper right, five slashes marred the stone. Converging lines lead from beneath both symbols, coming to a point at an inscription of four slashes.

Gralyre ran his fingers across the cryptic marks, guessing that they were the formula for the correct weight to extend the drawbridge.

Gralyre circled the edifice, looking for more inscriptions, but each of the four sides of the spear of stone held precisely the same marks.

"From eight comes four," Gralyre mumbled to himself. "Or three and five equals four?" He shook his head grimly, at the obtuse markings.

Back at the well, he picked up the smaller of the crystal decanters, and as the angle of the light refracting through the glass changed, he saw that it had three slashes inscribed on its side, and sure enough, the larger one was etched with five. He circled the well, trying in vain to find the container marked with four slashes, but there was none, and no smashed crystal crunched underfoot to indicate that such a container had ever existed.

He glanced up at the sky, beating back his urgency, as he worked through the problem. The counterbalance of the machine needed the weight to equal four in order to activate the controls for the bridge, but with a container for three, and a container for five it could not be done!

It had to be done!

Gralyre had to create the weight of four from the crystal decanters provided. It was a riddle.

He moved to the edge of the well, and stared suspiciously down at the liquid shimmer. It appeared to be ordinary water, but mindful of the contents of the moat, Gralyre took the liberty of dropping a stone into it. With a hollow splash, it sunk from sight, with no bubbling or boiling involved.

A slight humming began to shimmer through the air, and it could mean only one thing. Outside the labyrinth, the sun was beginning to set. Soon the portals would move apart, and the way back to the world would be shut to him. There was no time! He had to act!

Clenching his jaw against the danger, he dipped his pinkie finger into the liquid, and hissed out a breath of deep relief, as cool water momentarily embraced the digit to the first joint.

Gralyre dipped the large decanter, and held it aloft, squinting in concentration, as he carefully poured dribbles until it appeared one fifth of the water had been removed. Was it close enough that its weight would now activate the bridge?

He left the well and eagerly moved to the bridge controls, yet he hesitated to place the container upon the counterbalanced platform. He had most certainly made a mistake, for he had not used the container marked three, as was instructed upon the obelisk. His solution had been too obvious and simple. Gralyre scowled and dumped his careful work to the ground. If it was not an exact measurement, he would destroy the controls to the bridge, and his one chance to reach the sword.

He set the crystal decanter back on the lip of the well, and stepped back, eyeing the two containers for inspiration. Three added to five equaled four? How was he to make four by adding three to five? That made eight, and there was no container for that.

The answer was suddenly there in his mind, and he marveled at the brilliance and simplicity of the solution to the riddle. His heart filled with hope. That had to be it! 'Twas the only way!

Gralyre took up the decanter marked with three slashes and dipped it full to the brim. Careful not to spill, he poured it into the larger container then he repeated the exercise, leaned back, and smiled. The decanter marked with five slashes was now full to the brim, which did not matter, because the smaller container now held exactly one unit of water. He emptied the larger container, and replaced the liquid with the perfect portion from the small decanter. *'One.'*

Gralyre refilled the small decanter so that the water was level at the top, and slowly added its contents to the one unit of water already held by the larger container.

"Three added to five equals four," Gralyre grinned in triumph.

The humming was gradually gaining in volume as Gralyre, careful not to spill even a drop, bore the large crystal decanter to the pulley system, and settled it in place upon the platform.

At first, nothing seemed to happen, and Gralyre felt a bead of sweat trickle down his chest, as he began to pray to the Gods of Fortune that he had made the correct measurement. If he were wrong, it was over, and Catrian's life was forfeit.

With a grinding sound of age and disuse, the platform depressed and the counterbalance activated the pulleys and ropes. Gralyre shouted with victory, and shook his fists at the large, flat, arch of rock that descended out of the fog on the far side of the moat, and slammed down onto the landing at the edge of the old, stone path. It came to rest with a heavy splash, spraying acid in a wide arc, and immediately began to dissolve. The stones fronting the drawbridge landing pitted and sputtered from the acid that had spattered them.

Shielding himself as best he could from the geysering liquid to either side, Gralyre sprinted across the rock bridge, and arrived unharmed on the far shore. He jogged up the knoll, and directly towards the sarcophagus in its ring of columns, leaving behind the bridge, as it snapped and groaned and dissolved. He had to retrieve the sword quickly, for his avenue of escape would soon vanish and leave him stranded!

The buzz in the air continued to gather volume, and Gralyre fought back a wave of dread, as the sounds of the slowly dissolving stone bridge vied with the increasing hum of the labyrinth preparing to seal for another year.

The sarcophagus was roughly eight feet in length, and the capstone rose to the middle of Gralyre's chest. Worn with age but still visible, the exterior marble was intricately carved with scenes of battles. Unfortunately, the pulleys that had extended the drawbridge had not opened the tomb. Had the ancient mechanism failed in some way? Had Gralyre used the wrong measurement of water?

Shrugging his heavily muscled shoulders to loosen them, he wedged his back under the lip of the capstone of the tomb, braced his arms against his legs, and he heaved upwards with all his might.

Nothing happened. The stone did not so much as tremble, let alone slide from place. Gralyre was trying single-handedly to shift a capstone that would take six strong men to throw off. Releasing his effort, he allowed himself to sag to a squatting position while he recovered his breath.

The bridge emitted a tortured groan, and the spewing acid further mocked his failure. The stone pavers beneath his feet began to vibrate with the approach of the realignment of the portals.

His time was up.

Gralyre reached into his tunic, for the precious token he had carried over his heart for all these many months of hardship. He raised the plait of Catrian's hair to his lips. "I am sorry," he whispered.

ഇന്ദ

FENNICK'S ISLAND

Aneida signaled Trifyn to release the deadfall. This was the final trap, and there was still the equal to a squad of Demon Riders making their way cautiously through the narrow canyon. The first two ambushes had worked very well, felling many of the enemy, but since then, the 'Riders had grown overly cautious, watching the heights for falling stones, and though Trifyn and Aneida had winnowed their numbers significantly, they were still facing at least twenty of the enemy. Two more twists to the narrow ravine, and the remains of the Demon Rider forces would be free of the canyon. Then things would get bloody, as they battled for control of the cages and the portal.

When the dust from the rockslide cleared, six more 'Riders lay buried under stone. Trifyn and Aneida ducked the rain of arrows that smacked against the rocks behind which they hid. The 'Riders did not know exactly where they were, but that did not stop them from trying to kill their tormentors with a lucky shot.

As Aneida waited for the arrow storm to cease, she was already devising the next plan of attack. She popped her head up, and did a quick count, ducking down again before she could be spotted. The Demon Riders now numbered a baker's dozen. Against their four, it was not the odds she had hoped for after their labors on the death traps for the better part of the afternoon, but it was far better than what they had faced when the barges had landed. Of more concern was what would happen at sunset, when the Deathren left behind in the canyon awoke, and came hunting.

With any luck Aneida, Saliana Mayvin and Trifyn would already be dead before the Deathren began to howl.

A rattle of stones skidded into her hiding place, and Aneida flinched from her musings, reeling in alarm. She relaxed when she saw it was Saliana, but the pounding in her heart made her tone terse and unfriendly. "What are ye doing here? Why are ye no' at the cages? Has something happened t' Mayvin?" Aneida fired off the questions. "And get down!" she ordered, tugging Saliana's arm to pull the woman flat, as another barrage of black fletched arrows smacked into the surrounding rocks in response to the sound of her voice.

Saliana dropped to her belly. "Listen t' me!" she forcefully silenced Aneida's questions.

Aneida's eyebrows shot towards her hairline, for she had never heard this little mouse squeak before, and now suddenly she was snapping orders like a lion.

"Six more barges have arrived from the mainland. There are more 'Riders coming through the canyon. Many more! Mayvin counted six hundred. And they will be here any moment!" Saliana gasped out her message, winded from the climbing and running it had taken to reach Aneida's position.

"Gods, no!" Aneida snarled, slapping her hand against the rock. As she glared back along the twisting, narrow canyon, towards the direction of the beachhead, her eyes widened, and a sound of disgust growled out of her throat, as she realized what had happened. "'Twas all a ruse! They knew about the deadfalls, and sent an advance party t' force us t' trigger them all, so that when the bulk o' the 'Riders arrived they would traverse safely through the canyon!"

"Should we return t' the cages and await them?"

Aneida shut her eyes for a moment, as desperation and weariness slashed through the sweat and dirt on her face, and her mouth thinned and turned down at the corners. "No. Come with me!"

Grabbing Saliana's arm, and dragging her along, Aneida was up and running along the rim of the canyon, as sure footed as a cat. Far below, the surviving Demon Riders continued their cautious march forward. They had never been meant to reach the valley of the portal. They were nothing but the goats that had been sent to tempt them to exhaust their only advantage.

On the opposite rim of the canyon, Trifyn caught sight of Aneida and Saliana flitting through the rocks, and saw from their body language that something urgent had happened, so he kept apace with them on his side of the gully. After springing this last deadfall they were to have rendezvoused at the lookout, but he could see that the women were working their way down to the canyon floor instead, so he altered his course to match theirs.

Mayvin, who was waiting on the road at the exit to the canyon, met him when he arrived. "What is wrong? What has happened?" Trifyn asked.

With quick hand gestures Mayvin told him of the additional forces that had landed. Moments later, heralded by a small shower of dirt and rocks, Aneida and Saliana skidded onto the canyon floor.

"We are finished here! Quickly, back t' the cages!" Trifyn urged.

"No!" Aneida snarled. "Ye go, I will stay here!"

Trifyn followed her gaze towards the one deadfall that had been too dangerous for them to even consider using. "'Tis suicide!" Trifyn breathed, staring up at the towering columns of rock to either side of them. Attached to ropes, a small keystone was set on either side of the canyon and held tons of loose rock wall suspended to either side. When pulled, the cliff would collapse inwards, burying whoever had pulled the linchpins, as well as any enemy, and sealing the exit to the canyon. To be entirely effective, the trap would have to be triggered when the enemy had almost surrounded the ambusher.

Trifyn shook his head in denial, as fear clutched his vitals, making his palms sweat and his knees weak, but he knew, as well as the others did, that it was their last chance. Someone would have to make the sacrifice. If the approaching 'Rider army made it through the canyon, the small group of defenders would be slaughtered at the cages. There would be no one left to protect the retreat should Gralyre and the others make it out of the labyrinth alive. He drew a deep breath. "Alright we need a longer rope, and we will pull it from far enough away that..."

Aneida slapped his face lightly, her challenging grin fierce. "There is no' enough time. Get the others t' safety right now!"

"No, Aneida, we need your sword. I will do it." He had always feared death, but now that it was here, he wanted it to mean something, not in a vain quest for a mystical sword, but in protecting his friends.

"No!" Aneida made a sharp gesture. "It has t' be me! We need your bow t' protect the cages at the end. I will do it!"

"No, I will." Saliana breathed fearfully. She was the only one, and she knew it. "We will need your sword in the fight at the cages Aneida, and Trifyn's bow, no' my healer's touch! I am the expendable one. I have no warrior skills. I am expendable," she repeated. The others said nothing, just stared at Saliana's stubborn face, as though seeing her for the first time.

Aneida was shamed by her previous opinion of Saliana, as she saw for the first time the quiet courage that this woman had, and she swallowed heavily. "Ye are right," she agreed, and her voice caught. "Ye are right." Aneida stated with more strength. "Let me show ye how it works." Aneida turned away so that Saliana would not see the grief upon her face, and a small rock hit her in the middle of her back, turning her around angrily to see that Mayvin had something to add to the matter.

Wait! Mayvin's hands wove urgently. *I, and no other, must do this. I am dying, Aneida, and choose not to die in my bed, but killing as many of them as I can to protect you.* So weak was she that she wavered where she stood.

"Mayvin," Aneida breathed, as tears welled in her eyes. "Ye have no' the strength."

I have the strength! It is my due! It is my right! Her eyes blazed with fanaticism and fever. *I am dying! Nothing can stop that now! It is my right to choose how I shall die!* Her eyes challenged them all to deny her.

"Mayvin, please...no." Aneida cried out brokenly.

There is no time. I love you, my sister, more than anything in this world. I would never cause ye pain, but in this ye will respect my wishes! My wound has poisoned me. Let me do this. You live a little while longer, and defend the portal. Mayvin's expression turned pained, as she looked at Trifyn and Saliana's stricken faces. *We will all die this day. I claim this death for my own.*

Aneida hung her head, her shoulders heaving with rough sobs, as the approaching sound of marching feet echoed from within the canyon. What remained of the vanguard of the Demon Rider army would soon be upon them, and upon their heels were six hundred more of the hated enemy. Panicking at the thought of Mayvin's sacrifice, she roughly embraced her sister, her face contorted with her anguish.

Trifyn turned away, and began to climb back up the canyon wall, using the scant hand and footholds to gain the upper pathway.

"Where are ye going?" Aneida hissed after him through her tears.

"If this last deadfall is t' decimate the approaching six hundred, then we must first finish off the rest o' the vanguard t' give Mayvin the room t' spring it on the ones behind," he reminded as he climbed higher. He reached the top of the canyon wall and unslung his bow. He had more than enough arrows to do the job, as he had been collecting them every time the 'Riders had shot at him during the long day.

Aneida continued to embrace Mayvin for long moments, her face reddened, and wet with tears of pain. "I must go help Trifyn," Aneida sobbed.

Mayvin's good arm wrapped tightly around her sister's back, and her injured arm dangled loosely at her side until finally, she pulled back. Holding her sister firmly by her shoulder she smiled encouragingly. *Fight well Aneida! Hold them back. Give me the time I need t' show them the way t' the underworld!*

Aneida dashed the tears from her eyes, leaving dirty smudges upon her cheek. Her mouth firmed as she allowed the warrior within to harden the woman. "I will, sister!" She turned away, hesitated and turned back. "Die well, Mayvin," A wistful smile lifted her lips. "Father would approve."

Mayvin's face brightened with a fierce grin. *I will await ye beyond the veil. And Aneida?*

"Yes?"

Make sure 'tis a long wait!

Aneida nodded, her face hard and blank of emotion, as she turned away to climb back up the rock wall opposite to the side Trifyn had taken.

Saliana stared after her with indecision, uncertain what role she should play in the coming fight. Finally, as she watched Mayvin struggle to pick up one of the lengths of ripcord she recognized where she could do the most good. She sighed heavily, and collected both rope ends, and dragged them to Mayvin's side, dropping them heavily into the dust for the moment.

"Can ye move your arm at all?"

No, Mayvin winced. *It has been dead for a day.*

Saliana considered the problem for a moment. "If ye wrap the ropes around your body, like this," she proceeded to anchor the cords around Mayvin's hips, "then ye will no' have t' use your arms t' pull at all. The weight o' your body will do the work."

Mayvin smiled at her. *Well healer, if you are going to keep me alive until I can die, you had better take this!* She passed her sword into Saliana's trembling hands.

"I...I am no' very good," Saliana sputtered with surprise.

Do not worry, Mayvin reassured, and then pressed Saliana's hands upon the hilt. *This sword has a memory, and it knows the way. You just need hold it, and it will do the rest!*

Saliana's returned smile was sickly.

Mayvin suddenly doubled over with a fit of coughing, and the hand she used to cover her mouth came away bloody.

"Mayvin!" Saliana pulled out her water skin, and held it to Mayvin's lips. "Drink! Take as much as ye need," she urged.

Mayvin drank weakly from the skin then pushed it away violently. *Save it for the others. Do not worry, healer! I will not die before I do my duty.*

It hurt Saliana to think that Mayvin mistook her deep concern for a venal motive. "See that ye do!" She snapped, dropping the water skin to the dirt at Mayvin's feet and, head high, stalked into the narrow exit of the canyon, holding Mayvin's sword aloft in a two handed grip, as she had seen Rewn do on numerous occasions. She had watched him wield his sword so often she had the moves practically memorized.

Mayvin watched her go with grim amusement, for it was better for Saliana to go into battle angry than scared! She sagged her weight into the ropes, conserving her strength for the right moment.

Saliana's head snapped up at the twang of Trifyn's bowstring and the answering scream of death, as his arrow found its first mark. On its heals came the sounds of rocks striking bodies, and cries of alarm and pain, as Aneida heaved stones over the lip of the steep canyon wall to fall upon the last survivors. Saliana tightened her grip upon Mayvin's sword, staring intently at the curvature of the canyon wall that hid the fight from her gaze, determined that no 'Rider would make it past her.

Another whistle of an arrow, and another death. She heard a flurry of deep thrums as the 'Riders returned fire. Then another clatter of stones, as Aneida threw more rocks upon the enemy. Disembodied echoes bounced eerily in the confined area of the canyon floor, making Saliana shudder with dread, her mouth going dry as, finally, she heard pounding footsteps coming towards her.

She stepped to the side, and drew Mayvin's sword back behind her head, priming herself for a vicious swing. The Demon Rider rounded the curve at a run while glancing back over his shoulder, and never saw the small woman waiting with a deadly sword in her hands, and never had a chance to raise his shield.

Saliana swung with all her might. Mayvin's sword was very sharp, and bit deeply through the neck of the 'Rider as he ran past. He staggered onwards for a few more paces, his head listing on his neck, before collapsing into the dirt.

Over the pounding of Saliana's heart she could here another soldier fast approaching, and readied her stance.

She was just in time, and did not even aim, just swung in panic. The Demon Rider skidded in surprise, as he rounded the corner, but it was to late. She jumped back to avoid the geyser of blood, as the Demon Rider lost his head. She fought back her gorge, reminding herself that she could not fail. She was all that Mayvin had for protection.

Taking a deep, steadying breath, she raised her sword and took up her position again. More rocks fell; more arrows were heard to reach their mark, and Saliana had a long wait, for the 'Riders were having trouble fleeing the killing ground in the crossfire between Trifyn and Aneida. The sword jittered and shook as her arm weakened, but Saliana was too scared to relax her stance for fear that she would not be ready when the next 'Rider appeared. And then, faster than she could believe, two of them rounded the corner in front of her.

Saliana swung her bloodied sword, but she was too slow, and her target easily blocked her inexperienced swing. She slashed out again and again, with wide sweeps of her blade, holding them both in front of her, preventing them from moving around her, but doing them no damage. She was in terrible danger for the element of surprise, which had been her only weapon, was gone.

Over the ringing of their swords on hers, they snarled, bloody and berserk with their own fear. One of them aimed a heavy overhand blow at her head that clanged on Saliana's weak defense, and drove the flat of her own sword against her temple.

Saliana stumbled back, her ears ringing from the blow, as the skin split and blood gushed out to soak her face. Using both hands, and whimpering with the effort, she weakly raised her sword to parry another slash, and gasped in relief as a black fletched arrow whistled through the throat of her attacker, and prompted the second 'Rider to turn and flee.

Aneida launch herself from the canyon wall to land upon the back of the soldier. Her dagger flashed, and the 'Rider dropped, gagging on the blood from his own slit throat.

Trifyn landed awkwardly on the canyon floor, and tripped into the dirt. "That is all o' them!" he yelled, as he headed towards Mayvin. He wobbled under the burden of a large bundle of black fletched arrows that he had collected throughout the day from those that had been shot at him. He stooped on the run to pick up three wooden shields that the dead 'Riders had been carrying. "Take these!" he stacked them into Saliana's arms hurriedly. "Come on!" he shouted back over his shoulder. "The second wave is almost upon us!"

He paused to drop the burden of arrows, and place a hand of farewell on Mayvin's shoulder. "Good luck t' ye," he stated awkwardly. "And... thank-ye." He wanted to say more but could not think of a thing.

Mayvin silently laughed, and slapped him gently across his face. *Promise to kill what escapes me.*

Trifyn attempted a smile, "I promise." He cupped her face, unable to find more words, to say how glad he was to have known her, how grateful he was for her sacrifice. His face contorted with grief, and he pressed a kiss to Mayvin's cheek. He spun away, reclaimed his arrows, and limped out of the range of the rockslide, taking the road down the hill towards the distant cages.

Saliana stopped long enough to try to return the borrowed sword, but Mayvin would not hear of it. *It is yours now. Learn how to swing it properly afore you take it into battle again!*

Saliana's jaw jutted out mulishly. "I did kill two o' them, ye know!" she boasted, juggling the sword and the three shields awkwardly.

Aye, I saw. You did well, healer! I am proud of you.

Tears stood in Saliana's eyes, and her lips trembled as they spilled over. "Farewell, Mayvin. I will miss ye." She spun with a sob, and ran after Trifyn.

Aneida was left alone with her sister, and gripped Mayvin's good hand. Together they listened to the sounds of the approaching army.

Go! Mayvin ordered.

"No!" Aneida snarled. "I am no' leaving ye t' die alone!"

Mayvin's eyes narrowed with fury, as she balled up her fist on her good arm, and knocked Aneida to the ground. *I am not doing this just to see you sacrifice yourself beside me!*

"I am no' leaving!" Aneida shouted back. Her face crumpled, as she picked herself up from the dirt, and hard sobs racked her body.

And if you do not, who is going to protect the cages from the 'Riders who escape? The boy, or maybe the healer? We all saw how good she is with a sword!

The fight drained from Aneida, and her shoulders heaved as she tried to contain her sobs. "She...did...kill...two o' them!"

she joked darkly, raising tortured eyes to her sister's face.

Mayvin smiled painfully. *Go!* Mayvin's jaw flexed, as she gritted her teeth, and her own tears overflowed her eyes at her sister's pain. *Please, Aneida, let me do this for you. I am dying, wound poisoned, I am already dead, and you cannot save me, but I can save you. Let me save you. Please.*

Aneida embraced her sister, holding on as though she would never let go, while the sound of marching feet reverberated around them, drawing ever nearer. "I love ye. I love ye so much!"

Mayvin pushed her gently away, and wiped the tears from her sister's eyes with tender care. *I love you to. Go now, go on, before it is too late.*

Aneida turned blindly and ran, as the first soldiers in the second wave of 'Riders rounded the bend of the canyon. She screamed in anger, refusing to look back, as she heard them jeer at the lonely figure of Mayvin standing heroically in the centre of their path, bound in the ropes leading to the linchpins of stone that would soon drop tons of rock upon them all. She tried to keep her attention upon Saliana and Trifyn, who were working their way down the slope towards the floor of the bowl shaped valley.

'What am I doing?'

Aneida skidded to a halt, and turned back. She could not, would not, leave Mayvin to die alone! Before she had taken three strides to return, the walls of the canyon started to collapse inward.

"NO! MAYVIN!"

Tortured stone roared and screeched, drowning out her cry, as the wall gave way and fell. A billow of dust boiled out of the mouth of the canyon, blowing back her hair. Aneida shaded her eyes from the debris, and staggered back a stride, sobbing as it washed over her. Her knees loosened, and she collapsed to the ground. Pain filled howls ripped from her throat. The roar of stone went on and on, as though the entire canyon were folding in upon itself.

'She is gone! Mayvin is dead!' Aneida shook her head in denial, bowing under the weight of her grief.

"Goodbye, Mayvin," she whispered. She hung her head for a moment longer, overwhelmed, before she screamed her anguish, and pushed to her feet, sprinting to catch up to Trifyn and Saliana, joining the footrace for the cages. The surviving 'Riders would soon be climbing over the rockslide, and they had little time to ready themselves for their attack. If she were able, she would personally usher each and every one of them to their deaths!

Aneida quickly overtook Saliana and Trifyn, who were burdened with arrows and shields. She wordlessly shouldered half of the bundle of arrows, before noticing that Trifyn was flagging. Aneida glanced downwards and grimaced.

"A scratch!" Trifyn snorted boldly. "They thought I needed a souvenir for killing all o' them!"

She frowned at his words, for any fool could see the broken arrow shaft in his upper leg, and the sheen of sweat that had nothing to do with the exertion of the run. His grin faded, as they stared at each other. Aneida slung his free arm over her shoulder, supporting his damaged leg, as they started to move quicker.

"Why did ye no' tell me ye were injured!" Saliana chastised, as she did her best to lend her own support. She propped her free shoulder firmly under Trifyn's but she was already overburdened with the shields. She made to drop them, but Aneida bade her not to.

"Keep them. They will be our only protection against archers. I will help Trifyn. Go on! Hurry!"

As quickly as possible they hobbled towards the cages, and Aneida was surprised by Trifyn's fortitude. He was handling his wound better than some seasoned veterans would, but then, perhaps he realized it was not worth crying over a wound when you were fighting a battle for your life.

They reached the cages, and turned back to watch, as the first few Demon Riders trickled out of the collapsed canyon. The dust from the cave-in still settled slowly over the small figures in the distance, dulling their red coats to grey. The still captive Demon Riders screamed and howled triumphantly, as they saw that their reinforcements had arrived.

"Climb! Go! I will hand up the shields and arrows!" Aneida ordered.

Saliana climbed to the top of the empty cage first, and lent a hand to Trifyn who was having trouble making the effort with his wound. Together they reached down to Aneida, and dragged up bundles of arrows, and the shields. Relieved of her burden,

Aneida quickly scaled the bars to join them, and they began their shuffling crawl across the iron grid, dragging their pilfered armoury along with them, and down into the empty square surrounding the glowing portal.

Far up on the rim of the valley, more and more of the enemy boiled out from the distant canyon, clambering over Mayvin's rocky tomb.

Aneida and Trifyn sprinted like a strange three-legged beast across the empty square towards the humming, shimmering portal, followed closely by Saliana.

"Here!" Aneida cried over the din of the shouting caged 'Riders. "Give me your arrows!" She relieved Trifyn of the burden, and relinquished him to Saliana's care.

Trifyn winced as he took up more of his own weight, and his hand hovered over his wound. Now that they had reached the relative safety of the cages, he was feeling the pain.

"I will bind it, but no' so tight that it will interfere as ye fight," Saliana, promised. She grabbed Aneida's arm, as she would have dashed away. "Aneida...I am so sorry.... Mayvin..."

"Yes, me too, Aneida..." Trifyn joined in awkwardly.

Aneida's face collapsed for a moment, but she did not wait for them to finish their stuttering condolences. "NOT NOW! It was what she wanted! I will no'..." She clenched her eyes and her fists, fighting back tears. She jerked her arm free from Saliana's compassionate grasp. "Hurry! We have precious little time t' prepare!"

Saliana nodded and turned to her pack to get her medicines to dress Trifyn's wound.

"Is it me, or is the portal's humming louder?" Trifyn asked.

Saliana spared the glowing gateway a secretive glance. "It will soon be sunset."

If Rewn did not emerge by day's end, and she yet lived, she would enter the labyrinth before the way closed. She would be trapped for eternity but she would be with him at the end. As Mayvin had claimed her death, so too had Saliana.

ഇരു

THE LABYRINTH

Their only hope now lay with Little Wolf's dedication to Gralyre, and his exceptional sense of smell.

Dotch's gut told him the hour was late, for they had travelled many leagues. He did his best to keep up with the younger men, but his years were telling on him as the forced run continued, and he was gratified when it was Jord who finally panted out a complaint.

"Gods! When are we going t' take a rest!"

Rewn grunted agreement, too spent to waste breath.

As suddenly as that, Little Wolf halted then backtracked several yards. The men staggered to a stop.

Jord glared at the wolfdog, as it ran back towards them, nose to ground, stopped abruptly, and turned around once more. After Little Wolf's second circuit, he groused through tight clenched teeth. "If he makes us turn 'round, and run back the way we came, I think I will kill 'em!"

Still unable to speak, Rewn merely nodded in concurrence, his chest pumping hard for air, as he hunched over to rub his cramping legs.

An excited whimper came from Little Wolf's throat, and he jumped up onto his hind legs, pawing at the empty air.

"What is he doing?" Jord demanded, snapping forth a dagger, and stumbling back several paces.

Rewn grinned in excitement. "'Tis the sound he makes when Gralyre comes back from being away! I think he has found him. He has found Gralyre, just like he found Dotch!"

Jord's shoulders slumped. "Then 'tis over. Gralyre will soon be joining us, and the sword is lost beyond our reach. We are well and truly trapped!"

"Do no' be too hasty," Dotch entered his voice of reason. "We know how thin the veil is between this graveyard and the labyrinth. Perhaps Little Wolf can see his master, where we can no'?"

The graveyard had begun a soft hum, something they had not previously noted within the snapping, bone breaking noise of their pace. "In any case, I will run no further. This is as good a place as any t' await sunset." So saying, Dotch dropped to the ground, and made himself comfortable with a settling shuffle of his rump amid the clacking bones.

Rewn heaved a sigh, and plunked himself down next to Dotch. He watched Little Wolf anxiously, as he pushed back his sweat soaked hair.

Jord's face contorted. "So this is it! We just lay down like these stinking, rotting corpses and die?"

Rewn looked at Dotch.

Dotch looked at Rewn.

Rewn looked at Jord. "Water?" he asked, holding out the skin.

Jord sheathed his blade with a growl of dissatisfaction, and snatched the waterskin from Rewn's hand. He threw himself to the ground next to his two comrades, and took a long pull, swallowing heavily before passing the water back to Rewn. "Too bad 'tis no' something stronger. 'Tis a shame t' toast our deaths with warm as piss water!" He squirmed for a more comfortable seat, dug a skull out from under his left buttock, and tossed it aside.

"Well now," smiled Dotch, reaching deep within his shirt, "It just so happens that I have been saving a little something for a special occasion." His hand appeared with an innocent looking, carved, wooden flask, not the usual one he had been sucking on these many weeks.

His smile faded nostalgically, as he fingered the carvings. "I whittled this myself, as my wife brewed her berries." Another melancholy smile chased across his face, as the memory filled him, and he cleared his throat noisily, pulled the cork free, and passed the flask to Rewn.

"Now ye be careful with that, lad. It be liquid fire. Burn the cold out o' your bones like the purist sunshine, and knock ye on your arse like a blow from a club if ye disrespect it!" Dotch boasted.

Rewn's eyes bulged, as the smooth fire burned down his throat, sweet and hot with the tang of bog-berries. The taste of summer chased the graveyard away. Wordlessly he passed it to Jord.

"Dotch," Jord toasted, smacking his lips in anticipation, "ye are the best man I have ever met!" He upended the flask in an ambitious swig. Manfully, he swallowed, as the liquor exploded in his mouth and empty belly. Dotch chuckled, as Jord handed back the flask with all the reverence of a man handling a rare jewel.

"T' my darling wife, Ella!" Dotch toasted the air, "She sure knows how t' preserve bog-berries!" They all laughed.

"T' Dotch's darling wife, Ella!" Rewn toasted in turn. "Maker o' the best medicine I have ever had t' take!"

"T' the bog-berries!" toasted Jord.

"T' the pot that brewed this!" toasted Dotch. And so the flask was passed back and forth, the toasts getting wilder and crazier with each swig. In the air, the hum increased its strength, as the end approached.

Little Wolf ignored the impromptu party. His gaze remained locked upon the ghostly image that only he could perceive, of Gralyre, slumped against a stone sarcophagus, in a circle ringed in mist and shadow.

CHAPTER SIXTEEN

THE HEATHREN MOUNTAINS

The sun was slanting heavily towards dusk when Dara awoke from her exhausted slumber. She sat up and rubbed the lingering sleep from her eyes, blinking at the makeshift camp that had sprung up around her in the grove where she had killed the Stalker. She did not remember much after the second creature had been driven off. The old man had taken Dajin from her arms, and given her something to drink, but she remembered no more. Someone had thoughtfully thrown a cloak over her, though truthfully she doubted that the coolness of the spring night would have disturbed her.

The strange warriors of the night before wandered about on various tasks, or sat fletching arrows. Cook fires teased her nose and stomach with the promise of food, but she was uncertain of her welcome to partake of the simmering contents of the pots. Her experiences in the Rebel fortress had taught her caution when approaching strangers for succour.

She decided to find her brother instead. Dara stood and drew the cloak tighter around her while she bit her lip, and glanced around for something to remind her which way to go. She vaguely remembered the old man taking him away, while another carried the Sorceress, to a tent that had been erected in record time to his demands. Was it this way? Or that?

She spied a large singed circle, and realized that it was all that remained of her dead Stalker, where it had lain until the sun had arisen to sear its evil from the skin of the world. Thinking about the events of the previous night made her head hurt and her heart pound. It was as though it had happened to someone else. That could not have been her, armed with naught but a dagger, standing alone against a Stalker! She shook her head. No, she had not been alone. The strange warriors had appeared. If their arrows had not weakened the beast, she would certainly not have lived to tell the tale.

She would have to ask directions to the sick tent. Dara nervously shivered, and walked to the nearest campfire, standing far back, and prepared to bolt should the several warriors who sat around it turn on her.

"Your pardon, sirs? Do ye know where my brother is?" The men gave her their attention, and conversation in their strange language ended, but they did not answer. Perhaps they did not understand? "My brother?" she asked again, slower.

One of the warriors nudged the man next to him, and said something in a smirking voice. The rest of the men laughed. The man who had made the joke gave her an assessing glance that made Dara bristle. She had seen such looks before, and recognized the tone of voice that needed no translation for their insult! Her face flushed red, and her hand instinctively sought the hilt of her dagger.

The warriors saw the move and froze, their mirth fading.

Dara backed away, and noticed their eyes flick to look over her shoulder just before she stepped into someone. She whirled around, but had no opportunity to draw her dagger before a strong hand over hers prevented it.

"Be at ease. You are in no danger here," the warrior comforted. His fingers trailed across her hand, as he released her, but Dara had already twisted away from his touch. "They find you beautiful, and strong."

He was standing too near. Dara took a step back so she could see his face clearly. He stood as tall as the other men and had much the same look; brown hair, and eyes that were smiling kindly at her. There was no guile in their clear depths, leaving her confused and off balanced.

He ended her musings by lightly touching the edge of the cloak. "Did my cloak keep you warm last night?" he inquired in his strangely accented voice. His head was bent low to talk to her, and a heavy lock of hair fell forward over his strong forehead.

Dara swallowed heavily, and blushed at the simple question, feeling equal parts threatened and protected. "Yes, thank-ye," she stammered. "Ye will be needing it back." Her fingers went to the fastenings at the throat, only to find his had beat hers there.

Her gaze jerked upwards to his, as her brows lowered into a frown. She did not like the way he was casually touching her, it made her nervous, frightened, but his eyes were still warm and kind. Dara was confused by the dichotomy of messages that she was receiving, and was uncertain if she was acting normally, or suffering aftershocks of her experiences at the hands of the Stewards. The rapes had shattered her trust in men.

"You must keep the cloak, now," he smiled down at her.

Despite herself, she smiled shyly at the kindness he was showing her. "Thank-ye," she replied. At her words, his eyes seemed to ignite with heat. Was she missing something? He was standing too close again. She sidestepped, taking herself out of range of those too casual hands. "I was wondering if I could see my brother now?"

The men seated around the fire broke into guffaws of mirth. She turned to see what they were laughing at and realized it was at the man standing beside her. This time, when she turned back, his smile was tight on his face. There were undertones she was missing.

"This way," he indicated with a sweep of his arm.

She preceded him, and missed the glare he threw over his shoulder at the men around the fire that started another round of mirth.

He led her to a large round tent in the middle of the camp, and entered first, turning to hold the flap back for her to enter. The space was carpeted in soft furs. Catrian and Dajin lay on opposite sides of the circle, upon comfortable pallets, and the old man of the night before sat cross-legged in the center near a glowing brazier. His hands rested lightly on his knees, and his eyes were closed. She would have thought he slept save for the lightly mumbled words that escaped his lips. Sunshine pooled around him from the smoke hole at the top of the pole.

"Your brother," the warrior announced with another sweep of his arm, ignoring the old man. The warm smile was back on his face.

Dara smiled back, but it felt strained and false. She was not aware that, as she moved towards her brother, she kept her body angled towards the stranger, hyper alert to attack, and that even after she knelt down next to Dajin she remained facing the warrior.

She touched Dajin gently upon the shoulder, and her brother awoke with a start. "Shh," Dara whispered. "'Tis me. How are ye?" She brushed the hair tenderly from his forehead, feeling for fever.

"Ye bitch! How could ye?" Dajin slapped her hand away.

Dara leaned back on her heels in confusion and hurt. "What?"

"Ye fought the Stalker afore I could, and labeled me coward again! Perhaps ye would like t' embroider it on my shirt collars?" Dajin griped snidely.

"Dajin! What are ye saying? If I had no' fought it we would be dead!"

"Get from my sight. From this day on I have no sister, for no sister o' mine would have shamed me so!"

Dara sprang to her feet, and narrowly prevented herself from kicking her brother in his obstinate head. "Obviously, ye are no' yourself. I will come and see ye again later!" She strove to keep her voice calm for the benefit of her audience, but knew her anger was leeching through, as Dajin rolled to his side, giving her his back.

She spun to leave, and saw the old man had arisen from his chanting, and was now standing next to the warrior. The warrior's brows were knit tightly, and judging by the scowl on his face, and tight clenched fists, he looked ready to do battle. The old man held a cautioning hand upon his arm to keep him back.

Dara edged towards the tent entrance, and remembered her manners just in time to prevent her from bolting. "I thank ye for looking after my brother." Tears at Dajin's behavior threatened but she would not betray herself in front of these strangers. She took a deep steadying breath. "How is the Sorceress?"

"Not good," the old man murmured, as the young warrior moved to Dara's side.

She grew worried at how welcome the man's silent support felt after her brother's unwarranted attack, and stepped nearer to the light of escape offered through the tent flap.

"It would help if I knew how she came to be afflicted." His white brows rose in query.

Dara's forehead wrinkled into a frown. "I do no' know much more than rumours. I think that it happened almost a week ago, the day o' a terrible storm. 'Twas rumoured that Catrian exhausted herself, and was left defenseless t' a Stalker's attack. She killed the Stalker, but it left her…" Dara indicated the prone Sorceress, "…well… like this."

"A storm?"

"Yes. It tore up much o' this forest as it moved south. I heard that she had made it t' help the ones journeying t' Fennick's Island." Dara's gaze slid away to where the Sorceress lay so still. "She was trying to help them, my eldest brother Rewn, Gralyre, my friends Mayvin and Aneida. Is today the Solstice? If they made it t' the island they might be…"

The old man grabbed her arm in excitement. "Gralyre was here?"

Dara gasped at the grip, for she did not like to be touched, but stopped herself from pulling away, as this was obviously very important to him. "That is what he calls himself, but he has no memory o' who he is. He travels with a wolf," she hinted helpfully, not certain if they spoke of the same warrior.

The old man said something rapidly in his language to the man at Dara's side. Then to her he asked, "The sword! They travel to Fennick's Island to reclaim the Dragon Sword?"

Dara frowned and nodded. "I am so sorry, if Gralyre is important t' ye. My brother Rewn said the quest is hopeless," she dropped her eyes in distress. "They will no' be returning."

The old man spoke more foreign words to the warrior at her side then returned his attention to Dara. "This is my son Jacon. He will make sure that you are kept safe." The old man finally performed introductions, before glancing away to look at Catrian, mumbling something under his breath before he addressed Dara again.

"I am Gedrhar y'Traydeyon. Among the Dream Weavers, I am what you would call a..." here he paused, as though searching for the correct word "...a wise man. You are correct.

Today is the Solstice."

"My name is Dara Wilson, and this is my brother, Dajin," Dara introduced herself, trying not to let her voice quiver at the excitement of being confronted with legends. Dream Weavers! It could not be! They were nothing but mist and shadow. Their people had not been seen in the lands for generations.

Words bubbled out of her, unstoppable in her excitement, shades of the girl she had once been. "Will ye know if they find the sword? Can ye tell if they yet live?" Dara was eager for news of Rewn, and her stomach clenched, as she said a brief prayer to the Gods of Fortune to keep him and the others safe.

"We will know that they are successful by nightfall." Gedrhar steepled his fingers before his chest, and smiled benignly at his son and Dara. "She wears your cloak?"

Jacon grinned, and without another word, grasped Dara's hand, and pulled her from the tent.

Dara squeaked in panic, and tried to free herself, twisting and struggling for a moment. Jacon turned and looked at her in surprise. "Let me go!" Dara ordered, as she tugged.

He frowned and released her.

Dara quivered as she drew in gouts of air to control her need to run, somehow finding the courage to look up into his face. She expected rage and braced for a blow, but instead saw naught but kindness and concern. "What did your father mean?"

"Do not concern yourself. You are safe," he reassured. "I will take you to eat now?" His brow rose questioningly.

Dara felt foolish and broken, unable to trust any of her own reactions. She nodded and looked at the ground, following quietly behind him. Gedrhar had said that his son, Jacon, would keep her safe and she believed him, but who would keep her safe from her own, terrifying insanity of mistrust. It was as though her fears were worsened by his attentiveness to her. Was she doomed to never feel normal again? Had normal become men who brutalized her?

He led her to a cook fire, and made certain she had food aplenty, fussing over her while the other men smirked, and nudged each other. Dara felt as though she was missing something, and turned to ask Jacon what they said, and found him sitting too near to her again. She edged away. "Jacon, will ye teach me t' speak your language?" If she knew what they were saying, she would no longer be left out of the joke.

"Of course," he murmured to her through a warm smile. "It is good that you should learn my language." He touched her cheek. "Belitar." The word rolled off his tongue like a purr, the r's rolling exotically to her ear.

"Bel-ee-tar… What does that mean?" she asked, trying to act casual, as she shrank back from his fingers, unable to control the finely tuned protective movement honed over months of torturous abuse.

"Beautiful," he smiled at her.

A deep, trembling fear shivered through her, and she shied away. He would not think her so beautiful were he to discover what the Stewards had done to her. Without saying a word, she fled, tears of shame and rage blurring her vision.

CHAPTER SEVENTEEN

THE LABYRINTH

Gralyre's worried gaze was locked upon the dissolving bridge, as he fingered the plait of Catrian's golden brown hair. He could not move the capstone he acknowledged, as he placed the token back within his shirt above his heart. There was no way around the fact that he would have to use his magic to open the tomb though he was deeply exhausted, and did not know how much Godsmagic remained within after the efforts of the past few days.

He heaved himself to his feet, and stepped back to gain a perspective on the entire structure, trying to pick the right spot to apply force. The hum permeating the air increased to a buzz that he could now feel through the soles of his boots, urging him to act quickly.

He shut his eyes, taking deep breaths to settle his rioting urgency, quieting his mind, before seeking within for his power. His eyes flew open, as magic flowed into his veins, and burned away his fatigue. Gralyre raised his hand imperiously, and directed a blunt force of air against the capstone, fully expecting to see the lid of the tomb shatter, and fall to the ground.

But something went wrong, and the magic rebounded upon him. Gralyre yelped, as the force of his own will sent him soaring upwards, shooting away, as though his energy had been reflected back from a mirror.

He hit the ground some distance away, against the side of the small hillock, and scrabbled to halt his roll downhill that could only end in the acid moat. He slid to a stop, and gasped for air like a fish out of water, for the breath had been knocked from him by the long fall. He was finally able to lift himself shakily up upon one elbow, to assess the damage.

The force of his magic had tossed him almost as far as the acid moat, and he shuddered at what would have befallen him had he landed in the caustic fluid instead of against the hillside. Painfully he twisted his head, looking over his shoulder at the slowly disintegrating bridge. There was not much stone or time remaining!

With more willpower than strength, he staggered back up the short hill to the tomb. It was completely unmarred by his recent assault. There had to be a way to open it! Strength was not the answer, nor was magic. What had he missed?

He draped himself upon the sarcophagus, and blood dripped from his nose to the surface of the capstone, as he searched for a hidden latch or lever about the edges. Coming up empty, and fearing that his wobbly legs would betray him at any moment, Gralyre circled the tomb, paying closer attention this time to the embossed figures in the carvings along the sides of the stone. He ran his fingers carefully over each figure, feeling for any imperfection that might indicate a switch that would start a mechanical shift of the capstone, or for another riddle that he would be obliged to solve.

He was examining the third side when he discovered the jewel. Barely visible, coated as it was in the grime that only years of exposure could deposit, he had previously mistaken it to be part of the carving. About as large as his fist, it was set in the hands of one of the carved figures, from which thunderbolts radiated outwards, decimating beasts of darkness on a grim battlefield.

Gralyre rubbed the filth from the jewel, trying to see if it was indeed the trigger, and if it were, how it might work. As he polished the gem, it caught the light, and revealed itself to be a ruby that radiated a deep, red light. Gralyre knelt low and poked and pried at the jewel, trying to figure out how it worked. Finally, he slapped his palm over it and pressed, thinking that perhaps it would unlatch some counterbalance.

A jolt of electricity surged from the crystal into his hand, cementing his palm to the jewel so that he was stuck fast. Gralyre jerked back on his heels, trying through the force of his weight to tear his palm from the magnetism of the jewel, but no matter how he struggled, he could not win free. Under his palm the ruby's glow intensified until he could see the bones and sinews of his hand through his flesh.

A bolt of magic, as deeply red as the jewel, shot through the back of his hand, and grounded into his forehead. Gralyre screamed and jerked from the power of the elemental force that tore aside the puny mental resistance he mustered, as though he had not made the effort, and overcame his mind.

The power rushed through his memories and crashed against the dark wall of his amnesia, the deep blackness that hid his past, that even Catrian and he, working in concert, had been unable to pierce. Gralyre put his free hand to his head, howling as the pressure built against that wall, built until he thought his skull would explode with it! His eyes rolled back in his head, and he went into convulsions.

The jewel would not be denied. The dark wall shattered, releasing a torrent of images and memories, releasing Gralyre's past. His body locked, arching with the force of the impact, as more information than he could handle overwhelmed him, and he lost consciousness.

The acid continued to erode the stone drawbridge.

ಬೂಂಡ

FENNICK'S ISLAND

The dust of the canyon's cave-in billowed slowly about the Demon Rider army, now hiding their numbers, now revealing them, as they swarmed from the mouth of the canyon to the echoing booms of battle drums. Doaphin's double serpent standard, black snakes on a red field, holding a crown suspended between their viperous jaws, snapped malignantly in the breeze as they advanced. To the three who awaited their doom, the distant army of hundreds seemed a lone creature of singular intent.

"I thought the collapse o' the canyon would have taken more o' them," whispered Trifyn in acute disappointment, as he took in the teeming numbers marching down the road towards the cages. Better than half still remained.

All emotion had fled Aneida's voice when she announced, "There is a Demon Lord with them." The Lord was plain to see, even from a distance for he was riding the only horse on the field.

"He must have protected the army from the falling stone, and cleared them a path through t' the valley," Saliana put forth. Her tongue darted out to moisten the dry fear on her lips. "We should take refuge within the labyrinth!" The thought of flight seemed the best idea to her, even to someplace that would see them dead, for at least she would die with Rewn.

"We canno' hide from a Demon Lord's magic. It would find us." Aneida vetoed the idea. "Besides, we agreed t' hold the gate, t' protect our retreat. We must give the others time t' get free!" The shadows on the ground slanted in long black bars away from the shimmering portal, as the sun inched towards the top of the surrounding hills. "'Tis no' so long t' hold the ground now." The sun would be down in a matter of minutes.

"T' what purpose? So that when they emerge, that Lizard Lord out there can kill us, and take the Dragon Sword?" Trifyn snarled.

Aneida glared at the bowman, as she was struck dumb by his words. They were no match for this army, and were doubly less a threat to a Demon Lord. If Gralyre, Dotch, Rewn and Jord somehow made it free of the labyrinth with the sword, it would only be to deliver unto Doaphin all that he had craved for hundreds of years! The Demon Lord would effortlessly pluck the sword from their grasp! They would have wasted their own sweat and blood to give it to him! *'Our dearest blood,'* she thought bitterly.

"If we enter the labyrinth, we are dead. If we stay here, we are dead - but we might delay them long enough t' prevent them from passing through the gate afore sunset." Aneida suggested, as her hands worked on the hilt of her sword.

Saliana swallowed audibly. "And the others?"

"If they make it out afore the labyrinth seals itself, and they have the sword, we must ensure that the Demon Lord does no' get it. They will have t' throw it back through the portal afore it seals. They will have t' leave it behind."

"All o' this will be for nothing! All o' us dead for nothing!" Trifyn lamented. Tears stood out in his eyes at the hopeless situation. To have come so near to success only to fail now was an unspeakable tragedy!

Aneida gripped Trifyn's shoulder with enough force to bruise. "Get your head out o' your arse! Do ye no' yet understand? We were ne'er meant t' survive this. That we came as far as we did, is nothing but dumb blind luck, and the strength and leadership o' Gralyre. We will die here. But at least we can die by our choice, just as Mayvin did. This is the death o' my choosing!" Aneida growled through tears. "I stand!" Her burning gaze challenged Trifyn's.

Trifyn nodded jerkily in agreement, though he swallowed hard to contain his fear. "We stand."

They both turned and looked at Saliana, whose chin rose courageously. "For whatever good it will do…I am with ye both. T' the end."

"T' the end." Aneida and Trifyn vowed.

"Quickly, they are almost upon us! Ready yourselves. Trifyn, until they breach the cages, it will be up t' your skill with the bow. Saliana and I will provide ye with cover, and collect any arrows they shoot at us." Aneida looked up at a sky that was beginning to paint a delicate blush against the clouds. "We need no' last long."

Trifyn gave a short nod of assent. "I will aim my assault towards the Demon Lord. Mayhap I will get lucky."

Spinning on his heel, Trifyn limped to his pack and removed a new string for his bow. Carefully he strung it, plucking the gut, and listening to its tone like a maestro tuning his instrument. The women watched on in silence as Trifyn, even more intent now, examined the arrows he had collected. Sighting along their shafts, the slightest flaw caused him to put them aside. In the end, he selected six that met his criteria for straightness of shaft and smoothness of fletching.

He planted them tip down in the ground for ease of access. By the time he finished readying himself, the army had reached the cages, their numbers great enough that they could move to surround them all. Trifyn calmly nocked his bow with the first arrow, holding it ready at his side, as he rolled his shoulders, and set his balance against his injured leg.

The Demon Lord rode out to the forefront, a sneer on his human face. 'Riders parted ranks for him, cowering back from his horse. An uneasy silence descended through the troops, as they awaited the words of the fearsome leader. Even the weakened prisoners of the cages fell silent. His face was stamped with arrogance and power, and no mercy lived in his eyes. The evil that oozed from him seemed to reach through the bars, and attach a hand around the hearts of the defenders. The Demon Lord was pale and slight, almost effeminate in his gestures and poise, yet the reaction of the 'Riders proved that he was someone to dread. He wore no armour, only a red cloak that snapped smartly in the breeze in complement to Doaphin's banners. The stillness was the calm before a terrible storm.

"Why does he no' just slay us with his magic?" Saliana whispered fearfully out of the corner of her mouth.

Aneida frowned. "Do no' give him ideas!"

"Remember what Gralyre said o' magic?" Trifyn muttered quietly. "He may be too tired from having used much o' it protecting his soldiers from the rock slide."

The Demon Lord made a show of glancing around the area. "This is it?" he sneered, his words amplified by the natural amphitheater of the bowl shaped valley. "The Master led me to believe that I would be facing a great Rebel force, not two women and a puny bowman!" He laughed uproariously, cueing his troops to join in. The laughter echoed from all sides, even from the surviving Demon Riders in the cages.

Trifyn lifted his bow and drew his string back to his ear, his gaze keen upon his target. It would be a difficult shot, for he had to navigate between the layers of bars of the cage to hit his mark. Gods be with me, he begged, as he sighted down the shaft of the arrow at the smooth throat of the Demon Lord, exposed as he threw his head back in laughter.

Calm descended. The throbbing pain in his leg receded along with his fear, and everything in his life narrowed to this one moment, this one shot. It was as though he had been born to perform but one task, and this was it. He was ready. He drew his breath, held it for a heartbeat, and let fly his arrow.

The Demon Lord turned his horse slightly to address his troops. "Take them!" he ordered with a negligent wave of his pale hand. With a roar, the army surged forward just as their commander flew from his saddle from the impact of the shaft embedded in his left eye, halting his brays of triumphant amusement.

There was a great indrawn, shocked breath from the Demon Riders, a silence that was crushing in its intensity. Their attack stumbled to a halt, and they milled aimlessly for a moment. Several 'Riders rushed forward to check on the body, and a pushing and shoving match ensued as they began to squabble over the Lord's boots and cloak.

Aneida let out an explosion of sound, somewhere between incredible relief and disbelief. "That was a one in a million shot, bowman!" she slapped Trifyn on the back. "I have ne'er seen anyone sight and shoot so quickly!"

"Quickly?" he wondered, for to him he had taken all the time in the world to make the shot. Trifyn shook his head abashedly. "Actually.... I was aiming for his throat," he admitted.

"Well I will no' tattle on ye, bowman!" Aneida chortled.

"Get down!" screamed Saliana, barreling into the two, and knocking them to the ground. The army had recovered, and their archers had let fly.

At the approaching wind-whistling volley of arrows, the three huddled under their stolen shields, wincing from the impacts upon their scant protection. The bars of the cages deflected most of the missiles, for none of the enemy had the talent of Trifyn, but many of the enemy bowmen were savvy enough to aim high to send their arrows up over the cages to rain down on the square from above.

Aneida yelped as the mettle tip of an arrow penetrated her shield, and gashed the flesh of her upper arm. Saliana made a move to go to her, but Aneida waved her off.

When the arrow storm passed, they looked up to see that the 'Riders had begun their attack in earnest. Under the cover of their archers, the army of evil was scaling all four of the cages. Without a Demon Lord to open the locks, the penned 'Riders would not be joining the attack, and the three defenders thanked the Gods for the small mercy.

Without a commander to guide their assault, they were all trying to clamber the bars at the same time, their numbers interfering with each other in their bid to reach the enemy first. The 'Riders at the front of the line were being crushed against the bars of the cages before they could ascend, as more and more pushed forward from the rear. Their screams now had as much to do with pain as battle rage.

"Will the pens hold against their weight?" Saliana yelled in horror to be heard over the din.

"'Twas designed t' withstand an attack. 'Twill hold!" Aneida's voice added both a threat and a plea to the words. "Follow me!" she shouted. Under the cover of their shields, they maneuvered themselves toward the glowing, buzzing archway, so that their backs were to the shimmering ripple of the magical portal. Any missiles fired at their backs, would enter the labyrinth instead of striking them – at least until the sun set.

Aneida and Saliana lifted their shields to the fore, interlocking so they had a makeshift wall to huddle behind, and protect Trifyn, as he fired arrow after arrow into the swarming mass of the 'Riders. He could not miss. He slowly rotated his aim to spread out the lethal shots to all of the surrounding cages.

The 'Riders at the forefront seemed to realize they were easy targets for the expert bowman. Screaming in panic they tried to move back, but the masses piled up behind would not allow it. So they died, pinned to the bars. They did not fall but remained hanging, a fleshly shield behind which the second line of 'Riders took refuge, as they began to climb.

Trifyn altered the trajectory of his shots, raining arrows down from above in an effort to get past the shield of bodies, but for every one killed, three took his place. And by the time he circled back to the other three cages, the attackers would have advanced ever further. They were easily targeted, for navigating the bars was a slow and clumsy process, but it was getting easier for the enemy to advance with every body that draped across the iron grid, providing a fleshy platform to walk upon, and a shield against Trifyn's deadly aim. Their numbers would see their success, and they did not care how many died in the process, as they stormed over the cages.

Saliana watched the depletion of the bundle of arrows Trifyn had collected in the canyon with concern. It was only the strength of his arm that protected them now. Her gaze spread to the field of black shafts surrounding them like a crop of ugly flowers. "We need more arrows!" She shouted to Aneida and Trifyn over the din of the 'Riders.

"No! Saliana, wait!" Aneida yelled, realizing too late what she intended.

By then, Saliana had lifted her shield, and darted out beyond the shelter of the portal to gather arrows.

"Watch your back!" Aneida sucked in her breath fearfully at the healer's stupidity. She picked up her own shield, and ran to stand back to back with Saliana, as more arrows thudded into the ground around them.

"Keep them coming!" Saliana laughed at the dangerous hailstorm. "Give us the weapons t' kill ye all!" She screamed at the surrounding 'Riders.

"Hurry!" Aneida yelled, using her free arm to pluck and toss the arrows back towards Trifyn. Saliana would not stop until her arm was as full as she could carry. Only then did she allow

Aneida to lead the way back to Trifyn.

"Good work," he congratulated breathlessly, as they returned. Sweat rolled down his face, and dampened the cloth of his shirt. He grunted now with the effort, as he leaned into his bow and fired, knocked and fired, a tireless rhythm of death.

"She almost got us killed," Aneida snarled.

"What does it matter? Ye said it yourself, we are already dead, and I will choose how I spend my last hours!" Saliana raised her chin mulishly.

"Ye sound like Mayvin," Trifyn laughed.

After a moment, so did Aneida. It was a pale imitation of her usual brazen battle challenge, but it was something.

Trifyn fired salvo after salvo into the sea of 'Riders, until his arms trembled, and every arrow they had was spent. "'Tis the last of them!" he cried, as he crouched down behind his shield. "I wonder why they do no' shoot at us again?"

Aneida smiled grimly at him. "Even 'Riders learn eventually. They know they will no' hit anything, and ye will only send them back with death attached!" The enemy bowmen had finally realized that their arrows were just more ammunition for the defenders.

"I did no' think 'Riders were that smart!" Saliana spat in disgust. She looked up at the sky, now turned a darker blue, as the sun slid deeper into the horizon. The undersides of the scant clouds burned orange and red, and the ground had begun a soft tremor. Not much longer now. Soon she would rejoin Rewn.

ഇരു

THE LABYRINTH

Dotch corked the now empty flask, and returned it to his vest pocket, pausing to rub his fingers gently over the fine stitches his wife had made in the fabric to mend a tear. He surely wished he could have kept his promise to her, and returned. He would give everything to hold her and his wee boys, just one more time.

The three men had grown quiet and withdrawn, as the end approached. Their brief joust with hilarity had vanished, as quickly as the intoxication from the liqueur. Now there was only death to look forward to.

Rewn looked into the far distance, trying to distract himself from the tremor that had begun to rattle the bones around them. "I wonder how my brother and sister fair?"

Dotch patted his shoulder awkwardly.

"There is so much I would have said t' them. My brother Dajin… he marches in the war under General Matik. I suppose I will see them both soon…on the other side…"

"Ye know," Jord murmured, weaving his knives in their intricate dance. "I ne'er believed we would fail." He glanced up at the other two, a quiet smile on his face. Sorrow and pride washed up on the shore of his face. The tide of it churned moisture in his eyes.

Rewn's returned smile was sad. "Gralyre had a way o' making it all seem possible, did he no'?"

Jord nodded, and looked down. "I have no family, have no' for a long time," he said haltingly, "but travelling with you all," he shrugged, his hands busy with the knives, "'tis as close as I have ever come."

Jord's knives stopped so suddenly, he actually dropped one. Rewn heaved a large sigh, as he plucked the blade that had narrowly missed his boot, from the fragile bone of an old skull, and passed it back.

Dotch held up a cautioning hand, silencing the younger men. "Do ye feel that?" From all around them, the low drone of the labyrinth had increased to an angry buzzing. The bones on the ground leapt and bobbed, as the tremor increased, animating them with false life. Boney legs attached at a pelvis were thrown upwards to stagger a pace or two before collapsing.

The men clung to each other struggling to keep from being buried in generations of shifting bones. With nothing to cling to in the barren graveyard, it was all they could do to ride out the waves in the earth, and try to stay on top of the layers.

This was it. This was the end. The labyrinth was sealing.

Little Wolf began to wail, pawing at his ears, as he had done that morning. He cowered down, as though attempting to escape, gnashed his teeth and cried, pawing at the image only he could see.

"Brace yourselves, lads! Here it comes!" Dotch yelled over the wolf's howls.

₧₧

Gralyre awoke, his body aching, and his flesh glazed in sweat. His hand was still locked firmly to the ruby even though he had slumped to the ground next to the sarcophagus. His thoughts were a chaos of noise and confusion, as memories of his childhood, his family, his first loves, favorite foods, everything, flooded his mind at once. He growled in resistance to the pounding in his head, and the discordant thoughts, gritting his teeth against the buzzing hum of noise.

Though it resisted him slightly like the sticky pitch of a tree, he jerked his palm free from the jewel, and pushed himself to a seated position. The ruby was alive, pulsing with an inner light that spread a red radiance over the face of the stone, and made the age worn carvings of war come alive with a wash of gore. The surrounding mists also adopted the crimson glow, undulating thickly against the ground like a river of blood.

All of this made little impact upon Gralyre when measured against the enormity of the return of his past. He drew up his knees, and cradled his head onto his arms, sobbing as he tried to ride the crest of the tidal wave of knowledge lest it drown him. It was difficult to make sense of the pandemonium, as everything he was, everything he had ever hoped, dreamed, or cared for, cavorted confusingly through his thoughts. He gripped his hair with a guttural moan, rocking his body, as he was overwhelmed by the vibrancy of his rediscovered life. Nothing existed outside this moment, and his eyes fluttered shut in utter devastation.

Lightning slashed the air and thunder cracked, jerking Gralyre back to awareness. His gut clenched, as he noted that the noisy buzzing he had thought part of the return of his memories, was not inside has head but was the heralding noise of the closing of the portals. The lightning was the oncoming storm that would seal the labyrinth for another year!

Gralyre swung around to check his escape route, only to see the stone bridge slump into the acid moat in a mocking geyser, as it disintegrated completely. His feint had lasted just long enough to see him trapped!

The lightning grew in violence until the sound of the thunder rumbled without interruption, and the strobes of light made his eyes burn and water. The ruddy mists swirled and boiled with the quickening wind, lashing Gralyre's hair into his eyes. The temperature began to drop, and the sweat of moments ago now chilled him, making him long for his lost shirt.

He shoved himself to his feet, and only then saw that the capstone to the sarcophagus lay in shattered pieces. His last chance for escape lay with the sword! Perhaps its magic could save him from the power of the labyrinth! But he needed it for so much more than escape, beyond even the need to save Catrian. He had a purpose and responsibility that he was only now coming to realize, to remember.

The ground heaved mightily, and Gralyre teetered and staggered, falling forward to grip the edge of the tomb to steady himself. Wind whipped hair blinded Gralyre's eyes, as he boosted himself up to drape over the edge of the box, confirming what he already knew, when the contents were revealed in the strobes of blue lightning. There was no body.

The tomb was filled with swords, hundreds of swords, of every shape, size and description; rapiers and broadswords, claymores and scimitars. Gralyre scrabbled through the pile, searching frantically until his fingers closed over the familiar hilt, his arm hefted the familiar weight, and the great Dragon Sword of Lyre lifted in his hand.

With a surge of triumph, Gralyre stabbed the magnificent blade high into the air, screaming his victory.

Four and a half feet of polished blue Maolar gleamed in the flashes of light. A bolt of lightning struck the tip, bouncing off to detonate against the surrounding ring of pillars. With cracks and groans the stone columns shattered and toppled. The lightning writhed down the metal and, for a moment, the snaking neck of the dragon undulated against the blade, its metal mouth opening in a roar to rival Gralyre's.

The energy pooled into the ruby jewels of the dragon's eyes, making them glow with power and menace, as the wings of the guard spread wide, as though to take flight before folding back into position on the guard. The ruby cabochon set in the end of the hilt glowed richly, mirroring the eyes of the dragon.

Power flooded Gralyre. Magical energy, such as he had never felt before burned into his mind, and saturated his flesh. In his now remembered past, the power had never been present, but then he was no longer the same man.

"What is your command?" a voice whispered into his mind. It was dry and cold, and sent shivers skittering over his skin. Gralyre almost dropped the sword in sudden revulsion. If his

recent life had taught him anything, it was that no good came of having another inside your thoughts without invitation.

"Who are you?" Gralyre yelled, although he need not have done so, as the entity was firmly entrenched in his head. He could feel it there, burrowing in and carving a place for itself. The metal of the blade had never been more than it was, had it? Had this whispering voice always been present? He searched his newly revealed memories but the past and present collided in rioting discord.

"I am what was Fennick."

"Fennick is dead! 'Tis not possible that you are he!" Gralyre challenged, his hands strangling the hilt of the sword as though to force it to reveal all of its secrets. "He died at the battle at Centaur Pass!" Gods! The memory was as clear to him as if it had taken place yesterday! The battle! Men being turned to stone! Gralyre blinked rapidly to clear his thoughts of the familiar nightmare. No, not a nightmare. Memory!

"All that was Fennick's to call his own, as he left behind his life, I have become!"

Memory, a more recent one, flitted across his mind's eye, of Catrian describing the mechanics of a Wizard Stone. The more one used the magic stored in one's Wizard Stone, the more of one's power and soul became trapped within, until death completed the transformation. It was the price of power and long life. So it was true! The Dragon Sword was Fennick's Wizard Stone. It was how the sword had escaped the clutches of Doaphin, then created the labyrinth upon the island to protect itself. It had a soul!

"What is your will?" the sword asked once more.

All of the sword's power, Fennick's power, was now Gralyre's to command. An exultant smile flitted across his face, for he knew that he had won, knew that he was going to live, and he was going to escape the labyrinth. Catrian would live.

"Find my companions, and see us clear of this cursed place," Gralyre ordered. If he were to be granted a wish, this was the one at the forefront of his needs.

Immense magical force surged through Gralyre, as the power gathered itself.

"Gods!" he shouted, panting at the rush of it through his blood, even into his bones.

The knowledge of how to direct the energy seeped into his mind, and he lifted the sword, and aimed it at a point in the air. With a flex of his borrowed might, the landscape around him tore open and there, waiting on the far side were his lost companions with Little Wolf.

The wolfdog yelped, overjoyed, as Gralyre stepped through the tear in the fabric of the labyrinth into the bone yard. Little Wolf cavorted and danced around his legs, so excited to be reunited with Gralyre that he could not form language, only elation whirled into Gralyre thoughts.

"By the Gods!" yelled Rewn. "He did it! He has the sword!" All three men leapt to their feet at his unexpected appearance. They surrounded him, slapping him on the back excitedly.

"Can ye use it t' get us free, lad?" Dotch asked urgently, as the ground shifted and roared beneath their feet.

"Hurry!" Jord yelled.

Gralyre was unable to respond, for he was still possessed of the magic's power. Briefly he wondered if he used it, or if it used him, but the thought was distant and smothered, unimportant to the moment. It felt as though a thousand bees were stinging his skin, itching and burning, and making his muscles ache painfully, pleasure and pain combined. The power was within him, yet he was also sensing it as though another was wielding it, which accounted for the crawling at the base of his skull.

The droning sound of the closing gates was escalating in volume, and the lightning was at a frenzied pitch. If they did not leave immediately, they would be trapped forever, beyond the help of even the sword's magic!

Gralyre hefted the blade, and instructions on wielding the sorcery reappeared, unsummoned, in his thoughts. He reached for his newly augmented magical muscles, and watched a bubble of blue light spread from the tip of the erect sword, out to encircle them all, not unlike the energy shield that Catrian could create.

The sphere levitated, gathering up his comrades, and surprising yelps and cries of equal parts excitement and alarm. With a lurch of acceleration, that threw them onto their backs against the walls of the energy bubble, it shot forward. Gralyre, caught firmly by the magnitude of the energy, was unable to acknowledge his companions' questions and panic, as they passed through gate after gate with shocking velocity. They exited the labyrinth in a thunderous clap of displaced air, and lurched to a halt as the sphere popped, tumbling them into the square clearing within the cages.

Lightning spat venom, as the gates continued to close. Saliana, Trifyn and Aneida lay huddled under shields, doing their best to stay out of the way of the bolts that snapped against the metal cages, killing the 'Riders that were clambering over the bars with devastating blasts of electricity. Amidst the turmoil, they seemed not to notice the new arrivals until Gralyre's glowing blue sphere of magic expanded once more to add them to his collection. He sought Mayvin until he caught the scent of grief that clung to Aneida and the others, and knew she was dead. Turned mute by the demanding grip of the magic, he could do nothing but grit his teeth and ride the pleasure-pain to the end.

The electrical storm fell silent, as the passage into the labyrinth closed with the sun's last rays, and the shimmering portal dimmed its radiance to become again, a plain stone archway. Inside the hovering sphere, the echoing, panting breaths of the companions rasped loudly in the sudden silence, as though they were contained within a small room.

"Gralyre!" Trifyn gasped. "Ye have the sword!" Joy and wonder lit his eyes with tears of thankfulness, as he collapsed back in exhaustion.

Saliana closed her eyes, holding back sobs of relief that Rewn was safe. Let them think she was happy about the timely rescue.

"Where is Mayvin?" Rewn demanded.

Aneida crumpled with anguish, and she fought valiantly to hold on to her composure. Time enough for grief when they reached safety. "Dead."

"Ah, damn the Gods, Aneida. A terrible loss!" Jord murmured regretfully.

"So sorry, lass," Dotch added.

"Aneida, there are no words…" Rewn whispered.

Aneida nodded her acceptance of their regrets, but it was the unfamiliar sense of belonging that maintained her strength in the moment of tragedy. The weeks of travel and struggle had knit them into a family of sorts, and she knew that her loss was also theirs.

Outside the glowing blue sphere, slain 'Riders were rising again, rising as Deathren. Without a Demon Lord or Stalker to hold them to heel, their mindless hunger drove them to turn on their own. 'Riders broke and ran to escape the reanimated corpses of their own troops. Most were unsuccessful. They died under the ravenous mouths of the unnatural beings only to rise again in their own Deathren form to add to the chaos.

All of this Gralyre observed in the time it took deploy his borrowed magic. The world tilted sickeningly, as they launched into flight again, leaving the island far behind.

Within moments, they were standing safely upon the rocky shore of the mainland staring out at where they had only just been.

Gralyre released them from the bubble of energy, and heard

their murmurs of surprise and no little fear, as they milled around him in confusion. Still pulsing with the power of the sword, finally able to feel the grief of Mayvin's death, Gralyre knew the need to wield the magic again. Mayvin would be avenged!

He pointed the sword at the island, and a ball of energy gathered at the tip, bursting out with such force that it slammed the sword backwards from the recoil of its momentum, jerking the blade in Gralyre's grasp. The plasma ball arced over the inlet to the island and detonated. The concussion travelled across the water as a great wind, and lifted them all from their feet, throwing them to their backs, as though they had all been hit with a mighty fist. Gralyre lost his grip on the sword as he landed, and felt the power of its magic drain away from him, severed like a new arm he had grown to love.

He resisted the urge to pick up the blade, frightened by his avarice for more tastes of its massive power, forcing himself to leave it where it lay. Its power was a drug he would not allow himself to grow addicted to.

The ragged group lay upon the rocky beach, wordlessly watching as Fennick's Island burned. Ash began to rain down upon them, as the warning bells of Elevor sounded, far in the distance down the coast from their position.

Twilight deepened, and Rewn gave a snort, then a soft chuckle. He glanced towards Jord, working to keep the grin from his face, but as their eyes met, their merriment burst. Within moments the hilarity had infected the entire group. Only Little

Wolf seemed immune, cocking his head inquisitively, as the mad humans contorted with glee, a manic release of gladness at having their lives returned to them.

Dotch swiped a tear from his eye, as his laughter wound down, and he gasped for breath. He gripped Gralyre's shoulder and shook it. "Well done, lad, well done!" he praised.

A lightness of spirit gripped Gralyre for the first time in weeks. They had survived, they had the sword, and his past had returned, though for the moment, he would hoard the knowledge to himself. He was not ready to share his good fortune; it was still too new and precious to him.

"We should move. It will not be long afore the 'Riders start patrolling the beaches looking for survivors," Gralyre advised.

Aneida smirked and shook her head. "I doubt there is anything but the cook left in the kitchen. They sent a thousand 'Riders o'er the seas today."

The sword's spell had carried them to where they had made the crossing all those nights ago, and they were fortunate that their abandoned gear was still hidden in the rocks, undiscovered by the Demon Rider patrols from Elevor.

Rewn lifted some rocks and revealed a sealed packet of salted meat. "Ah," he smiled. "'Tis still here! I left a package behind," he glanced up at the others, "ye know," he waggled his brows comically, "just in case." Carefully, he dolled out the meager portions, for none of them had eaten in over three days.

Trifyn groaned as he chewed. "I conno' believe how good this tastes!"

"I wish we had horses," Aneida griped, as she chewed on the preserved venison. "I do no' fancy a walk through what is left o' the Bleak."

Jord glanced at Gralyre with a smirk on his clever face. "I bet the Elevor patrols have horses…"

Gralyre's dimples flashed, as he grinned with a nod. "I will take that bet." He closed his eyes to send his consciousness winging outwards, and found a mounted patrol less than half a league down the beach. He soon had the horses freed of their demonic riders, and galloping in their direction. "They will be here soon."

"What shall we do with the sword?" Dotch asked, as he walked to where it still lay upon the rocky beach, and bent to retrieve it.

"Do not touch it!" Gralyre snapped, and Dotch recoiled in surprise at Gralyre's unexpected possessiveness.

"I meant no harm t' it. Are ye alright, lad?"

Gralyre's, mirth fled, and he was ashamed at snapping at his friend, yet was unable to curb his covetousness; the thing both beguiled and repulsed. "I am sorry Dotch. It is very powerful, and very dangerous. Keep clear of it." He scanned the group. "All of you."

The flames from the burning island reflected within the bejeweled pommel stone, mirroring Gralyre's blazing longing. The lure of the power frightened him as nothing else had in a long, long time. The sword was dangerous and nobody was safe in its presence – especially him.

From the depths of a recovered pack, he pulled a worn bit of canvas tarp and, careful not to allow his flesh to touch any part of the weapon, wrapped the sword, binding the package with strips of leather. In the distance, the island continued to burn and the bells of Elevor continued to ring, almost drowning out the whispers of the sword's magic.

Rewn paced the beach. "How soon before the horses arrive?" After witnessing Gralyre's possessive reaction to the sword, he was trying to wrap his mind around the means by which they had escaped the bone yard of the labyrinth. Disquiet hummed through him, and an intense need to flee took hold.

Gralyre sought the horses through the mind link he had established with them. "Soon. We should start packing what we are taking."

Saliana fussed over Aneida and Trifyn, binding their wounds, and applying salves. The tasks kept her from betraying her joy that Rewn was safe, though she kept stealing looks at him when she was sure he was not watching.

Aneida finally punched her in the shoulder, drawing her attention back to the wound on her arm that Saliana was supposed to be tending. "Why do ye no' tell him o' your feelings, healer? These moo-cow eyes ye are making are sickening," she muttered quietly.

Saliana's gaze narrowed in irritation, and she tightened the bandage with far more force than was necessary. Aneida winced. "For the same reason ye are no' talking t' Jord," she retaliated.

"Shut your trap!" Aneida snarled. A hot blush washed over

her face, as she realized where her own gaze had been resting. She was tired, that was all. But her eyes returned to watch Jord where he was silhouetted against the darkening sky with the red light of the burning island burnishing his clever face. The ever-present knives that he played with when he was thinking flashed in his hands. Severely irritated, she pushed Saliana away. "I will do the rest myself!"

Saliana lifted her eyebrows smugly, and walked to where Trifyn lay resting his leg.

Jord turned away from the spectacle of the burning island, looking around at his exhausted friends. "When the island sinks, what do ye suppose is going t' happen?" he asked to no one in particular.

"It will sink. If it sinks, it will sink," Aneida snapped harshly. She could not help being irritated by his odd question.

Dotch jumped to his feet in sudden panic. "By the Gods!" he yelped. Jord nodded at him in agreement.

Gralyre glanced up from where he sat on a bolder with the strapped bundle of the sword resting across his knees. The sudden dawning of understanding was matched by his anger at himself. "Gods-take-it!" he snarled, as he surged to his feet. The horses were still too far away. "Gather what you can carry. We must meet the horses halfway."

"What? Why?" Rewn asked, as he began to organize their packs.

"Yeah, what is the rush?" Trifyn whined, massaging his leg above his wound in an attempt to ease the pain. He was in no shape to walk. He would rather stay here to await the horses.

In answer, Jord tossed a large stone into the shallows, sending up a spray to spatter Trifyn. He cut through Trifyn's complaint with a simple, "Now imagine that rock as the size o' an island. How much greater do ye suppose the splash is going t' be?"

Trifyn paled, and without further complaint, struggled to get to his feet. Saliana moved quickly to help him, and Rewn took up his other side.

The packs were light, containing little more than spare bedding and some lanterns, having been culled of food and essentials when they had travelled to the island. What was too heavy was immediately abandoned, for speed was of the essence.

They ran raggedly down the beach towards where Gralyre said that the horses would meet them. They glanced frequently at the burning island, trying to judge the time remaining before it sank.

"How much further until we reach the horses?" Rewn panted, as he half carried, half dragged Trifyn, hanging tightly to the bowman's arm over his shoulder, as they limped along. His eyes went to where Gralyre jogged easily in the lead, and the long bundle of the sword that bounced across his shoulder.

"They are almost here," Gralyre promised.

"How much longer until the island sinks?" Dotch asked.

"No' long now," Jord gauged, side-stepping for a few yards, as he evaluated the flickering fires across the inlet. The flames were dying. That could only mean one of two things; either the fire had consumed all there was to burn, or the island was beginning to sink.

"How much distance must we place between us and the coast?" Aneida threw the question out that nobody had an answer for.

Materializing out of the flickering darkness, the light from the inferno across the channel reflecting from off their frothy hides, the horses met them with whinnies and nickers of greeting. They still bore the saddles and reins from their lost riders.

Murmuring their thankfulness, the band mounted and urged the horses into a gallop inland. They pushed for as great a speed as they dared in the darkness, aided by Gralyre's mental contact with the animals. Behind them, they heard a roar that slowly increased in volume.

"The island has sunk! The wave is coming! Faster!" Gralyre urged them onwards.

The drubbing of the horse's hooves was barely heard over the fearful pounding of their own hearts. Gralyre led them up the only rise in the area. His magical connection to the creatures that had already begun to return to the freed lands that had been the Bleak, provided him a superior knowledge of the terrain.

Throughout their frantic dash, Gralyre cursed his stupidity continuously under his breath. There was no excuse for his recklessness, save that the power of the sword had seduced him. Again he wondered if he had been wielding the Dragon Sword, or if it had been wielding him.

In the far distance, the bells of Elevor abruptly silenced.

Gralyre spared a glance, and realized that the garrison was gone. Though the darkness hid the crest of the oncoming tidal wave, the roar of water grew louder, chasing them inland.

"Are we safe? Are we far enough away?" Saliana yelled, bent low over her steed. No one answered her, saving their strength for the race. They reached the summit of the hill, and there was no place left to go but down the other side.

"This is it. This is as high as we can get!" Gralyre reined them in, and turned to watch for the oncoming wall of water.

೫೦೧೩

DREISENHELD

Bed sheets rustle and toss. The dreamer speeds through nightmares to a sarcophagus adorned with a glowing jewel…

…A flash of lightning, a strobe of light reveals a face. 'Tis Him! The face glows bloody, as a palm presses to the ruby. Bones show through flesh. Lightning crashes violently, and the sarcophagus splits.

The sword boils out of its grave, and materializes into His hands. He presents it to the forked tongues of the storm, bellowing a challenge, as the point stabs the sky. Dragon eyes in the sky, blue-black and merciless, glare at the dreamer. He is coming…

Awakes with a cry of joy!

The Rebels have the sword! No! Not just the Rebels! Gralyre has the sword! Finally, after three hundred years, Fennick is free of the labyrinth!

Throws off clammy, sweat soaked bed sheets. The sword is free, is coming! Everything is as planned! It is time.

A powerful surge of magic floods the world, and the Master staggers, catches the golden bedframe for support to keep from falling.

The Rebel Sorcerer! He has used the sword to escape Fennick's Island unscathed!

The Sorcerer mus die! The sword is mine!

'Tis time to kill the humans, and draw Gralyre out! 'Tis his weakness, Gralyre will seek to protect them, he will come.

And if the Rebel Sorcerer gains power enough through the sword to defeat all of the Demon Lords sent against him?

Snorts with giggles.

Let him spend all of Fennick's magic killing them. They are nothing. Only one thing matters, the most important thing. Gralyre must come. He must give up the sword willingly.

Sobers. Sly, cunning.

The bell pull summons a dark shadow.

"Fetch Doaphin, and assemble in the throne room! Now!"

"By your will, my Master," the shadow's sibilant words echo hollowly, as it backs from the room.

Gralyre is alive. The sword is freed. Fennick is vulnerable, only shadow and mist. The endgame begins.

CHAPTER EIGHTEEN

SOUTHERN SHORES

"Here it comes!" Trifyn yelled. They were trapped on the summit of the hill. The tidal wave caused by the sinking of Fennick's Island, struck the distant shore with a roar, chewing through the dead forest, rising higher and higher as it came. The consumption of rotting trees did nothing to appease its hunger, as the water rose with shocking speed up the slope they had barely had time to climb themselves.

The rising moon traced the forefront of the salty crest, dancing its light upon the foam, until the moon itself was blocked from view by the oncoming wall of death.

"We are no' high enough!" Rewn yelled warning over the approaching thunder, measuring the speed and force of the waves towering above them. Trees that had been dead for centuries in the Bleak, were easily ripped from the ground, their roots bobbing roughly in the swells, tumbling and shattering, as the water forced them up the slope. If the wave did not kill them, the debris would.

Gralyre felt the inevitability of their death settle deep into the pit of his stomach. By his arrogance, they would all die when they had been so very near to escaping victorious with the sword! Remorse rode heavily upon his shoulders, as he stood tall between the wall of water and his companions in unconscious protectiveness. He should never have used the Dragon Sword to destroy Fennick's Island, there had been no reason in it, only the addictive power working its will through him.

The sword! Excitement and eagerness blasted through him. He had to use the magic again! 'Twas the only way to save them all!

Yet he hesitated, as something deep within screamed that to use the sword again was too dangerous. No, not the sword, the Wizard Stone. The power was too coercive, and he was too tired to control it. But if he died here, so too would his friends, as would Catrian, and all hope of defeating Doaphin. The thought decided him.

His life for theirs, whatever the risk.

Gralyre had a creeping sense that he needed little excuse to wield the power again, but there was no choice. None. It had to be done.

Behind him, the horses stamped and snorted, thoughts of flight assaulting his concentration as, in a quick, economical move, he pulled the bundled sword from across his shoulder, and went down on one knee. He drew his sharp dagger from his boot and slit the thongs that bound the weapon. The light of the moon caught against the polished Maolar blade.

For a moment, his fingers hesitated to touch the hilt, and shame pressing down upon him, as he glanced up at the approaching wave. He schooled himself on what power used without forethought of consequences accomplished. They were about to be buried under an ocean of water. The sword's magic was their only hope, but he could not allow it dominion over his will again!

Shaking the Dragon Sword free from the canvas cloth as he gained his feet, it took all of his concentration to keep from succumbing to the intensity of the insane power. His breath hitched, as the hum of magic set his nerve ends screaming. Holding the sword aloft he paused, as the others became aware of what he was doing, bunching together with fear etched onto their faces; fear of him and the Dragon Sword, not just of the oncoming tidal wave.

'What is your command?' Fennick's Wizard Stone asked.

Instead of answering immediately, Gralyre took a moment to think. They wanted free of the water, and he knew that he could transport them all to safety. But perhaps he could do better than that?

"Take us to Catrian... No, wait! Take us, all of us, to where Catrian's body lies!" he quickly amended, unsure of how literal the sword could be. Catrian, her soul, her essence, was now in a place of spirit, not flesh, imprisoned within her Wizard Stone, and the powerful magic might trap them there with her if Gralyre were not careful.

Power, stronger than anything he had ever felt, even that used to free them from the island and then sink it, blew through him, surprising a cry of pain, as he convulsed. He felt his control usurped, and began to struggle against the magic, but was as ineffectual as a fly buzzing inside a jar; too little, too late. The

Dragon Sword took complete command, not giving him the smallest control over directing the energy of the spell.

The world shifted, and Gralyre was swept into the current along with his companions, a river of colours that blurred with the speed of their passage.

For a moment Gralyre was back in the void, the empty place of his worst nightmare. What had he done? In his arrogance had he erred again? Gralyre cried out, and thrust away the horrific memory, staving off his fear by noting the differences of this journey from that of his nightmare's.

Here and now, unlike his nightmare, his senses had not deserted him; he could still see, he could still feel his body, he could hear the screams of the others, and the panic of the animals. His hands yet gripped the hilt of the Dragon Sword, solid and heavy, as it bucked and jerked in his sweaty grasp like a living creature. He was terrified that he might drop it, and strand them all in this mad kaleidoscope, as they travelled north in mere moments, what had taken them long weeks of horseback riding south.

Even in the black of night, the colours of the world were jeweled and smeared. The moon rose, oddly seeming to hang steadily above them, while the colours around them deepened further. It had its own beauty, not that the roughness and speed of their passage allowed them to concentrate on aught but staving off their disorientating vertigo.

After a time, the blur of movement slowed, and the colours swirled brighter, tighter, becoming clearer as they resolved into bright dots of fires, tops of trees and sparkling rivers that spun past. The maelstrom rent with a booming clap that spat them out into a wooded clearing.

The flickering light from many cook fires lent a sense of unreality, as the horses bucked and screamed, running dangerously amuck, as they escaped into the surrounding trees. Little Wolf, snarling and snapping, fled after them into the moonlit forest at a ground-scratching run.

The ragged party lay in the loamy dirt, sucking in harsh breaths. Gralyre released the sword from numb fingers, and shakily raised his head, checking that everyone had made the journey intact.

Saliana was sobbing quietly, rocking back and forth on drawn up legs, her head buried in her hands. The sound of her terrified cries cut Gralyre to the quick, though he was physically unable to summon the strength to rise and go to her. At her side, Trifyn, the injured bowman, was lying on his back, unmoving. Gralyre decided that the lad had feinted, for thankfully, his chest still rose and fell.

Rewn was on hands and knees, puking and retching. His brown hair was disheveled, and clung wetly to the sweat on his face as he heaved. His eyes were brown stones of dismay that rose to meet Gralyre's for a devastated moment, before he was surprised by another gag.

Gralyre, unable to watch, as his stomach heaved in sympathetic warning, looked away to Jord who was also swallowing hard to hold back his motion sickness. His face was white, and his hands dug deep into the dirt, as though to anchor himself to the real world. He gurgled raggedly upon the air like someone had kicked him hard in the side.

Aneida was on her feet, staggering aimlessly, as tiny, quiet mewls escaped her throat. Dotch caught her in his arms, supporting them both even as his eyes rolled white with his own terror. She pushed him away, and clumsily drew her sword on her friend. "Do no'…Do no' touch me!" she shrieked.

"Sorry…sorry," Dotch mumbled, and grabbed a tree for support instead. He wiped a hand over his sweat-slicked face. "Sorry," he continued to whisper long after Aneida had stumbled away with her sword dragging behind her in the dirt.

They had landed in a large, wooded clearing. Tents were staked in neat clusters around cook fires, and men were stilled in their various tasks, shocked into silence by the small band's sudden, loud arrival.

A pair of old, worn boots appeared in front of Gralyre's nose, as movement returned, and men sought to recapture the careening horses before they could destroy the camp.

Gralyre forced himself to his knees, and then to his feet, dragging the sword after him to use as a crutch. His eyes came level with brown faded trousers, an old gnarled staff, a neatly trimmed white beard, an age-wrinkled, yet lively, tanned face, and finally piercing blue eyes.

"Humph," stated the old man. Gralyre staggered and almost fell, and the stranger reached out a surprisingly strong hand to steady him. "Welcome to the camp of the Dream Weavers, my lord Prince."

Blackness folded around Gralyre, and he did not feel the ground that hit hard.

"Humph," Gedrhar, the Dream Weaver Seer, stated again, staring down at Gralyre's laid out body.

Dara came running from the tent that she had been assigned, wondering at the loud clap of thunder she had heard. She screamed joyfully when she saw the travellers. "Rewn!" She ran to her brother, pulling him into a hug. "Gods! Ye are safe! Thank-ye! Thank-ye!"

From the tent that she had exited, Dajin limped to the entrance, his face stark white, save for the blackened bruise that spread from temple to jaw. As he stared across the clearing at his sister and brother, he hesitated upon the threshold, before stepping back inside, and letting the flap of the tent fold back into place.

ഇരുജ

Sethreat hides from the killing rays of sunlight, and nurses Its wounds. It cannot remember so terrible a defeat. From allowing Speckle Tail the opportunity to attack, to the wound on Its back suffered by a simple human weapon. And the Dream Weaver arrows! The stench of putrefying flesh in the infected Maolar wounds taunts Its failure further.

Now, just after nightfall, It emerges from Its den to inform the Master of the return of the Dream Weavers. It hopes that the information will buy back Its life.

Sethreat bows Its head, waiting for the judgment of the Master. It regrets that Speckle Tale is dead, killed by the Dream Weavers, for now It cannot shift the blame.

"Dream Weavers, you are certain?"

"Yes, my Master. And they bear Maolar."

Even across the great distance, Sethreat feels the Master's disquiet.

"And the Sorcerer?"

"Sorceress, my Master. She yet lives. The Dream Weavers protect her."

Sethreat feels the Master's power gather yet does not seek to flee, for there is nowhere It can go that the power of the Master cannot find It. The ill news has only made Its punishment worse.

The Master's might is all. The Master is right to punish It, for only see how It has allowed mere humans to make It bleed.

The Master's magic reaches out across the lands and smites It.

The Stalker tumbles like a dandelion seed in a strong wind, slams into trees, smashed by the magical hand of the Master. Sethreat's death will be slow and painful. The Master makes an example, as warning to the others.

The Master's word is law. The Master's will is all, and Sethreat has failed it.

CRACK-BOOM!

The earth shakes. Nesting birds and forest animals alike startle from their sleep, and take flight.

Sethreat thinks that It imagines the noise in Its bleeding ears, but the Master pauses the execution, for the sound, the great magic, is even felt in the far throne room of Dreisenheld.

The Stalker lays in a twisted heap, pants in anticipation of the killing blows that are not yet falling. It waits, cowed, bloody, beaten.

∞❧

DREISENHELD

Gasps for breath! Power! Such power as never felt in the land, even wielded by the slack white hand now reaching for a bloodied cup of sustenance. Shaking hands. The rapture in the Stalker's torture evaporates in the glowing light of this new disturbance.

Doaphin stands upon the lowest step. "My Master, 'tis the Sorcerer who travels with the Rebels! He has used the power of the sword again. If Fennick finds a new body afore Gralyre delivers us the sword, if he usurps this Rebel Sorcerer as his new vessel…"

"Silence your mewling!"

It has not been a consideration until mentioned. Damn Doaphin to the darkest pits, he is right.

Blood, still warm from a slave's throat, fills the mouth and gives back some calm, sloshes over the rim of the bejeweled goblet, spatters the floor. The drops join ancient stains upon the stones at the base of the throne, an intricate pattern, an augury that has yet to be deciphered.

Steady. Steady the chalice. Do not let the creatures see the panic and fear.

Swallows, thinks.

The minions are astir. They mutter restlessly, fearfully. The reverberations of power still rasp painfully across nerve endings. The unknown Rebel Sorcerer has wielded such power that every creature in the land with a hint of magic ability has felt it.

Envy! Fear! Lust for the sword, for the power! More power. All the power!

Where? From where has he unleashed his magic?

Seeking. Questing. Not the island, the island is gone. Destroyed in their escape... But no matter! The source has come from farther away... in the mountains....

Laughter starts low in the chest, booms out over the assembled creatures, cows them. The sword must be recovered before Fennick can leap into a corporeal host, and, blessed by fortune, there is a trusted Stalker less than a league away.

Doaphin stumbles back down off the steps below the dais. The Master's laughter is more terrifying than rage.

"Doaphin. Our troops march tonight. They are ready?"

Doaphin bows low. "Yes, my Master."

The Master leans forward on the throne. "Kill. Kill them all. Leave one alive in each township to carry the message."

"What message, my Master."

"Return the sword to Dreisenheld, and humanity is spared."

ഓരു

NOTHERN HEATHREN MOUNTAINS

"Sethreat!" the Master's voice revives It. The presence is no longer angry. The Master has forgiven Its sins.

The Master is great and terrible. Glory the darkness of the Master!

"Seek the Man! He is but a league away from you! Seek him in the Dream Weavers' Camp! Return him to me, unspoiled, with the Dragon Sword. Beware, there are two sorcerers protecting the blade. Kill them both! Glut yourself on their magic, my pet!"

A gift instead of death! "Thy will is all, my Master," It grovels.

It lives to grovel. It lives.

ഓരു

A sharp scent seared Gralyre's nose, and he raised a weak hand to bat it away. It left momentarily but as he began to sink back into his dark exhaustion, the pervasive odor returned, and a demanding voice ordered him to waken.

Summoning what strength he had, Gralyre opened his eyes. He was still lying in the dirt, and the old man was waving a wooden flask under his nostrils.

"Awaken, Gralyre! You cannot rest yet!"

"I am awake," Gralyre mumbled groggily, spitting out dirt

and twigs, as he lifted his head. He attempted to sit up, but lacking the strength for even that, he pushed himself to one elbow, and flopped onto his back. The flask disappeared, and Gralyre considered sinking back into blissful oblivion.

"Come, my Prince! Catrian's time grows short. We must act now if we are to save her."

At the mention of Catrian, such a surge of adrenaline went through Gralyre's heart that he was able to lever himself back up to his feet. How could he think of rest while she was still in danger?

The old man got a shoulder under Gralyre's arm just in time to prevent him from pitching over upon his face again. Gralyre dragged the sword ignominiously in the dirt as they walked, for he lacked the strength to support its weight.

"This way." The old man directed Gralyre's tottering steps towards a tent in the middle of the camp.

"You called me *'Prince'*," Gralyre mentioned quietly. He had told no one of his returned memories. Chaotic. Disjointed. But all his memories were there for the asking, for the first time since he had awakened alone in a forest covered in the gore of a battle he could not recall.

"My name is Gedrhar y'Traydeyon, and I know who you are, for I am your mother's sister's great, great..." he waved his hand to indicate more greats, "grandson."

Gralyre was suddenly awash in the memories of his mother...

...Dark hair hangs in braids around a strong oval face; blue-

*black eyes smile, arms hold in comfort, a whiff of scent, sweet,
floral...*

Gralyre blinked rapidly, as sorrow and poignant nostalgia
assaulted his senses. How could he have forgotten his own
mother? In forgetting her, he was now unprepared for his
enduring grief at her loss. Tears burned hotly in his eyes. "She
was very beautiful," he volunteered awkwardly into the
conversation gap.

Gedrhar looked at him kindly. "You have her look. The look
of our people. And it would seem that your journey through the
ages has awakened your mother's power as well."

"I always had it..." Gralyre's words stumbled awkwardly. Or
had he? A disjointed memory, a fragment without context...

*...Pain from a lash. Count of four. Count of five. Then the
dark and the rats.*

"So you will forget, boy!"...

'*...so I would forget,*' Gralyre shivered, coming back to the
present with a flinch for the memory of pain. He averted his eyes
from Gedrhar's concerned gaze. The trip through the void of
time had made him forget to forget...what?

He was confused, and assaulted upon all sides by disordered
thoughts. After the empty desert of past, his newly returned
memories were as so much noise to his exhausted mind, a
verdant jungle he was too tired to try to navigate. Time enough

for that after he had saved Catrian.

They stumbled to a halt in front of the large round tent, and Gedrhar held back the flap for them to enter. There Catrian lay on a pallet of soft furs, illuminated by a lantern hung against the central pole. It was a moment that Gralyre had doubted would ever come again on this side of the veil of life.

The soft lantern light played over her face in an illusion of life, but Gralyre could clearly see that she was too still, her face sunken, waxen. Breath barely stirred through her dry, cracked lips. Her glorious hair was matted with sweat, lank and lifeless.

Gralyre left Gedrhar's support, and stumbled to Catrian's side to fall to his knees. His chest contracted, as though his heart had been struck with an arrow, making him hiss from the pain of seeing her like this. His hand shook, as he laid his palm against her clammy forehead, brushing back her limp, dark hair. He had seldom seen her hair out of its practical braids, and he indulged himself to stroke his fingers through the silky length. His trembling fingers clenched into a fist, Catrian's locks held firm in his grasp, as if to anchor her to this world, and to him.

"How did this happen?" he asked brokenly. He eyes narrowed in anguish, as Gedrhar told him all he knew.

"I am told that she was attacked by a Stalker, and expended too much of her magic to defeat it, used even that little bit needed to keep her body alive." Gedrhar was as dispassionate as possible. It did not take a wise man to realize the depth of feeling that was involved here. "She had just created a storm. The Stalker must have tracked the scent of her magic to find her, and attacked her while she was weakened and vulnerable."

Gralyre's head bowed, his attention narrowed to the texture of her skin, as his hand smoothed compulsively down Catrian's cheek. She had used up her magic for the storm, to give him a chance to survive the quest that should have claimed his life. She was trapped in her Wizard Stone because of him. His heartache stole his breath, made him swallow thickly. "How do I reach her?"

"Gently. You cannot force her to return. Instead you must tempt her back, convince her that her life is better here than within her Wizard Stone."

"If that is all there is to it, why did you not help her?" Gralyre snarled viciously over his shoulder, while his hands remained gentle in the caresses upon her cheeks.

"I do not have the power at my command that you do, my Prince. You have the sword. Only it is mighty enough to give her soul the power to return. She cannot reunite with her body until her Godsmagic is replenished enough to sustain life. If you or I alone were to attempt this, it would save her, yet doom us for we would be sacrificing our own life force for hers. But the sword is not alive, it's magic can replenish her body's Godsmagic without consequence."

Gralyre nodded his understanding, finally tearing his eyes from Catrian to look up a Gedrhar. "That is all I must do?"

Gedrhar looked troubled, as he shifted anxiously. "No. That prepares the vessel, but it is the soul's choice to return or not. If she will not consent to leave her Wizard Stone, then you will not be able to save her, no matter that her body lives. If this occurs, 'tis better that you end her body's life quickly, and release her forever."

"Do not ask it of me!"

"This is naught but an empty vessel. Her essence is within her Wizard Stone. You will make the right decision, my Prince."

Gralyre's full attention returned to Catrian, and he barely noted Gedrhar leave the tent. Back on Fennick's Island it had seemed so clear; get the sword and return to save her. He had not allowed himself to think of failure, but looking back he saw that the odds against their success had been insurmountable.

Now, watching Catrian, as she lay dying with every breath, he almost wished himself back in that maze, fighting for his life and hers. It seemed infinitely simpler than what he was about to attempt. He was a warrior, what did he know of healing?

'Nothing!'

But what he did know was that to go on without her by his side, would halve his soul. To never again see her eyes spark with anger at him, or soften in passion was the most heinous torture that he could imagine.

Gralyre leaned forward, and brushed Catrian's dry, cracked lips with his own, before laying his cheek to hers in a gentle caress, and vowing softly in her ear, "I am here now. Everything is going to be alright." He slid down beside her on the pallet and, treating her as if she would shatter, drew her into his arms, nestling her slack head into the hollow of his throat in order to feel her every labored breath against his skin. With his free hand, he placed the Dragon Sword between their entwined bodies, maintaining his grasp upon the hilt, as he sought the power within.

'What is your command?'

The whispery voice from the Wizard Stone sounded strange to Gralyre's ears, coloured by an emotion he had not expected. Avarice? Still the power beckoned him, like a sunlit lake on a hot summer's day, though he found himself leery of what lurked beneath the still surface. In such a short time, he had come to crave this rush of power. Dare he use it again, when the last time it had stolen his will?

It was needed to save Catrian's life but Gralyre was reluctant to allow the magic to work directly upon her, as if its touch would somehow corrupt her, as it had already begun to corrupt him. That whisper of emotion from the Wizard Stone concerned him, making him instinctively seek to place himself between Catrian and possible danger. "Replenish me, as I give her body back the Godsmagic it needs to sustain her soul when it returns," he whispered.

Immediately, he felt the addictive surge of power work its way from the hilt of the sword, up through his arms, and into his body. As gently as possible, Gralyre released his Godsmagic into Catrian's body, and as it drained away, he was renewed by the power of the Dragon Sword. A soft radiant glow surrounded them both, fusing their energy together. The power of the sword seemed to call the power of Gralyre's own life force, replenishing and building it, before releasing into the shell of

Catrian's body. This was unlike the raw power that had been unleashed upon the island. Instead of overwhelming him, the sword gave a steady, warm glow of strength.

When the magic had run its course, Gralyre felt renewed as though he had wakened from a long, cleansing sleep. Already, he could feel that Catrian's breathing had grown stronger. He placed a hand over her heart, measuring the steady beat. Now he had to call back her soul.

'What is your command?'

Gralyre fought the feeling of invincibility with which the sword sought to lure him.

"No!" he snarled. "You will not touch her! I will do this myself." He could feel the sword's discontent and something more - anger? Repulsed, Gralyre tossed it to the side. The dull clang it made as it struck the furs on the floor of the tent, seemed an ominous rebuke.

But Gralyre paid it no mind, for all his being was bent to the task of saving Catrian. Drawing on his renewed magic, Gralyre merged his mind into hers.

What he found frightened him to his core, for where once there had had been a glowing landscape of thoughts, emotions and memories, there was now nothing, an absence of life within an echoing darkness. Even during the early days of his amnesia, his mind had never been so empty. Gedrhar had been right. Without her soul, her body was but a husk. How was he to find her?

"Catrian!" He called her name, but the sound seemed

dampened by the dark. There was no answer.

Was he too late? Was she gone forever?

No! She might be trapped in her Wizard Stone, but there had to be a link to her body somewhere, else she would already be dead. Fear made him frenzied, as his consciousness darted deeper and deeper within hers, like a silver fish in a dark still pool.

He remembered the last time that he had sensed her, how he had almost reached her from so far away on the island, but had lacked the strength to save her then. Mere days had passed, and already she was so much further away. Failure was a scavenger of faith, chewing at his soul, but he forced himself to keep exploring, to keep seeking hints of Catrian within the inky void.

"Catrian!" he howled. A hint of her, a whiff of a remembered scent perhaps, tickled his senses. He turned in a slow circle, and spotted it; a small flaw of silver luminance that marred the infinite darkness.

With the quickness of thought, he reached the light and discovered a silver pool, so small he doubted that it could encircle his boot. From the pool, a silver strand arose into the darkness, pulsing slightly as it drew upon the last of the light, the last of Catrian's Godsmagic. Gralyre's heart flipped with fear, as he realized that this silver light represented last the vestiges of his Sorceress, and that when the pool was gone, so was she.

Gralyre followed the strand, his dream body flowing effortlessly after it. He could sense Catrian at the other end; her presence was growing stronger! He had found her!

"Catrian! Can you hear me?" He felt her awareness center upon him. The strand that he followed vibrated, a deep note that made the darkness hum for a moment. Even as his heart surged with hope, her attention turned, and left him bereft. Her disinterest in all that came from outside her new realm smote him like a blow, as her presence faded once more. With a spin of vertigo, he arrived at the end of the silver ribbon, into the prismatic land of Catrian's Wizard Stone.

The terrain was a deep, milky blue, the colour of a clouded glacier lake, and was devoid of vegetation. Crystalline facets with hard angles did nothing to divide sky from land, as though it were all the same material, as though Gralyre and Catrian were caught within the facets of a rare jewel. All this he noted with a glance. His attention was all for the woman seated before him.

"Catrian," he whispered in aching relief. He had found her!

She sat upon a crystal ledge, clasping the fragile end of the silver strand in her hands. She was naked, her long, brown hair flowing over her body in a gentle wave to pool at her hips. Her bare toes scraped lightly at the hard crystal under her ledge, as she swung her legs. She seemed so innocent, like a little girl playing cat's cradle in aimless boredom.

Gralyre felt the cold of stone beneath his bare feet, and glanced down to see that he was also naked. But in this landscape of Catrian's Wizard Stone, the landscape of the soul, he did not wonder at the lack of clothes.

"Do ye know what this is?" Her voice was without the curiosity that would give her words the inflection of a question.

"I have been holding it forever, and I would like t' let it go, but 'tis hard t' put down. Soon, I think, I will be able t' drop it." She shook her hands, as if trying to remove a spider's web from her fingers, only it was the silver line flowing wide onto her hands, wreathing them in silver light.

Gralyre's sucked in a harsh breath of fear. Instinctively he realized that were she to drop the silver strand, all would be lost; her soul's final connection to her body would be severed forever. Not wanting to spook her, he slowly approached, and touched her shoulder. "Catrian, come back to me. Please, love. Do not do this. Do not leave me."

Catrian ignored him, concentrating on ridding her hands of the wreath of silver light. She was so cold to the touch, as cold as if she herself were made of stone. The warmth of life was absent from her flesh.

"Catrian?"

She momentarily left off trying to drop the silver cord, and looked up at him. Her eyes reflected the blue glaze of the landscape, cold and unnatural, no longer the soft mossy grey-green that Gralyre recalled. Even her flesh now mirrored a cyanotic blue; a beautiful woman who was beginning to turn into the same stone that made up the rest of this world.

"Who are ye? Why are ye bothering me?" Again, although the words were confrontational, they were said stonily, without inflection or emotion.

Life was emotion and chaos. Life was unpredictable, joyful, and painful. Here, in her cold realm, Catrian was the goddess, untouched and untouchable. To draw her back to her body, back to the land of the living, he was going to have to reacquaint her to life, reintroduce her to emotion, and tempt her back with the pleasures that were to be had there.

"Why do you not enter my mind? Then you will know me," Gralyre offered while gazing steadily into her eyes, willing her to join with him.

She cocked her had curiously for a moment, but it passed. Ignoring him once more, she continued her struggle with the remnants of the silver strand.

Stymied, Gralyre knelt at her feet, as despair gripped him. "Please. Please do not give up. Please come back to me. Do not leave me!" His fierce plea was ignored, and did not produce any further reaction.

Gralyre could not reach her in this realm of her Wizard Stone where even curiosity had been stripped from her. As he watched, the silver light of Catrian's lifeline dimmed further.

Through the shimmer of his grief, his eyes narrowed upon the silver strand dangling before him. There was only one point by which he knew she was still connected to the realm of the living. Via the strand, would she be able to feel the emotions that beckoned her to live again?

Concentrating hard to radiate everything that he was feeling, Gralyre placed his left hand around the fragile cord, and forced his emotions to flow into the lifeline.

Her reaction was immediate and extreme. Catrian gasped and flew to her feet with her fingers splayed wide. Her head fell back, her eyes huge and staring, as she experienced Gralyre's love and despair surging into her through the length of silver that bound them. The tinsel-thin lifeline thickened to the width of a rope. It was working!

Catrian's head snapped down, and the glare she gave him came from eyes that now spun with a hint of green. "What are ye doing?" she snarled, emotion flowing through her words for the first time. "Who are ye?"

Gralyre retained his grip on the silver cord, as he gained his feet to confront her. He continued to pour emotion at her, everything he was feeling, and everything that he felt for her. "Enter my mind, and see for yourself!" he challenged.

"No!" The howl echoed back from the sharp angles and walls of the Wizard Stone prison. *No-no-no-no-no!* "Ye are trying to trick me. This is a trick!" She tried to back away from him, but was anchored by his grip upon her silver lifeline.

Ruthlessly, Gralyre brought her up short, and forced his memory of their first turbulent kiss up the silver strand. He smiled in satisfaction as he watched her mouth go slack with the heat of secondhand lust. The silver strand thickened even further, radiating more light, subverting the unnatural blue of Catrian's Wizard Stone.

Unrelenting in his effort to reach her, he reminded her of their parting, when he had been sentenced to seek the sword, a suicide quest. The agony and grief of the remembrance roughened his voice. "Remember! Remember!" he chanted, he demanded.

"No! Stop! No more!" Catrian cried out in empathy for the

pain of a parting she did not recall. "No more!" The plea was softer, less certain.

Gralyre was fiercely unflinching in his demand, "Come back to me!"

"I remember… I think…" She drew nearer once more. "Do I know ye?" Her hands wreathed in their silver light moved hesitantly to touch him, danced lightly over his bare chest. "I think ye died. Ye are dead."

"I am not dead. I am here. I am waiting for you to return to me!" he cupped her face with his free hand. Was her flesh warmer? He looped his arm around Catrian's waist, and pulled her nearer, leaning his forehead against hers, as he laid his soul open to the strand of light, to her.

He knew that nothing short of this was going to bring her back. She was with him, as he relived the trials of the labyrinth. She was with him when the sword restored his lost memories. She was with him when he returned to save her.

The silver light that wreathed them grew stronger and stronger, until it blazed. The strand thickened to the point that Gralyre could no longer hold it. As he released it, the silver light dimmed slightly. Their contact was broken. It was up to her now.

Catrian's breath came in short pants, and her hands clasped his shoulders for support, her fingers clawed and kneading like a scared kitten. Her flesh was warmer, stimulated with life, but though she was experiencing emotion, it was all secondhand, originating within Gralyre. If she were to return, she had to be forced to experience her own feelings, remember why her own life was worth living.

With deliberate seduction, Gralyre pressed little biting kisses up the side of her neck. He could not afford to let her mind start to think, to reason. Reason would not save her, only emotion would. She had to feel!

"Catrian," he breathed her name into her ear, letting the heat of his whisper diffuse his desire into her.

A small gasp escaped her, and she shivered. The silver light increased once more.

Gralyre smiled, and wrapped his arms tightly around her, melding her to his flesh, forcing her to feel the heat of him, his life force. He rubbed his hands over the silky skin of her back, tangling his fingers in her flowing tresses, as he massaged more heat into her.

"Mmmm," she hummed in pleasure, as her body undulating against his.

Gralyre pulled gently on her hair, tilting her face up for his kiss, a light, teasing pass that made her shiver, and raise on tiptoe to seek his lips when he moved away.

Her eyes fluttered open, and she looked at him, really saw him for the first time. "Gralyre?" Catrian whispered in remembrance, in recognition, uncertain, as though awakening from a deep dream. Her hands travelled up to his head, tilting his midnight-blue eyes towards her, searching his gaze for the familiar to cling to.

"Hello, Sorceress!"

"Gralyre!" She gave a glad cry, as more awareness returned. Her lips parted and sought his, clung to his, biting, taking, consumed by her unfiltered emotion.

Wrapped in the silver light of Catrian's life force, Gralyre could feel her reawakening. He keenly felt the moment when she recovered her own memory fully.

Her mouth was hot and demanding where it clung to his, her dream body now burning with life, as her mind hesitantly sought a connection.

The silver light exploded around them, wrapping their nakedness in the warmth of life.

She pulled her mouth free of his, so that she could pepper sweet kisses against his cheeks, his brow. "I thought ye were dead!" Crystalline tears sparkled in eyes that were warm with life, green and aware as they should be.

Gralyre brushed the wetness away, and was amazed when she did the same for him. "I was afraid I would not reach you in time," he confessed brokenly. Overcome by relief and desire, he pulled her close once more, and heard her laugh in gladness as he lifted her high in his arms, and twirled for the joy of it.

Her lips parted softly, as her eyes met his, and the playfulness vanished in the heat that they found for each other. They sank together into the silver light, bodies, minds and thoughts merging. The landscape of Catrian's Wizard Stone receded, disappeared. Together they made the journey back, ecstasy exploding through their minds, as they bonded themselves forever with their love.

Gralyre's eyes snapped open, as the contact was broken, and he returned to his own body. He was slick with sweat, his breathing harsh and strenuous. He pulled back to look down at the woman he held in his arms.

Catrian's eyes were open, and she was smiling a tired, siren's smile at him. There was no need for words. They were closer now than any two beings that had ever lived. More than lovers. They were one. With trembling fingers, Gralyre gently brushed her hair back from her face, watching as she sighed and fell asleep, a deep healing, natural sleep. He nestled her nearer and allowed himself to finally succumb to the luxury of his own exhaustion.

The End

of

The Sorcerer

Lies of Lesser Gods - Book Three

Coming Soon

The Prince

Lies of Lesser Gods - Book Four

About the Author

L.G.A. McIntyre grew up amid the lush forests and mountains of central British Columbia, Canada in the City of Quesnel. Here were histories and tall tales of the Goldrush and ghost stories that fired the imagination.

McIntyre trained in Media Arts and Communications and enjoyed a successful career in television before accepting a position supervising digital media production at the University of British Columbia.

After years of writing scripts, for documentaries, television and film - telling stories through images – L.G.A. McIntyre decided it was time to publish the novels that had been waiting patiently to see the light of day.

"There comes a time when, looking into your Writing Drawer, you realize that creating stories has become more than a hobby, and is now flirting with an Obsessive Compulsive Disorder."

Connect with the Author

Visit our website for insider news and giveaways
www.lgamcintyre.com

Like us on Facebook
www.facebook.com/lgamcintyre

Follow us on Twitter
@LGAMcIntyre
#theLOLG